THE NIMMY NIMMY DANCE

THE NIMMY NIMMY DANCE

TOM GEIER

The Nimmy Nimmy Dance

Paperback: 978-1-7367745-0-2
Hardcover: 978-1-7367745-1-9
Ebook: 978-1-7367745-2-6

www.tomgeierauthor.com

www.TheNimmyNimmyDance.com

Edited by Carrie Bolin, The Inspired Pen

Book Cover Design by Megan Katsanevakis, Deckle & Hue Design Firm, LLC

Cover Art by Vicki Wade, Vicky Wade Fine Art

LET THEM PRAISE HIS NAME IN THE DANCE:

(Psalm 149:3 King James Version)

ACKNOWLEDGEMENTS

The decision to write a novel was both easy and exciting. Making it happen proved to be extremely difficult and protracted. I owe a tremendous debt and enormous gratitude to those who helped:

My wonderful wife, Paula, who joyfully coined the phrase "nimmy nimmy dance" many years ago and patiently endured my long hours in front of a computer.

My children, Kevin, Beth, and David, and their spouses, Laura, Kirk, and Nicole, who gracefully refrained from rolling their eyes whenever I talked about the book and rallied me forward.

My grandchildren, Ansley, Annabelle, Gibson, Zaile, Gabriel, Charlotte, and Anastasia, who inspired the song that inspired the book.

Carrie, my editor, who taught me how to shape a manuscript full of words into a story worth a read.

My beta readers who fastidiously plodded through the early versions and gave me invaluable feedback.

Jesus, the Author of all our lives.

THE NIMMY NIMMY DANCE

We'll stomp our feet as fast as we can
Pump our arms, wave our hands
Twirl around, we're in a trance
Let's all do the Nimmy Nimmy Dance

A stitch in time saves nine, lives a cat does have
Earned is a penny saved, a laugh the greatest salve
All's fair in war and love, makes the world go round
Indeed, is a friend in need, and you're the one I found

If you love me, I'll love you too
Who cares what crazy things we do
So, come with me and take a chance
And do the Nimmy Nimmy Dance

A journey of a thousand miles, a single step must start
If absence makes the heart grow fond,
the best of friends must part
Good things come to those who wait,
true love will find a way
So, laugh and dance and sing and shout,
tomorrow's another day

We'll stomp our feet as fast as we can
Pump our arms, wave our hands
Twirl around, we're in a trance
Let's all do the Nimmy Nimmy Dance

Part One

A JOURNEY OF A THOUSAND MILES,

A SINGLE STEP MUST START

CHAPTER 1

Penny strained against reality's tug with every fiber of her being. But the carefree laughter in her head evaporated as she was defiantly dragged into wakefulness. She'd been drifting in and out of this dream all night, and like an addict clinging to a high, Penny desperately wanted to savor every moment. Murmuring in her sleep, she tugged on the bedcovers and tightly drew them into a warm cocoon around her shoulders.

Although already half awake, the moving pictures in her mind were still vivid. Best friends, at the energetic age of six, Penny and Henry were almost home from the last day of school. First grade in Mrs. Linden's class hadn't been all that bad. But the start of summer meant freedom. They raced through the grassy field that separated the edge of their quiet neighborhood from the school grounds. Soon, Penny and Henry reached an area where the bricklebutter bushes grew high and formed a small, haphazard maze. The sweet scent of the tiny, white flowers hit their nostrils, and they instinctively breathed in a satisfying gasp. As they slowed to a walk, Penny grabbed Henry's hand and started singing their special song.

"Come on, Henry, dance with me," she pleaded, singing louder as they gradually made their way through the overgrown bushes.

Penny knew he would, and before long, both were waving their hands and twirling around.

"If you love me, I'll love you too," they shrieked and squealed with laughter. "And do the Nimmy Nimmy dance."

Sleep inevitably yielded and surrendered to the day. So did Penny's dream. Desperate to dwell longer in the fun, contentedness, and unabashed happiness of a time long ago, Penny savored the memory. With a quick giggle, she reluctantly opened her eyes and released her mental grasp on the fading sights and sounds of two kids singing and dancing.

Although dawn, it was mostly dark in her bedroom. The only light was the reddish/orangish glow outlining her window as the sun's rays intensified. Miniature prisms, the frost on the window captured the beams and spread them outward like tiny lasers. Stifled only by the heavy curtains that blocked the winter draft, the rays sneaked through the gaps between the drapes and the wall and danced defiantly at the darkness of the room.

Penny ventured an arm out from under the blankets and stretched for her cell phone on the nightstand. The room was still chilly. Her thermostat was set to switch from the brisk nighttime setting she enjoyed to the warmer daytime one at six a.m. She pressed a button on the phone. Twelve minutes to six. Her alarm was set for six thirty, so she had some time before needing to get ready for work.

Twisting again onto her back, she stared at the ceiling. Somewhat hypnotized by the slow-motion prancing of the light, Penny contemplated the dream. She knew it was triggered by the phone call with Kate the night before.

"Henry Taylor," Penny muttered to the departing shadows as the room continued to lighten. She smiled, picturing her childhood best friend and fluffed her blanket. Then she remembered the wedding invitation.

Carefully clenching the covers, Penny sat up on the side of her bed, turned on the nightstand lamp, and glanced over at the dresser. Sighing heavily, she raced to it, shuffled through some papers, and grabbed an envelope. Shivering, she pulled it close and bolted back to her bed. She stacked her pillows together so she could prop herself up and pulled the blanket snugly around her.

Now warm again, Penny slipped the envelope from under the covers and studied it. Opening the flap, she emptied its contents onto her lap. Lifting an elegantly printed card, she scanned the formal wording. Two months from now, Kate Taylor would marry Robert Anderson, and Penny and a guest were invited. She had already mailed back the response card with the "Yes, I will attend box" checked. She had even handwritten, "I'm so excited," next to it.

Penny lived in Frankfurt, Germany, and worked for a consulting firm that specialized in corporate transitions. Her company helped organizations navigate complex reorganizations and integrations. Located near an international airport, and central to the area, the city provided a convenient base for her assignments.

She had planned to leave for the wedding on a Friday afternoon, flying from Frankfurt back to her parent's house in Atlanta, Georgia. That Saturday, her brother, Tim, was graduating from college. She'd spend a few days there, and then fly to Indiana for Kate's wedding. The Tuesday after, Penny would be back in Frankfurt. She'd only miss eight days of work.

Unfortunately, all that had changed. Penny's employer suddenly announced an accelerated schedule for the completion of a critical project. They canceled all vacations for the next three months. Although everyone involved would get a hefty bonus as compensation, it didn't soothe Penny's anger, then sadness, at not being able to get home.

After sliding the invitation card back into the envelope, Penny picked up the photos that Kate had included, most likely taken at her engagement announcement.

The first one was Kate and Robby. "They're going to have beautiful babies," Penny mumbled.

She then flipped through the others. Robby, Kate, and her parents. Robby, Kate, and Henry. Kate and Henry.

Kate and Henry were twins. Their similarly streaked blond hair and facial similarities gave this away. Personality wise, though, they couldn't be more different. Kate was talkative, spontaneous, and personable, while Henry was quiet and sometimes aloof. Highly intelligent, Henry preferred facts and figures. "Likely the reason he's still single," Kate had teasingly informed Penny.

She picked up the last photo and stroked it affectionately with her thumb. Kate, Henry, Alex, and Sean, with their arms interlocked.

"Gosh, how long has it been since I've seen them in person?" she asked herself. "I was eleven when we moved, so 15 years," she sighed.

Penny, Henry, Kate, and Alex had grown up on the same street within a few houses of each other. Their backyards faced an open field that seemed to shrink every year from the encroaching bricklebutter bushes. All four, or parts thereof, could inevitably be found together. School, sports, and other activities kept them busy. At some point, a new kid, Sean, moved into the neighborhood, and the four friends became five.

Penny pushed her head back into her pillow and closed her eyes. "Hmmm," she pondered. "Why weren't Kate, Alex, and Sean in my dream? We were always with each other."

A sadness welled up inside as she remembered moving away from her friends. It was during middle school that Penny's dad was transferred. A "for sale" sign popped up in front of their house, and the family prepared for the moving vans to arrive.

The day before Penny was set to leave, she asked her four friends to meet for one last time in the bricklebutter patch. Winding their way into the center, they sat down under a canopy that had grown higher over the years. Sean, the tallest, could reach up and touch the golden branches. The white flowers emitted their sweet scent.

They took turns asking questions about Penny's new home and made her promise that they could come see her. They talked about going to a new school.

"Have you met any friends there yet?" asked Kate.

"Yes, I went with my mom to register at the school. The

principal showed us around, and I met some classmates," answered Penny.

Glancing around, Alex wondered, "Do they have brickle-butter bushes there?"

"Well, so far I haven't seen any," said Penny.

"So, you're really leaving tomorrow?" asked Kate as she choked up a bit.

"Unfortunately, yes. This is my last time in the patch. I'll miss it."

Penny stood up and stretched her arms out to Henry. "Will you dance with me, Henry? One last time? Like we used to do when we were little?"

Mortified, Henry's face turned red, and he looked at Alex and Sean. "No, I'm not doing that," he said.

"We're not either," said Sean, speaking for Alex and himself.

"It's a stupid song anyway," said Alex.

"It is not!" protested Penny. Offended, she turned away.

"Just what is a nimmy?" asked Sean.

"Yeah, it's not even a word," Alex added.

"It's my grandmother's word. She made it up," answered Penny, facing them again.

"You can't just make up words," proclaimed Alex.

"She did," insisted Penny.

"Well, what is it then?" asked Alex.

"A nimmy is something that makes you so happy, you need to let it out."

"Oh," said Henry and Sean simultaneously.

"Then what's a nimmy nimmy?" snorted Alex.

"A nimmy nimmy is even more intense," explained Penny.

"Like a nimmy squared?" offered Henry.

"Why does everything have to be about math with you?" scolded Kate. "It means you're so happy and excited you're ready to burst. So, you dance."

"I like Henry's description better," said Alex.

"Me too," agreed Sean. "It makes more sense."

"Besides, we're not happy. Nobody wants to dance," said Henry.

The boys' deflection had almost worked when Kate looked up at Penny and then at Henry. "Well, maybe sometimes the dance makes you happy," she mumbled.

Kate hopped up. "I'll dance with you, Penny!" she exclaimed.

She grabbed Penny's hands. They were soon singing and twirling around. Pausing for a second, both girls clasped one of Henry's arms and pulled him into their circle. Anger quickly turned into a smile. He helped Penny and Kate drag both Alex and Sean onto their feet. Holding hands and singing, the five of them bounced and swayed in an awkward and ungraceful gyration.

After a few rotations, Alex's foot caught Henry's leg and the five of them plummeted to the ground. They were howling with laughter as they untangled themselves.

Standing up, Kate threw her arms around Penny. "I'll miss you."

Henry, Alex, and Sean just stood there frozen, not knowing what to do. Penny hugged Alex and Sean for a moment, which was all they would tolerate. She then turned to Henry.

"I'll miss you, Henry," said Penny.

Henry shyly met Penny's eyes as a few tears trickled down

her cheek. Henry's stomach churned as an odd feeling rose inside him. He put his arms around her and squeezed. "Me, too."

Promptly at 6:30, Penny's alarm rang. Not sure which had jarred her more, the memory, or the alarm, Penny hastily opened the envelope and dropped in the photos. Her room had warmed considerably, and she threw off the blankets. "I've got to get going," she mumbled to no one. "I've got a full day of meetings." Resolutely, she hopped out of bed and began her morning routine. She had soon dressed, eaten, and was out the door.

That evening, Penny washed the few dishes from her dinner and settled onto her sofa. She briskly rubbed her feet for a few minutes. The throng waiting for the subway was larger than usual, so she had walked. She didn't mind as she found she did her best thinking when trekking.

Not owning a car, Penny relied on public transportation, friends, and the infrequent car rental to get around. Fortunately, her apartment was downtown and close to work. She had sublet it from the person who had held her job before her and done her best to make it feel homey.

Although small by American standards, the rooms were cozy and comfortable. Besides, Penny's goal was to spend as little time as possible in her apartment. There were enticing places she wanted to see and interesting people to meet. Furthermore, her job kept her busy. The travel demands of each project meant the flat was empty for weeks at a time.

Penny reached for her cell phone and checked the time. She'd been dreading this call all day. Her mother worked mornings for the county and would be home by now. She sighed and hit the button.

"Hi, Mom!" said Penny cheerfully.

"Penny! How are you?" asked her mother.

"I'm good. How are you and Dad?"

"We're fine. Your father's embroiled in the usual drama at work. He's sorry he took that manager's slot. Now he's supervising his friends, which he isn't fond of doing."

"That's a hard adjustment. I've got some information we use to help with those transitions. I'll email it to him."

"He'd appreciate any help at this point. He's monopolizing our prayer time at church," she chuckled.

Penny laughed with her. "I can see Dad doing that!"

The apartment grew darker as the sun's intensity shifted farther away from Penny in Europe and closer to her mom in the U.S. The timer on the lamp next to Penny clicked loudly and filled the room with light.

"What was that noise?" asked her mom.

"Just my lamp turning on. It's almost dark here."

"Oh, yes, the time difference," said Penny's mom. "Is work going well?"

"That's one reason I'm calling. I won't be able to get home for Tim's graduation," said Penny gently.

Her mother gasped faintly, and Penny could hear her disappointment. "I was afraid of that."

"Major crisis at work. They've canceled all vacations for the next three months. I can't get away. I'm really sorry."

"We were all hoping."

"I know. I'm sorry. I'll call Tim at his dorm and talk to him. But I do have an idea. I'd like Tim to fly over and spend some time here. He'd love it. He could hang around with my friends and play tourist."

"Well, I'm sure he'd jump at the chance. I'm not so sure I'd like that, though. He might meet someone over there, and then I'd have both of my children living away. My grandchildren, too."

"Then you and Dad could move over here with us," Penny suggested halfheartedly.

Her mother changed the subject.

"What about your plans for Kate Taylor's wedding?"

"I can't go to that either. I already called Kate and explained."

"I'm sorry, Penny. I know that was hard."

"Yes, it was. Kate was disappointed and a little upset at first. But she understood."

"I know you were hoping for a reunion with your friends. Are you okay?"

"Yes, I'm fine. I'll admit, though, I wasn't very gracious to my boss when she told me. But everyone else needs to reschedule plans, too. The office isn't the cheeriest place right now."

"I'm sure there'll be other opportunities," consoled her mother. "Did Kate say anything about Henry?"

"Just that he's working at a lab and very happy there."

Her mother chuckled, "You kids were always running off to that bricklebutter patch. Remember that?"

One of Penny's fondest memories was of Henry and her in the patch. They had both been lying on the soft ground. Looking skyward, Penny had wondered why Henry made her feel so special. She was soon lost in a fantasy. She and Henry, wandering through a magnificent castle, surrounded by vast mountains. They would live there together forever, doing whatever fun things they chose.

"Penny! Penny! Are you there?" her mom's voice broke through her reverie.

"Oh, sorry. Got distracted." Penny shook her head, snapping her mind back to the present. "Yes, I do remember that."

"Your father and I wondered if the two of you would end up together one day."

"Mom, I don't see that happening. We're friends. Plus, there's an ocean between us. I have a life over here." Penny's voice rose along with her irritation.

"You're right," admitted her mother. "I'm being selfish. You do have a life over there."

"Thanks for that. I miss all of you."

"I know. We miss you too."

Penny rearranged her legs on the sofa. She was getting hungry, but knew her mom needed to talk. Especially given the bad news.

"How was your visit with the Lindens?"

"Wonderful. It was so nice to spend time with them again. Ned and your dad went to two ball games. That gave Eileen and me plenty of time to catch up."

"Is she still teaching first grade?" asked Penny.

"No, they move her around based on the student population. Last year she had third grade, and this next one, fourth grade. We laughed and laughed at her stories of you and your friends in her first-grade class."

"I'm sure," chuckled Penny. "Although I don't think it's fair to have a teacher who is best friends with your mother!"

"She loved having you in her class. Henry and Kate, too.

Although Alex was a handful. Do you remember how he used to make fun of how I called you home for dinner?"

Penny reflected for a moment and laughed. "I do. He could be so annoying."

Henry, Kate, Alex, and Penny would usually play outside after school until Penny's mom, Mrs. Stevens, would open the back door and shout, "Penelopeeee, Penelopeeee." That was the signal for them to stop whatever they were doing and head home.

Alex would sometimes mimic the call with his own high pitched "Penelopeeee," with an emphasis on pee. Alex would start laughing at his pee joke so hard that he would hold his stomach and almost fall. The first time, Kate and Penny got angry and, together, pushed Alex over onto the ground. However, Alex insisted, in a way only kids would understand, that he was not making fun of his friend. Pee, poop, and farts were funny, weren't they?

Laughing along with her, Penny's mom agreed, "That he could! Eileen told me the story of how he fell out of his chair. I hadn't heard that one."

Penny tilted her head and frowned as she tried to remember the incident. She grew somber. "That wasn't exactly the best of times."

"I know what you're thinking. Forget about that. I made it through, and I've had no problems since. But you're right. That was a challenge for us. I'm sorry you had to experience that."

Penny's mother had been diagnosed with cancer. It was a scary and confusing time. Her mom and dad had assured both Penny and her brother that everything would be fine. However, because of complications, Mrs. Stevens took a turn for the worse.

As one of Mrs. Stevens' best friends, other adults would frequently pop into Mrs. Linden's classroom for an update. Anytime an adult would mention Mrs. Stevens' name around the kids, they would get a pained look on their face and speak in hushed tones. You could tell they were worried and concerned. This was not lost on the children, as they, too, wondered about Penny's mom.

The tension came to a head one week during class. Penny had fully rotated her upper body to explain something to both Alex and Kate, who sat behind her. Penny had not heard, or simply ignored, the three requests from Mrs. Linden to turn around and pay attention to the lesson. Mrs. Linden grew exasperated. Alex and Kate, too, were so engrossed in what Penny was explaining to them that they were oblivious to Mrs. Linden's instructions. Only Henry, sitting next to Penny, could see the angry expression on the teacher's face. Henry nudged Penny.

"I definitely need to separate the four of you," Mrs. Linden grumbled out loud, and moved toward the children.

Henry nudged Penny again.

Annoyed at Henry for interrupting and poking her, Penny turned and faced forward again. But it was too late.

"Penelope Stevens!" said Mrs. Linden emphatically. "If you don't stop that talking and start paying attention, I'm going to call your mother and . . ."

The class froze.

Mrs. Linden did, too. She saw the hurt expression on Penny's face and mouthed some words, but nothing came out.

Paralyzed, no one moved.

Then Penny quickly slid out of her chair and ran up to Mrs.

Linden and threw her arms around her. "Mom will be okay," she assured her mom's best friend.

Mrs. Linden regained her composure and hugged Penny back. "Yes, she will."

Suddenly, Alex let out a loud holler, "Penelopeeeeee!" Again, emphasis on the pee.

This broke the spell, and the entire class giggled simultaneously. This only encouraged Alex, and he was soon doubled over, laughing as hard as he could at his joke.

Unfortunately, he fell out of his seat.

The class thought that was hysterical. So did Mrs. Linden.

It took a while for Mrs. Linden to stop her own laughing and regain control of the class.

Penny chuckled into the phone. "Now that I think back on it, that was pretty funny. I'm surprised Mrs. Linden remembered that."

"Oh, Eileen remembers everything. She's been a loyal friend to me." Her mother paused. "Eileen's oldest daughter is married now and has kids of her own. So, she spends lots of time with her grandkids. We're fortunate they could visit."

Penny braced herself, ready to defend, once again, her move to Germany. "I hope I get to see everyone back there sometime soon, too."

"Well, you know my feelings about that. I wish you'd settle down and find someone special," her mother said wistfully.

Penny rolled her eyes. "Mom, I will. I'm not just traipsing around Europe haphazardly. I have a job I love and friends who love me. I'm happy here."

"Well, I wish you weren't!"

"You don't want me to be happy?"

"You know what I mean. Of course, I want you to be happy. But over here," her mother said facetiously.

"Oh, I see," Penny laughed. "By the way, I'm still dating Ethan."

"Oh, that sounds promising," her mom teased. "Tell me more about him."

They talked for another half hour before Penny's mom became concerned over the length of the call, and they hung up.

CHAPTER 2

With his travel coffee mug settled into its cup holder and cell phone linked to the car's sound system, Henry began his morning commute up the mountain to Fusion Lab. The drive was now second nature, and he'd sometimes arrive at the Lab's gate not at all conscious of his trip but having resolved some of the day's issues in his head.

"Ugh!" Henry let out a frustrated sigh. A large truck had just turned onto CR17 about a quarter mile ahead of him. He'd have to follow it all the way up. "If only I'd been five minutes earlier!"

Fusion Lab's Research Complex stretched out over approximately 70 acres on a plateau surrounded by the foothills of the Blue Ridge Mountains. The complex had at one point been a town built by successive railroad companies to support the great expansions of the track lines of the late 1800s. It was reachable by following State Road 86 along Lake Genevieve and up the winding, two-lane County Road 17. The Lab's entry gate stood at the top of the highland. The plateau looked out over massive culverts and canyons that lured the admiring gaze of all visitors.

Theodore Granger, Henry's boss and mentor, scooped up the entire parcel, over 5,000 acres, when the opportunity arose. He traded a sizable chunk of valuable research hours to the holding company who owned the rights to the land. The many buildings had been vacant for decades, needed costly renovations, and, in some cases, demolition. The holding company eventually tired of the taxes and upkeep on an unused asset.

Over the years, Ted had invested a small fortune into refurbishing the complex. Driving through the Lab's entrance gate, you could still see the enormous rock, steel, and concrete skeletons of the historic rail town fabrication areas and old wooden rail piling structures. However, instead of decaying, abandoned ugliness, they provided the buttresses for an artful, modern complex of buildings.

Henry had joined Fusion Lab right out of graduate school. It was his only career job and became all he knew and loved in business. Over the next ten years, Henry had drawn upon his smarts and analytical skills to rise rapidly within the Lab. Inevitably, despite his youth, he had now become the Lab's Research Director, answering only to Ted.

Henry grabbed his mug out of the car cupholder and took a few sips of coffee. As he lowered it, his cell phone and console lights both flashed, announcing a call. "Alex," he muttered. He debated ignoring it, as he knew why he was calling.

"Hey, Alex, what's up?"

"A little cranky this morning, aren't we?" asked Alex. "I guess you've heard?"

"Yes, Kate called me last night," answered Henry, regretting taking the call.

"So, Penny's not coming to the wedding?"

"No, she's not," confirmed Henry. He shifted his eyes from the road and caught the view on his left of the valley below. The sun was warming up the night's dampness, forming patches of mist that rose like smoke from a snuffed-out campfire.

"I was sure she would," said Alex. "It's been a long time."

"Penny called Kate. She's committed to a project at work and can't get the time off. I'm disappointed, too."

"You sound a little ticked off to me," countered Alex.

"No, I'm fine. I was hoping we'd all get to see her."

"Maybe you should call Penny sometime."

"You sound like Kate. Maybe I will."

"Yeah, yeah. You've been saying that for forever," groused Alex. He hesitated before adding, "Look, I know you're busy. Just wanted to check in. Sean's coming into town the week before Kate's wedding. We're planning on a couple rounds of golf. Are you up for that?"

"Sure!" answered Henry, his mood brightening. "I'll be there the whole week. Can you check with Kate on the schedule, though? She has a list of things she'd like help with."

"I'm sure she does," said Alex. "I'll let you know the details once we figure it out. Talk to you later."

Henry hit a button on his steering wheel to end the call. Noting the time, he realized he'd be a lot later to work than he wanted. He'd been matching the acceleration of the truck in front, followed by the stuttering shifting of its gears as it slowed for the turns. Steady progress, but very slow.

The delay did, however, give him extra time to stew over the news about Penny. Alex was right–Henry was miffed. Although he'd never admit it to anyone else, his feelings were hurt. And that annoyed him even more.

The last time he had seen Penny's face was over a year ago. His sister Kate had shown him a photo on social media. An attractive brunette, Penny was smiling brightly in front of Munich's famous Glockenspiel. Around her waist was the arm of an equally impressive man, obviously her boyfriend.

"They look happy together," Henry had remarked.

His sister had sighed and frowned at him. "You should call her sometime."

Although not as striking as his sister, anyone looking at the photo would insist Penny was as beautiful. With shoulder length, brown hair, and eyes to match, it was Penny's smile that perfected her shapely build. It was that smile that had tugged at Henry from the time they first met.

Attempting to quash his foul mood, Henry thought about the fun times he'd had with Penny as kids. Without a doubt, his favorites were of the bricklebutter maze. They'd run and laugh together until, out of breath, they'd collapse on the soft mat.

Although loved by Penny, the landscapers in town hated the pods. For when bricklebutter pods mature and are ready to release their seeds, the outer casings disintegrate, leaving behind a custardy substance a lot like creamy butter. Over many seasons, the pod clumps meld into a nutty colored sod pad that squishes to the touch like memory foam.

Surrounded by the hedges, Penny and Henry oversaw their own little world. Lying on their backs, they could see the blue, puffy-clouded sky above. The height of the bushes and the wooly-leaved branches created a sparse awning that shot out in every direction. Bright, yellowy gold in color, the branches resembled lightning bolts that splintered out and created haphazard cracks in the teal blue sky.

Often, Penny would roll over on her stomach and nestle her chin in her hands, supported by her elbows. She and Henry would then talk about their latest happenings. Sometimes, their eyes would meet, communicating something, although Henry could never figure out what. He'd feel uneasy and glance away.

The truck slowed to a crawl at the apex of the hill. Henry sighed as he was forced to stop while the truck turned at the curve. "Why doesn't he pull to the side so I can pass him?" grumbled Henry, his gloomy frame of mind returning.

His sullenness surprised Henry. Normally a positive person, he'd never let events master his mood for long. Yes, he'd been elated with the anticipation of Kate's wedding and Penny's return. But Kate's wedding would still be a blast, even if Penny won't be there.

Now at a long straightaway, the truck's speed picked up. So did Henry. Calmer, Henry wondered if he had ever before felt this upset with Penny. "The day she moved away," he muttered to himself. He was, what, eleven or twelve?

He and Kate had stood in the driveway as Penny and her family drove off. Kate had grabbed Henry's hand as they waved goodbye. Henry then went about his days as if nothing had changed. If anyone asked him about Penny, he just shrugged his shoulders. He didn't want to talk about it with anyone.

The only person he couldn't brush-off was his grandmother, Ruth. Henry had a special relationship with her. Even as he grew older, he still enjoyed talking with her and looked forward to her visits.

One day, soon after Penny had moved, Ruth knocked on his bedroom door and asked, "Can I come in, Henry?"

Henry lay across his bed tossing a small rubber football up in the air and back into his hands. "Okay," he answered.

"Your mom says that you're not feeling well and didn't go to school yesterday. I'm sorry about that. Can I get a hug, anyway?"

"Sure, Grandmom."

Henry rolled the football onto his bed, rose slowly, and turned to reach out his arms. His grandmother smiled at him and gave him a firm hug. They both sat down on the bed. Henry then slumped back and reached for his football.

"It's Saturday. And beautiful outside, too. I'd think you'd be out playing with your friends."

Henry grunted.

"Well, can you explain to me what the problem is?" Ruth asked. "Is it your stomach? I sometimes get heartburn if I eat too many beans. They give me gas. How about you? Did you eat beans for dinner last night?"

Henry snickered at the thought of his grandmother passing gas and averted his head so that she could not see him laughing.

"No, I don't know what it is," said Henry.

"I bet you have a fever. Let me check your forehead."

Henry protested at first but gave in to his grandmother's request. She stretched her arm out a little further and cupped her hand over his forehead.

"No, you seem alright to me. How is Kate? You both seem to always get sick together."

"No, she's fine. She's around somewhere."

"Well, if you're not sick, tell me what's going on."

Henry gave his grandmother a blank look signaling that the visit was over, and he now wanted to be alone. Ruth shifted on the bed as if to rise and then settled back again.

"Oh, I meant to ask you. How is Penny? Have you talked to her?"

Henry froze as the football he had just tossed into the air drifted down and hit him in the face. He grunted exasperatedly and rolled the ball onto the floor. He then turned onto his side so that his back was toward his grandmother.

She paused but expected no answer from Henry. "I bet she misses her friends here. I wonder if she is a little worried about meeting new people."

"No, she's not worried. Kate and I talked to her on the phone the other day. She and Kate blabbed for most of the time. They have a pool at their house, and she's swimming every day. She was eager to tell us all about it."

"I bet you're happy for her," said Ruth as she watched Henry out of the corner of her eye.

Henry rolled over toward his grandmother. "I want to be. I know she was sad to leave, but she was excited, too. I could tell. It makes me angry."

"I bet that does hurt a little." Ruth reached over and patted Henry's shoulder.

"Everything's different," continued Henry. "All of us would walk to school together and Penny would sit next to me in class.

I'd help her with math and stuff."

"Who do you sit next to now?"

"I'm between Alex and Sean," moaned Henry.

"Do you help them?"

"Yes, but Alex is annoying. He's difficult to explain things to."

His grandmother laughed softly. "Yes, we need to pray for that boy!"

Henry laughed with her.

They were quiet for a few moments. "Sounds like a big change for you," offered Ruth.

"It'll never be the same," Henry griped.

"I'm sorry for that. But I bet you'll work it out," his grandmother assured him. "Remember, Henry. There's always hope, no matter what."

"If you say so," mumbled Henry.

"You know, I miss Penny, too. She has the most wonderful smile. Don't you think, Henry?" asked Ruth with a twinkle in her eyes.

Henry didn't respond. A picture of Penny's face crossed through his mind. Yes, she did have a magnificent smile. His mood brightened somewhat.

"Well, I'm going to be on my way," said his grandmother. "I'll see you tomorrow, though. I've invited your family over for dinner. Your grandfather is grilling hamburgers and hot dogs, and I'm thinking of making a pie. I can't decide between apple and cherry. What would you choose?"

"Apple, of course."

"I thought so. Apple it is, then."

Henry looked at the walls and sighed. His room bored him.

He wanted to get outside. Alex and Sean had been calling all morning.

Timidly, he rose from the bed and found the football on the floor. He palmed it and leaned forward and kissed his grandmother on the cheek.

"Thanks," he said, smiling, as he ambled through the door on his way to meet his friends at the ball field.

The red flashing of brake lights caught Henry's eyes and snapped his attention back to the road. Crunching and grinding its gears, the truck ahead downshifted to slow its speed for its descent down the hill.

"Oh, I'm here," Henry announced to the back of the truck. The entrance to the Lab was just ahead. Relieved, he nosed his car slightly to the right and onto the turn lane.

Remembering his grandmother, Henry chuckled to himself. He knew she'd admonish him to shake off these bad feelings and give Penny the benefit of the doubt. Yes, Penny would've done her best to make the wedding. After all, she'd originally said she was coming. By herself, without a guest, Henry recalled.

Most likely, she was as disappointed as he was. She had an important career, with responsibilities and commitments at work to uphold. Henry could understand that, couldn't he? "Sometimes circumstances occur that're out of our control," Henry muttered.

A reminder from his phone popped up on the dash screen telling him he had ten minutes to get over to the east lab room. Jolted back to the priorities of work, Henry sped up slightly. As he pulled into his usual parking spot, he waved at Rhonda and a few others as they hustled to get to the lab room on time.

Fusion Lab had been a perfect fit for Henry. Theodore "Ted" Granger had started the firm over 30 years ago. Ahead of its time, the Lab performed research for which many corporations paid handsomely but were unable or unwilling to do themselves. People trusted Ted. He was honest to a fault with his clients and possessed a brilliant mind. Ted imprinted these traits on his firm as well, and his clients knew it.

The complex itself fascinated Henry. It looked more like a college campus than a business center. Over many years, Ted had preserved, refurbished, and restored the old railroad buildings, making sure that any new additions blended into the surroundings. What once was dilapidated was now beautiful and boasted of the latest technology and conveniences.

Most Fusion Lab employees, like Henry, lived in the city down in the valley. But for visitors, the complex core offered a small group of studio apartments and cottage suites, a cafeteria, movie theater, gym, and urgent care medical suite. All were apportioned within the large cabins adapted from the railroad village of long ago. The complex had hosted hundreds of clients, researchers, and many other guests.

Henry's newfound enthusiasm for Kate's wedding proved justified. He was able to take two weeks away from the Lab and had a fantastic visit with his family and friends. Putting thoughts of Penny behind him, he now threw himself into his work.

One afternoon, Ted called Henry into his office. Settling into a comfortable chair facing Ted's desk, Henry waited patiently while Ted finished shuffling through a stack of papers.

"Henry, I'd like your input." Ted raised his head and squinted at Henry through his wire-framed glasses. "A few days ago, I took a call from Agnes Mallort at Chemclone. She wants us to collaborate."

Ted removed the glasses, rubbed his forehead, and continued, "She's twisting my arm a bit, and it's making me uncomfortable. They want us to work with an energy company I'm not familiar with. Now, according to Agnes, Chemclone's onto something that could be game changing, as she puts it. Your graduate paper was on unknown energy sources, and you researched most of the notable companies around. This company's name is Emerson Energy, and it's run by a guy named Hyatt Emerson. Ever heard of them?"

"You know, I'm familiar with the name," answered Henry. He leaned forward toward Ted's desk. "They aren't a major player in the industry, though. They're mainly on the fringe of things. But I don't recall anything negative about them."

"Well, good. Agnes already has a meeting set up. I'd like you to go with me. If we like what we hear, you may have a new project on your plate. A significant one. There was an excitement in Agnes' voice that I've not heard before. I've got a good feeling about this!" Ted slapped his hand on the top of his desk for emphasis.

Henry laughed. "I hope you're right. I'll dig up some information on Emerson." He rose to head back to his office.

"It could work, you know," said Ted to Henry as they drove back from the airport. Both Ted and Henry were animated by the meeting they'd had. The idea was to take liquid petroleum gas, mix it with a chemical media, and pressurize it into a solid.

"Yes, but it's a daunting challenge. It could take years to hit the exact formulation needed, and that's after the equipment is designed and built," Henry countered. "It'll consume a lot of the Lab's resources."

"I know, I know. That's why no one else has produced something like this yet. But Agnes is right. She's been in this business all her life and sees the potential. It's worth a feasibility analysis."

"Definitely," agreed Henry. "Can you imagine if we succeeded? It'd be a monumental breakthrough in energy delivery!"

"Wouldn't that be something?" chuckled Ted.

Henry pulled the car into a parking spot. As they walked into the office building, Ted put his arm on Henry's shoulder. "Come on up to my office. We've got to think this through. Obviously, we're both super excited by it." Ted then stopped in his tracks and looked at Henry. "My worry is that it may be too enticing. If we start down this path, it could be impossible to stop. We'd better be sure."

"I agree," said Henry. "We need to consider all the risks. Let's weigh this carefully."

The feasibility study proved formidable, but hugely successful. Within three months, Fusion Lab, Chemclone, and Emerson Energy agreed to proceed. They formed a holding company, Solidane Energy, as the entity to control the project. The "Wafer Project" as it eventually would be called, was born.

It was another few months before the equipment requested by Chemclone was in place. The Lab's design was flawless, and everyone raved at how well it functioned.

The next phase was the search for the correct media to capture, bind, and confine the pressurized gas. Henry had guessed that this phase would take over a year. Progress was slow until Henry hit upon the "wafer" concept. Now, with a workable media in place, they needed to stabilize the absorption. That proved elusive.

As the challenges of the project grew in both complexity and number, so did Henry's passion for it. Unlocking the enormous potential of this new venture kindled an excitement within him that he hadn't yet experienced in his career.

Henry was sifting through some reports when the alarm rang on his cell phone. He hastily silenced it, reorganized the reports, and locked them in his desk. He had a meeting to get to. The phone on his desk beeped.

"Henry?"

"Yes?"

"Sorry to bother you, but Mr. Granger asked me to remind you of your call with Matt and Marie, scheduled for two p.m. It's the only time all of you have available. He doesn't want you to miss it."

"Thanks, Eva," said Henry. "Please tell him I'm on my way."

Henry popped into Ted's office a few minutes later.

Ted was just settling back in his chair when his computer sounded a tone that alerted him to an incoming video. The face of his son popped onto the screen. "Hey, Dad! How are things?"

"Matty! You look good, from what I can observe on this old screen." Ted waved at Henry to grab a chair.

"Dad, please set up the new computer I sent you. It's leading-edge technology. Marie and I don't get to see you enough, and when we do, it'd be nice if we didn't have grainy spots over our faces."

The computer beeped again, and another image popped up on the video screen. "Hi Dad!" a familiar voice melodically announced her presence. "Is Matty dialed in yet?"

"I'm here," answered Matt flatly.

"You don't sound very happy to hear from me," Marie teased.

"No, Dad is complaining about his old computer again and I'm just wondering where the new equipment you and I gave him for his birthday went."

"Okay, you two, give me some slack here," said Ted. "I have a happy team over at the laser optics lab using my birthday present. Best present you've given me! Things are tight financially, and I'm allocating most resources to the Lab. I promise I'll move it back to my office soon. Did you know it has a satellite connection?"

"Yes, as I said, state-of-the-art. My company just got access to them," answered Matt.

"Well, I might be connecting my phone to it so I can make calls from the veranda. It's so lovely there. Who knows, maybe I'll move my office outside," Ted chuckled. "Henry, can you get my phone set up? Yours too. It's smart to have backups."

Henry nodded. He mentally added it to his long to-do list.

"You said things are tight financially. Is everything okay there?" asked Matt.

"Couldn't be better," Ted assured them. "That's why I suggested this call. I've mentioned we're involved with a major new project. Well, it's gone extremely well. But it's at a critical juncture. To proceed means taking some substantial risks. Risks for the Lab, for me, and therefore, the family."

"That sounds a little ominous," said Marie tentatively. "Can you explain what you mean?"

"Well, hold on. I've invited Henry to join us. I'll let him explain the project, and then we'll talk about risks."

Henry walked around Ted's desk and dragged a chair to face the computer screen.

"Here's Henry now. I'll tilt this around better so you can see."

"Hi Henry," said Marie cheerfully.

"Hi Marie," answered Henry. "Good to see you."

"How are you doing, Henry?" asked Matt. "Is Dad working you and your team to death?"

Matt and Henry had become close friends. About the same age, they had met at one of Matt's visits to see his father. Over the years, their friendship grew deeper.

"He's fine," interrupted Ted. "Now, Matt and Marie, this may be the most important project of my career. I want you to grasp enough of it to gauge both the rewards, if successful, and the consequences of failure. Are you okay with that?"

"Yes," they answered after a few moments.

Ted breathed out loudly. "Okay, Henry, could you give them a rundown?"

"Sure," said Henry. He moved to the right so the camera could pick up his face as Ted backed away. "Stop me if you have a question."

"We will," said Matt.

"I know you've heard your dad talk about Chemclone," Henry began. "Agnes Mallort, your father's friend there, asked for help with the design of equipment that would pressurize liquid petroleum gas, that's propane, and mix it with solids to stabilize it. We discovered a process that would concentrate the propane into a cake. We call it a wafer."

"Can you explain why you and dad are so excited about that?" asked Marie.

"Well, imagine going camping, taking out one of our wafers, lighting it, and cooking your entire dinner. Then, that same wafer could provide campfire light and some warmth for the night. Or a few cases of wafers might heat a cabin in Alaska the entire winter." Henry paused for a few seconds. "Our wafer would be a game changer from an energy delivery standpoint."

"Oh, wow. I had no idea!" exclaimed Marie. "And you've done this already?"

"No, not yet. But we're close," answered Henry. It took a moment for the frustration that rose inside him to pass. "The gas keeps wanting to escape. We need to stabilize it, and that's the challenge right now. We'll get there, I'm sure."

Ted stuck his face back into the line of view. "Yes, we will! I get dizzy envisioning the applications for such a product! We tried a multitude of media to hold the gas. The pressurized wafer was Henry's idea."

"I definitely see the upside. What are the risks you spoke about?" asked Matt.

"From a practical standpoint, we're dealing with gas. We're taking every precaution, but you can imagine some nasty outcomes," answered Henry.

"Then there's the financial one," interjected Ted. "Already, this project is eating into the emergency reserves I've set aside over the years. There's no revenue supporting it. And the more resources I throw at this one, there's less available for new, profitable projects."

"I see your dilemma," said Matt.

"If this goes sour, it could take the whole Lab down with it. We'd lose everything," said Ted gingerly. "I'm most worried about how this could affect you two. And your mother, of course."

Henry shifted in his chair, not sure if he should offer to leave so Ted could talk privately with his family.

Sensing his unease, Ted glanced at him. "You're fine, Henry. We can use your advice here." He then faced Matt and Marie again. "Have you heard from your mother?"

Ted and his wife had divorced. Confident, attractive, and self-assured, Margaret encouraged and supported Ted as he built Fusion Lab. They were most happy when they were struggling financially in their early years. But as Fusion became more successful, providing ample income, they grew apart.

The affection Ted and Margaret felt for each other gradually became replaced by Fusion Lab for Ted, and affluence and luxury for Margaret. Exclusive parties, charity events, and mingling with the most fashionable crowd afforded Margaret with increasing emotional affirmation as her relationship dimmed with Ted.

"Yes, she's planning a visit here next month," said Matt. "She's still seeing Randall, if that's what you're getting at."

"Well, I want her to be happy. I miss her sometimes. I wish it could've been different, but here we are," said Ted. "I hope that once we prove this wafer concept, we'll have a fine celebration dinner. All of us together, including your mother. She can bring Randall, too," Ted said mischievously.

"That sounds wonderful," Marie chimed back.

"What do you need from us?" asked Matt. "We'll help if we can."

"Well," began Ted, "I'd like you to weigh over this wafer project. If you sense that it's too much, say so."

"I don't think you should worry about me," said Matt.

"Me, either," said Marie. "No matter what, we'll be okay."

Matt and Marie had successful careers of their own. Matt, the oldest, was a software conversion manager with an international computer firm in Atlanta. Marie was a hospital administrator at one of Florida's largest medical facilities.

"As for mom, you know her financial situation better than we do. She seems well provided for," said Marie.

"Her lawyers saw to that," chuckled Ted.

"What's your recommendation, Henry?" asked Matt.

Henry took a moment to weigh his answer. He cared deeply for the Granger family and didn't want to steer them into any danger. However, just like Ted, the wafer project had captivated him.

"I can only speak for myself. You both know me. I'm not a big risk taker. But I've considered this thoroughly, and I know I couldn't turn down an opportunity like this one. I'm all in."

"Knowing Dad, he is too," said Matt.

"Yep," agreed Marie.

A heavy knock sounded at Ted's door and Eva stuck her head in. "I'm sorry, Mr. Granger, but Hyatt Emerson is on the line insisting on speaking with you. What should I tell him?"

Ted sighed and waved his hand in dismissal. "That I'm on an important call with my family, and I'll call him back right afterward."

"I already explained that to him. He keeps calling," said Eva.

"Then let him keep calling," said Ted gruffly. "Give him the same message each time."

"Will do," answered Eva. She hurriedly ducked out of the door frame and closed the door.

"What was that?" asked Matt.

"Oh, that was Hyatt Emerson, with another crisis. I'm sure it can wait until we finish our call," said Ted. He swiveled his chair back toward the computer screen.

"Who is he again?" asked Marie. "Is he involved with this somehow?"

"Yes, Agnes, Hyatt, and I formed Solidane Energy Corporation as a holding vessel for the wafer. The way it works is, Fusion Lab's task is to design and prove the wafer. Agnes and her company, Chemclone, will produce the wafer. Hyatt and Emerson Energy will take care of regulation and marketing."

"You mean all the time and money you're devoting to this wafer isn't for the Lab?" asked Marie.

"Well, it is," answered Ted. "Just indirectly. It's complicated. We agreed that to be fair based on contributions, I would own the majority of shares of Solidane. They each split the rest. So, if the wafer is successful, the Lab stands to benefit accordingly. Plus, my majority position puts me in the role of CEO."

"So, you call the shots," said Matt.

"Supposedly." Ted shook his head back and forth. "I'm not sure Hyatt would agree."

"Well, good luck with that, from what I just heard," offered Marie.

"Yeah, good luck with that," said Matt.

"Now you sound like Henry. He's not a fan either," laughed Ted.

"I'll say!" chimed in Henry.

"I'd better go save Eva from Hyatt," grumbled Ted. "I'm certain she's gotten an earful by now." Ted moved closer to the screen to see Matt's and Marie's faces more clearly. "Now, about this wafer project. I admit, I've never been more excited by an opportunity. But you think about it. If there are no objections, I believe we're 'all in,' as Henry said."

"Will do," said Matt. "Thanks for being on the call, Henry."

"Good to talk to you! Hope I see you in person soon," said Henry.

"I'll be praying about this," said Marie. "It's a big decision."

"Please do," said Ted. "Thanks for taking time to chat. I always enjoy this. Give my love to your families."

CHAPTER 3

A light burning at the end of the office area caught Clara's eye. With a huff, she hustled down the hallway and walked through the open door of Penny's office. It was sparsely furnished and had few decorations, a mirror image of those of the firm's other project managers.

"Penny Stevens!" she stated sternly. "What in heaven's name are you still doing here?"

Startled at first, Penny recognized the voice of her boss and stopped typing on her computer. Laughing, she turned her head and looked at Clara. "I could ask you the same question!"

"I didn't have a choice," muttered Clara. She walked over and sat in the chair in front of Penny's desk. "You should be out enjoying yourself. Where's Ethan?"

"Ethan's away. I'm catching up on my reports."

"Is that project going any better?" asked Clara. "I'm getting concerned."

"No, and I'm frustrated. I don't think those two VPs want

this to succeed. We agree on a plan, and they do the opposite. Here, look at this. I just updated the timeline. We'll be battling this out for another month." Penny turned her laptop around so Clara could see.

"That's not good," agreed Clara. "Stephan called just as I was leaving. He asked about your project. Seems the client's CEO is getting impatient. He doesn't understand the hold-up."

"Well, tell Stephan to have the CEO call me. I can give him an earful."

Clara laughed. "I'm sure. If you could do a quick status note, I'll get that to Stephan. I think it's time this CEO lit a fire underneath his VP's. Either they support the reorganization they agreed upon or say why they won't. This undermining is not acceptable."

"Gladly," affirmed Penny. "How'd I get assigned to this project, anyway? Shouldn't this have gone to Rory? He's miffed at me. He thinks I hijacked his assignment."

"I wish you'd all trust my judgment," asserted Clara. "I don't play favorites."

"Obviously!" moaned Penny. "You stuck me with this project!"

"Rory doesn't have the experience yet to maneuver through a complex reorganization. Those two VPs would eat him alive!"

"Possibly. Maybe it would've been an excellent learning experience?" Penny tilted her head and smirked at Clara.

Clara and Penny had known each other for over ten years. Clara had hired Penny after her internship with the firm. She had mentored Penny, helping her to adjust to both a new job and a new country. They'd become great friends.

Leaning back, Clara waited for Penny's attention. "Stephan and I also discussed another matter. He said he's retiring and putting the firm up for sale," sighed Clara.

"Again?" asked Penny.

"Supposedly, this time he means it. We'll see. In the meantime, I don't want any of you to get distracted. We've been through this before and nothing came of it. However, knowing this office, everyone will be buzzing about it within the week."

Penny nodded in agreement. Neither one spoke for a while. Penny sensed Clara wanted to ask something and waited. Usually, after catching up on work issues, they'd move onto private matters.

"So, Ethan went somewhere without you?" Clara inquired gingerly.

"That's kind of a personal question. And you complain about the office!"

"Don't give me that. We've been friends for too long," said Clara, dismissively waving her hand. "You two are always together lately. What's going on?"

"It's the World Cup. Ethan is away with a group of his friends. He told me I shouldn't expect to see him until it's over." Penny closed her laptop and packed it in her travel bag as if preparing to leave.

"Oh, right, that began," affirmed Clara. "Why didn't you go along?"

Penny laughed. "Me, no. Ethan took me to a match when we first started dating. Teasingly, I told him that the best parts were the histrionics when someone got injured. Ethan wasn't amused. He hasn't invited me to one since. I'm okay with that."

"Have you met this group of friends?" asked Clara. "Any alarm bells going off?"

"You're so cynical, Clara!" exclaimed Penny. She shook her head.

"Comes with this job," said Clara matter-of-factly. "I'm just looking out for you. Ethan has the looks and the charm."

"Yes, he does," Penny said sharply, now growing agitated. "What are you getting at?"

"I'd think he'd have a ring on your finger by now," answered Clara.

Penny's face turned crimson, and she glared at Clara. "I think that's between Ethan and me." She began packing the remaining items on her desk into her computer bag.

"I'm sorry, Penny," said Clara, softly. "You're right. That's none of my business. I've overstepped." She reached over and grabbed Penny's arm. "My job here is to watch, observe, and head off problems. I do that very well. Unfortunately, I guess I do that with my friends, too. I'm meddling."

Penny laid the computer bag down on the desk with a thump and sighed. "I know you're just concerned about me."

"I promise I'll mind my own business and stick to work related topics from now on."

"We both know that won't happen," laughed Penny. She reached over and patted Clara's hand. "Besides, I value your friendship too much." Penny sat back again and looked intently at Clara. "What problem are you trying to head off, if I dare to ask?"

"None, I'm sure. I know you both love each other. My only concern is, at what point does Ethan make a commitment? I think you deserve that."

Penny looked away. "Funny you should say that," sighed Penny. "We had an argument before he left about our relationship. We've dated a long time now. I asked him where he saw it going."

"And he said?"

"We'd discuss it when he got back."

"Well, I guess that's fair, the World Cup and all." Clara rolled her eyes so Penny could see.

Penny laughed. "We'll work it out. I'm not asking for a ring. At least not yet." Giggling, she shrugged her shoulders at Clara. "I only want to know what our future looks like."

"That's reasonable," agreed Clara. "Keep me posted on how that goes. Now let's get out of here. The Rathskeller next door is open. Let's grab a fast drink."

"Gladly!" exclaimed Penny, and they hurried out of the building.

"What's this?" asked Adrianna. She picked up a colorful envelope Penny had left on the kitchen table.

"It's a birth announcement. You can open it," replied Penny.

"People still send these?" asked Adrianna, more a comment than a question.

Penny didn't reply. She put the container of leftovers in the small refrigerator and brusquely closed the door.

"I've got to get that door fixed. Know anyone that does appliance repair?"

"Call our landlord. It's their fridge," answered Adrianna.

She and Penny lived in adjoining apartments. About the

same age, they met while riding the elevator together and easily developed a longstanding friendship.

"Oh, you're right. I hadn't thought about that. Are you ready to go?"

Penny had just finished breakfast when Adrianna had knocked on her door. It was Saturday, and they decided to spend the day together. This morning, they were headed to some of the local shops.

"Oh, how cute!" exclaimed Adrianna as she inspected the photo of the newborn baby on the card inside. "Wow, big baby," she mumbled as she read the birth stats.

"Baby Joy! I love that name." She glanced at the return address. "So, this is from Kate, your friend in the States?" asked Adrianna. She held up the envelope as if Penny needed to see it to confirm.

"Yes, we try to keep in touch," replied Penny, reaching to take the card out of Adrianna's hand.

"I'm so envious," said Adrianna as she clung to the card. "I want one!"

Penny laughed. "I thought you and Raf wanted to wait until he finished his deployment with the military? I have a hard time envisioning you with a baby by yourself. Now let go of it."

Penny quickly won the tug of war and put the card into the envelope. She returned it to the table.

"But they're so cute! You'd help me, wouldn't you?"

"Of course. But I'm out of town, too, most of the time. And look at my plants. You're supposed to be watering them when I'm gone." Penny pointed to a few potted plants on the windowsill, most drooping.

"Hey, that's the cold air from the window," Adrianna rebutted. "I told you it's impossible to keep them alive. You'll notice mine are all artificial."

"I noticed," said Penny.

"So, you're saying I'll be a negligent mother?" With a tilt of her head, Adrianna gave Penny a challenging look.

"No, that's not what I'm saying. You'll be a wonderful mom." Penny grabbed Adrianna's arm and spun her toward her. "Are you trying to pick a fight with me this morning?"

Adrianna chuckled contritely. "No, I'm sorry. I just miss Raf. I hate it when he's away."

"Well, you stay cooped up in this building. We need to get you out of here. Let's go have some fun!" said Penny brightly.

Adrianna headed into Penny's living room, grabbed one of Penny's framed pictures off the end table, and flopped onto the sofa. Penny followed behind.

"I thought we were going out?" asked Penny, standing in the middle of the room, hands on hips.

"We are, but I'm curious. Kate's the one whose wedding you missed a couple of years ago and you didn't get to see your friends?" asked Adrianna.

Penny groaned in frustration and moved toward the sofa.

"I remember all that," Adrianna muttered, mostly to herself. She held up the frame. "And these are those friends here in this picture," she announced like a detective who had just discovered a clue.

"Yes," sighed Penny. She sat next to Adrianna and took hold of the picture frame. "The girl here is Kate, who's just had the baby. That's Henry, her twin brother, next to her."

"I can see the resemblance," said Adrianna.

"These two boys are Alex and Sean," said Penny, pointing to the faces. "That's me in the middle. We all lived on the same street and were close friends."

"I'm so impressed that you stay in contact! And you live in different countries! I couldn't tell you what happened to most of my friends from childhood. I'd have to find them on social media," said Adrianna. She turned her gaze up from the picture. "So, Kate was your best friend from that time of your life?"

Penny looked away. "Actually, her brother, Henry, was my best friend."

"Do you keep in touch with him, too?" asked Adrianna, wondering why Penny had suddenly withdrawn.

"Unfortunately, no. I don't know why. We've just lost touch," explained Penny, somewhat apologetically.

"That's a shame. You obviously aren't happy with that. Why don't you call him?" suggested Adrianna. "When was the last time you talked to him?"

"Hmmm," Penny sighed. "Let's see. The last time I spoke with Henry, I was at my parents' house, packing to move over here."

"So long ago," Adrianna sighed back. "I guess it was an upsetting goodbye?"

"No, in fact, it was very nice," whispered Penny as she remembered back to Henry's call.

A muffled ringing had caught Penny's ear as she carried a loaded suitcase down the stairs. Reaching the bottom, she patted her pant leg, satisfied it wasn't her cell phone. She propped the suitcase up against the hall wall and looked about. Nothing. Moving into the family room, she pinpointed a sound coming from the side cushion of the couch. Spotting the glint of silver from the antenna of the family's portable phone, she yanked it out of the sofa's snug grasp and looked at the display. "Out of Area." Penny hesitated to answer the call, but thought better. It could be someone her mom or dad expected.

She pressed the answer button. "Hello?"

"Mrs. Stevens?"

"No, she's not here. Can I take a message?" Penny sighed, assuming it was a sales call.

"Penny?"

"Henry?"

"Penny! Great to hear your voice. I was calling your mom to get your number. How are you?"

"I'm so glad I picked up. No one usually calls this phone anymore. I guess I'm doing well," said Penny excitedly. She switched the phone to her other ear as she settled onto the couch.

"It's been a while. I didn't recognize your voice at first. Sorry I haven't called sooner," said Henry.

"I'm just as guilty," admitted Penny. "No apology needed."

"Kate tells me you're headed to Europe on an internship. I wanted to wish you luck."

"Yep! I leave on Saturday. Mom and Dad are both at work, so I'm all alone here at their house finishing my packing. I'm really glad you called."

"You're finally doing it. I guess all those language classes will come in very handy now," chuckled Henry.

"We'll see. I know I can invite anyone I meet to the library in Spanish, French, or German. And English, of course," giggled Penny.

"I barely remember my Spanish class from high school. But I think I remember those memorization lines!"

"I'm headed to Germany first. I hope I'll understand enough to figure out if someone is saying something bad about me!" laughed Penny.

"I'm sure you'll be fine. Are you excited?" asked Henry.

Penny paused, and her shoulders slumped. She pressed her head into the soft padding of the sofa back. "Honestly, yes and no. This has been my dream for so long. But now that it's a reality, I'm second guessing my decision. You're the only person I've admitted that to, by the way."

"You'll never forgive yourself if you don't jump at this opportunity. You love your adventures. We've all known that since we were kids. I'm sure it's just the goodbyes that are so difficult right now."

A wave of emotion raced through Penny and caught her voice. "Yes," she cracked. "I'm dreading those with my family."

"Well, I've been sitting here in a chair staring at a blank TV for the last hour," confessed Henry. "I wanted to call, but I'm not sure what to say."

"You're saying the right things," Penny assured him in a stronger tone. "Are you still living on campus?"

"Sort of. I live just off campus with most of the grad students. Three courses to get under my belt, and then I'm out of here."

"Any idea of where you'll end up?"

"I've got three or four strong possibilities," revealed Henry. "There's a lab I've heard a lot about and I'm hoping to tour the facilities in the next couple of months. The guy who founded it keeps calling me. We seem to have hit it off. I'll see what develops."

"I'm positive you'll find the perfect fit," said Penny. A rustling sounded from the garage door as a car pulled in.

"I think Mom or Dad just got home."

"Say hi to them for me. And Penny, go live that dream. You've put a lot of hard work into making it happen. An internship that special doesn't get offered to just anyone."

"Thanks, Henry. I needed to hear that." Penny let out a sincere sigh of appreciation at Henry's encouragement.

"Good luck and stay in touch," said Henry. He paused, unsure of what to say next.

"Thanks for calling, Henry," said Penny. "It means a lot."

"Bye, Penny."

"Goodbye, Henry."

"Oh, Penny, that's so sweet!" said Adrianna once Penny had recounted the conversation. "Why don't you call him? You obviously still have some kind of connection."

Grimacing, Penny looked away. "So much time has passed. We've gone our separate ways, and I doubt we'd have much in common anymore. Besides, my life is over here." She waved her arm around her room.

"I see your point. Well, at least Kate stays in touch." Adrianna picked up the picture and returned it to the table. She sat back down next to Penny. "I admire you so much, Penny. I'd never have the courage to move across an ocean."

"I don't have many regrets. Sure, I miss my family and

friends. But the last ten years have been amazing for me. It's been a wonderful adventure," said Penny confidently. She lifted her legs off the carpet, swung them gracefully onto the sofa, and rested her head on the plush cushion.

"And you have your family here, too. Me, Raf, and Ethan!" exclaimed Adrianna. She copied Penny's shift of her body, but with her legs now more underneath her bottom.

"You and Raf, for sure. Sometimes I wonder about Ethan," said Penny wistfully.

"Trouble in paradise again?" Adrianna quizzed.

"If I think of our relationship like a car, sometimes we're moving along fine. But then we suddenly slip into neutral. Like we're stuck in place. I'm finding that Ethan seems happier when we're in neutral than drive. Also, I feel like the times in neutral are getting longer, and the drive times shorter. I've tried to ignore it. That's getting harder to do."

"You and your analogies!" sighed Adrianna. "A car?"

"I learned that technique at work. It's very effective in explanations," defended Penny.

"If you say so," said Adrianna dismissively. She shifted a leg and leaned closer to Penny. "Look, you both love each other. I'm sure you'll work it out."

Penny drew in a deep breath and let it out slowly. At the last puff of breath, her eyes grew brighter, and she smiled.

"I think so, too," she said optimistically. "When we're together, we have the best time. We love traveling with each other, and we've explored so many places already. We've had so much fun!"

"See there!" Adrianna said encouragingly. "Ugh! My feet are falling asleep. How about we get out of here?" She unfurled her legs and stood. Reaching out a hand, she helped Penny.

"Ooof!" gasped Penny as she stood and stretched. "Let's get moving. We don't shop together that often. Let's make the most of it!"

CHAPTER 4

Deep in concentration, Henry rapidly flipped through a wordy project report spread out over his desk. These updates were important. They allowed him to stay abreast of the many projects he handled. Most of his managers got right to the point with pertinent facts. However, this one, Rhonda, seemed to hurl bursts of data at him, like popcorn cooking without a lid. It was up to him to gather these scattered kernels to determine if her project was on task. It consumed a lot of his time and he didn't have any to spare lately.

Frustrated, Henry sighed and silently mouthed the question, "Why can't Rhonda simply give me a quick recap?"

"Henry, I've got great news!" Ted shouted as he dashed into Henry's office.

He rushed up to the desk and straight-armed aside all of Henry's reports. As sheets of white flew in all directions, he plopped down a poster sized printout, jammed with color charts, graphs, and column after column of data.

"Look at this, Henry! It worked. Only briefly, but we got a 955 degree burn for three seconds!"

Ted leaned over the edge of the desk and stabbed his finger at one specific section. "See here, right here Henry. Look. Just look at this!"

Ted kept poking the sheet. Finally, he slammed his palm in the desk center, right where he had just pointed.

"Yes! A three second flare!" Ted straightened up and almost twirled as he moved around the side of the desk and toward Henry.

Henry recovered from his initial shock at the unexpected interruption and grasped the significance of Ted's elation. He didn't need to see the numbers. The Lab had finally coaxed a wafer to retain gas long enough to ignite.

"We did it!" Henry exclaimed, the true realization sinking in.

Henry jolted out of his chair, sprung upright, and met Ted's extended arms. They embraced in a bear hug and clapped each other on the back.

Henry and Ted chuckled with excitement. Henry returned to his chair, and Ted began pacing in front of his desk.

As Ted's march back and forth slowed, his twinkling eyes narrowed and the huge, gleeful grin melted. Mapping out the next moves in his head, Ted's demeanor changed from one of celebration to anticipation, bordering on impatience.

"Now Henry, three seconds won't do. We need a sustained burn. I'd love to pull everyone off the projects we have going, but that'd be a mistake, I fear. Can you free up any time, Henry? Delegate anything?"

Henry grimaced at the thought of a heavier workload. He

was already working late at night. He'd have to work some weekends.

"I'll figure something out."

"Sustained. Sustained, Henry. We need a sustained burn. That's the next challenge," Ted proclaimed. He rubbed his beard again and then leaned both hands on Henry's desk. "How do we keep it lit, Henry? Can we do that?

Ted slowly turned to face the office widows and gazed out over the valley. He never tired of the majestic view, the calmness and strength of the mountain guarding the teeming life in the broad canyon at its feet. He grunted and then turned to Henry.

"My instincts tell me this'll be the most laborious task. I hope we can do it. It may take a year, based on the time needed to reach this point."

"I agree. We've come to the most arduous step. But one foot in front of the other," Henry said, doing his best to imitate Ted's low voice. "That's what you always tell us."

Ted laughed and brightened. "You're right! No, I'm right! One foot in front of the other. Next step, a longer burn. A sustained burn." Ted straightened and headed out of Henry's office.

At the door, Ted half turned and said to Henry, "Great job! Tell everyone. This is a marvelous accomplishment."

"Thanks! I'll let everyone know. They've worked doggedly on this."

"By the way, I saw Rhonda on the way over," said Ted. "She noticed me and ducked down the hallway and into the conference room. Problems?"

Henry smiled and pointed at the pile of papers scattered to the right of his desk.

"As you can see in her report there . . ."

Ted turned fully and stood in the doorway. He glanced over at the strewn, tangled white heap of paper and began chuckling.

"Sorry, Henry. I guess I was a little excited."

Replaying Ted's paper storm in his head and noting how out of character it was, Henry burst out laughing. Ted soon joined him, shaking so hard he had to prop himself against the door frame.

Settling down, Ted moved back into the office. "Here, I'll help you pick that up," he offered.

"Don't worry about it," insisted Henry. "It was worth it."

"If you say so," said Ted. He headed for the door. "Have a good night, Henry."

"I will," said Henry. He focused once again on his computer screen as Ted disappeared.

The excitement of the wafer flare intensified over the next months as Henry's team worked harder to run extra simulations. Every additional second they coaxed out of a wafer ignition seemed a reason to celebrate. But the long hours and intense concentration were taking a toll. Henry grew increasingly tired and frustrated.

The phone on Henry's desk buzzed and he heard Ted's voice. "Henry, can you meet me on the porch?" asked Ted.

Henry looked at his desk and sighed. So many things needed his attention, but Ted sounded tense.

The "porch" was the veranda at the west end of the Fusion Lab corporate office building. A short path led to a semicircle of bright-colored, cushioned lounge chairs, as well as a few small tables, each surrounded by four straight-back, but amazingly comfortable chairs. Toward the front, a gas-powered fire pit stood ready to warm and brighten.

The veranda had a wooden pitched roof built out of old, reclaimed railroad ties. Flower beds made of the same ties lined the path to it. Various hedges and bushes garnished a well-designed landscape. The veranda's face opened to one of the most spectacular views in the county. The mountain ridges far off to the north intersected with the lower hills to the south, creating a magnificent background to the valley below.

Ted spent a lot of time out on this veranda. It was where he went to mull over problems, usually while smoking his favorite cigar and sipping a generous glass of brandy. It was one of his very favorite places to be.

"Sure, Ted. I'll be out there in 15 minutes," Henry finally answered into the phone. He put down the batch of reports, rose from his seat, and headed down the hall.

"Hey, Ted, what's up?"

Ted motioned for Henry to sit in the chair next to his. He had already poured a glass of whiskey, which Henry accepted. Stretching out on the lounge chair, Henry soaked in the incredible view.

"Some things are bothering me, and I want to get your input," began Ted. "I'm trying to plan for the next few years.

Henry began to speak, and Ted waved a hand at him.

"This is going to take some explanation, some of it very personal. Let me lay it out for you before you comment. Okay?"

Henry nodded and sank back into his padded chair to listen.

"Everyone who knows me understands that Fusion Lab is

my great love. Just look at my past—it has come before everything else. Even my marriage. Margaret suffered through the early years of round-the-clock work here until my neglect of her became intolerable."

He paused, taking a sip of his brandy and another healthy pull on his cigar. He breathed the smoke out in a long exhale and turned to face Henry.

"Then there's Matty and Marie. I missed so much of their lives. They're grown now and have forgiven me. They know I love them completely."

Ted paused and took another sip from his glass.

"When we divorced, Margaret, as well as her lawyers, realized my weakness and negotiated accordingly. For me to keep control of Fusion Lab, I had to buy back Margaret's share of the corporation with other assets. She got the house and most everything else, and I had Fusion. When the divorce was finalized, I ended up with eighty percent and she with twenty. She will never admit it to me, but her twenty percent is worth a tidy sum today."

Ted looked at Henry and chuckled, acknowledging his self-praise.

"You're aware that I own fifty-two percent of Solidane, and Agnes Mallort and Hyatt Emerson own the rest. I'm the CEO due to my majority stake. I thank my attorney, Chester Worthington, for that. He helped with the negotiations back when we formed Solidane. His instincts proved correct. I'll explain that at another time."

Ted took a sip of his whiskey. Henry also raised his glass and waited for Ted to continue.

"I've given this a lot of thought. Too much, perhaps. But once we prove the wafer will hold its burn, of which I'm certain, I'm considering turning over the Solidane CEO role to Hyatt Emerson," said Ted, somewhat cautiously.

Henry froze for a moment and then leaned forward in his chair.

"So, Hyatt would lead Solidane? Why would you do that, Ted?" asked Henry. "Hyatt Emerson is an arrogant tyrant. You know what a pain in the butt he's been to our team. You're the only one who can keep him on a leash. He scares everyone else."

Ted laughed.

"It's not funny, Ted. I'm certain we'd be much further along without him. Why do we need Emerson Energy?" Henry asked, his voice rising with concern.

Ted took another sip and patted Henry on the arm.

"I realize he aggravates you, Henry. Especially after that battle about the additives."

Henry was still smarting from the video conference of four days ago. Henry and his team had just re-charted the project milestones to get consensus on the next phase. He had been working around the clock for the last week. The next steps to be taken were crucial.

On the video call, as Henry and the other managers were discussing the rollout for the next phase, Emerson's marketing manager joined the call and tossed in a hand grenade. He insisted on testing additives for color adherence. There was an audible collective sigh from the other nine participants.

Henry could refuse the request, stand firm, and get Ted involved if necessary. But Henry deduced that Ted wouldn't see any value in this battle. Or Henry could agree to the additional testing, which he did. The marketing manager had smirked as the video went dark. Henry and his team were furious over the resources wasted. Even now, it still annoyed him.

Ted stared out at the mountain ridges and shook his head. "Hyatt is certainly difficult, and I understand your feelings about him. Let me explain a bit more. This wafer has become an obsession with me. It's obvious to everyone. But my devotion to our project has had a considerable cost. I don't like to let on, but it has impacted me physically and financially. My relationships, as well."

Ted reflected for a moment.

"Sometimes, I'm just drained. But then, think about it, Henry. If we succeed, if we can do this, what an accomplishment! It would be the most significant achievement of my life. Possibly the lives of everyone on the team."

Ted continued, "Matty calls it my baby. He's right. I'm like an expectant father. Once this baby is born, it'll be wonderful. But Henry, I'm over seventy years old now. I need to turn the responsibility over to someone younger to build Solidane into what it should become."

"But why Hyatt Emerson?" asked Henry.

"Once we succeed at this, Henry, its appeal will be seductive. We've said it before, this is a game changer. The potential for disruption of industry is immense. The potential for financial gain or loss even more so. Already, I have people sniffing around, trying to elbow their way into whatever we're doing here. I don't have the energy or the inclination to fend them off. Hyatt does."

Henry considered that. "Hmm," he muttered as he forced

himself to assess the traits of Mr. Hyatt Emerson. Vain, overbearing, devious, deceptive. Henry deliberated on the multitude of negative attributes that popped into his mind. He then compelled himself to examine the positive ones. Smart, aggressive, tenacious, gritty, brawler. He sighed. He couldn't agree with Ted's perspective on Emerson. Where was the benefit of the relationship?

"It's probably unfair of me to take you out of the picture, Henry. You'd be next in line, in my place, as Fusion Lab's representative on Solidane's board. With that comes the CEO role. By rights, you've contributed as much as me to this endeavor. After all, a wafer vessel was your idea. We spent too much time pursuing that liquefactions/sludge process before we trashed it for the wafer."

Ted paused while he reminisced on the inception of the wafer concept and then began again, "You're young, Henry, and extremely capable. You could do it, I'm sure. I should put you in charge, if only to frustrate Hyatt! You'd be giving orders to Hyatt as his boss!"

Both Henry and Ted began laughing at the idea. Henry imagined for a moment the satisfaction of saying no to Hyatt Emerson and Hyatt being forced to accept it. Not that he would.

Ted emphatically patted the chair with his hand as his laughter ebbed. "Yes, that would be some display!" He took another generous sip of his drink.

The enormity of exactly what Ted was inferring hit Henry. Sometime in the future, Hyatt or Henry could lead Solidane.

"Ted, if I'm hearing you correctly . . ." began Henry.

"Yes, you are," interrupted Ted. "If the product, or should I say, when the product launches, I'm stepping down. My home is here at Fusion Lab. Solidane is not my future. The two entities will go their separate ways. But should Solidane be your future? Or Hyatt Emerson's? Think about it. Let me know what you feel is best for you."

Ted rose from his lounge, looked out at the view, and sighed.

"Henry, I never tire of that!" he exclaimed as he gestured toward the mountains where the sun had just shifted its rays to a dusky red. "Let's get back. And thank you for listening and strategizing with me. We're onto something good here."

They were stumped. No matter what process they attempted, the goal of a "sustainable burn" as labeled by Ted eluded them. The longest ignition they'd been able to induce was 22.6 seconds. Nothing worked. Henry had never experienced this level of frustration.

Over the past weeks, Henry had tried everything. Swimming, running, lifting weights, beer, wine, whiskey. Nothing could calm the swirling fragments of information that ran through his brain. He tried to relax and let his thoughts settle, hoping to piece together a coherent solution to the problem of the wafer burn. Zilch.

Maybe it was an impossible task. Maybe science had to progress a bit more to provide the exact materials needed. In theory, the computer simulations proved the possibility. In practice, the gas absorbed by the wafer escaped too quickly.

The entire team was losing patience. Tempers flared and smiles were now few. They needed a victory, a breakthrough, no matter how small. Could they force a few more seconds out of the next attempt? And the next, and the next?

Henry sat at his desk, scrolling through the latest results that he had uploaded on his computer. Nothing. Nothing. Nothing. He sighed in exasperation.

At that moment, Rhonda knocked on his door jamb and poked her head through the doorway.

"Henry, I've had it. I'm done. I can't take any more. It's not just the late nights, I get paid well. I'm missing out on life!" she exclaimed as she walked over to a chair near Henry's desk and collapsed into it.

"I hate to say it, Rhonda, I'm right there with you," answered Henry. "I'm out of ideas."

"Is that the printout from the lab?" asked Rhonda. She pointed to a small stack of papers on the corner of Henry's desk.

"Yes, I'm going through the uploaded numbers on my screen. But go ahead and look at the reports."

Rhonda pulled herself forward enough to reach the reports. She slumped back into the chair and thumbed through them.

"Nope. Nope. Nope. Nope," she stated as she reviewed each new page. When she got to the end of the bunch, she growled and threw the entire pile across the room.

Henry froze.

So did Rhonda.

"I'm so sorry, Henry. I've never done anything like that before," she stammered.

At that moment, Ted appeared in the doorway. He looked at Henry and Rhonda, and the papers scattered around.

"I'm not picking those up," he said calmly.

Henry laughed, as did Rhonda and Ted.

"Go home," said Ted. "That's an order. Tomorrow's another day, right Henry?"

A week later, Henry was finishing shutting down his computer to grab some dinner when his cell phone rang.

"Hey, Mom, what's up?" asked Henry. He sat back in his chair and gazed out the window at the night sky. A million sparkly points of light stared back at him.

"Not much Henry. Your father and I are getting worried about you. We haven't heard from you in a while. Kate told me the same. Is everything okay?" she asked.

"Just really busy. It's good to hear your voice. We're all a little overwhelmed up here at the Lab. We can't seem to get to the end."

"I'm sorry about that. I wish there were something we could do."

"Don't worry, I hope we'll figure it out. Although we could be at the point of declaring failure. I'm not sure how many more resources we can devote to this. The lab's not generating any revenue. All the focus is on this," explained Henry.

"I wish you could tell me more about it, but I understand the confidentiality issue," consoled his mother.

"What are you and dad up to lately?" asked Henry.

"Your father's still clearing out the garage. This week he's been sorting through his old tools and such. He's also found more boxes of stuff for you and Kate. Next time you visit, could you sort through that or take it back with you?"

"No problem, I can do that." Henry assured her. He glanced over at the two boxes against the far wall of his office he'd brought back last visit. They held remnants of his old chemistry set and records he had made of his childhood experiments. He knew they weren't of much value, but he couldn't part with them. He smiled as he thought back to Alex and him creating crazy concoctions.

"Mom, I have to go," Henry said eventually. "Tell Dad I'm sorry I missed him. I'll talk to him next time. Love you."

Not wanting to jump back into work, he eyed the boxes again. He shrugged his shoulders. Still seated in his office chair, he rolled over to the boxes and lifted the lid of one. He scanned through some papers, recognizing the handwritten lines. It surprised him how organized and precise he had been.

"Wish some of our researchers were this diligent with their notes," he mumbled.

One of the file folders had "formula" scrawled across it. Chuckling to himself, he remembered the contest for the bricklebutter pod killer. The potion he and Alex had hatched had won. Leaning back into his chair, he balanced the folder on his lap and retraced time back to his high school days.

"I think you should call Penny and ask her," said Kate.

"Ask her what?" Alex responded indignantly. "She doesn't even live here."

"But she likes them. We all do."

"Not anymore. That was kid stuff. Besides, they're weeds. It says so right here." Alex held up a news clipping on the struggle the public golf course was having with bricklebutter pods.

Henry considered what Kate was suggesting and decided she was wrong. Why would Penny have a problem with this year's Junior Year High School Contest? The rules were to find a problem that people complained about, and to propose a workable solution. All three high schools in the area competed. The grand prize was $200, a lot of money for a sixteen-year-old.

Henry and Alex signed up as a team. The weekend paper had run the story on bricklebutter pods and both Henry and Alex thought it was the perfect problem, one they were familiar with. The reporter for the paper had already done a fair amount of research. Bricklebutter bushes were found only in the county where Henry and Alex lived. A non-native species, they were thought to have been brought over as seeds from another continent. How they ended up in Henry's neighborhood, no one knew.

The local landscapers eradicated the bushes by spraying a herbicide. Many died off after a few treatments. But the bushes were stubborn, and often, new sprouts would shoot up among newly sodded lawns. For golf courses, this was a troubling problem, as bare, brown greens and fairways were not acceptable.

Alex and Henry, along with help from their biology and chemistry teachers, drew up a project plan. Henry wrote down all their teacher's explanations about membranes, osmosis, and evaporation, as places to begin. They then divided up the tasks they deemed necessary to win the prize. Alex would fetch and Henry would test. Henry would identify the buds, flowers, branches, roots, and pods that they would need to examine. Alex would scamper off to the grove and get the samples. Henry carefully transcribed everything they did.

Certain of success, they wondered why no one had figured this out already. Henry's observation was that the bushes grew only in a few areas. If bricklebutter bushes were such a small, local problem, maybe it wasn't worth the effort for a business to find an alternative to herbicides. Well, they would!

Henry wondered if something was unique about the ground where they grew. He sent Alex to dig up some soil, both in areas with the bushes, and neighboring patches of grass where there were none. Alex persuaded the county extension office to waive the fees on the soil tests and expedite them. Time was running out, though. The school term, and therefore the contest, ended next month.

"Have you found anything yet?" asked Alex as he bounded down the basement stairs of Henry's house. He saw Henry crouched over a worktable, drew up next to him, and peered at the sheets of paper.

"No," Henry answered sharply. "The soil tests don't tell us anything."

"I'm finished then," growled Alex. "I'm tired of this project and want to do something else. Everyone's out having fun. I'm starting to hate bricklebutter bushes."

"We haven't found a solution to the problem yet," countered Henry.

"Yes, we have. Spray twice as much herbicide on them. That will kill them for sure."

"We won't win the prize if that's the best we can do."

"I don't care about the prize. This isn't fun anymore."

"It's not meant to be fun, it's a school project. We need to finish it."

Alex stared at his friend as if he was crazy. He then shook his head back and forth in disbelief and dismay, shrugged his shoulders, and huffed.

Henry ignored him. "It's got something to do with the pods. I think that's the answer. Can you collect a bag of them?" Henry gave Alex a pleading look.

They spent the next two weeks soaking the pods in various solutions. Their biology teacher had suggested that instead of trying to kill the bushes, they should figure out a way to stop them from reproducing. The seeds came from the pods. The pods had to be the answer. With this fresh approach in mind and the help of their chemistry teacher, they thought up various formulas. None worked.

Back in the basement, Henry showed Alex the soaking pods.

"You were right. Nothing's working. I'm sick of this project, too. Let's clean this up and get out of here," said Henry. He dropped the container haphazardly onto the table.

"Maybe Kate and her friends will go to the movies with us. That would be fun," offered Alex.

"Okay," sulked Henry.

They combined the bowls together when a pod suddenly turned red as it absorbed the solution.

"What was that?" exclaimed Henry. They dropped more pods into the solution with the same result.

"It's doing something!" said Alex. He smacked Henry's back.

The next day, the pods had shriveled up into hard cakes.

At school, Henry and Alex excitedly demonstrated their pod experiment to their teachers. They gasped when the pods turned red and congratulated the boys.

They did win the contest. The school received a plaque with their names on it, and Henry and Alex received a check. The newspaper ran an article complete with photos of the winning team.

Snapping the folder with his finger, Henry exhaled sharply. He remembered how upset Penny had been. “Kate was right. I should have called Penny,” he mumbled.

Crossing his arms, he wondered what Penny was up to these days. Maybe he should call her. Quickly calculating the time difference, he guessed she’d be at lunch. A brief wave of excitement enticed him to look around for his phone.

But then the photo of Penny and her boyfriend popped into his head, smothering the idea. “She’s probably engaged by now,” he told himself. He shook his head forcefully to rid it of thoughts of Penny.

Focused again on the folders, Henry grazed through the papers, assessing the amateurish calculations. The notes read like a recipe, complete with ingredients and measurements. Preparation steps were meticulous. It impressed Henry. He read the description of the expected results, “after absorption of the solvent, the pods will harden into a dry cake.”

A thought passed through his brain and then a completed puzzle picture rose out of the shadows within his gray matter. “That’s it!” he shouted to no one.

Henry stood up quickly and brought the folder with him to his desk. He hurriedly called Rhonda and asked her and the team to meet him at the computer lab. He raced out of his office to the other building.

Not waiting for Rhonda and her team to arrive, Henry sat before a large screen and furiously keyed in instructions. He caught himself, ceased typing, and took a few deep breaths. He was rushing, and most likely would make mistakes.

Once he had scanned the bricklebutter notes, it surprised him at how much of the formula he remembered, having worked on it for months in his parent's basement. The challenge here was inserting it into an intricate process already coded.

Rhonda and the other analysts buzzed the door lock and entered the room. They maneuvered around computer screens, terminals, and various other IT paraphernalia. Some were old and useless; some newly purchased. They spotted Henry and steered toward the long rectangular table that served as the perch for his keyboard. Henry did not acknowledge them.

"Henry, what's the matter? Why the frantic call?" asked Rhonda.

Henry looked away from the screen for a second. "Oh, hi," he muttered. He then focused on the screen and his fingers spewed out a rhythmic clackity clack on the keyboard.

"Tracy, you're our best coder. Look at this and tell me what you think. Are my instructions clear?"

Tracy took Henry's place in the chair and soon all of them were peering over her shoulder, watching. They were silent while Tracy clicked a few keys, halted, and then clacked a few more.

"There, the code is fine. What is that formula?" she asked.

"It's a stabilization formula. If we add this one ingredient to the wafer and then begin the absorption process using this program, we may get a burn we like," explained Henry, bubbling with excitement.

Rhonda looked at him questioningly. "Where did this come from?"

"I'll explain later. Let's get this code into the simulator and run it," responded Henry.

The team shared a few dubious glances and got to work. After an hour of set up, the simulator was ready. Rhonda hit the start key. Five pieces of equipment executed the strict instructions, while two others monitored and recorded the results.

The team let out a distinctive gasp when the green light lit. "Simulation successful" flashed onto the screen. The monitoring equipment then started spooling through lines of test data. "No errors detected" appeared.

"Run it again," instructed Henry eagerly.

Another hour later, Rhonda hit the start key.

This time, when the green light blinked, they all cheered.

"It works!" Rhonda shouted. They took turns hugging one another.

"Let's go tell Ted!" whooped Henry.

The bunch moved hastily out of the lab room and swiftly approached the administration building. Henry buzzed them in and held the door for them to file through. They almost ran to Ted's office.

His door was open, and they piled into the room. Ted heard the commotion, raised his head from what he was reading, and stared at the group now facing him. His immediate reaction was one of fear. Have they had enough and are quitting? He saw smiles. As if on cue, they started clapping.

Ted stood up. "Green light?"

"Yes," confirmed Henry.

Ted moved over to them, almost in a dance. More high fives, hugs, and cheers.

"Tell me, what caused the variation?" asked Ted.

"Henry came up with a stabilization formula," Rhonda exclaimed.

Ted patted Henry on the back. "Smartest kid around, I say!"

The team agreed wholeheartedly.

"Well, congratulations, everyone! Job well done! I'm so proud of all of you!" answered Ted. "We're going to celebrate this milestone tomorrow. Take the day to relax. Have some fun. Then we'll get the specs to Chemclone so they can run a batch. If that goes well . . ." He raised his eyes and upturned hands and made a delighted face.

CHAPTER 5

Penny let out a tired huff and opened the door to the office building. She had just completed the last on-site session with a new client this morning and had taken the train back from Munich to Frankfurt. She normally would have gone straight home, but Clara, her boss, had asked her to stop by the office.

Clara was on the phone when Penny tapped on her door. She waved her in. She quickly ended the call and greeted Penny.

"Thanks for coming by. I know you must be exhausted," said Clara.

Penny slipped out of her heavy coat and laid it on a chair. She grabbed the chair beside it by its arms and pulled it closer to Clara's desk. With a grunt, she slumped into it.

"I am," agreed Penny. "I'm getting texts, emails, and calls from everyone. So, I guess the rumors are true?"

"Yes, it's official. Stephan has sold the business. I wanted to let you know before the announcement. We've been friends a long time, and we should talk about what this means to you."

"Have many of the details changed since the last time we talked?" asked Penny.

"Not really," Clara assured her. "The American firm met all of Stephan's terms. Quite surprisingly. They're very enamored with how we do things."

"So, we'll all keep our jobs?" Penny shifted her legs and tilted her head.

"Yes, even me," laughed Clara. She pushed her keyboard to the side. "It's all in the contract. Stephan sent it out to the Directors. I've read through it thoroughly and he did an amazing job. I thought for sure they'd force me into early retirement, and you know I'm not ready yet. I love what I'm doing."

Penny straightened up. "They'd be foolish to let you go. I know I'd have never lasted this long without you."

"Well, I appreciate that, but you've earned your keep!" chuckled Clara.

"What's the timing on this? Have they worked out a transition plan?" Penny leaned back in her chair, suddenly realizing how her clients must feel.

"It'll be a while, yet. Four to six months, I'm sure. You've seen how these things drag out on your own projects."

Penny nodded.

"Now, let's talk about the possibilities ahead." Clara placed her arms on the center of her desk. "Because you're an American, you'll have an edge. I may be fluent in English, but my accent is severe. I imagine they'll ask you to be an intermediary for the transition."

"I'll help however I can," said Penny confidently.

"Once the sale closes, they want our staff to take 90-day

rotations to their home office, a few at a time. Stephan has already requested that you help organize this."

Startled, Penny drew her head back. "You didn't mention anything about rotations before!" she exclaimed. "Three months?"

"That surprised me, too. I'd assumed they would send teams over here. Which they are. But they asked for our help on the best way to build connections with their team, and Stephan suggested this."

"Are you going with us?" asked Penny.

"No, no. The rotation is for project managers," answered Clara. "You're used to being away for extended periods. Think of this as your next project."

Penny nodded, but said nothing.

"I'm flying over with Stephan in three weeks, though. We have four days of meetings and then I'll be back. You know things will fall apart around here if I'm gone any longer," chuckled Clara. She studied Penny's face and then crossed her arms.

Penny was listening to Clara while trying to assess the many ways this information might impact her. Although the rumors had been circulating for months, she was determined to wait for certainty before she'd give it much thought. Especially considering it had been over five years since Stephan first expressed a wish to retire.

"You remember their home office is in Atlanta?" asked Clara. "Isn't that where your family lives? I thought this would be a wonderful piece of news for you."

Clara's tone of voice and the mention of her family grabbed Penny's attention. "Yes, it is," she answered. Smiling, Penny leaned forward and rested an arm on Clara's desk. "I may get to spend three months with them?"

"That's what I'm hearing. After that, they'll assign each manager to another project back here. Business as usual. For you, though, longer-term, possibly not. You have experience and insights that the rest of us don't. It could open many wonderful opportunities for you."

Penny was now fixated on returning to her home. Her family would be ecstatic. It might be just the recharge she needed before returning here and launching the next phase of her career.

"It sounds very positive. Why is everyone so panicked?" asked Penny.

"It's the unknown. What do we tell our clients? Communicate! Otherwise, we'll create all kinds of monsters out of fear of the future." Clara patted Penny's hand. "It's another reason I wanted to speak with you. If you're excited about this change, it'll spread to others. You're well regarded here."

"I can't help but be excited now!" Penny promised her.

"I think once Stephan outlines the plan for the next six months, everyone will get on board." Clara grabbed the arms of her chair and shifted closer to Penny. "Now, on a more personal level, I'm thinking it might help you with Ethan, too. Last we spoke, you were having some intense disagreements."

"We still are," said Penny. Her eyebrows furrowed into a face that told Clara she didn't want to discuss that right now. Clara ignored it.

"A 90-day hiatus might bring things to a head. Maybe you'll finally get the commitment from him I think you deserve."

Penny looked away. "You sure have a matter-of-fact way

about you, Clara."

Clara laughed. "You mean blunt. It's why I've done so well here. There's never enough time in the day to beat around the bush."

Penny laughed, too. "I've heard that often from you." She leaned back into her chair. "But we've been away before. I have my projects; he has his own assignments."

"Yes, but most are within a short travel distance. You see each other anyway. This is different. It's across an ocean, and the place you grew up. And with a packed schedule, you won't be able to fly back for a weekend. Ethan would need to travel over there."

Penny sighed. "I see what you mean. This is different."

Clara felt bad that she had dampened Penny's excitement. "It'll be fine, Penny. I know it'll work out. Stay focused on the positive. You're going home!"

At that thought, Penny smiled. "Thanks for being my friend. I needed one when I first moved here. I still do."

"That's a two-way street. You've been there for me too, as you know." Clara had gone through a nasty divorce and Penny had helped throughout. "Now, go home and get some rest. We've got some exciting changes on the way."

They both stood and drifted to the door. Penny gave Clara a big hug and headed home.

Adrianna knocked forcefully on Penny's door. After a few seconds, Penny opened it, dressed, but with her hair wrapped in a towel.

"Sorry, Adri, I'm running late," she said, and led Adrianna

into her hallway.

"Take your time. We have an hour before we have to meet up with the others. Ida can't make it. The kids are sick."

Adrianna made herself at home, sitting in an easy chair and leafing through a magazine, not attempting a conversation over the roar of Penny's blow dryer. After a few minutes, Penny appeared in the doorway.

"I'm ready," she announced.

"You look nice. I like those jeans. When did you get them?" asked Adrianna.

"Yesterday. I need something for my trip with Ethan."

"Oh," Adrianna said softly. She examined Penny's face. "You're really going through with this. Can we sit for a bit?"

"Sure, I'll get us a glass of wine." Penny turned and disappeared into the kitchen.

Holding two glasses of red wine, Penny returned and carefully handed one to Adrianna. She then sat on the sofa.

"Speaking of Ethan, he called me," said Adrianna as she lowered her glass. "He's worried. He wanted to know if you said anything to me about the weekend."

"I'm sorry he did that," Penny said matter-of-factly. "He knows we need to decide. This is between Ethan and me."

"He wants me to lobby for him," Adrianna added quickly. She reached up, grabbed a chunk of hair that had fallen into her face, and vigorously twisted it into a knot.

Penny scrutinized the technique. "I thought you were going to get that cut off?"

Adrianna giggled. "I know! I keep changing my mind. Maybe I'll wait for Raf to get back from deployment and see what he thinks."

"When is that again?"

"Two months." Adrianna patted the bun that now rested comfortably on her head, satisfied.

"Good, he'll be back before I leave."

"Yes," said Adrianna. "Now back to Ethan."

Penny let all her weight settle into the cushions. She turned her head toward the window, where the sunlight brushing the curtains dimmed for the evening.

"I know it's over."

"You're sure?"

"Yes. We've been here before. We've dated for four years, and I know he loves me. He feels pressure now, though. Once it's off, we'll slip right back into our old relationship. I can't do that anymore."

Overcome by a sudden surge of sadness, Penny suppressed a sniffle. A few tears leaked down her cheek.

"I'm so sorry, Penny," said Adrianna. She came over and gave Penny a hug. "I hope the weekend goes so well you'll feel differently."

"Thanks, Adri." They sat huddled together on the sofa. "But I don't think so." Penny dabbed her face with her napkin and then continued.

"All my life, circumstances have separated me from people I love. Some of my choosing, some unavoidable. But my feelings didn't change. I still love them. This is different. I'd hoped Ethan and I would stay together no matter the circumstances. Am I asking too much?"

"No, of course not. It's his choice if he lets you go," said

Adrianna.

"That's the thing. It's my choice too. Ethan hinted I could use this buy-out as the opportunity to find a new job here. We could be together."

"True," said Adrianna. "But you don't want that?"

"I guess not," answered Penny. "Ethan wants his life a certain way and expects me to adapt to it. He's fitting me into a box. I can't do that."

Penny drank the remaining wine in her glass and exhaled pointedly. "Hold on," she muttered and disappeared into the kitchen, returning with an opened bottle of wine and some cheese and crackers. Topping off their glasses, she began speaking again as she settled back onto the sofa.

"Last year, Ethan and I drove up to Berlin to see one of his firm's new buildings. The builders had constructed this amazing maze of scaffolding around this complex block structure. They were attaching this gorgeous, veined marble cladding. As I was admiring the intricate design, it hit me why I was discontent. I'm just this scaffolding around Ethan's life."

Adrianna drew her head back. "That's quite a bit." She crunched on a cracker while she pondered. "So, Ethan's the blocks?"

"Yes."

"Maybe you're the beautiful cladding?" Adrianna suggested.

"No, I'm the scaffolding."

"Do you want to be the blocks?"

"I want both of us to be the blocks."

"You're confusing me with this. I'm trying to follow."

Penny laughed and spat out some cracker bits. She put her

hand to her face. "It's the wine. I'm not sure what I mean."

"You're certain then?"

"I don't know," Penny sighed. "I might cave. One kiss and we could be back to where we were a month ago."

"Hmmm," said Adrianna. "Don't see that happening. I guess this buy-out came at a good time?"

"Yes, it's what finally forced our hand. I consider it a blessing."

"Well, three months away from each other should prove telling."

Penny sipped some wine from her glass. "I admit, I'm looking forward to lots of time with my family. I miss them."

Adrianna moved her arm and pointed out the furnishings. "Can I live here while you're gone? Your furniture is nicer than mine."

Penny didn't respond and instead took another sip from her glass. Again, she slumped into the plush pillows on her sofa in deep thought. Conflicting emotions, some new, others very familiar, battled within her as thoughts raced through her mind. Excitement. Anticipation. Sadness. Heartache.

"You know, Adri," Penny almost whispered, "I feel like I'm always on a journey. When will I know I've arrived at my destination?"

Straightening her back, Adrianna leaned forward. "Penny, it's going to be fine, no matter what you and Ethan decide. I just know it. As you said, there's plenty of people who love you. Me included."

Penny nodded her head and forced a smile. "Thanks, Adri. You're a wonderful friend."

"You really will be fine, Penny," insisted Adrianna. After a few moments, she stood, pulled Penny to her feet, and hugged her. "Now enough of this drama!"

Penny laughed. "You're right. There's always hope." She smoothed out her white blouse, studied it, and then shook her head disapprovingly. "So drab," she muttered as she grabbed Adrianna's hand and tugged her toward the bedroom. "Help me find something fun to wear with these jeans."

"What happened in here?" asked Adrianna. She looked around the room. Clothes were tossed all about. "You're usually so neat. I've always hated that about you. Has my messiness finally rubbed off?"

Penny laughed. "No, I had trouble deciding what to wear."

"Obviously!" chuckled Adrianna. "What's wrong with this?" she asked as she held up a colorful knit sweater to her chest.

"It's just that most of these outfits I wore with Ethan. He liked them all, and now I don't think I do."

Adrianna rolled her eyes. She picked up various garments off the floor and chair and hung them back in Penny's closet. Opening the top drawer of Penny's dresser to put in a blue silk scarf that had been piled up on top, she spotted a glass covered case.

"Oh, wow! What's that?" she asked Penny. She reached in and removed the box. Inside, a golden branch sparkled in the light.

Penny giggled. "That's just a silly gift from long ago." She took the box from Adrianna and opened it.

"Who gave it to you?"

"Henry Taylor. My friend from Indiana. I've told you about him."

"It's beautiful! So, your 'just a friend' gave you this?"

"Yes, we were all in high school. It's a funny story. Let me tell you."

Penny had had a rough day. She'd been driving cheerfully down the road to the local mall with her three friends from high school, when Jayla in the backseat shouted, "Look, there's Tyler!" All heads turned to the left. Penny faced back to the front, but not in time to see the car ahead stop suddenly. She slammed on the brakes, but her car smacked the bumper of the other. Fortunately, there was no damage to either car.

Angry and embarrassed with herself, Penny sought refuge in her bedroom. She was seated at her desk, peering at her computer screen, when a knock sounded at her door.

"Penny, you have a call from Henry and Alex," announced her mom as she opened the door and walked in. "They have some exciting news. Here's the phone."

She walked over to Penny's desk and handed her the cordless phone.

"I'll let you talk," she said. She left the room and closed the door behind her.

Penny brightened immediately. "Henry?" she asked into the phone.

"Yes, it's me and Alex. We won the Junior Year Contest!" said Henry excitedly.

"We won $200!" said Alex, talking over Henry.

"What contest?" asked Penny, trying to hear.

"It's a contest among the schools. They do it every year. The task this time was to find a problem and craft a solution," explained Henry.

"We're in the newspaper, too!" said Alex.

Penny switched ears, hoping she could hear better. "That's really cool!" she exclaimed. "What was your project about?"

Henry paused, but Alex charged in. "We found a way to get rid of bricklebutter bushes. They're a real problem."

"Bricklebutter bushes are a problem?" asked Penny guardedly. "I love them."

"They're a problem for golf courses," said Alex. "We found a way to kill them."

"You killed the bricklebutter bushes?" asked Penny in horror.

"No, we haven't killed any. We figured out a way for other people to do that," responded Alex proudly.

Penny could hear Henry tell Alex to stop talking and let him explain.

"I'm sorry, Penny. Alex is running at the mouth again. We came up with a formula that stops bricklebutter pods from seeding."

"Why would you pick that as your project, Henry? Why would you do that?" Hearing the hurt in Penny's voice, Henry couldn't answer.

Alex jumped in. "We didn't think you'd care. You don't even live here anymore," he offered as justification.

Kate walked into the room and caught the conversation. She frantically waved her arms at Henry as she ran over to the phone.

Too late, they all heard Penny's loud voice. "I don't want to talk anymore, Henry. In fact, I don't know if I ever want to talk to you again." Penny hung up the phone and burst into tears.

A little over a week later, Penny was again in her room doing her homework when her mom yelled up the stairs. "Penny, Henry Taylor is on the phone. He says it's important."

"Ok, I have the cordless up here," Penny shouted back down.

Penny reached for the phone on the far side of her desk.

"Hi, Henry. How are you?"

"Fine, Penny. I'm sorry Alex and I upset you. We didn't mean to."

"No, I'm sorry, Henry. I've been meaning all week to call you and apologize. I had a terrible day and took it out on you. To be honest, I'm not sure why it hurt my feelings so badly."

"Kate says we're insensitive. Alex doesn't agree and thinks you were rude to hang up."

Penny laughed. "Tell Alex he's right. It was rude."

"Okay," chuckled Henry, relieved to hear Penny's laugh. "How about I promise I'll share the prize money with you?"

"You don't need to do that," Penny assured him. "Like I said, it was a bad day. I had an accident with my mom's car, and I was angry at myself. I'm happy you won!"

True to his word, Henry used his prize money for Penny. About a month after his call, an overnight carrier delivered a package to Penny. She raced to her room and opened the box on her bed. She gasped when she saw the tiny, golden, bricklebutter branch. With multiple flowers and buds sprouting out, the finished golden twig was beautiful. Henry had found a local craft store that hand dipped roses in gold and convinced them to dip a bricklebutter branch.

She ran to her dresser, removed a small glass jewelry case from her top drawer, and emptied it. Carefully, she settled the branch on the black felt at the bottom of the case and closed the glass lid. Setting it gently at the back of her dresser, she admired the sparkles where the room light reflected off the shining leaves.

Her mind raced back to the memory of her favorite spot, with her favorite person, lying on their backs under a canopy of bricklebutter branches. She twirled around in a circle and then collapsed, giggling, onto her bed.

Suddenly, she popped up and raced over to her desk where the phone lay. She dialed Henry's number and was startled when he answered.

"Henry?" she asked.

"Penny?" he answered.

"It's so beautiful, Henry. Thank you so much. That's the nicest gift I've ever received."

"I wanted to do it," he offered awkwardly. "How are you?"

"Good," affirmed Penny, as she strolled back to her bed and settled onto it.

They talked about the things happening in their lives for the next half hour until Henry had to leave to meet Sean and Alex.

"That's so romantic!" blurted out Adrianna. "Will you see him when you get over there? He can help you forget Ethan."

"I don't think so," Penny answered, casually shrugging her shoulders. "It's been so long. And I'll soon be heading back here, after the training. We'll always be friends, I'm sure of that. But I don't see any possibility of anything more than that."

"But you've thought about it!" blurted Adrianna. She carefully put the glass case back into the drawer. She then looked straight at Penny and shrugged. "Well, maybe one day he'll invite you to his wedding."

"Adri! That was nasty!" growled Penny. She threw a bunched-up blouse at her.

"Hit a nerve there, did I?" asked Adrianna, laughing. She tossed a pale-blue cardigan top at her. "Here, wear this. You'll look fine."

Penny held it up in front of her and checked the mirror. "You're right. It'll do." She pulled the top over her head and fluffed her hair. She checked the mirror again, satisfied. "Let's get out of here and meet the others," she said cheerily. "I'm ready for a fun night out."

Various shades of green, interrupted by the occasional car, rushed by Penny's window. "Beautiful!" she sighed to herself. "I wish I could enjoy this."

Seated on the passenger side, Penny kept more space than usual from Ethan, who was driving. "Did you say something?" asked Ethan.

Drawn out of her daydream, Penny turned her head toward him and shook it gently. "No, just thinking."

Penny and Ethan were returning from a long weekend visit to Salzburg. They had planned it as a business outing, but knew it meant more. Decisions needed to be made about their future.

Ethan, although trained as an architect, referred to himself as a scout. His job was to find and collect ideas for distinct and innovative architecture. He'd present these novel approaches to his employer for evaluation and enhancement. They would then market the resulting high-caliber designs to their wealthy clients who craved one-of-a-kind builds.

This weekend Ethan planned to photograph the ornate balconies of the Salzburg cathedral. A client wanted something similar included in the plans for their new home.

Penny loved Ethan. He was fun, adventurous, and spontaneous, just like herself. She knew he loved her, too. They had enjoyed the weekend as they played tourist and took in Salzburg's sights.

The two avoided any hard conversation until the drive home. Penny braved the topic, hoping for a happy outcome but not expecting one.

"I had a wonderful time, Ethan," she began.

"Me, too," he agreed. Turning his head from the road, he smiled at her. It quickly melted as he saw her serious expression.

"We need to talk about my job," said Penny.

"I'm in denial. How will I get through three months without you?"

"It's more serious than that, Ethan. My company's being bought out and I have no say in the matter. The 90 days is only for training. After that, they could transfer me anywhere." Penny paused and then added, "I could even end up back in the States permanently." Penny watched as the outline of Ethan's face sharpened.

"I know that!" Ethan sighed in frustration. He slowed down so he could give more attention to Penny. "So, where's that leave us?"

"Yes, where does that leave us?" Penny repeated softly.

Ethan tightened his grip on the steering wheel. "I've been up front with you. You know I'm not ready to make a move, at least right now. I can't make that commitment."

"I know. You love what you do."

"Quit your job and travel with me. We could make that work," pleaded Ethan. He turned to meet Penny's eyes.

"I could do that, but so could you," she countered. "Come with me to the U.S. That'd be an adventure."

Ethan frowned at Penny. They both knew that would not happen.

"That's not the issue," pressed Ethan.

"I know it's not. The issue is us."

"We could get married," offered Ethan.

"Are you asking me to marry you?" challenged Penny.

"No, you know what I mean. That would be the next step in our future. We love each other."

"And if that happened, we'd end up right back here, eventually. I want a family. I want a home."

"I know," sighed Ethan. "And I don't."

After a few moments, he grasped Penny's hand. "I'm a selfish jerk, aren't I?"

"Yes, you are!" said Penny with a quick laugh, unable to remain annoyed at him. She pushed his hand away in feigned anger. "Though at least you're an honest one," she added.

Ethan gently re-grabbed Penny's hand. "I'm sorry we've come to this," he said, wishing she would back down, knowing she couldn't.

"Me, too," whispered Penny.

Both Ethan and Penny grew somber, frustrated with the outcome of their discussion. Neither wanted to voice out loud their mutual conclusion. They drove for a long while in silence.

Their decision today was not a surprise to either but stung, nonetheless.

"Are you okay?" asked Ethan, finally. "Do you want to talk some more?"

"No, let's enjoy the scenery for a while," suggested Penny. "This is hard for both of us."

Relieved, Ethan let go of Penny's hand and returned his to the steering wheel. Penny moved hers to her lap. Gradually, they leaned away from each other.

Penny lost herself in thoughts of the future. There were so many unknowns. What would this new company be like? Could she stay in Germany? She loved her life here, at least until now. Would it be easier for Ethan if they transferred her? What would a return to the U.S. mean?

The tension between Ethan and herself, and the stress of so many unanswered questions, soon took their toll. The deep, staticky sound of the wind rushing past her window acted as white noise, taunting her eyelids. Arching her eyebrows as supports, she tried to pin her eyes open.

They rounded a curve, and Penny caught her breath. Enveloped by a canopy of overgrown trees, the sun shot through the branches, creating golden spikes. The reflection of the rays formed tiny white speckles on the leaves as they raced by. "Oh! Just like bricklebutter bushes!" thought Penny. A fresh shot of adrenaline quashed her tiredness.

Memories of her young friends raced into her head, and she smiled. Henry, Kate, Alex, Sean. So many good times together. "I wonder how Henry's doing?" she mused to herself.

Eager to discard the worries of the present, she settled back into her seat and stared out at the images flashing before her. Fueled by her imagination, they cast comforting scenes of a little hideaway from a time long gone.

Part Two

If Absence Makes the Heart Grow Fond, the Best of Friends Must Part

CHAPTER 6

With the new absorption formula in place, the entire Solidane project team functioned flawlessly. Fusion Lab would run simulations of the wafer with varying size, absorbency, burn rates, heat emissions, etc. The team then conveyed those formulations to both Chemclone and Emerson Energy. Chemclone would produce a batch of wafers and expedite them back to Fusion Lab for further tests.

Emerson would analyze the specs to see if they met the required parameters for actual sales. Wafer size and heat emissions would impact usage by industrial companies. Any retail applications would require reliable safety precautions. Emerson also verified regulatory and legal issues in real time.

The wafer breakthrough could not be understated. Ted Granger, Hyatt Emerson, and Agnes Mallort therefore allotted two days a week for a conference call discussion to maintain the progress. The excitement was palpable.

As the prospects of the wafer expanded, so did the need

for tight confidentiality. The three executives agreed the wafer could not only delight and entice others with diverse new opportunities but also threaten and endanger some existing businesses. They took additional measures to assure security throughout the three enterprises.

Henry's most tasking headaches during this phase were production problems. Chemclone could process small quantities, however, any increase in output caused defective wafers. In fact, three minor fires had hatched from a cluster of abnormal wafers. With each complication, Henry and the Lab's crew needed to reconfigure the formulation and run additional simulations. This took time.

Eventually, the team decided that the project would target only industrial applications for the wafer. This would narrow the tests and dedicated resources to that one product. A consumer wafer, although touted by Emerson as having the most profit potential, had too many safety concerns. Simple issues, such as packaging for delivery and retail shelf display, had to be factored into product design. Adding to the complications were creating appropriate product instructions for use and legal liability disclaimers.

As the project continued to move rapidly, Ted slowed down. He grew tired easily and had difficulty catching his breath when walking from building to building at the Lab. Concerned for her father's health, Marie convinced him to take a break and visit her.

Ted was straightening up his desk when Henry poked his head into the office. "All set?" asked Henry.

"Mostly, yes. I leave in the morning," answered Ted.

"Anything I can help with?"

"No, I don't believe so. I've got this all organized. How about joining me for a drink in the courtyard?" asked Ted. "It's a beautiful evening and the sunset should be splendid."

Henry hesitated, as he had hours of work still ahead of him. But he enjoyed his conversations with his mentor and friend too much to say no.

"I'd love to," answered Henry. "Let me lock down my office, and I'll meet you there."

Henry headed back down the corridor to his own office and hit a few keys to secure his computer. He called out to his administrative assistant that he was joining Ted on the veranda if something came up.

When he reached the seating area, Ted was comfortably sprawled out on a chaise with a glass of whiskey held to his lips. He pointed to an additional one sitting on the serving table designated for Henry.

Ted was right. The sun was slipping slowly through the clusters of billowy clouds. It created a crimson glow on the curved peaks of the mountains in the distance. The rays broke in and out of the thin strips of white now forming on the horizon. As the sun settled further, it broke free of the clouds, a reddish, pinkish ball that appeared to be swallowed by the hills.

"Beautiful!" remarked Henry as he sat in the chaise.

"Yes! What a sight!" agreed Ted.

They both watched as the light of the sun faded and the lamps surrounding the grounds popped on.

"I hate to leave you like this, Henry, but Marie insists. She has me scheduled to see a specialist next week."

"Try not to worry about us, Ted. Although, I'm certain you will. Everyone agreed to do what's needed to help you. We're all concerned about you."

"Well, I'm looking forward to a brief break. I'm stopping to see Matty along the way. I'll spend a few days with him and his family. Then off to Marie's."

"It'll be good for you to catch up."

"Yes, it's been a while. I'm hoping to see my grandson play. He's in a soccer league. Matty says he's quite the athlete. Must have gotten that from his mother's side. He's much better than I ever would've been," laughed Ted.

"Well, Matt's not bad either. He's whipped me in way too many tennis matches!" said Henry.

They both laughed and sipped their drinks.

"I'm at a good place, Henry. We've succeeded. The wafer's future is limitless, but I expect my part is complete. We've proven it could work and have created an amazing thing here. I'm immensely proud of this Lab."

Ted turned, looked him in the eye, and paused for a moment. "I'm immensely proud of you."

Henry looked off into the distance, self-consciously. "Thanks, Ted."

"We've discussed this before, but for the production phase, I'll be handing the reins over to Hyatt Emerson. We've had our share of internal battles, some very severe. But that next phase will embroil us in conflicts with the outside world. I portend external parties will both love and hate the wafer. I, myself, have no appetite for that kind of warfare. Hyatt will relish it."

"You'll get no argument from me. That's Hyatt's forte. He's

the best person to capitalize on everything we've accomplished so far."

"Now, I've told you before, you could give him a challenge. You've thoroughly considered that?"

"Yes, I honestly don't see that as the best role for me," Henry said confidently. "Just like you, I'd be miserable. I love what I'm doing at Fusion Lab. My future's here, not at Solidane."

"You obviously love it here! Lately, you rarely leave," chuckled Ted. "For now, though, it's vital that I keep a tight grasp on the project. We need to abide by the plan. We're almost there. I promise, I'll stay at the helm until we sign off on development. Hyatt can lead us once production begins. God help us!"

They both laughed, followed by another span of silence as they emptied their glasses.

"Forgive me this one splurge here. I'm having another!" He refilled his glass.

"Go for it! You've earned it!" encouraged Henry. "I'd join you, but I still have some reports to approve. One's my limit."

"This is magnificent!" exclaimed Ted as he waved his hand across the last bits of the skyline visible to them.

"Heavenly," agreed Henry.

"I want to bounce some of my plans off you for Fusion Lab. Once Solidane is effectively operating and on its own, I want to return my attention to the Lab. Now, these plans are pipedreams, but exciting ones to me."

Ted nestled back into his chair. "Unfortunately, the Lab's stressed financially. That should change once the wafer is in production. However, I can't underestimate the challenge that poses. In the meantime, I may have a solution." Ted shifted in his seat. "We own all that land on the plateau at the other end of the property. I've put out some feelers to a developer. They're considering buying that parcel from us and putting in a planned community. The proceeds of the sale could save us from our financial bind. What do you think of that idea?"

Henry mulled it over, and then spoke out. "A friendly neighborhood in which to raise a family up here on the hill would be enticing. The drive back into the valley is taxing for me and most of the others here at the lab. I'd have to think some more. Though I'm so consumed with this project that I'm not sure I can give it fair scrutiny."

"No need for that, Henry. I wanted to get your reaction. If you were set against it, I'd reconsider."

"Seems like a suitable solution to me," Henry responded.

Ted glanced at Henry. "You mentioned raising a family. Is that important to you?"

Flustered by the question, Henry shifted uncomfortably in his chair. Now that he was so engrossed in his work at the Lab, Henry didn't foresee any prospect of a relationship anytime soon. He took a long swallow of his drink before answering.

"I've always thought so. Now, I'm not so sure. My career here is gratifying and important. Sometimes, after visiting my sister, Kate, I get a little envious. She and Robby already have one child, and I know they want more. I feel like I want that, too. But then I get back to the Lab and I reconsider. I love this place and what I'm doing here."

Ted reached over and patted Henry's arm. "I'm fortunate to have you here! And we're both blessed to love our work. But relationships are important too. Ever since Margaret and I divorced so many years ago, I've been living the single life. I'm enormously happy. I wouldn't change a thing. But I still try to make time for friends and family."

Henry leaned forward. "I agree with you. I do my best to stay in touch with my friends and family, too. I'm just saying, I don't see any romantic prospects in my future. And I'm okay with that."

A brief surge of guilt shot through Henry as he thought of Penny. For so long now, he'd successfully blocked her out of his mind. He hadn't kept in touch.

The guilt was quickly replaced with a tinge of resentment. Penny's career offered her many opportunities to meet new people. His, here at the Lab, did not. Besides, he expected to hear from Kate at any time that Penny was engaged. It's best to keep Penny in the past, he had decided.

Ted sensed Henry's discomfort with the conversation and changed the subject. "I'm also worried about morale. Our financial stress has meant no raises or bonuses for years now. I'm running out of ways to keep people happy."

"We're receiving our bonuses, Ted, just not in cash. Speaking for myself, I'm convinced the stock options are worth considerably more, anyway. I'm sure the other managers agree. Otherwise, they'd no longer be here."

"If we're successful, they'll be worth a great deal more," said Ted. "I'm certain of that! The Solidane stock that Fusion Lab will continue to own will spit out nice dividends. Over time, that could grow into a tidy sum."

Both were more comfortable now talking about finances. Gravitating to more pleasant topics, they spoke for another two hours. They reminisced about Henry's first years at the Lab and how things had changed. Ted recounted some funny stories, some Henry had already heard, while some were new tales. They chatted about the people who had come and gone.

The night chill set in around them and they reluctantly rose and said their goodbyes. Ted left early the next morning for the airport.

After a wonderful visit with Matt and then Marie, Ted underwent extensive tests at Marie's hospital. Ted's specialist then explained to him why he was so tired. His heart was failing. The condition was grave. Margaret Granger flew to Marie's to see him. Less than two weeks later, Ted passed away at the hospital during the night.

The memorial service for Ted was scheduled at the Fusion Lab grounds. Remarkably, Margaret Granger organized the testament to her husband. She arranged for accommodations for guests either at Fusion Lab or at various hotels in the valley. Condolences and tributes poured in. Those who could not attend relayed their expressions of sorrow. The day was a tremendous honor to Ted.

When Ted purchased the Fusion Lab land, it included a graveyard that was the resting place for those who had passed on a century ago. It was located on the east side of the vast hill that the Lab sat upon. The railroad had originally carved it out of the stone mounds that protruded from the mountain. Small granite monuments seemed to sprout out of the ground in circular grottos. Similar rock shelters were spread out over the ten-acre cemetery.

Ted added the cemetery to his plans for revitalizing the property. He had the graveyard border tastefully delineated by discarded railroad ties. He added landscaping and trees, plus pavers to mark paths for strolling among the monuments. Bright-colored flowers now dotted the open field areas. It was beautiful. Ted's ashes would rest in an area that he had designed and set aside for himself.

Chester Worthington, Ted's attorney, had requested a meeting at Fusion Lab immediately after to discuss Ted's will. They scheduled the meeting for four that afternoon, allowing time for those that needed to get back to the airport.

Chester entered the room last and noticed that Ted's usual position at the table's head had been left open for him. Hyatt Emerson and Agnes Mallort sat on the right. Henry Taylor and Matt and Marie Granger sat on the left. Margaret Granger had declined the invitation to attend and asked Matt to represent her. Chester silently slipped into the chair.

"This is a sorrowful occasion that brings us here," began Chester. "Ted Granger was an extraordinary man, and I was blessed by our 30-year friendship. Ted always spoke of hopeful futures. I think we can honor him by taking Solidane forward and completing the vision he and the rest of you had. To accomplish that, Ted established a trust for management of Fusion Lab. The trustees he selected are me, along with Matt Granger, Marie Granger, and Henry Taylor."

Chester waited a few moments to be certain that everyone understood his comments to this point. He then continued.

"The trust controls the estate of Ted Granger. Now, Margaret

Granger will continue to own her shares of Fusion Lab that were acquired as a result of their divorce decree. In my conversations with Margaret, she has made it known that she intends to maintain the arrangement she had with Ted while he was still alive. That is, as a minority stakeholder, she'll defer to the trustees as to matters that affect Fusion Lab."

Again, Chester paused and looked around the table. With all eyes on him, he proceeded.

"The trustees of Fusion have met and concur with Ted's request to appoint Henry Taylor as Executive Director of Fusion Lab, Ted's previous title. He'll follow the trustee's instructions and manage the day-to-day functions of the Lab."

Chester placed the sheets of paper he had been referencing delicately on the table. He cleared his throat and then began again.

"Now we come to Solidane. Ted Granger was the CEO of the company, as elected and appointed by Solidane's board. The board comprised you, Agnes, and you, Hyatt, and Ted."

Chester tilted his head to recognize both Agnes and Hyatt. They nodded back.

"After the settlement of Ted's estate, Fusion Lab's fifty-two percent interest in Solidane now is in the hands of the Trust and Margaret Granger. Agnes and Hyatt, your companies still represent twenty-four percent each. At the direction of Ted Granger, the Fusion Lab Trust requests that a meeting of the Solidane board be immediately called."

"I agree," said Agnes.

"I also agree," said Hyatt.

"Then this meeting of the Solidane Board is now called to

order," Chester announced.

"The purpose of this meeting is to name a successor to Ted Granger as Chairman and CEO of the company. As per the wishes of Ted Granger, the Fusion Lab Trust nominates Henry Taylor for those roles."

Chester surveyed their faces. No one spoke. Agnes Mallort finally broke the awkward silence.

"Because this is what Ted wanted, I'll go along with that, for now," stated Agnes. "I'd like Hyatt, Henry, and I to discuss at another, more appropriate time, the best roles going forward. At the moment, I need to mourn the death of my friend."

Hyatt understood that this was not a fitting time to jostle for power. Besides, Agnes had already cast her support for Henry and Hyatt had no means to counter it.

"Agnes said it perfectly," began Hyatt. "Let's honor Ted's wishes. Henry, you'll fill Ted's shoes for now. Let's digest this sudden change in our lives and meet again."

Agnes reached across the table and patted Henry's hand. "Henry, are you okay with this? Ted regularly commented on how much pressure you and your team were under. This would be another considerable responsibility."

Henry shuffled in his seat. He smiled at Agnes.

"Thanks, Agnes," answered Henry. "I agree with you that this is a heavy load. I've discussed it with the others at the Lab and with the trustees. Rhonda and the project leaders consented to take on a few of my tasks. Ted walked me through his schedule right before he left for Marie's. I believe I can manage them if we stick to the outlined strategy. We've been successfully doing that so far. Our focus would be on signing off on an industrial use wafer product."

Hyatt started to say something but caught himself.

"If the Board has confidence in me, I'm willing to keep going," said Henry.

"We do," reaffirmed everyone except Hyatt.

"Okay, then," pronounced Chester. "The Board of Directors of Solidane has elected Henry Taylor as Chairman and appointed him as CEO. I'm sure you'll keep in close contact in the coming weeks, but a formal meeting should be scheduled for a couple months or so from now. This has been a trying time for us all. I hope that your efforts are rewarded, and Ted's dream for this wafer is actualized."

The next few months were fierce for Henry. Ted's funeral had been painful, but it was good for Henry to see his family and friends. Henry's mom and dad, Kate and Robby, as well as both Alex and Sean, had made the trip to Fusion Lab. The pleasure of engaging with familiar faces helped dull the ache of the loss of Ted.

But since that day, new tasks piled up faster than he could handle. His list of "to do's" turned into "must do's." Not just Henry, but the entire team grew tired and exasperated. Tempers flared regularly and feelings were hurt. The collegial atmosphere that Fusion Lab was known for dissipated.

"Henry!" called out Rhonda from down the hall.

Henry stopped typing into his laptop and looked toward his door. Rhonda burst through, holding a wad of paper crushed in her hand.

"Henry!" she hollered. "You won't believe this! Emerson sent this over during the night. Not even the courtesy of a heads-up call." Rhonda slammed the small pile of notes on Henry's desk.

Knowing not to interrupt Rhonda until her anger simmered down, Henry looked from the papers back to Rhonda.

"They changed the specs again! We wasted the last three days of verification runs! And for what? A minor tweak? Any moron could see that these new requirements don't add a thing to the product. We need you to call Hyatt and get him to sack those idiots in marketing!"

With a final, loud breath of air, Rhonda plopped into a chair in front of Henry.

"Let me look," said Henry. He calmly retrieved the papers from the far edge of the desk and began to uncrumple and smooth them out on the hard surface closer to him. With each piece, Henry made a show of ironing the creases. Rhonda was silent. After he leisurely pressed flat two more crinkled pages, Rhonda snickered.

"Maybe I should read those to you?" Rhonda chuckled.

"Might be a good idea," said Henry. He, too, laughed.

"I'm sorry, Henry," said Rhonda, now composed.

"No need to apologize, Rhonda. I'm as annoyed as you."

"We've been wondering over at the workshop why Emerson has turned up the heat. Something's different. They aren't taking our calls when we need them to. And we're getting these new edicts. Everything seems fine in our weekly status calls, and then we get those." Rhonda pointed to the stack of papers.

"I agree with you. I see it too. In fact, I just got off the phone with Hyatt. We discussed the expanding number of modifications and how it's delaying the project. He said he was unaware and will dial back the marketing aspirations to those crucial."

Henry suspected Hyatt was having a tantrum over Henry's rank on the board. Hyatt talked a good game of support, but the actions coming from the Emerson team said otherwise. And after the week Henry just had, he'd happily give Hyatt those three letters, C.E.O.

"Look at these!" Rhonda exclaimed as she lifted the pages from Henry's desk. "They're all marked CRITICAL at the top." She flipped through the rumpled papers.

"Let's see if Hyatt comes through for us. In the meantime, scrutinize any deviation or modification requests. If you consider it frivolous, bring it to me and I'll bounce it back to Hyatt. We can only do so much."

"No offense, Henry, but I miss Ted," said Rhonda wistfully.

"None taken. I miss him too."

"When Ted was here, I had faith that this was all going to work out. Now I'm not so sure," Rhonda said softly.

Henry was quiet for a moment. Rhonda had voiced his own worries. He couldn't validate them by agreeing with her.

"While Ted was alive, he convinced us that this design and this project would succeed. 'Stick to the plan' he would say. Or 'look how far we've come.' He was right. We've had amazing success. We can do this."

"Thanks, Henry. You're right," said Rhonda. "But Emerson had better adjust." Rhonda then reached across the desk and palmed the stack of papers. As she stood up, she mouthed to Henry, "Guess we won't need these."

In a matter of weeks, an all-out war had broken out between

Emerson Energy versus Fusion Lab. Chemclone maneuvered to hold neutral territory. The teams had lost their focus on the end goals.

Henry called Agnes Mallort for help.

"You have to understand Hyatt's motivations, Henry. He's not going to make it easy for you, even when it seems counter-productive," said Agnes. "I talked to him yesterday. His business is hurting. His managers are screaming for more people, and he doesn't have the resources for more hires. The wafer project has been more consumptive than any of us had expected."

"I do understand. Fusion Lab is in the same predicament. We all are," protested Henry.

"Yes, we are," agreed Agnes. "But the fact is, every one of us sees the potential of this wafer. Otherwise, we would have pulled the plug long ago. We're not fools. You've done incredible work, Henry."

"Thanks," said Henry. "So, how do I stop this war?

Agnes chuckled. "That won't happen until Hyatt is running Solidane. Ted and I used to discuss that at length. He was convinced Hyatt would make a horrible leader for the development phase of the project. I wholeheartedly agree. That's why I supported you when Ted passed. You're doing fine, Henry."

"Again, thanks, Agnes. I thought about calling a board meeting to hear Hyatt out. Maybe in that setting, he could release some of his frustrations. Especially if you wouldn't mind umpiring."

"I'll do what I can," said Agnes. "A meeting may help."

"He won't talk honestly with me on the phone. I'm certain his animosity has spilled down to his people. I'm worried about the project."

"Me, too," Agnes said softly. "Let's give it a try. Hopefully Hyatt will lay his cards on the table so we can resolve this."

The board meeting was arranged, and Henry had waited impatiently at the large oval oak table centered in the Fusion Lab conference room. Alongside of him sat Rhonda and Doug, both now executive managers on the wafer project. Each had a substantial pile of documents in front of them, as well as individual laptop computers displaying complex charts.

To save time and money, most of the board would call from their own offices. Matt Granger was the first on the line, and Henry exchanged small talk with him. Calls from the rest of the board were shortly patched in. As usual, Hyatt Emerson was the last to join. "Sorry, had to finish an important call. How is everyone?" asked Hyatt.

Various "fine" and "good" comments overlapped each other as the members responded.

"I guess we can get started then," said Hyatt. "Is Fusion Lab ready to give us some good news?"

Henry fumed. This was not the agenda they had agreed to. Rhonda and Doug shook their heads. They had been issuing almost daily progress updates to everyone involved. Hyatt, as well as everyone else on the call, understood that they still had not achieved a production burn from the wafer. After a hundred permutations of the process, still no success. Besides, Henry was the Board Chair, not Hyatt.

"Okay," Henry began. He felt it best to answer Hyatt's challenge directly. "If you'll turn to the report we emailed to you yesterday, you can see exactly where we are. We've made progress and are narrowing the possibilities significantly. As we've said many times, we need to get through these simulations. Once our system identifies the correct sequence, we should be able to conduct the in-lab experiment to confirm. We're fortunate that we can run these simulations and tweak them in real time. If we had to prove each one with actual tests, it could take years."

"But, Henry," interrupted Hyatt acidly. "You've been telling us that for months now. We need results. It's time we changed course."

Hyatt paused for effect and then continued, "You sound like Ted Granger. No offense, but his stubbornness led us here. I believe it may have contributed to his passing. You all know I cared for Ted, but his iron-handedness could be irksome."

Silence. Hyatt guessed his remarks were offensive to most of the board, but he didn't care. The only way to move forward was to make some major waves. "As I've been recommending for some time now, we should be discreetly making overtures to other players in the industry. They have resources we can only envy. For example, Henry, some larger research facilities have super computers at their disposal. They could perfect your calculations in hours instead of months."

"Hyatt, I appreciate your viewpoint," Henry calmly responded. "However, we've discussed this thoroughly. As Ted astutely pointed out over the years, this must remain private. Our plan is solid. Ted continually reminded us that the process requires patience because of the copious failure rate. I remind you of his analogy that we're looking for a needle in a haystack. But every run of the formula removes another piece of hay from the stack. Every ineffective run takes us closer to that needle. That's always been our consensus, and I believe it still is."

"Well, I'm not sure the rest of the board agrees. If I'm not mistaken, Fusion Lab was in dire financial straits before Ted passed, and I doubt the prospects have improved."

"We're doing fine," insisted Henry.

"We'd all like to believe you, I'm sure. I've been hearing some grumbling. Has the consensus changed? Anyone want to speak up?" asked Hyatt.

The rest of the board members were torn between their loyalty to Ted and the pressure from Hyatt. Hyatt's facts were indisputable. In his pre-meeting, one-on-one phone calls to them, Hyatt had lobbied for a new direction. He'd hoped they would now take his side. Ted had been a powerful presence. He held considerable sway over them. But he was gone now, and Hyatt saw an opportunity.

Matt spoke up. "I admit my father was stubborn at times, but it was always because of his confidence in his decisions. Most of us can agree that he'd proven his judgment repeatedly. The success we've had so far, in fact, is his success. We've been along for the ride. Yes, all have made considerable contributions, some more than others."

Matt cleared his throat. "I have to say, though, that my dad was never iron handed. He always asked for opinions and welcomed opposite viewpoints. I have full confidence in Henry and the team. For my part, I want to stick to the plan. I reviewed the timeline, and we've accomplished much. As my dad would ask, let's be patient a while longer."

A chorus of accents then followed from the remaining board

members on the call.

"I have to express my dissent. I believe we're making a mistake," reiterated Hyatt.

Henry took the opportunity. "Excellent discussion. Note to the secretary that we've voted to stay the course, with one dissent, as usual. We need to get back to our lab, so thank you for your time."

Henry pushed the end button on the conference console and the line went dead. The phone immediately chirped. Henry saw that another call was on the line and hit the answer key. The caller ID said it was Matt.

"Do you believe that guy?" demanded Matt.

Rhonda and Doug took the question as their cue to pack up their belongings and head back to their desks. As they filed out, Henry let out a loud, exasperated sigh. "I know!"

"Why did Dad get involved with him? Such an arrogant . . .!"

Henry interrupted Matt to avoid a string of obscenities.

"I asked your dad exactly that at one time. He told me his challenge was to keep Hyatt on a leash, but that we would need Hyatt's hubris and aggressiveness at some point. He saw Hyatt as the guard dog that would keep the competition at bay. I don't see it just yet, but I have faith that Ted was right."

"Well, good thing we didn't have a video connection. I made some great gestures."

Henry laughed. "I appreciate how you spoke up. I was speechless for a minute. Rhonda was ready to toss her glass of water on me, I was so heated. You saved the day. Your dad would've been proud."

"Thanks, Henry. Let's see what happens next."

Henry sighed. "That was an unfortunate waste of time. If anything, it increased the hostilities. The opposite of what I'd hoped."

"Are you okay there at the lab?" asked Matt. "I didn't realize the finances were so bad."

"We're managing," Henry assured him. "Let me get back to work. Thanks again, Matt. Say hi to Connie and Marie. I'm sorry I've been so out of touch."

"Believe me, we all understand. Take it easy, Henry."

"This is unacceptable." Hyatt was aggravated by the call but still composed. Nora Brumfield, as well as a few more members of Hyatt's executive team at Emerson Energy, stayed seated at the conference room table and watched him for his reaction. Before the call, Hyatt had run through a few potential scenarios of outcomes. This was the least desirable of them.

Hyatt had become confident that the timing was ripe for a change of direction in the wafer plan. His prior conversations with the other board members had confirmed that they, too, were extremely concerned. However, he hadn't foreseen that Matt Granger would be on the call and make such a coherent defense of Henry and his team. In hindsight, he shouldn't have denigrated Ted. His strategy was to diminish the hold Ted had on the project, even after his death. He accomplished the opposite.

"Everything I said about Ted Granger was true," Hyatt insisted. He paused and glanced at each of them. "It appears as if he continues to be held in too high a regard."

Hyatt looked over at Nora. He could usually read what was on her mind and knew that she was always honest. Nora looked away. "So, Nora, you disagree?"

Nora hesitated to make sure she chose the right words.

"Well, Hyatt, I was fond of Ted Granger. He and my father studied together, and I'd known him from that relationship, as well as our current business dealings. I had great respect for him. I had suggested in our pre-call strategy meeting that the emphasis should be on Henry, not Ted."

Nora watched as a brief wave of anger crossed Hyatt's face and then disappeared. Hyatt knew Nora was correct and should have given more weight to her advice. His momentary irritation at being proved wrong surrendered to his pragmatism.

"Of course, you're right, Nora," Hyatt continued. "Henry Taylor is the logjam. Ted put him in place and, in effect, still represents him. However, he'll never be as accomplished as Ted. We should direct our energies to him."

Hyatt was no fool. He believed he could size up any individual, given enough information and time. Henry was impressive. His most obvious talent was his intelligence. Hyatt was conscious of, but would never admit, that Henry was smarter than himself. In Hyatt's evaluation, at ten years his junior, Henry lacked Hyatt's upbringing, experience, and pedigree. Under different circumstances, he could envision Henry as a valuable employee. Not anytime soon, though. Taylor had to go.

"Conrad, I'd like you to trickle out that information we discussed."

Conrad was Emerson Energy's VP of Marketing and had extensive industry contacts.

"Be discreet," said Hyatt faintly. "Remember, we've all signed iron tight non-disclosure agreements regarding Solidane and the wafer. If this backfires on us, I want the fingers pointed elsewhere."

He turned toward Ben Stentson. "Ben, I think it's time to have a talk with Margaret Granger. Can you set that up?" Ben nodded, rose, and left the room.

Hyatt turned forcefully in his chair and surveyed the skyline silhouette of the city in the broad expanse of glass enclosing one side of the room. After a few moments of silence, he faced the remaining group again and proclaimed, "Emerson Energy is suffering due to this wafer. The future of Solidane needs to be taken out of the hands of Fusion Lab and into more capable ones. We have too much invested and too much to lose because of Fusion Lab's present debacle. Let's get moving."

CHAPTER 7

Henry was headed out of his office on his way over to the lab building when his admin called after him.

"Henry! Wait up!" Eva shouted. "It's Hyatt Emerson. He says it's an emergency."

"When isn't it?" Henry muttered. "Tell him I'll be right there."

Rushing back into his office, he slumped down into his chair and picked up the line. "What's up, Hyatt?"

"I've got Agnes Mallort on the line, too. Have you seen the article?"

"Sorry, Hyatt. I don't know what you're referring to."

"There's information about the wafer that appears in one of the industry trade publications. And just hours ago, marketing got a call from a reporter asking about Fusion Lab and the wafer. You have a security leak!" Hyatt practically yelled.

"That's impossible!" objected Henry. "We've dealt with proprietary research since the Lab started. Everyone knows the protocols and follows them."

"If I may interject," said Agnes calmly, "This news is extremely alarming. It's the first time details about our project have escaped into a public forum. Henry, if you don't mind, would you give Chester Worthington a call? He would know how to investigate this."

"Absolutely!" affirmed Henry. "We'll also do an audit of our security procedures at the Lab. That's going to be consumptive."

"I know Emerson Energy is airtight," insisted Hyatt. "I pay a fortune to our outside consultants."

"Would you call them and ask if they could do an audit of Fusion Lab?" asked Henry. "If you already have a relationship with them, they might get here quickly. And they'd be familiar with how sensitive the wafer project is. If we have a problem here, I want to find it."

"I'll call them as soon as we hang up," agreed Hyatt. "I'm sure we can keep this breach contained. But it confirms how important it is to get this wafer into production."

"Yes, Hyatt," muttered Agnes. "We're all well aware."

"Thanks for everyone's support," said Henry. "Let's get the security team hired. We'll get this resolved."

When his cell phone rang, Henry surmised it was Matt. He was in the middle of a huddle of lab analysts and IT experts in one of the larger testing rooms. During their verification of the privacy measures throughout Fusion Lab, the security team that the board had hired apparently damaged some equipment.

Henry and the technicians hunted down the problem as a communications connection between two metering devices.

The break in the flow of data caused the entire spectrometer to shut down. After they restarted the machine, Henry somehow needed to soothe the four infuriated analysts who had just lost that morning's testing log.

"Hi Matt, can you hold on for a second?" asked Henry as he put the phone close to his chest. "Are we okay here now? I'd like to take this call, if possible."

The cluster of men and women griped a few more moments and then made their way back to their stations. "Call me if you have any more problems," Henry shouted to them as he bounded out of the lab and toward the footpath to his office in the other building.

"Sorry Matt, putting out fires here. What's up?" Henry asked as he raised the phone back to his ear.

"I just got off the phone with Chester. Are you somewhere we can talk?"

"Yes, I'm walking over to my office, but can talk as I go."

"It's not good news. You know Hyatt called my mother, right?" asked Matt.

"Yes," said Henry. "And your mom then called Chester."

"Well, Chester called the bank. He verified that everything Hyatt told my mother is true. The bank's loan committee is now reviewing Fusion Lab's loan for non-compliance with our loan covenants."

"How did Hyatt know this, and we didn't?" fumed Henry.

"Chester intends to find out. In the meantime, because all the assets of Fusion are pledged as collateral, if they call the loan, the Granger family will lose everything my dad built . . ." Matt's voice trailed off.

"I'm sorry, Matt."

"It's cruel," mumbled Matt. "So anyway, Chester also reached out to the private equity firm Hyatt's dealing with. They're ready to infuse some cash into Solidane and give some assurances to Fusion's bank. But only with Hyatt in charge."

"Why wouldn't Hyatt bring that proposal directly to the Board? Why get your mom involved?" asked Henry.

"Because if he can finagle Mom's vote, Hyatt will take your place as CEO," answered Matt angrily.

"I feel bad for your mom," said Henry. He stopped along the path and leaned against a support post.

"She doesn't have much choice."

"We're so close now, though. If Hyatt would just cool off for a little while longer . . ." Henry offered, and his voice trailed off. "I've tried calling him directly recently, but somehow he's always out. He'll only interact with me through the board. I've even asked Agnes Mallort to help me gain Hyatt's confidence. I've set up conference calls just between the three of us, but Hyatt always cancels at the last minute. Agnes and I have a fine relationship, at least for my part. I sense she has her own apprehensions regarding Hyatt."

"Hyatt had problems with my dad being in charge. He's certainly not going to respect you in that position. No offense," said Matt.

"None taken. Hyatt won't rest until he's in control. I try not to take it personally. Ted certainly had his misgivings, too."

"Makes you wonder how much farther along we'd be if Hyatt was supporting the team instead of working against it," said Matt.

"Yep. A source of great frustration."

"You realize, Henry, with Hyatt in charge, anything can happen," asserted Matt.

"Yes, I guess we'll have to see what he has planned. Hopefully, nothing too drastic."

"How are things going there? Is there any progress we could present to the bank that might forestall Hyatt?"

"I wish I could say yes, but we're still in the middle of the safety testing schedule. Unless we ascertain its constraints, we can't produce the wafer in any quantity. Last week, a wafer exploded during an emulsion. Well, it really didn't explode, it just had an unusually rapid burn. By that, I mean about eighty times above normal, which would appear to anyone as an explosion.

Henry shifted his weight against the post as he switched the phone to his other ear. Two technicians passed him on the walkway, and Henry smiled and waved to them.

"Sorry, Matt, I'm drowning you in detail. Once we can sign off on the safety issues, we can get the formula to Chemclone to produce trial batches. After that, we're free and clear. I'm guessing, a couple more months."

"And that's too late," said Matt, discouraged.

"I'm afraid so," confirmed Henry.

"I guess we'll see how this plays out. Try to stay positive."

"You too, Matt."

Henry tucked the phone in his pocket, turned, and headed back to the lab. He needed to make sure that everything was back in operation. If necessary, he'd shoo away the security techs so they'd no longer interrupt the lab's routine.

Walking along the path, he rehashed the call with Matt

in his head. "Well, there's another one for you, Lord . . ." he muttered in a halfhearted prayer.

Rhonda hesitated as she approached Henry's office. Tensions at the lab had been rising all week. Although the tests on the various wafer alternatives were progressing extremely well, rumblings and rumors swept through the lab staff.

She knocked gently on the door frame. Henry looked up from his work and nodded to her. No smile, no scoff, only a blank expression. Rhonda's stomach knotted up. In a slow, fluid motion, she shifted her weight and leaned her shoulder against the doorjamb. Something dreadful was brewing.

"Hey, Henry, sorry to interrupt," Rhonda said, then paused. "We're making substantial advances on the tests. I thought you might want a status report," she finished timidly.

"Come on in, Rhonda. I pulled up the stats a while ago and agree with you. Particularly good progress," Henry told her in a flat voice.

Rhonda strode into the office and sat gingerly in a chair in front of Henry's desk. The bright, harsh light of his computer screen seemed to frame Henry's face. He looked terrible.

Henry caught the shocked look on Rhonda's face, even though she quickly masked it with a forced smile. "Is everything okay?" she asked.

"How to answer that?" mused Henry to both himself and Rhonda.

No, everything was not okay. He had not slept in days. He had not changed his clothes in the same amount of time. Eating? This morning he'd tried to convince himself he was hungry. He had wandered over to the employee lounge and rummaged through the cupboards. Nothing appealed to him. He then drifted over to the refrigerator. He opened the door and stood peering into it. After scanning its contents, he sighed and casually closed the door, uninterested.

Henry then walked to the back of the lounge and spied a bag of pretzels left on the counter. He grabbed it. The bag crackled and crunched as he made the opening big enough to plunge his hand through. He pulled out a few pretzels and emphatically bit down on one. Some pieces fell away from his mouth and scattered onto the floor as he returned to his office. That was today's breakfast, lunch, and dinner.

Rhonda's fellow managers had met and decided that she would be the best person to confront Henry to find out if the rumors were true. They had considered meeting with him together to show their support, but didn't want to gang up on him. Remindful of her charge, she summoned the courage to proceed.

"Henry, some very nasty rumors are floating around the lab. Are you at liberty to tell us what's going on?"

Sitting up straight, Henry smiled affectionately. "So, they sent you in here solo, huh?"

Rhonda let out a short laugh. It heartened her to see Henry's face light up and for him to joke with her. "Yes, they're all huddled over at the lab. If I don't return, they'll draw straws to determine who's next."

They both laughed.

"I appreciate everyone's concern," said Henry, as he gradually grew serious. "You deserve some answers. Let's walk over there, and we'll discuss this with everyone."

Rhonda rose cautiously. Henry turned off his computer, placed the paper reports he had been viewing in a drawer, and locked it. "Security," he whispered.

Together, they walked out of the administrative office doors and out onto the path to the interconnected lab. The rest of the project managers were waiting for Rhonda in the lab meeting room. Drawing up to the door, Henry gestured for her to go in. As she opened the door to the room, the managers all turned in anticipation. It surprised them when Henry followed her in.

"Hi, everyone," began Henry. Again, Henry was cognizant of the fleeting looks of distress at his appearance. Most had not seen him in at least a week, as they were buried in their own tasks. He pulled out a chair from under a table, faced it toward the group, and sat down.

"I guess I let events progress too far without discussing them with you. I apologize. Some things won't go away if you just ignore them, I guess."

The group shuffled in their seats, and most avoided Henry's eyes. They stared down at their feet or off into the distance. Henry waited until he had their attention.

With all eyes now on him, he continued, "About a month ago, an industry trade publication reported some proprietary information about the wafer. It was limited but surprising to see. The next week, a reporter called asking the marketing team to confirm additional confidential data. It was obvious we had a leak. This could not come at a worse time.

"The board agreed to have a security team hired to investigate. That's why we have these IT personnel crawling over the building. We've conducted our research and development for years now without a peep. We all understand the dangers of outsiders gaining access to our secrets. That's why we're so careful and take so many precautions. In addition, our intense loyalty to each other, as well as to Ted Granger, protects us.

"However, the information escaped from somewhere. The cybersecurity specialists examined all our outbound and internal data lines to make sure they were secure. They found one not to be. The computer in the laser optics lab has its own uplink to a satellite line. That computer belonged to Ted Granger, and he let the lab borrow it. His son, Matt, gave it to Ted."

Henry paused and looked at them. "We gave the security auditors access to the link and my cell phone number is listed in the history. I've used the satellite link when out by the fire pit. There is spotty cell coverage there. Ted used to do that often. The security firm is convinced I'm the one who is divulging information. Either knowingly or unknowingly."

The group sharply drew in their breaths. Then a unified, "You, Henry?" They became angry. "That's absurd!"

"I assure you; it was not me," said Henry forcefully. "The issue is that there is personal information on that computer that mentions my name. The inference is that I'm using lab property for personal use. That violates our rules."

"Why would anyone accuse you, Henry?" asked Rhonda.

"Oh, it's just a friendly power struggle," said Henry angrily.

"We've heard," stated Rhonda.

"Hyatt Emerson has called for another emergency board meeting to discuss the security breach and has recommended my removal as CEO of Solidane."

The group gasped.

"He can't do that!"

"Actually, he can."

"This is more horrible than I expected," moaned Rhonda. "I'm so sorry, Henry."

"Thank you, all of you," answered Henry. "Let's not get ahead of ourselves. It hasn't happened yet. Also, we're making great strides on the wafer. If Emerson would just be a little more patient, this would work out to his benefit. Fusion Lab is only a few more tests away from releasing the wafer to production. Wouldn't you agree?"

"Yes," they replied together.

Rhonda added, "We only have three more milestones on the project flowchart to complete."

"Well, as soon as that happens, our part of the project will conclude, and we can celebrate!" said Henry cheerily. "I wish Ted were here to see this through with us. He'd be incredibly proud of this team."

The group started talking excitedly among themselves. A definite end of the project did not seem concrete until Henry voiced it.

Henry's stomach growled, and the group laughed. "If it's okay with you, I'm going to go home, eat some dinner, take a shower, and crawl into bed. I'm exhausted."

They all seconded that and filed out.

Later that week, Henry was in his office gazing intently at the computer screen. He'd been trying to verify a simulation they had run that morning. With each try, his computer would answer with the rudeness of a buzz, signifying another failed attempt. The incessant beeping felt like the computer games of his youth whenever his on-screen icon got devoured by whatever evil monster he was trying to overcome.

Except for the irritating sound, Henry's office, like the rest of the building, was dark and quiet. The others had left for the night, like most nights lately, not that Henry cared anymore. He was tired, frustrated, and ready to give up.

Scanning the list on his page of notes, he did a few quick calculations in his head and then entered another series of instructions to the complicated program. Too engrossed in his work to notice, two figures appeared in his doorway, paused, and studied him. They watched his head bob up and down as Henry glanced from paper to screen and back again. They nodded to each other and then snuck around the outside area of the office.

With obvious military experience, the two figures crept closer, silently advancing on each side of Henry seated at his desk. The computer again emanated its shrill buzz, confirming another rejection. Henry let out an embittered sigh. It was then he noticed the slight shadow and reflection of the strangers on his screen. Too late. He jumped out of his chair and tried to turn to face them. But each had grabbed an arm and together, they tackled him to the floor.

Henry's face was ground into the carpet as he toppled into a heap. The larger of the two, with the precision of a combatant, pinned Henry's arms against his back. Henry couldn't move. The other figure hurried to the light switch and flicked it on.

The bright white light from the overhead fluorescents

engulfed the room. Henry turned his head and blinked his eyes quickly in order to identify his attackers. The bulky one on top of him began to shake. Just then, the other one moved into his frame of vision.

"Alex! What the heck?" Henry shouted. He then realized the one on top of him was laughing. "Sean! Get off me!"

Alex let out a loud laugh that infuriated Henry. He pushed with all his might to roll Sean off his back, but to no avail.

"Hi Henry," chuckled Alex as he strolled over to Henry sprawled on the floor. "Nice to see you. What's new?"

"I'm gonna . . ." began Henry.

"Sean will let you up once you calm down and promise not to punch either of us. Especially me."

Sean leaned over so that Henry could see his face. He had a big smile, as if this were the most fun he'd had in a long while.

"Henry, you should've seen your face," said Alex, and he began laughing again. Sean joined in and soon they were both laughing so hard, Alex had to lean against the desk. Holding his side, Sean rolled off Henry.

Still simmering, Henry now sat up and glowered at both. This only made them laugh even harder. Alex could scarcely breathe. He doubled over and lost his balance. Falling forward, his head smacked into Sean's with a loud thump. That stopped their snickering.

Ever since their high school days, Alex and Sean openly competed. Sean had always been, by far, the tallest, strongest, and most fit of the two but with a slowness that accompanies extra muscle. However, Alex was the most athletic. A "born athlete" as they say. Better golf swing, brutal tennis serve, and higher jump shot on the basketball court. But when force or muscle was needed, such as in any brawl, petty or serious, all bets were on Sean.

"Ouch!" hollered Alex, as he glared at Sean. "Watch that fat head of yours!"

"Silly me!" Sean barked back sarcastically. He scowled at Alex and massaged his forehead. "You're so darned uncoordinated!"

Henry chuckled, "Serves you both right."

The two looked at Henry and all three laughed.

"We had to do it, Henry. You were so engrossed," explained Sean.

"Yeah, we came up here to capture you and get you out of this place for a while," said Alex.

"Thanks for that, but you didn't need to scare the heck out of me," answered Henry.

"Sorry about that, but we need to cut you loose from this office. Let's head out to that courtyard. The firepit beckons," suggested Sean.

As they escaped out of Henry's office toward the front of the building, Alex reached down and grabbed an oblong bag.

"We brought our own provisions just in case the fridge in the cafeteria isn't stocked anymore," said Alex as he jostled the bag.

"Well, we haven't had many get-togethers up here recently," answered Henry.

All three were silent as they thought of Ted. They then headed over to the outside terrace.

The night was dark, and the air was just cooling as the heat from the valley below them dissipated. The glow of millions of bright stars and a rising moon provided enough light along the pathway.

"Let's get that thing going," said Alex. He pointed to the fire pit and shifted his direction to the bank of cabinets where the controls were located. After unlatching the protective hood, he fiddled with a few control valves and hit a starter button. With a sudden poof, flames shot out of the fire ring. The pit soon glowed as the blaze caressed the fake logs.

The three men each dragged a wooden lounge chair closer to the fire. Alex handed out the cans of beer.

"I love this place," said Sean. He waved his arm around the area. The slight glow of the moon, gaining height and intensity, highlighted the tips of the far-off mountains.

"So, Henry, Sean and I are headed upstate to the big game this weekend. We have tickets. You're coming with us," Alex stated matter-of-factly.

"No, I'm not," answered Henry. "I shouldn't even be out here. I have work that needs to get done."

"Come on, Henry. You've ignored my calls and texts for weeks now. Sean called you and you snubbed him. Sean never calls anyone. This isn't good."

Henry looked at Sean, tipped his beer toward him and mumbled, "Sorry."

Henry turned to face Alex. "Why are you on my case? You attacked me and dragged me out here. I should be at my desk finding a way to get that blasted wafer finished."

"It's not just us, Henry. I've been getting calls from Kate, your mom, your dad. They haven't seen you or heard from you. That's not like you. What's your problem?"

"I don't have a problem," insisted Henry. "Everyone realizes

I need to get this done. You know how important this wafer is."

"It's not the end of the world, Henry. It was Ted's dream, not yours."

Henry became annoyed. "Well, Ted's not here anymore, and all of this is now on my head."

The three were silent again. Sean took a slurp of beer and then opened a new one. He tossed a cold can to both Alex and Henry.

"Well, you became my problem. Everyone's calling me. I think Kate is madder at me than at you," objected Alex.

Sean chuckled, "I wonder why?"

"She insisted I do something, like she couldn't do the same. She kept telling me how upset your mom was. I told her, of course, your mom is upset because you're her favorite and she's worried about you. Kate didn't take that so well and told me to get up here."

Sean chuckled again, "You know what buttons to push, don't you?"

Henry laughed too. "Actually, I think Alex is my mom's favorite."

Alex agreed. "I think so, too. I'm very lovable."

Deflecting the conversation to avoid any more conflict, Henry rubbed his chin and shifted to Sean.

"What's with the beard?" he asked.

Sean attempted to respond, but Alex interrupted.

"It's his new girlfriend. She likes it," announced Alex. "They've been dating now for over three months! Can you believe that, Henry?"

Henry sat up. "Really! Someone hooked Sean? Hard to

conceive."

"Her name is Angie," volunteered Sean meekly. "If you hadn't been such a hermit lately, you would've met her by now."

Henry sat back, lost in thought. He wondered how much he'd missed in his friends' lives. His family, too. But they couldn't comprehend the pressure he was under. How would they ever understand? Ted's torch had been passed to him. He was determined to see it through, even though it looked bleak. The lab was running out of money, the wafer would not perform as needed, and the intrusions by Hyatt Emerson and his horde were becoming aggressive.

Alex noticed Henry's grim facial expression. "Henry, did you read about our new coach? Long overdue, nobody's surprised. Well, possibly you are, as you have your head buried in work. The college will pay the rest of his salary on his old contract."

Alex didn't wait for a response and began listing the pros and cons of a new coaching staff. The three of them spent the next hour debating the prospects of the top college football teams in the country. Football had always been one of Henry's favorite sports, and usually he could rattle off a string of statistics most pertinent to the moment. He felt out of touch and a bit discouraged as Alex and Sean led the conversation.

However, this familiar banter drained the stress from him. Helped by the alcohol, the iron grasp of burdens and obligations melted. The familiar drone of Alex's voice, punctuated by Sean's grunts of agreement or disagreement, drew Henry's body deeper into the comfortable chair. He fell asleep.

Alex prattled on for another twenty minutes before Henry let out a snore. Sean and Alex paused, laughed, and then stood up. Alex walked over to the firepit controls, turned the dials, and slowly snuffed out the steady, flickering flame. Sean gathered up the empty beer cans and flipped them into the flexible cooler pouch. Then, together, they hoisted Henry up, a shoulder under each arm. They carried him along the winding path to the cottages where some of the staff, including Henry, briefly lodged because of their tedious hours.

Henry woke the next morning refreshed. After breakfast, he followed Alex and Sean out to their car and saw them off. Henry had made it clear that he couldn't join them. He had too many obligations and no time to spare. He made promises to stay in better contact.

Alex watched Henry's face in the rearview mirror as he drove off. Henry waved and then lowered his head and turned away. Alex saw the smile fade and a look of what he concluded was fear, replace it.

The car sped up and Alex grumbled to Sean, "This is not good."

CHAPTER 8

The board meeting was infuriating. All the board members had flown or driven to Fusion Lab to be present in person. Even Matt Granger, generally opting for a call in to these meetings, had arrived. After they dispatched the usual housekeeping items, Hyatt took the floor. He self-assuredly laid out his case for why he should replace Henry as CEO and President of Solidane.

He explained that the financial condition of Fusion Lab, the significant delay in the wafer schedule, and the security breach left them no alternative. For dramatic effect, he called in the security experts to present their findings on the breach. They alleged, with an extremely high level of certainty, that the transgression came from Henry's use of Ted Granger's computer. Either wittingly or unwittingly, Henry Taylor injured Solidane.

The other board members issued their rebuttals and assurances that Henry could not have done such a thing. Henry, himself, remained silent. The outcome was preordained, so there was little to gain by protesting. The confidence in him that the others vigorously articulated heartened him.

Hyatt then spoke, "I appreciate everyone's viewpoint, but there's another voice to consider." With somewhat of a flourish, he revealed the proxy Margaret Granger had signed.

"I must tell you I've been in contact with Margaret Granger. After discussing the situation, she agreed with me that a change is necessary."

Matt Granger started to interrupt, but caught himself. He did not want to malign his mother. But he also wanted to protect Henry.

Henry spoke up, "Hyatt, tell us specifically what changes you'd make in the direction of Solidane if you take the helm."

Hyatt, caught off guard for a moment, looked at Henry. He studied Henry's face and concluded that Henry was not laying a trap.

"The adjustments necessary are not dramatic. I've endorsed the wafer project plan wholeheartedly in the past. We have received the latest update and the testing has turned the corner and is improving. What's needed are additional resources. I've said this emphatically over the last year. Once the security breach occurred, a private equity firm approached me. They're highly interested in Solidane, even knowing only the vaguest of details about our wafer. They're already heavily invested in the energy space. The numbers they're suggesting they could infuse are staggering."

Henry glared at Hyatt. If only he could somehow prove that Hyatt, or someone in his employ, caused that leak. He accepted it was too late to make any difference.

"Solidane presently exists only on paper. There are no

employees, no offices, no product. Its future depends on a wafer that Chemclone, Fusion Lab, and Emerson Energy have collaborated on for years to develop. Ted Granger led the program with outstanding success. We're remarkably close now. As Ted's protégé, Henry here has done his best to fill Ted's shoes. However, such a daunting task has caused some missteps, as the security team just outlined."

Matt squirmed in his chair and his face grew hot. He held his tongue.

"My leadership would provide a fresh course, only in that we would expeditiously partner with the private equity firm and build the foundation of Solidane. We need facilities, manufacturing systems, and assets in place. We can't do that without their help."

Agnes Mallort interrupted. "We already have Chemclone's largest plant re-outfitted and ready to go. That was my responsibility we agreed on at the beginning. It's what I brought to the table and got me this seat here. It's costing Chemclone a hefty chunk of capital."

She looked around the table for assent. "Ted committed the resources of Fusion Lab. Combined over the years, I'd hate to tally the total costs to the Granger family. Obviously, Ted pledged every dime.

"I need to remind you, Hyatt, your share of this odyssey was to use your connections and expertise in the energy business to open markets for the product. So, you are only doing what you already have pledged. I feel the sacrifice has been a little unequal."

Hyatt grimaced and responded hotly, "I assure you; Emerson

Energy has suffered tremendously from the focus my employees devoted to the wafer. My contribution is steep. I'm as committed as anyone. Let me state again, without my contacts with the private equity firm, our journey, as you call it, will end abruptly. Do you agree?"

They fell silent. Hyatt was correct in that fact. The other fact was that saving the wafer came with Hyatt in control.

Henry raised both his hands as would a referee. "I think we have all the information we need to decide. Let the secretary take the roll call vote."

A few short minutes later, the Board named Hyatt Emerson as the new CEO and Chairman of the Board of Solidane.

Immediately after the board meeting ended, Hyatt had asked Henry and Matt to remain. Hyatt was no fool. He understood Henry was the glue that held Fusion Lab together. He needed Henry's cooperation to keep his plan on track now that he was directing the business of Solidane.

Hyatt broke the tense, awkward silence. "Henry and Matt, I hope we can put this event behind us and move forward. We've had, and I'm sure we still have, differences of opinion on the correct path for our venture. But now that the board has come to a consensus with me as the skipper, so to speak, I'm asking for your support. As the primary trustees for Fusion Lab, you have the say so on what happens next.

Henry and Matt remained motionless.

"My mandate is to create a company out of the shell that is, right now, Solidane Energy. However, that task would be pointless unless we had a marketable product. Henry, the last update from your team shows excellent progress. And my team at Emerson, along with the production crew at Chemclone, have been synthesizing the exact specs for the first wafer. We need you, Henry, to keep this machinery rolling. Your lab personnel must conclude the testing.

Hyatt paused and studied their faces for reaction. Seeing none, he continued.

"Solidane and Fusion Lab are separate entities. As CEO of Solidane, I have no authority over Fusion Lab. The trust set up by Ted has that responsibility. In effect, nothing has changed for you, Henry, and your work here. All of us must work together for the good of Solidane. That was Ted's desire."

"You expect us to forget what just happened?" asked Matt incredulously. "Those security consultants trashed Henry's good name. You simply expect him to forget that?"

"That was an unfortunate outcome of the security break investigation, I concur. None of us believe Henry could do such a thing. However, the evidence did point there."

"What evidence? That was my father's computer, given to him by me. I've explained all the specifics to the examiners," protested Matt.

Henry interrupted. "Thanks, Matt, but you don't need to defend me."

Turning to Hyatt he said, "Hyatt, you have my support. However, I'd like your help in return. You might've heard, Fusion Lab has had some trouble with our bank. We understand that they've gotten wind that a security firm is investigating our privacy protocols."

Henry stared at Hyatt to see his reaction. Hyatt looked

down at some papers scattered in front of him and gathered them together. He ignored both Henry and Matt until Henry spoke again.

"The bank construed the incident as a breach of our loan covenants. It's no secret that our financial condition is dire. The bank's aware, however, that the fortunes of Solidane and Fusion Lab intertwine. If they knew about that cash infusion you've promised for Solidane, it would go a long way toward mollifying their concerns."

"Of course," answered Hyatt emphatically, facing Henry again. "Send me the contact information of your banking representative, and I'll call them. I'm sure the bright prospects of our respective companies will placate them. Please reach out to them first, so I have permission to speak with them."

Matt then interjected heatedly. "Also, I expect you to address any concerns about our security breach. We all agree, as you said, that Henry did nothing wrong. I don't want anyone to presuppose otherwise. I expect you to clear his name."

"I'll make sure the final investigation report to the board shows the information that you, Matt, have provided. I'll make sure it explains the computer mix-up and states that Henry did nothing wrong. If it'll help, I'll convey that to Fusion's bank, too," said Hyatt.

"Okay, then. We're all-in," said Henry. "Fusion Lab will proceed as planned. The goal is the final wafer product. The sooner the better."

Hyatt and Matt nodded. They rose, shook hands, and left the conference room. Hyatt hurried back to his entourage lingering in the Fusion Lab lobby. They scurried into their waiting cars and headed to the airport.

Hyatt did not allow himself much time for celebration. Talk of work quickly replaced the festive mood following a brief toast on the charter flight back home. Much needed to be done, and Hyatt assigned the various tasks. They made phone calls that put in motion actions they had planned months ago.

After a week at Emerson Energy's Massachusetts headquarters, Hyatt was set to travel to New York. He had meetings pre-arranged with the private equity group, as well as various subcontractors who would arrange for office space, personnel, and furnishings.

The more time Hyatt spent in New York, the more he enjoyed it. People talked his language of business. Things were fast-paced, and action packed. He had never embraced the "sluggishness" as he phrased it of his many encounters with the Ted Granger's and Agnes Mallort's of the world.

Emerson Energy had a long history. Its roots were in electricity. Company lore told that Hyatt's great, great grandfather was a friend of Thomas Edison. Proof of the claim was non-existent. However, Emerson Energy emulated the success of the GE that Edison founded. Hyatt's father had once referred to the relationship as that between a whale and remora fish. Emerson profitably sought and mastered the minor projects that would not attract a larger enterprise.

The priority for Hyatt was to secure the funding for Solidane. After signing agreements, the board approved stock options to be issued to the private equity group in settlement of the financing. Solidane could now make draws against the funding commitment, based on the proforma financial forecasts supplied by Hyatt. That way, the equity fund could control and monitor its investment.

Office space was leased and furnished. Hyatt announced new Solidane executives and managers almost daily. The first batches were those he brought over from Emerson Energy. Key hires followed. After three weeks of frenetic activity, Hyatt ceased, pleased with the results.

The fourth week was when things unraveled. As promised, Hyatt had spoken to the bank officer in charge of the Fusion Lab loan. He assured them that Solidane would support Fusion Lab, as they were integral to the success of Solidane. The bank would finalize its review of the loan agreement. They expected a favorable outcome. All seemed fine.

However, the bank had requested the Solidane board meeting minutes to confirm the prospects of Fusion Lab considering the Solidane relationship. When the loan committee reviewed the minutes, they realized it was Henry Taylor who had committed the security breach, and that the board subsequently removed him as CEO. The bank was not happy. They called the loan.

The bank sent the notice by express carrier to the law offices of Chester Worthington, as the agent of record for the Fusion Lab Trust. Chester was livid when he read it and immediately dialed Hyatt.

"I just received a notice from Fusion Lab's bank. They've called the loan. You said you had resolved everything," said Chester angrily.

"I spoke with the loan officer. That's what he told me,"

Hyatt responded indignantly. He wasn't going to be harangued by Chester.

"Well, please call him again. This could be a disaster. We need to find out what this is about," said Chester. "Please get back to me soon." Chester didn't wait for a reply and hung up.

Flustered when the call with Chester Worthington ended, Hyatt grabbed his computer notebook. He scrolled through the tasks and entries he had noted over the last month. Something went wrong. What had he missed?

He finished swiping when he reached the notes of the failed board meeting. It was after that meeting that he had set in motion the events that led to Henry Taylor's ouster. As he read the entries, it hit him. After they removed Henry at the subsequent emergency board meeting, Hyatt had never ended the security probe at Fusion Lab. The security firm even now continued to investigate Henry.

Hyatt dialed Ben Stentson.

"Ben, what's the status of the security audit?" asked Hyatt.

"Their focus is on Henry Taylor, as we hoped," answered Ben.

"What does that mean? He's out. I'm in. What are they still doing? Why wasn't this wound up?"

"We don't think it should be yet. Suppose Taylor is a sore loser. We're not sure what he's capable of. He was accused of leaking information. What if he really does that now?"

"I'll worry about that. We need to end this audit right now. It's becoming a liability. Word is spreading to troublemakers and Solidane can't afford the negative publicity."

"Okay, they're installing a GPS device in Taylor's car. They wanted to keep track of his whereabouts. I'll shut it down."

"Good. I don't want to hear any more about this."

Ben Stentson immediately called his counterpart at the security firm. "Paul, Ben here. We're good with your last report and need to end our contract immediately."

"You mean stop the investigation?"

"Yes, immediately."

"Okay. We're working on Taylor's car right now. I'll call them."

Henry had handed over the keys to the car that morning. The security firm had sent out a notice that they would screen all Fusion owned vehicles that day for possible listening devices. They methodically opened each car or truck and waved a wand throughout the interior.

Now inspecting Henry's car, a technician had the panel open under the dashboard where the chips that controlled most of the automated features were located. He carefully pulled out a small IC chip. This one controlled three systems: the radar cruise control, the backup camera, and lane assist.

When ready, the technician opened a box from his tool case and gently lifted out a replacement IC. He grounded himself and snapped the tiny legs into the empty holes in the circuit board. As he pressed down, the phone rang. He jerked his head and hit it on the metal pole of the steering wheel. Cussing, he pressed the chip in harder. He did not see that he had misaligned the fragile strands, and four of them bent.

"I'm busy!" he yelled into the phone.

The tone of voice bothered Paul, but he calmly explained that the assignment was over and to pack up and leave.

"Gladly!" was the response.

The technician hastily replaced the cover and screwed back into place the decorative trim. He then slammed the door and hit the lock button on the key. The car chirped, and the lights blinked.

Over the next two weeks, Hyatt and Chester negotiated with the bank to reinstate Fusion Lab's loan. The private equity company agreed to increase drawdowns to Solidane. This allowed Solidane to pledge additional assets to support Fusion's loan and satisfy the bank. Fusion Lab was saved.

But Henry Taylor wasn't. The tale of the security breach had taken life, as gossip usually does. A reporter from a local paper had shown up at Fusion Lab and asked to interview Henry. Because of all the fallout, neither the bank nor the private equity firm would consent to allow Henry to remain. They couldn't demand his termination; however, they both made it clear that they would reach no deal without that understanding.

Hyatt called Chester.

"Chester, we've done our best, but the demands for Henry's resignation are not negotiable."

"Then you didn't keep your commitment!" Chester barked.

"Actually, I did. I promised that I'd save Fusion Lab. I did that. I never promised to salvage Henry."

"Watch yourself, Hyatt. Henry did nothing wrong."

"Henry allowed proprietary information to escape out of Fusion Lab. Now, he didn't intend this, but it happened."

"Matt Granger cleared that up. It was Ted's computer, not Henry's."

"Well, Chester, I've done all I can. The bank doesn't want

Henry employed at Fusion Lab, period. Neither does our equity partner. They're asking for his immediate removal from the premises."

"They don't have that authority!" bellowed Chester. "We need time for an orderly transition of duties!"

"You'll have to work that out with them. Please tell the trustees that the bank will release the loan when Henry Taylor is gone. This is now between the trust and the bank. I'm no longer a party to this negotiation. Goodbye Chester." Hyatt hung up.

"I'm sorry I can't do this in person, Henry," explained Chester, "But conditions are changing rapidly. Here's where we stand. The bank has agreed to reinstate the loan."

"That's terrific news!" exclaimed Henry.

"Somewhat. It's only a six-month extension. They'll review it again, then. I've gone through the Lab's financials with the bank. The last two years look terrible. One of their complaints is that Fusion has no pipeline. There's no revenue. The Lab has dedicated all its resources to Solidane and the wafer."

"Yes, that's a decision Ted was forced to make. He shunned many requests for our services. We're still unable to accept new business. We don't have the resources," added Henry.

"The Lab's banking relationship is built on confidence," said Chester. "Ted had been doing business with this bank for over thirty years. They knew him. Fusion Lab is unique. Selling research is complicated. They understand that. Ted's passing alarmed them, but they've been patient, given we have made every loan payment on time."

"And now, everything rests on the wafer," stated Henry.

"And on me instead of Ted."

"Yes," agreed Chester. "And the supposed 'security breach' was a shock to them. They're skittish."

"I understand why," said Henry.

"Now, here's the tough part of this conversation for me, Henry. Because the board removed you as CEO, the bank is nervous about you. They want to bring in an outside executive to oversee the Lab for the next six months."

"Are you saying they now want me out of the picture?"

"Yes, they want your resignation."

CHAPTER 9

"Kate? Hi, this is Matt Granger."

"Matt, nice to hear your voice. It's been a long while," said Kate. She shooed the girls out of the room.

"Yes. Sorry it has. Henry keeps me up to date on your family. He gets such a kick out of your girls," said Matt.

"And they love him, too. I wish we could see him more often," said Kate.

"I hope I'm doing the right thing. Has Henry spoken to you about the mess at the Lab?"

"Yes, he called me yesterday and told me about his resignation. I'm pretty confused about the whole situation myself."

"We all are. The bank is insisting that Henry resign from the Lab. It's baffling. Henry met this morning with all the Lab employees. They're terribly upset. They know this is wrong. To make matters worse, they need his help if they're ever to get this wafer completed."

"If Henry isn't there, how can he help them?"

"Well, Henry will no longer be an employee, but he's still a trustee, like me. The bank has no power or say in that. As a trustee, he's entitled to receive reports, just as I do. Henry and the Lab's managers have worked out a system to keep him in the loop. It meets the requirements of the bank, and Henry stays involved."

Kate wasn't sure she liked what she heard.

"Why would he agree to that? To be honest, Matt, I told Henry that maybe this is for the best. There're many other opportunities out there. He's so smart. He might be happier elsewhere."

"But Fusion Lab needs him, Kate."

"Fusion Lab is draining him!" Kate protested. "You've let him assume Ted's responsibilities as well as his own. The Lab can't even afford to hire help for him. He was in a terrible situation, and now it's gotten horribly worse."

"I'm sorry, Kate. You're right," Matt yielded. "I need to think of Henry."

Kate let her emotions catch up with her words. It frustrated her that her brother was in this predicament. But Matt was only trying to help.

After an extended silence, Kate began again, "I shouldn't blame you, Matt. Henry is incredibly talented and has made these choices. He understands full well the ramifications of his decisions. I'm sure he'll work things out."

"I know he will," agreed Matt.

"Henry said he'd be incredibly busy for the next four weeks. Alex and Sean volunteered to ride up to the Lab on Henry's last day. One of us should be there with him. They can snatch

Henry and do something fun," said Kate.

"I was hoping you'd say that. It's just what he needs. I'd go myself, but I'm committed to traveling for work. Our company is on an acquisition spree, and that means lots of additional duties," explained Matt.

"I'm insensitive sometimes, Matt. Henry told me how difficult this has been for you, too. All these calls, I bet you're as tired as Henry!"

"Not quite," said Matt. "I'm no match for Henry. He insists the wafer is almost ready. He's predicting that all this nonsense will die away once production starts and money is rolling in. I hope he's right."

"Ever the optimist," chuckled Kate. "You gotta love him!"

"You're hard to get a hold of," said Alex.

"I've been busy," protested Henry. He had shut down his computer about fifteen minutes ago and was walking over to the cottage that served as his sleeping quarters. The commute to his house in the valley would have chopped two to three hours off his availability at the Lab.

"Why are you calling me this late? It's one o'clock in the morning. Is something wrong?"

"I hear you're getting canned," said Alex nonchalantly.

Henry halted at the front door and used his key card to unlock the door. The cottage was small but amazingly comfortable for a building that was constructed so long ago by the railroad. He ambled over to one of the cozy chairs arranged in an alcove to the right of the room.

"Yes, Alex, I am. Did you call me just to confirm that?"

"No, actually Lukas texted me you were up. You won't answer your phone during the day, so I thought I'd call you now."

"Lukas texted you?"

"He's on the night shift tonight. I asked him to contact me when you were finishing up for the day," explained Alex.

"Wait, how do you even know Lukas, let alone his schedule?"

"Last time Sean and I were up there, Lukas let us carry you into that little apartment of yours. We had a few beers together while you crashed. Great guy. We keep in touch."

"Obviously," said Henry, irked. "Alex, I'm tired and need to get some sleep. What's up?"

"Not much. Kate told me your last day is Friday," reported Alex.

"Ugh!" Henry breathed into the phone. "Katie put you up to this?"

"No, she simply said Friday is your last day. Don't get all bothered. I thought you could come with Sean and me next week. We're going on a road trip to the Grand Canyon. Then Sean wants to stop by Vegas. He's never been."

"I can't go anywhere. I have too much to do here."

"I don't think so. Not after Friday."

Henry rubbed his head and looked at the clock. He really needed to sleep. Putting Alex on speaker, he dragged himself out of the overstuffed chair, unbuttoned his shirt, and headed toward his bed.

"I'm trying to get ahead of the project as much as possible. This is a lousy time for this to happen," he protested.

"Not your doing, Henry," insisted Alex. "Will you come with us?"

"No," answered Henry. He was ready to end the call.

"Even Rhonda agrees with me."

"What?"

"I talked to Rhonda, and she agrees a change of scenery is best for you."

"And how do you know Rhonda?"

"We met at Mr. Granger's service. She's funny. I like her. We keep in touch."

"Obviously."

"Tell you what," said Alex. "Sean and I will pick you up on Friday night. We'll do a hasty weekend trek. Just like we used to. There are great trails through that area. We'll have you back on Sunday night. Get the tent packed up. We'll need that."

Henry began to argue, but understood it was pointless. Besides, his bed was like a magnet drawing him to it.

"Okay, pick me up Friday night."

"Get to bed, Henry. It's late."

"You called me," groaned Henry.

"You answered the phone," countered Alex.

"Bye, Alex." Henry pressed the little red end button on the phone. He laid half-clothed on the bed. He grabbed a pillow and nestled it under his arm and head. In a blink, he was asleep.

Alex had been lying propped up on his own bed watching a rerun of a hockey game. He liked the fast pace and combativeness of the sport. Also, the teamwork, athleticism, and skill required to score a goal. His fingers moved quickly as he typed in a text message to Sean, "mission accomplished."

Pleased with himself having talked his friend into a weekend away, he mulled over various strategies to convince Henry to extend the trip. Alex was worried. It was very unlike Henry to avoid facing facts.

Henry was the most practical and analytic of the old friends. If Alex or Kate or Sean were in Henry's predicament, Henry would outline the best solution and talk them through a plan. But he couldn't do that for himself.

Alex thought back to the many occasions that Henry had supported him. It was Henry who had coached him through the ROTC scholarship process and encouraged him to persevere. The service requirements were not what had worried Alex. It was a nagging thought that someone more deserving and qualified should have gotten his scholarship. Let's face it, his selection shocked many who knew him.

When his service was up, it was Henry who masterminded potential career options. Alex had been ready to flip a coin. Knowing Alex as well as he did enabled Henry to suggest some good choices. In the end, Alex teamed up with Sean to start their own business. And they'd done well.

Alex already had seen the final score of the game and that his team had won. He reached for the remote and fast forwarded through to each goal. He eagerly watched the set up and shouted when the puck shot through the goalie. Once he had viewed the last one, even though time remained in the game, he turned off the television and the lights.

Somehow, he thought to himself, he had to snap Henry out of this obsession with Fusion Lab. Kate was right. Much better opportunities were out there. Although he didn't grasp all the details, he'd heard enough to conclude that his friend had been wronged. This weekend, he and Sean would try their best to refocus Henry. The great outdoors would be perfect.

The alarm sounded and woke Henry. Groggy, he looked around the cottage. He had to get moving. Today was his last day of employment at Fusion Lab. The bank had demanded his resignation, which he had given.

They had also wanted his immediate removal from the premises. That was a problem. Fusion Lab needed Henry. If they escorted him out the door, it would throw the entire project into complete disarray. Thankfully, Chester negotiated a month's time for Henry to wind down his duties. That month ended today.

Raising his hand to his forehead, he massaged his temples and searched for something positive. Maybe Kate was right. This was for the best. He could now move on from Fusion Lab and all its headaches. For Henry, however, that meant surrender, something he had difficulty accepting. He'd given his all to the Lab.

Ted's sudden passing thrust the full weight of responsibility for the Lab onto Henry. He was confident he could successfully manage the Lab's internal operations. What he couldn't surmount were the financial burdens Ted had left and the outside forces that wanted Henry gone.

"I've failed," Henry muttered.

A wave of anger, frustration, and exasperation swept through him. He shuddered. Although he wasn't cold, he drew the cotton sheet over his chest.

"It makes no sense," he insisted. "I love this place and I don't want to leave."

Henry then did something he had not done in a very long

time. "Father in heaven, please get me through this day," he prayed. He clambered out of the bed and into the shower.

After dressing, Henry meandered about scooping up small items and tossing them into a cardboard box. Opening the closet door near the bed, he gasped as he assessed the mound of dirty clothes. "How did that happen?" he mumbled to himself. He grabbed some plastic trash bags and stuffed them in.

Fusion Lab company cars were almost all hatchback run-abouts. The automatic lift gate made it easy to transfer lab equipment in and out. After three trips to the car parked out front, Henry hit the button to close the back lift gate. The car issued a whelp, but the hatch would not close. Henry reached up, grabbed the handle, and shut it himself. Going back inside, he did a quick scan of the cottage. He had everything.

The sun was now rising with increasing strength and brightness. Henry needed to get to his office. He slid into the car seat and drove the short distance to the administration building.

It quickly became clear that Henry would not get much done that day. Every few minutes, another person would poke their head through the door and ask a question. It was their way of confirming he was okay.

Word had spread of the arrangement made to stay in contact. Chester had suggested that Rhonda continue to provide "updates" to Fusion Lab's Trustee Board through Matt. As a trustee, it entitled Henry's access to this information. He could then respond again through Matt. Their hope was that the wafer would be finalized in a few months and the bank would back off. Possibly, Henry would then be welcome on the Fusion Lab campus.

"Are you leaving right now Henry?" called Lukas, the security guard. It was early afternoon. He had seen Henry exit the administration building and wanted to say his goodbyes. He hurried over, drew up next to Henry, and walked with him.

"No," replied Henry. "I need to get down to my place, drop this stuff off, and grab a few things. I'll be back. I need to turn in the car."

Lukas looked away. "I'm sorry this has happened."

"Thanks, Lukas, it's okay," said Henry. "My friends are meeting me here later. We're headed on a road trip. I believe you know Alex and Sean?"

Lukas brightened. "Yes, I talked to Alex this week. Great guy."

Henry smiled. "I'll take your word for it."

Henry tapped his pocket and verified that his key fob was there. As they approached his car, it beeped as if it knew him and unlocked his door.

"Don't worry, Lukas, I'll be fine."

Henry and Lukas paused as Henry reached for the handle and slowly opened the car door. Before Henry could enter the car, Lukas grabbed his shoulder, and they faced each other.

"I really don't understand," stammered Lukas. "First, we lost Mr. Granger. Now you. Two of the best people I've known. How can they do this?" Lukas paused before adding, "What's going to happen to the rest of us?"

"It was me they were after, Lukas. You'll be fine. I'll be fine, too. Please don't worry. Just remind everyone to stay on task, as always."

Lukas' distraught face and apprehension rekindled the

turmoil of the last month for Henry. The gravity of his circumstances, ending today, his last at Fusion Lab, brought up emotions he struggled to suppress.

Lukas dropped his hand from Henry's shoulder and took a step back.

"Henry, you don't look so good. Can I drive you home?" Lukas offered.

Henry answered from a foggy state of mind. "Thanks, but I think the drive might be what I need at the moment."

"Okay, I'll keep a lookout for your friends."

Henry smiled at Lukas. "Thanks, Lukas. See you soon."

He slid into the seat, closed the door, and started the engine. After a quick wave to Lukas, Henry began the drive out of the Fusion Lab complex, wondering if this would truly be one of his last views of the beautiful campus.

He moved slowly, soaking in the mass of buildings set against the mountain vista. Reaching the entrance, he sighed, and then turned onto the main road and aimed toward the valley.

Henry thought back to the first time he had driven up this way many years ago. The rolling hills had enthralled and captivated him, multiplying his excitement and anticipation of a pleasant career at the Lab. Now, the undulating horizon seemed a silent, dispassionate outline of his actual roller-coaster experience.

A sudden lurch in the engine snapped Henry out of his stupor. The cruise control light popped on and the car sped up. Henry immediately hit the brakes but could not disengage the cruise control. Pressing the cruise control lever did nothing. As the car sped even faster, Henry pumped the brakes. No effect.

He then pressed on the brake pedal with all his leg strength. The car shuddered as the brake pads squeezed against the brake disc multiple times per second as the anti-lock braking system deployed. He felt the forward momentum slackening. Gulping a breath of air, Henry calmed himself.

Henry glanced at the speedometer and realized he was now traveling at 72mph on a 35mph stretch of the road. He pictured the next few miles of roadway in his head, calculating how he would navigate it at this speed if he could not get control of the vehicle. The problem would not only be the precipitous, downhill slope, but the even more dangerous switchbacks.

His brain speedily weighed various options as they came into his thoughts. Turn off the engine? No, he would lose steering. Emergency brake? Of course. Henry grasped the emergency brake lever and pulled. The car shivered and let up a bit more. The car slowed until the cruise control fought back and accelerated. Trees and road signs whizzed by his window. Henry heard a loud pop, and the car lurched forward. The emergency brake cable had snapped. Up ahead was the first of five switchbacks.

Though not as steep and high as you would think of a typical mountain, the hills in this region had prominent elevations and tricky grades. One direct way to challenge the heights for road builders was to incorporate zig-zagged patterns that enabled cars and trucks to more gently climb or descend. Sinuous as snakes, switchbacks, as some call them, have long stretches of ascent, but then require sharp curves where the direction of travel is reversed.

Over a hundred years ago, CR 17 was just a dirt road. The

railroad built it, and it supported the small town that housed the railway workers, which was now Fusion Lab. Over the years, the road was asphalted, and guard rails installed. Although overseen in sections by two different county jurisdictions, with each county absorbing the cost for its territory, CR17 was currently decently paved and well maintained. Of course, Fusion Lab was a high-profile employer and a massive tax contributor to each county. The campus acreage significantly overlapped both.

After the railroads left and before Ted established Fusion Lab, CR17 was also noteworthy in town lore for what old-time residents called the "Bluff Gap." Still infamous among the locals of the area, the Bluff Gap got its name from a long-ago dispute between the county managers. The quarrel arose regarding the point at which the guard rails met at the county line. Or rather, didn't meet.

Both counties began their project at opposite ends of the boundaries and worked inward. When the installation projects ended at the dividing line at CR17, there was a twelve-foot gap between the last two sections. Each county had assumed the other would be responsible for that section. Blame and ridicule were quick and fierce. Newspapers wrote articles, and the county managers dug in their heels. The missing guard rail section soon became known as the Gap.

Many insist the Gap was intentional, pointing out that to this day, it has not been fixed. The theory is that no one wanted to block access onto the bluff. As it is, the twelve-foot expanse is the only entry.

This thrilled the teens in the area. The bluff at county line on CR17 was their meeting spot. The railroad had blasted an area about the size of half a football field out of the side of the mountain. They then used the stones as rock bed for rails. Hidden from view of the road by the mountain itself, it was the only level area until the top of the hill where Fusion Lab sits.

The blasting created a huge precipice that overlooked Lake Genevieve. The view was breathtaking. Teens would drive off the road and onto the rock terrace and then park. If the counties had installed the guardrail, access to the plateau by car would no longer be possible. Most of the adults in the valley below could spin a great tale about romantic times there.

If he could make it past the "Gap", there was a runaway truck ramp with an arrester bed a half mile past. Henry could drive onto the ramp bed, kill the engine, and let the deep gravel and sand in the pit grab his tires and dissipate the kinetic energy of his forward motion.

Henry's GPS showed he was now almost halfway down the side of the mountain, approaching the "Gap." Henry glanced once more at his speedometer. Sixty-one. Too fast to make it around the curve ahead. He gave up on trying to wipe out the cruise control malfunction and concentrated on slowing the vehicle. His best bet, he concluded, was friction.

Gently, he turned the steering wheel to the right and grew closer to the guardrail. His idea was to rub against it enough to decelerate, but not enough to ricochet off and crash into something. His grip on the wheel strong, he leaned the car into the rail. Sparks flew and metal screeched, but the rail rejected the car's hug and pushed Henry away. But the maneuver did help reduce his speed. He tried again.

This time, the guardrail accommodated the attempt. Again, metal shrieked and wailed as Henry pressed solidly into the rail. He tried his best to keep as much of the car parallel to the rail itself. It was working! Fifty-three!

More lights flashed on his dashboard and warning beeps sounded. His brakes were failing. The hydraulic fluid line had ruptured. As the emergency brake took on more of the work to slow the car, it, too, failed. A cacophony of noise pummeled Henry's ears as his car protested the torture it was enduring. His speed increased.

Henry pressed the steering even more into the guardrail. He was hoping his tires would shred, providing even more friction. Speed dropped again. If he could maintain this for the next half mile, the guard rail would pull him and lead him off the road and onto the runaway truck ramp.

Too late, he remembered the Gap. Like a magnet, the guardrail tugged at his car and then launched him through the Gap opening. Henry realized he was out of options and doomed to his fate as he shot onto the plateau. Fortunately, the gravel surface slowed his speed considerably. Unfortunately, it was not enough to save him, and Henry and his car plunged over the edge of the precipice, headlong into Lake Genevieve. After a too short feeling of weightlessness as the car descended, Henry lost sense of awareness as the car impacted the water and an airbag inflated into his face.

Fear, dread, and hopelessness were Henry's last conscious emotions. Anguish, finality, and doom were his last thoughts. Henry sensed a darkness, like a liquid, swirling around him.

It entered his toes and moved up his feet and legs. It also

entered his fingers and marched up his arms. It felt alive. It was alive, like millions of pitch-black bugs twitching together as they swarmed over a meal, determined to consume him.

As the inky blackness surged through him, the terror and hopelessness increased, and his destruction looked more certain. Churning, writhing, and slithering, it gloated in its certain victory.

Growing progressively confident as it gained territory, the darkness hastily conquered every cell of his body. Only one speck remained, deep in the pit of his stomach.

One tiny, bright dot.

It spoke to him.

"Henry, you must choose."

The blackness abruptly halted its roiling and whirling. It recoiled at the interruption of its conquest and attempted to choke Henry.

The white dot spoke again. "You must choose, Henry,"

The blackness froze.

"Do you remember me?" the voice inquired. "You knew me long ago. Do you remember when we first met?"

Henry willed his memory to unwind, searching for the answer. Years unfolded before him as he hungered to know. Back, back, back. A picture of Henry sitting on his grandmother's sofa flashed into his mind. "Grandmom!"

"I know her as Ruth."

"She told me about you," said Henry.

The dot fluttered for an instant and Henry felt a warmth that calmed him.

"It is time to choose, Henry."

The darkness retaliated and assailed him. Like an army of fire ants, they bit and stung him. It surged through his body, doing its best to obliterate the white speck of light.

Henry became afraid again. A sadness born of hopelessness gripped him. The darkness demanded victory. It must win.

Henry could resist no longer, and the tiny dot faded. In a last gasp, Henry whispered, "Help me, Jesus."

The tiny dot began to vibrate. Rotating and pulsating, vivid colors like thousands of rainbows glimmered from within it.

Suddenly, it exploded in a brilliant flash.

Part Three

GOOD THINGS COME TO THOSE WHO WAIT, TRUE LOVE WILL FIND A WAY

CHAPTER 10

Sean took his time driving the SUV up toward Fusion Lab. He and Alex were early and there was no need to speed, especially on these narrow, yet steep grades. Alex sat in the passenger seat, chatting about numerous subjects. As they came out of a tight curve of a switchback, Sean heard a shrill cry.

"What the heck is that?" he asked.

Alex stopped his rambling and listened. "Don't know," he answered.

Sean squinted through the windshield as he saw a car barreling toward them, alternating between smacking the guard rail and bouncing off it. The piercing noise was the sound of metal grinding against metal. Sean slammed on the brakes and guided the SUV as close to his side of the road as possible. The oncoming car shot past them. Sean gawked as the panicked driver fought the steering wheel.

"Henry!" shouted Sean. "That was Henry!"

Sean swiftly did a three-point turn and gunned the motor

to follow. He was gaining on the vehicle when it vanished into the hillside.

"Where'd he go?" asked Alex.

They sped down the hillside, and a hole in the mountain's side opened. A gap in the guardrail revealed the doorway to a flat expanse. They could see the outline of the lake in the distance.

Sean again slammed his brakes, and the SUV swerved into the opening. They sucked in their breaths as they watched Henry's car catapult over the edge and disappear. Both men bounded out of the car and ran to the edge. The tail end of Henry's car bobbed for an instant and then receded under the water.

"I'm going in!" hollered Alex to Sean. He attempted to take his shoes off. Sean grabbed his collar and held him back.

"It's too high," Sean screamed at Alex.

Alex hastily dialed 911 on his phone. Other people had now joined them. Henry had passed a few cars and one truck back up the road. All had turned to follow and help.

Together, they stared at the bubbles that popped out from the surface and sent small additional waves chasing after the huge one made by the car's impact.

A few hundred feet ahead of where the car had splashed, bits of foam from the hood insulation, some clothing, and dark bags popped onto the surface.

"There, what's that?" pointed Alex.

Again, they focused on the floating debris. They saw something tangled in a mass of plastic bags. Sean could make out arms and shoulders. The floating mass then flipped over in the water. It swelled and sagged as it now drifted forward more haltingly. A head with blond hair poked out.

"There he is!" yelled Alex to everyone.

Alex and Sean turned together and ran back to their car. They then raced down the hilly road and toward the plain. Once they reached the rim of the lake, they jumped the curb and scrambled onto the sandy shoreline. Sean gunned the SUV into four-wheel drive and toward the bank closest to Henry.

Behind them, they heard the loud sirens of rescue vehicles. Two Fire and Rescue trucks were approaching from the firehouse in the valley, and a County Fish and Wildlife vehicle approached from the lake access road.

Sean spotted the floating mass and ground the SUV to an abrupt halt. Alex hopped out before the SUV came to a stop.

The CFW truck drew up behind them. Two men hopped out and Alex pointed to the area where Henry hopefully was still afloat. He helped them unload their pontoon boat from the rails along the top of the truck. The four of them carried it as fast as they could to the water's edge, and Alex and the CFW officers hopped in. Sean pushed the boat deeper into the water and joined them. They fastened the portable motor into place and were soon roaring, thrusted toward the wobbling fragments.

The CFW officer manning the motor cut it about 20 yards away and they glided right up to Henry. Alex had seen his share of death in the military and had lost close companions before. He scanned Henry's battered head and had to look away.

Sean saw how jumbled and tangled everything was. A plastic strap was tugged up under Henry's armpit and wound around what looked like a large section of the leather roof covering. Numerous puffy plastic bags wafted around him. Sean donned a life jacket, snatched two others, and jumped in. Paying little attention to the coldness of the water, he carefully shifted the bags aside and propped the two vests underneath Henry. He then inspected for signs of life.

"He's alive!" he shouted to the others. "I feel a pulse and I can see shallow breathing. It's very weak. There's no way we can get him into the dingy. Toss out that rope. We'll tow him to shore. I'll stay here with him."

Hoping to get him out of the water quickly, they accelerated too much.

"Slow down!" hollered Alex, who was monitoring their headway. "You're pulling him under." With a few adjustments, they found the correct balance.

As they drew near to the beach, they saw the rescue team waiting. A stretcher was already prepared. One paramedic waded out to Sean and gently pushed Henry up close to the sandy beach, but still in the water. Moving him as little as possible, he did a fast survey of Henry's injuries. He untangled the various pieces of debris. After affixing a neck brace, they gently floated Henry onto an inflatable pad. When ready, six of them lifted him out of the water. They lowered him onto the stretcher and into the ambulance.

"How is he, Alex?" Kate asked calmly.

"Safe for now. How's your family holding up?"

"Mom's a wreck. She and dad insist we come there to the hospital."

"Please don't do that," said Alex softly.

"We just want to be there if . . ." whispered Kate as her voice broke.

"That will not happen, Kate. He's going to get through this. I promise you. I've seen worse and Henry will be okay. Trust me, Kate."

"Okay," she responded, as her voice grew stronger. "What's happening there now?"

"The doctors here say they've done everything they can for the moment. They have him stabilized, but they want him moved to a trauma hospital. I've been talking with Matt Granger. Marie is researching the closest ones that specialize in head injuries. She has some contacts that can recommend the best."

"So, he injured his head? Can he talk?"

"They have him sedated, so no, he can't speak. He's on a lot of medications, from what I can tell. They want to prevent severe shock. When his body warmed up after being in the water, the swelling started. They need to keep that under control."

"How about the rest of him?"

"They did an MRI. He may have a fractured skull and some internal injuries. Amazingly, they don't see any broken bones."

Kate breathed out loudly but couldn't respond.

"They're most concerned about his neck and head."

"Are you sure we shouldn't drive there?"

"No, by the time you reached the hospital, Henry would be on his way to another. Let's see where that turns out to be. I'll let you know as soon as I find out."

"Thanks, Alex. I don't know what we'd do without you."

"He'll be okay, Katie. I'll talk to you soon."

Alex slipped the phone into his pocket and looked around the waiting room. For a small-town facility, it was surprisingly comfortable. Many of the hospital staff had grown up in the valley and appreciated the contribution Fusion Lab had made to its growth. A few had met Henry. Everyone wanted to help.

Sean approached from down the hall. He had used the employee facilities to shower and change into dry clothes.

"How's Henry's family?" asked Sean as he lowered himself into a chair next to Alex.

"They want to be here, of course. That'd be a mistake." Alex and Sean looked at each other. Neither wanted to mention how beat-up Henry was. His body was bruised and bloated by the swelling. His face was unrecognizable.

"Doesn't one of them need to sign off on Henry's treatment or something?" asked Sean.

"No, I can do that," answered Alex.

"You?"

"Yeah, Chester had him do a medical directive as part of the Fusion Lab Trust. Henry named Kate and me. His mom and dad were okay with that at the time. I'm not so sure right now."

The doctor in charge of Henry's care interrupted them. "We've been speaking with Dr. Granger, and she knows a specialist at Hopkins in Baltimore. We're going to transfer Henry there. We'll move him to the airport by ambulance and then he'll fly to BWI. A team from the hospital will meet him. If all goes well, Henry will be at Johns Hopkins tomorrow morning. Can you notify his family?"

"Yes, I'll call them right away. They'll be happy to hear this," said Alex.

His phone rang. "Hey, Matt. The doctor was giving us an update. They're moving him to Baltimore."

"Marie has a close friend who's a neurologist there. Actually, she dated him, but that's beside the point. He's agreed to take on Henry and is arranging the admission. Could you get some flights booked for Henry's family? I'm sorry that I can't get out there right away."

"Yes, I'll do that now. And don't apologize, Matt. I'll keep you up to date, I promise."

A few weeks later, Matt finished up a call with his sister. "Thanks for making those arrangements for the medical equipment, Marie. Alex said Henry's family is so relieved."

"I wish I could do more besides pray. How are you holding up? I know you've got a lot going on there."

"I'm stressed, to be honest. I've got five new senior managers meeting our team for the first time bright and early tomorrow. I still need to go over the schedule to make sure everything's ready."

Marie recognized that tone in Matt's voice and tried some sisterly encouragement. "It'll be fine, Matt. You always get everything done. Dad would be proud."

"Thanks, I needed to hear that. But, Marie, I really have to go."

"Me, too. I'll call you again soon. Love you."

The company Matt worked for had recently acquired a medium-sized consulting firm. As an international enterprise software provider, his company offered one of the most technologically superior products on the market. The hiccups they encountered most always centered on product implementation, not the product itself. Clients loved the enormous capabilities of the software, but when it came time to use new tools, most employees of client companies resisted change.

His firm had spent sizable sums of money on methods to earn the support and buy-in of client teams during product implementation. They discovered this consulting firm whose specialty was fostering trust and benefit of the doubt for change within organizations. They were so impressed with their methods that they bought it.

The company charged Matt with integrating his IT team with the senior management of the consulting firm. Just as his clients need to embrace the change necessary for implementation of the enterprise software, his own team now needed to accept and welcome the new players.

The consulting firm itself had laid out the challenges to Matt and his bosses, so "his plan" was really "their plan." And it was a good one. Matt would assign each new consulting senior manager a corresponding IT manager, and the two would work together for the day. The next day, the assignments would shift until every new team member had a chance to work with an existing IT manager.

The task assigned to the teams was to do a postmortem on one of the company's worst installation disasters. Matt knew it well. He remembered as a young software coder on that project all the extra hours he needed to work as the demands of the client continually shifted. Eventually, his firm realized they would never satisfy the client and canceled the contract. The client sued for damages and forced the company to pay.

Although company lore told the story as the case of the crazy client, Matt felt his own firm bore much of the blame. Sure, communication was terrible between the two parties, but the company's salespeople had drastically oversold the capabilities. Once the client became disillusioned about the actual benefits available on day one, their employees dug in their heels on integration. Instead of working together, the relationship fell apart.

That was Matt's conclusion years ago, but now his teams had to discover their own. A slew of data was available from the period, including emails from most parties involved, project charts, logged status reports, and even the court depositions. Matt was curious to see how the new consultants would view the case.

The next morning, Matt welcomed the new team members into a large conference room that would be their workspace for the next week. There was room for the teams of two to work separately, but also, the entire project team was available for questions of each other. Each person on the team had their own laptop resting in front of them amid neatly stacked reams of old computer printouts.

Matt explained the task, rules, and objectives. The instructions concluded, Matt looked around the room and smiled at the group. "Okay," he said. "That sounds like the last question. Your first assignment is to take the next hour to get to know your teammate. There are refreshments over there on the buffet. Why don't you stand up and introduce yourselves? We'll get back to work promptly at ten."

Matt walked a few steps toward his new teammate and held out his hand. "Hi, I'm Matt Granger. You must be Penelope Stevens."

"Call me Penny." Penny smiled and firmly shook Matt's

hand. "I'm excited to be here. This is a great opportunity for us."

"And call me Matt. Based on your experience listed, I expected a European accent."

Penny chuckled, "It seems like I spent most of my life overseas, but no, I'm from Indiana. I interned at my firm while in college and went to work there upon graduation. I've been based in Frankfurt, but I've hopped around Europe for the last ten years. Believe me, it's been a fantastic experience. But I'm happy to be back in the States."

"So, no roots put down over there? Family?"

"No, unfortunately, I moved around so much on different project assignments that I never found a home. I have family here in Atlanta. We moved from the Midwest when I was younger. They find it hard to believe that I'm back! How about yourself?"

"I love it here," answered Matt. "Been here for over twenty years. My wife, Connie, is a schoolteacher and I have one son. But what's it like living in a foreign country?"

"I've met so many wonderful people. And Europe has such a vast history. It's such a contrast to realize how new things seem here in the States. A few of the buildings I visited there are over a thousand years old."

Penny and Matt exchanged more life stories and quickly became friends. They talked and laughed a bit more, and then Matt interrupted the chatter of the room. He asked everyone to grab a seat, and they all dove into the assigned task.

By mid-week, it was becoming obvious that each team was nearing their conclusions. However, Matt had instructed them to hold off final determinations until Friday. The teams still needed to discuss their findings among each other and share how the data was informing their stance.

The conference room had become stuffy, so most of the teams took breaks outside in a courtyard that opened to a grand view of the city. That afternoon, Penny and Matt sat at a round table off to the side, sipping iced coffee.

"So, Penny, based on what you've seen, what do you think?" asked Matt.

Penny gave Matt that disarming grin of hers and replied, "You probably don't want to hear this, but it's more and more obvious that your company extensively oversold your program. I think the client had a valid complaint. There may be more data that could show otherwise, but I don't see it."

Matt smiled back at her. "And I shouldn't tell you this, but I came to the same conclusion. We need your help to make sure we prevent it from happening again."

Matt's cell phone chirped. He glanced down at the caller's name and grimaced.

"I'm really sorry. Could I please take this call? It's important."

"Of course."

Penny moved farther away, to her side of the table, so Matt could have some privacy. Matt turned his shoulder away from her, but Penny could not help overhearing and felt awkward. She reached into her purse and withdrew her own phone, hoping to distract herself.

"Hey, Kate, how's Henry?" Matt waited for a reply. "I'm sorry to hear that, but it's still early. Yes, I talked again to Marie, and she's coordinating the entire room setup. Bed, machines, whatever Henry needs. The hospital already approved it. (Pause) Yes, yes, I'll tell her. How are Mr. and Mrs. Taylor holding up?

(Pause) Good. Please say hello to them. (Pause) No, don't do that. Alex called me last week. He and Sean are flying in next Tuesday to help move things around. I think between the two of them and Robby, you'll have enough muscle for the heavy lifting. (Pause) Thank you, Kate. I wish I could do more. (Pause) Ok. Sure. You too. Bye."

Matt sighed heavily and slowly turned to Penny. "I'm deeply sorry. A close friend of mine was in an accident a few weeks ago. He's in a coma right now, but we're all certain he'll be fine, with time."

He raised his eyes from his cell phone and saw that Penny had frozen in place and was a ghostly white. Her cell phone was in her hand, but she was staring right at Matt. She asked in a whisper, "Henry Taylor? Accident? Coma?"

"Yes, that was his sister, Kate. Do you know him?" asked Matt.

Penny nodded. Her eyes became moist.

The afternoon dragged by, as neither Penny nor Matt could effectively concentrate on the work project. Each was drawn back to the phone call and the shock of a tragic event they somehow had in common. Matt invited Penny over to his house after work. Penny had been clearly shaken. He already thought of her as a friend but hardly knew much about her. She was mostly alone here, though Penny did say she had family nearby. She accepted his invitation.

Penny followed Matt home in her rental car. She passed through very heavy traffic in the city streets before Matt turned onto a throughway that led to a neighborhood of newly built townhomes. Tall trees lined the street, designed to give the impression of age.

Matt drove down an alley that provided access to the backs of the houses. He turned into one and Penny pulled up right behind his car.

"Here we are," said Matt as he shut his car door and walked toward Penny to help her out. "We've lived here three years. My son goes to the middle school three blocks up this road, and Connie teaches at the high school another mile down the road. It's the perfect location for us."

Matt raised his arm toward the opened garage door that he had already raised from the car remote. As he led them through the opening, Matt chuckled nervously and said, "The one thing Connie dislikes about the house is we never use the front door. Even our guests enter our kitchen from the back. Except my mom. I drop her off at the front door and then drive around back here. There's just no parking out front. We get pizza deliveries through the front, though."

Penny laughed.

As they walked into a brightly lit kitchen, Matt's wife, Connie, entered from another room and warmly greeted Penny.

"Hi, Penny, I'm Connie. I'm so glad you could join us for dinner."

She gave Penny a quick hug and motioned for her to sit at a booth-like area on the side of the kitchen. "I thought we could have a glass of wine and get to know each other."

"That'd be perfect!" said Penny as she slid onto the padded bench seat.

"Matt knows much more about wines than me, but we have

a few choices. What do you prefer?"

"I recognize that cabernet right there. One of my favorites."

Connie reached for the bottle and poured three glasses.

"Our son will be home in a few minutes to see his dad and then he's spending the night at his friend's house." With that, the kitchen door swung open and two young boys ran in.

"Hey, Dad!" the first one yelled out as he spotted his father.

Matt walked over and greeted his son and his son's friend. "Where are you two off to?"

"I'm going to pick up some clothes and then I'm going to Craig's house."

"I'll give you a hand," said Matt as he followed them from the kitchen and into the living area. "Say hello to Miss Stevens here."

Both boys gave a cheery hello and ran off into the other room.

"I hope you don't mind," said Connie, "but we're having takeout tonight. I ran late at the school and, well, it seems, we do a lot of takeout."

Penny smiled and said, "When I moved over to Europe, I thought I would learn how to be the best cook. However, I never had the time. And there were so many little cafés, no matter where I lived. They had wonderful food that I knew I couldn't compete with, even if I'd wanted to."

They found subjects in common, and Matt joined them once he had made sure the boys were safely at Craig's house and thanked Craig's parents. Together, they emptied takeout containers into plates and bowls and enjoyed a delicious dinner.

Once they cleared the table, they sat again. Connie refilled the wine glasses. After an uncomfortably long silence, Connie glanced at Matt and then patted Penny on the arm.

"I hope I'm not intruding, but how do you know Henry Taylor?"

Penny was relieved to talk about it finally. "I grew up with him. Matt, all those names you mentioned on your call, Henry, Kate, Alex, Sean. We were close friends. My parents moved here when I was in middle school. We tried our best to stay in touch, but I think the distance was just too great. We spoke at various times on the phone during college, but once I moved to Europe, we lost all contact."

She sighed.

"I almost was able to meet up with Alex when he was in the service. He was transferring through Germany when I was living there. His flights were never definite and mostly last minute on standby. Unfortunately, I never got to see him."

Penny took another sip of wine and asked, "Can you tell me about Henry? You said he was in an accident and is now in a coma?"

"Yes," Matt answered softly. "I honestly don't know all the details. What I've been told is he was driving down a steep road and lost control of the car. He went off a high cliff and his car plunged into a lake. Although the car sank, Henry floated up with a bunch of debris. He has some pretty bad internal injuries. The worst is to his head. He was in an induced coma in the hospital for three weeks. They've now taken him off that medication. We're praying he wakes up soon. Once he's cognizant, they want to bring him home to his mom and dad's house. They're getting it set up."

"So, he hasn't responded at all?"

"Not yet. The doctors say it should be anytime now."

They paused the conversation for Penny to take in and absorb the information.

"Matt and Connie, how did you become friends with Henry?" asked Penny.

Both looked down briefly, but smiled back at Penny.

"Henry worked for my dad at Fusion Lab. Anytime I visited my dad, Henry was there. I consider him like a brother."

"He helped us so much after Matt's father passed," added Connie.

"I'm so sorry about your dad," said Penny. "And now this. What can I do to help?"

"Why not give Kate a call? She could give you a better idea. Do you have her number?"

Penny grimaced. "I have one from years ago."

Matt reached for his phone. "No problem. I'll text you her number. I'm sure she'd love to hear from you."

Penny gazed out of the plane's window as it descended toward the airport. The fuzzy splotches of various colors soon sharpened into the details of buildings, streets, and trees. Her stomach sent her sensations that reminded her of the time she became seasick in a rough Mediterranean Sea. It was not nearly as bad but still very unsettling.

She knew it was not the flying, as she had done so much traveling for her job. Years of onsite client projects developed into an inner confidence regarding most means of travel and the prospect of meeting new people. No, this was an internal battle between nervousness and excitement.

She had not seen Henry since she had moved away over twenty years ago, a difficult time for her. The pain of leaving often obscured the many wonderful memories of the fun-filled days as a child. But wounds heal. Life had bestowed incredible opportunities on Penny, and she had embraced them.

However, during her breakup with Ethan, she had grown disenchanted with her life. The variable and shifting locations of her work responsibilities made for shallow roots. She had hoped a future with Ethan would nurture deeper ones.

Leaving Europe was harder than she expected, though. Saying goodbye to friends proved the most difficult, and doubts about her decision sprouted up in those moments. She would miss her friends terribly.

Penny would visit the hospital. Kate had explained that, because his doctors had removed Henry from the induced coma, they were hoping and expecting him to awake at any time. His family had done their best to stay with him in Baltimore. However, the long weeks had stretched and strained the rotation schedule and budgets. Henry's mom and Kate were there now. Penny immediately offered to fly there over a long weekend to help.

As the plane's tires grabbed the runway, Penny felt a lurch. Startled out of her daydream, she waited for the aircraft to reach the terminal and hook up to the gate. As the passengers deplaned, Penny reached up into the overhead for her one piece of carry-on luggage. Her years of flying had taught her how to pack efficiently. She didn't know how long this trip might last, though. Grasping the handle, she expertly guided what she called the strolly down the aisle and out into the terminal.

Penny briskly walked with the other travelers toward the terminal exit and the arriving passenger pickup, where she had agreed to meet Kate. She scanned the faces in the distance for any clue of recognition. Off to the left stood a blond-haired woman frantically waving her arms. Penny headed right for her, knowing immediately it was her friend.

"Penny? Is that really you? It's so great to see you! Thank you so much for coming here!" exclaimed Kate. They hugged each other. Penny's apprehension evaporated.

"I'm so excited to see you, Kate! It's been far too long!" answered Penny.

Kate steered them to the parking area where her car awaited. "I'm glad you agreed to stay with Mom and me. We're at one of those long-term suites right near the hospital. It has a kitchen, which really comes in handy. We'll head there now and get you settled in."

They exited the airport and merged onto the highway. Kate reached her hand across to Penny and patted her arm. "I'm glad you're here, and, um, I'm sure you'd like to see Henry."

The flutters in Penny's stomach returned.

Once they had dropped off Penny's luggage, they walked over to the hospital. Sensing Penny's nervousness, Kate made small talk, chatting about Joy and Ellie. When they entered the hospital room, Mrs. Taylor quickly hugged her.

"Penny! Oh, my! You're all grown up!" Mrs. Taylor stammered.

Penny smiled. "I wish circumstances were different." She looked down, trying to keep her emotions in check.

"Me, too." Mrs. Taylor then turned her head to where Henry lay on his hospital bed. She took Penny's hand and led her closer to the side. "Each day he gets stronger. We're all praying he wakes soon."

Except for his blond hair, Penny didn't recognize Henry. The crash left his face still bruised and somewhat swollen. Penny reached down and grabbed his hand. She squeezed it slightly. As she leaned forward, she then lifted it and kissed it gently.

Kate and Mrs. Taylor came up close on each side of her. They held her as she softly cried.

"He'll be fine," Mrs. Taylor consoled her. "In fact, we've seen some movements over the last week. His fingers, his legs."

"Last night, I was telling Henry about the girls. Robby told me Joy had all her dolls, and Ellie, in time-out. She's become quite the disciplinarian. I swear I saw Henry smile."

Penny forced a slight laugh. After a brief span of silence, the women became comfortable peppering each other with questions about the past and renewing their friendships.

For the next two days, they took turns sitting with Henry. Penny would watch TV, read, or attend to her laptop. She also prayed Henry would wake. Hopefully with the smile she had not seen for a long time.

CHAPTER 11

Henry slowed his trot. He then paused and looked down a short stretch of bricklebutter bushes. "How do I get out of here?" he muttered to himself. He didn't know how long he'd been wandering through the maze. He was not tired, only perplexed.

The wonderful fragrance of the white flowers whirled around him, sometimes so powerful that he had to pause just to breathe. Other times, just a faint wisp reached his nostrils.

Henry wondered how he even got here, as he had no memory of leaving his house and arriving at the patch. "Mom's going to get worried and be mad at me," he murmured.

Walking again, he reached the end of the section, only to face another row that veered off to the left. He tried to remember. Fragments of information slowly entered his mind. He knew his name was Henry Taylor. He was six years old and lived at 638 Dunlowder Street. This was the bricklebutter bush patch right near his school.

Moving faster, he soon jogged to the next split in the overgrown bushes. Much higher than himself, the bushes here and there grew together at the top, obscuring the sky and subduing the light. "Dad must be home from work by now," Henry mumbled. "I need to get back."

He stopped again as another memory emerged from somewhere beyond the bushes. His twin sister's name was Kate. "Now, where is she?" he asked himself. A pang of emotion flickered like a spark. He missed his sister. He missed his family. He wanted to see them.

Some tones of music, from way off in the distance, caught Henry's attention. It sounded vaguely familiar, but he could only distinguish bits and pieces. He strained to listen. It was outside the maze, but he couldn't tell which direction. He set about finding it, now running through the various paths as they appeared.

A voice filtered through the branches on the right side of the path. It was humming a song. He stopped and listened. The voice now sang some words.

"If you love me, I'll love you too. Do the Nimmy Nimmy Dance."

He smiled.

"Come on, Henry, dance with me," he heard.

He turned to the left as the path ended. He saw an open field. He ran toward it and, gaining speed, soon shot out from the bricklebutter patch and into the bright daylight.

"Penny?" he whispered.

"Henry! Oh my God! You're awake!"

Henry blinked his eyes and saw a form hovering over him. He blinked some more and focused harder. He recognized Penny's face but didn't understand. This was a woman, not his six-year-old friend.

"Penny?" Henry whispered again.

"Yes, it's me," Penny replied.

Henry smiled.

Penny leaned over further and kissed him. She then abruptly stood upright, rushed over to the hospital room door, and called, "Kate!"

Kate walked casually into the room, holding two cups of coffee. Penny pointed to Henry and Kate quickly noticed Henry's open eyes. When she saw the recognition on his face, she cried. She ran over to the bed and put her head against Henry's.

"Hi, Kate. Where've you been?" asked Henry feebly.

She kissed Henry's cheek and said, "Stay right there. I'm going to get Mom." She ran out of the room toward a small lounge area with a sofa and some comfortable chairs, yelling, "Mom! Mom!"

Mrs. Taylor ran into the room with Kate and two nurses on her heels. It was true, Henry was awake. Tears spilled down her cheeks as she realized Henry was going to be okay. She rushed over and kissed him.

"Mom, I don't know what's going on. Where am I? What are you all doing here?" asked Henry, his voice sounding small and weak from disuse.

Mrs. Taylor wiped her eyes. "It's all okay, Henry. We have plenty of time to explain everything." Turning to Kate, she said, "Kate, text everyone and let them know he woke up!"

Henry slightly lifted his hand and tried to turn his head. A throbbing pain instantly hit him, and he winced out loud.

"Henry, don't move yet. You've been hurt badly," explained his mother.

Relaxing his hand, it fell gently back onto the bed. Exhaustion overtook him. He closed his eyes, and he fell asleep.

After a few minutes, he woke up again with a start. "Mom?"

"Yes, Henry, I'm here," she answered.

The song echoed in his head. Though fuzzy, he knew the voice.

"The craziest thing. I thought I heard Penny," he whispered, and tried to look around.

"Yes, Henry. She's here," said his mom as she patted his arm.

"Okay." Henry closed his eyes and fell into a sound slumber.

Now that Henry had awakened from his coma, his family worked fervently to have him transferred from the hospital to his parents' house. They had outfitted his old bedroom with a hospital bed. The plan was for home health providers to visit at least daily. If Henry's condition improved as expected, family and friends could then fill in.

After a few days at home, Henry reawakened. He heard voices that sounded familiar, sometimes faintly and sometimes loudly. He willed his eyes to open, but they wouldn't obey. Thoughts that normally resulted in instantaneous action seemed to fizzle out and lose the strength of his command. With the sense of sight out of his grasp, he shifted his attention to sound. In his foggy, groggy state, he tried to match each voice to a recognized face.

A high-pitched chuckle was easy to recognize. Female. His sister Kate. A deeper laugh that joined Kate's. Yes, that was Robby, her husband. Another deeper voice eluded Henry. The tones of the laugh were familiar, but the voice just didn't sound correct. He searched through memories. Was he at work? No, Kate and Robby rarely came to Fusion Lab.

He rewound time as best he could, eager to access the memory. There were many gaps. Many dark spaces that Henry could not discern. He made a mental note of alarm, but returned to the task at hand that had him so focused.

Was he at college? No, his sister Kate had not attended college with him. She got a degree in business at the state college. Henry remembered she worked for a local shop. Then Robby opened his own business and Kate took over the management and financial details. Yes, she and Robby made a great team.

Henry heard a playful belly laugh. Again, he knew he recognized the voice, but it just didn't sound right. At last, a face popped into Henry's mind. Alex! Of course. The resonance Henry identified was from his childhood friend, but the deep tone was from Alex as an adult.

"Here's a picture of you and Sean," said Kate as she handed a photo to Alex. She, Robby, and Alex sat at the side of Henry's bed. They had dragged their chairs to the edge and were eating sandwiches as they sorted through a small box of old photographs. Henry's prone, covered body lay stretched out in the middle of the bed like an oversized centerpiece.

"Look how tall and skinny he was," said Robby. "Sure looks different now."

"Still tall, but definitely not skinny anymore," answered Kate.

Alex took a bite of his sandwich. "You still make the best PBJs around, Kate."

At that, Robby, too, lifted his sandwich and took a bite. He was about to agree with Alex when a big clump of jelly slowly oozed out of the bottom and fell onto the bed sheet. All three looked at the blue blob and then at each other. Robby quickly grabbed his napkin and blotted the sheet. The smudge smeared even further and made a blotch three times bigger. Alex started chuckling, joined by Kate. Robby finally shrugged and laughed, too.

Simultaneously, Kate and Robby shook their heads and muttered, "Those girls!"

Alex looked at them quizzingly. "What girls?"

Kate giggled. "It's what Robby and I say when either of us makes a mess. We pretend Joy and Ellie did it."

Two of Henry's favorite people on the planet were his little nieces, Joy and Ellie. At ages four and two-and-a-half, Henry was addicted to their squeals whenever they saw him of "Unca En Reeeeee!" as they ran at him with the wild-eyed joy and bright smiles only kids can summon.

"I know, it's horrible. We're blaming them. We're terrible parents. Even Joy is saying it when she spills something. We all laugh about it."

"Wow, I'm feeling like a little kid. Shouldn't Mrs. Taylor pop through the door right now and give me that look she used to? You know she'll think it was me instead of Robby."

"Yes, she loves me, Alex. You, I'm not so sure," said Robby.

All three laughed. "She loves me, too. Just thinks I'm a bit of a troublemaker," said Alex.

"Well deserved," agreed Robby.

"Remember the time you lost your swimsuit at that swim meet?" asked Kate. Her voice rose into a squeal of laughter as she slapped her hands together and then hit Alex's arm.

"You had to bring that up," chuckled Alex. "I did win the race."

"What happened? I've never heard this one," added Robby.

"I was running late for the meet," started Alex.

"As usual," interjected Kate.

"As I was saying, I was running late and forgot to bring my swimsuit. I had to borrow one of the practice ones in the locker room. I didn't look at the size label and put it on and ran out to the pool. They were introducing my freestyle event and Coach was already livid with me."

"As usual," Kate added again.

"The gun went off, and I dived in. Everything was fine until I did the flip turn. I knew something weird happened, but kept going. I could swim faster and touched the wall before anyone else. I won by a mile. I was pretty excited until I saw everyone laughing, even Coach. People were pointing to my suit bobbing in the pool. I guess I streaked that last lap."

"Only Alex!" said Kate.

Kate and Robby were laughing uncontrollably, subtly causing the bed to shake. "What did you do?" asked Robby.

"Ask that guy there," said Alex as he pointed to Henry. "Henry was in the next race and was standing right above me at the poolside. He was laughing so hard he lost his balance. When he did, he fell into the pool. With that splash, I dived underwater, retrieved my floating swimsuit, and pulled it back on. Most eyes were focused on Henry dragging himself from the pool. He said it was my fault he lost his race."

All three were now howling.

The feel of the hot sun on his skin and the smell of chlorine welled up in Henry's mind. A memory unveiled itself. A young Henry convulsing with laughter, slipping on the wet pool surface and doing a convoluted forward flip into the pool. As Henry savored the recollection, he smiled. It became a giggle which grew into a chuckle. Nerves in his throat and mouth fired, and a full-fledged laugh came from his body.

Kate, Robby, and Alex froze in place as they watched Henry's arm move to his stomach to soothe the imagined hurt he felt from laughing so hard.

Henry opened his eyes and lifted his head slightly. "I love that story," he said faintly.

"Glad you could join us!" exclaimed a surprised Alex.

"I didn't have much of a choice," whispered Henry, as he looked at their faces. "Impossible to sleep around here."

"Sorry, Henry. We're reminiscing," said Kate warmly. She reached for his hand and squeezed it. "How are you feeling?"

"Okay, I guess," answered Henry. He tilted his head and searched. "Where's Penny? Mom said she was here."

"She had to get back to Atlanta for work," said Alex.

"Atlanta? I thought she worked in Germany?" he asked, puzzled.

Kate squeezed his hand again. "You've got a lot of catching up to do."

Henry stayed awake for a few more hours, talking a little, but mostly listening. Eventually, he grew tired, and they left.

Henry drifted back to sleep, encouraged by his progress, and determined to get stronger every day.

The bedroom door hinges squeaked like the sound of a small mouse. Henry had become accustomed to that noise while he lay stretched in the bed, his strength slowly, but steadily, building each day. He cautiously turned his head a bit to greet whoever had entered the room, but could not glimpse anyone. Henry blinked his eyes a few more times to get used to the shallow level of light. He knew it was morning.

"I can't see," he heard a whispered voice say. The door squeaked again as it gently closed only halfway.

Henry felt a thump as someone hit the side of his bed.

"Owwie. You hit me!"

"You're being loud. You have to use your quiet voice."

"But you hit me. I'm going to tell Mommy."

Henry recognized the hushed tones of his nieces. He smiled to himself, yet did not move to greet them. The morning sun grew stronger, and the room brightened.

"I think he's awake. Let's look."

Henry heard a small step stool being pushed close to the bed and sensed a tug on his covers as little hands used them as a grip to climb up. He kept his eyes closed. After a few minutes of rustling and grunting, Henry could feel the warmth of his nieces as they lay next to him, one on each side.

"I think he's awake."

"No, he's not. Be quiet."

Henry felt a tiny finger poke his cheek.

"He's awake."

"No, he's not."

"Yes, he is. See?" The small fingertip moved up from his cheek to his eyelid and pushed it open.

"I want to do it," protested the other voice, whereupon another finger prodded his other eyelid open, and not so gently.

Two curious heads were positioned right over Henry's face. He had tried to keep still. But sensing a laugh he could not stifle, he suddenly lifted his arms, grabbed the two girls, and growled as loud as he could. Startled at first, the girls then shrieked in delight.

"Unca Enry, Unca Enry! Please come play with us."

Henry held his nieces close to him. "Joy, Ellie, what are you doing here today?"

The girls pressed their heads against his chest and snuggled with him. "We're here with Mommy," said Joy. "Mommy said we could play with you when you woke up."

"Are you all better now?" asked Ellie. "Mommy says you're getting better."

"Yeah, I'm getting better and better all the time," answered Henry.

"I didn't like it when you were asleep so much," said Joy. "Even when it wasn't nap time."

"Yeah, even not nap time," agreed Ellie, as she patted Henry's cheek.

"You got a hairy face, too," protested Joy. "I don't like that. Daddy gets scratchy too sometimes, but Mommy makes him stop. We don't like it."

"No, we don't like it," said Ellie as she parroted her older sister.

"I didn't like sleeping so much either. I missed you girls," said Henry.

"You wore a diaper," announced Joy.

Henry felt himself blush and then laughed out loud.

"I'm a big girl. I don't wear diapers," said Joy. "But Ellie still does. Mommy and Daddy say she should use the potty, but she won't."

"I do too!" objected Ellie.

"Do not!"

"Do too!"

Henry was ready to interrupt when the door swung open.

"What are you two ladies doing in here?" asked Kate as she surveyed the lump of covers, pillows, and bodies curled up on the bed. The girls jumped at the sound of their mother's voice, knowing she had caught them.

"Nothing," they both answered simultaneously in the sweet, singsong voices that Kate had heard many times. The girls then burrowed their heads as best they could into Henry's side.

"We were going to wait for Uncle Henry to wake up, remember girls?" asked Kate.

"He was awake, Mommy. We checked," answered Joy. "His eyes were open."

"We checked," repeated Ellie. "Eyes open."

"Well, Henry, what do you say about this?" asked Kate.

"Actually, I was already awake, Katie. I heard them come in. We've been having a pleasant visit."

"Why bother asking? Of course, you'll defend them. Girls, go back downstairs to see your grandmom. I need to talk to Uncle Henry," said Kate as she motioned with her arms for the girls to head out of the room.

"Nooooo," they both protested. "We just GOT here. We neeeed to talk to Unca Enry tooooo," they whined and then gave Kate the saddest faces they could muster.

"Okay, but just for a moment. Now, what did you need to say to Uncle Henry?"

They both giggled and laid their heads right beside Henry's on the pillow. Because Henry was still looking at Kate and smiling, Joy reached with her hand and turned Henry's face toward her. As she started to speak, Ellie, not to be outdone, brushed Joy's arm away and then turned Henry's head to her side.

"Girls!" protested Kate loudly. "Be gentle. You're going to hurt your uncle!"

"I'm okay. Actually," Henry paused as he lifted his head off the pillow, "No pain," he said surprised.

Kate glanced at Henry to make sure he was telling her the truth. "Henry, that's great. You're healing!" said Kate.

"Yep," answered Henry. "I need to get out of this bed and back on my feet."

Henry turned his head slowly back and forth and made faces at the two little girls on each side of him. They both giggled and began talking at once.

"I'm very angry," began Ellie.

"No, I am," interrupted Joy.

Henry stopped their protests by asking sympathetically, "I'm sorry to hear that. What happened?"

In sing-song fashion, each girl took their turn to explain the cookie saga.

"We made 'licious cookies with Grandmom and now they

are gone."

Henry looked at Kate and she mouthed the word "disaster."

"We made them just for you."

"But now they're gone."

"Daddy ate them."

"So did Grandad."

"Now they're gone."

"I'm so angry that Daddy and Grandad ate your cookies."

"Me, too. I'm so angry."

Joy and Ellie cautiously glanced up at their mom. Kate stood with her arms crossed, regarding them with a look that said Dad and Granddad weren't the only culprits.

With a guilty face, Joy quickly admitted, "I ate some."

Not to be outdone, Ellie chimed in, "Me, too!"

"They were so good."

"Now they're gone."

Henry interrupted, "That's okay. I bet Grandmom would love to make more with you two."

Kate snickered.

Henry continued, "Do you know what I'd like better than a cookie?"

"What's better than a cookie?"

"Will you promise to come in later and read a book to me?"

The girls suddenly perked up and began to wriggle off the bed.

"Wait," protested Henry. "I need a kiss to make me feel better."

The girls slid back on each side of Henry and gave him a peck on each cheek.

"Wow! I think I just got a sandwich kiss!" Henry exclaimed.

The girls squealed and shouted together, "We just gave Unca Enry a sanish kiss!"

Henry, smiling broadly, patted the girls' heads. They laughed and then squirmed off the bed. Hopping onto the floor, they scurried out of the room in search of the best book to read later to their uncle.

Kate opened her mouth to say something after them but realized it was too late. "They sure keep us busy, Henry."

"I'm glad I'm getting so much time with them. They just crack me up. I love them. Thanks for that," said Henry.

"Robby and I worry about spoiling them, as they're so precocious," said Kate. "But they crack us up, too. They're so funny sometimes. They can be a handful, though. For example, potty training Ellie has been a nightmare. She loves to just sit on the toilet and talk. I wonder if it's because she has my undivided attention then, without her sister. I've started setting an alarm on my phone, so she has to finish when it goes off."

They both enjoyed the laugh together.

Kate shifted in her chair beside Henry's bed and continued, "I wanted to talk to you. You know Penny's back home. She'd like to visit when possible. I'm wondering what you think about that."

A quick hit of adrenaline shot through Henry.

Seeing his face, Kate persisted, "I was expecting a suitable response. What was that?"

Henry remained silent.

"Henry, Penny wants to keep visiting, but only if you say okay. You've had severe trauma with a lot to digest. I know it was ages ago, but you took it extremely hard when she moved away. I worried about you then, and I worry about you now. What are you feeling? We don't know what to tell her."

Kate had realized she was rambling on and stopped and looked at Henry. For one of the few times in their lives, she couldn't tell what her brother was thinking.

Henry swiftly tried to process a swelling number of thoughts and emotions. How did he feel? He suddenly felt dizzy, almost like sea sickness.

Kate saw Henry's white face and became alarmed. "Henry, are you okay? I didn't mean to upset you." She rose out of her chair, leaned over Henry, and grasped his shoulder.

"I'm fine," answered Henry weakly at first, but then firmly. Facts. He needed some facts to ground his thoughts.

"I'm still processing what happened with the crash, Fusion Lab, everything. I remember a lot, and each day I remember more. It helps when all of you talk to me about what has happened. It makes it real. So much even now seems like a dream." Henry hesitated. "How does Penny factor into this again?"

"We explained how she came back to Atlanta, right?" asked Kate.

"Yes, her company overseas was bought out by Matt's. She ended up over here working with him. It's only logical that they'd figure out the past connections. But how did she end up at the hospital?"

"Well, we were all exhausted when you were at the hospital in Baltimore. Mom and Dad were a wreck, of course. To be honest, we all were. I don't know what was worse for us, your physical condition, or what people were saying about you. It was infuriating."

"I know," said Henry in a consoling voice. "Let's talk about that sometime later. Back to Penny."

"Oh, yes," said Kate. "When Penny heard from Matt about you and what we were going through, she volunteered to help. She asked me what she could do, and I told her. I'm so glad I did! I mean, it was so good to hear from her and see her again. And then you woke up when she was right there in the room! I know that was a shock."

"Everything's been a shock, Kate. It makes my head spin."

"That's what we're worried about. You're doing so well now, Henry. No one wants to overwhelm you."

"You know me better than that," countered Henry. "The more facts I have, the better."

"Normally I'd agree with you. But do you really understand how injured you were? Still are?"

Henry gave Kate a pained expression and then grinned. "I am doing much better, Kate. I appreciate your concern. But I need to get out of this bedroom." He waved his arm in a circle, pointing around the room. "Tell me about Penny."

"Well, you saw her! She was right there. You talked to her. I was telling Alex how weird it is to see her as a grown woman. She looks the same, but again, quite different. I thought she'd get married overseas and have a family and all that. What else would you like me to tell you?"

"She does look different, doesn't she? I remember that. The same, but different. Kind of attractive, don't you think?"

"She's beautiful, Henry. My God, of all the things you could ask about her! It's been over twenty years."

"Well, did she get married and have a family over there?"

"There you go. Now, that's the first question I expected from you. No, she did not. She's back in the States because of her job situation and to spend time with her family."

"I'm surprised. I assumed she'd be married. I thought she was when no one had heard from her."

"About that. Penny told me she regretted none of us kept in better touch."

"I should've called her."

"Yes, you should have. But you were so involved with Fusion Lab, you barely had time for any of us."

"That's not fair, Katie, and you know it. I only became inundated with Fusion after Ted Granger passed. Sure, I put in a lot of hours before then, but I tried to visit or call everyone."

Kate backed down. "I know. I'm sorry. Everything got so messed up. It still is." She slumped down into her chair.

"Let's not go there. If I think about all those problems, my head hurts."

"It's going to be okay. What did Grandmom always tell us when we were upset?" Kate asked.

Kate began and Henry joined her in mimicking their grandmother's voice and they both waved a pointed finger at each other. "That'll do. We'll have none of those sour faces. There's always hope."

"She always said that," said Henry wistfully. "And it made me feel better."

"Me, too," agreed Kate. "I miss her."

They were both quiet and then Henry ventured, "Penny?"

"Oh yeah, I was telling you about her," said Kate. "We've

had some good talks. When you first woke up, Alex picked up Dad and drove all the way to Baltimore."

"I remember seeing Dad, but not Alex."

"Probably all the better," chuckled Kate. "That night, Penny, Alex, and I stayed up almost the entire night reminiscing. It was good to laugh at the crazy things we did as kids."

"Sounds like I missed a lot," said Henry with hurt feelings.

"Well, yes, unfortunately. You've been sleeping!"

"Sorry," said Henry. "You know I hate to be left out."

"Alex mentioned that while we were talking. He said he appreciated your contributions to our conversations."

Henry laughed. "Alex. My loyal friend." He paused, "Penny?"

"She's had such an interesting life, Henry. Living in so many different countries, meeting so many different people. She's very impressive. In fact, I got a little intimidated listening to her."

"Did you fill her in on everything going on here?" asked Henry.

"Pretty much so. Between Alex and me. You know how he loves to talk."

Henry knitted his brows. "Between the two of you, I guess Penny's definitely all caught up."

Kate leaned in closer to Henry. "I think she still has feelings for you," whispered Kate. She drew back some and said in a normal voice, "So does Alex. When we talked about your crash, she cried."

"We were great friends, Katie. Of course, she has feelings for me. Don't make anything more out of it."

"I'm not trying to. According to Penny, she's had two serious, romantic relationships over the years. In her words, it 'just wasn't right.'"

"She did? She told you all this?" asked Henry. He propped his arms on his side and rose out of the bed.

"And how many relationships have you had, Henry, that unfortunately were 'just not right?'" asked Kate.

Henry lowered himself and settled into the covers. "I don't like where this is going."

"All I'm saying is that you were in a coma, and precisely when Penny was in the room, you woke up," Kate pointed out. "But you're right. I'm making too much out of this. Now, what do you want me to tell Penny? She would like to visit again."

Henry rolled onto his side and moved his legs toward the edge of the bed. "I need to get out of here."

"Um, are you supposed to be doing that, Henry?" asked Kate.

"Definitely. I need to be out of bed at least four times during the day according to my PT. How else will I rebuild my strength and endurance?"

"I didn't know that. Here, let me help," said Kate as she draped Henry's arm around her shoulder.

Henry and Kate walked slowly across the room, and Henry paused before the mirror. Tired eyes looked back at himself. His blond hair had grown much longer than he ever wore it. Some hairs were matted to his head, while others shot out like threads of hay. He needed a shave. His face was thin due to the loss of overall weight.

"I don't want her to see me like this."

"She already has," countered Kate.

"But I couldn't see her. At least not for long. I zonked out again. I don't want her to see me like this, when I can see her seeing me like this. Look at me. I look horrible."

"Yeah, you do," huffed Kate. She straightened up to make herself as tall as possible. She was still three inches shorter than Henry, but firmly grabbed his face with one hand and started wagging the finger of the other at Henry. "We'll have none of those sour faces, now."

"Stop it!" growled Henry, and he playfully swatted his sister's hand away.

Henry's shoulders then slumped, and Kate helped him back to the bed. As they passed the nightstand, Henry reached out for his cell phone.

"Could you give me Penny's number?" asked Henry nonchalantly.

"You're going to call her?" asked Kate. "Can I . . ."

"No, you can't," said Henry firmly. Seeing Kate's disappointment, Henry added, "I'll let you know how it goes."

With a sigh, Kate pulled out her own phone and scrolled down the screen. A beep told Henry that Penny's contact info was now on his phone.

"Tell Penny I said hello," said Kate, as she turned her back to Henry. Grinning broadly, she scooted out of the room.

CHAPTER 12

Grunting, Penny maneuvered a small table over to the wall and rearranged the chairs around the remaining tables. She knew exactly how the meeting room functioned best and wanted it set up perfectly before any participants arrived. Her cell phone buzzed from across the room. Hurriedly, she raced over and grabbed it. Expecting a call from her mother, she answered it quickly.

"Hello, Mom?" she asked.

"Hi Penny, this is Henry Taylor. How are you?"

"Henry!" said Penny excitedly. "It's so good to hear from you."

"Did I catch you at a bad time? I know it's early."

"No, I'm just prepping for my session today."

Penny tugged on a chair she had just nestled snugly under the table. She gracefully sat on the edge and rested her arm on the cool surface. With her free hand, she nervously fidgeted with a rubber band clasping a bunch of pens.

"I won't keep you long," promised Henry. "I wanted to thank you for helping after my accident. Everyone can't stop talking about how wonderful you were."

"I felt so horrible for you and your family. I'm glad you're doing better."

"It was so great to see you," said Henry, his voice lowered. "I have to admit, I thought I was dreaming."

Penny laughed. "I'm sure it was a bit of a shock."

"A good one," Henry assured her. A tumble of voices grew louder, and a group of people meandered into the conference room. "I hear a bit of commotion. I'd better let you go."

"Yes, my training class is arriving. Can we talk again soon?" asked Penny eagerly.

"Sure!" answered. "Call me whenever it's convenient for you. Believe it or not, I'm pretty easy to get a hold of lately."

Penny laughed. "I will. It's so good to hear your voice. Get well!"

Buoyed by the encouragement of his family and friends, Henry focused all his energy on regaining his health. Still mostly confined to his room, he worked hard with the help of his therapists. If he overdid, his body would protest with pounding headaches and dizziness. That would force him back into bed for a few days. His toughest struggle was to subject himself to the excruciating pain all over again in the next therapy session.

Henry and Penny spoke a few more times on the phone. Mainly small talk, and to let Penny know how he was doing. Within a month, Penny called to let Henry know she had a gap in her schedule and hoped to visit. She was relieved at Henry's excitement when she told him.

Kate picked up Penny at the airport, and they hugged and giggled, happy to see each other.

"How was your flight?" asked Kate, as they walked along the brightly lit corridor to the parking area.

"Fine," said Penny. "As we were descending, I saw how much the area has grown. There are houses everywhere now!"

"Yes, we're definitely blossoming!" agreed Kate. "You'll be surprised, though, at how the old neighborhood is just the same. I know you'll recognize everything. Mom and Dad can't wait to see you."

"Are they expecting us?" asked Penny.

"Oh, of course. Mom is fixing dinner for all of us. She's been busy all morning."

"That's so nice of her!" said Penny. "How's Henry?"

"He's doing well. His good days are gaining on the bad days all the time."

"That's good news!"

"Dad took him to the medical center last week for some tests. His headaches concern his doctor, but overall, Henry is getting much stronger."

"I hope my visit isn't a burden."

"No, absolutely not!" insisted Kate. She hit a button on her key fob and the lights of the car blinked. "Here we are."

Now settled in the front seat, Penny reached down to her feet and pulled up two dolls.

Kate laughed. "Just toss them into the back. I can't keep up with those girls. I find things everywhere."

"I can't wait to meet them."

"Oh, they've already grilled me on who you are and why you're visiting."

Penny let out a buoyant laugh. "It was nice to see everyone in Baltimore. I hadn't realized how much I missed you guys. I wish the circumstances were different, though."

As they drove along, Penny peered out the window, trying to find some similarity to the way she remembered the area. Turning down a street lined with large trees, Penny grew nervous. As they approached a group of houses, Kate stopped the car in front of a well-maintained one with a broad porch. Penny recognized it as the house she grew up in.

"My old house!" she exclaimed.

Kate stayed silent as she reached over and squeezed Penny's hand.

"And that's Mom and Dad's there," Kate pointed to the house next door.

"It looks so different than I remember," Penny gasped.

"The roofs are all new and the colors have changed," explained Kate. She pulled the car forward and turned into the Taylor's driveway.

Kate's mom, followed by her dad, bustled out of the front door.

"Penny!" they shouted together.

They all hugged and led Penny and Kate to the door. Penny moved sluggishly, looking around.

"I know," said Mrs. Taylor. "It's a lot to take in. Let's get you inside."

Henry was sitting in an easy chair in the living room and stood painfully and haltingly as Penny entered.

"Hey, Penny!" Henry called out, beaming.

Penny hurried over, and they hugged. They held onto each other until Penny felt Henry tremble from the exertion. She let go and helped him settle back into his chair. She was elated at how much Henry had improved since she saw him last.

The Taylors peppered Penny with many questions, and they heartily chattered on. Although he said little, Henry was happy and content. Soon, Mrs. Taylor noticed Henry's head drooping. She caught Kate's attention.

"Well, sorry to break this up, but I need to get home. And Henry looks like he could use some sleep. Penny, can I drop you by the hotel?"

"Sure," said Penny, and she stood up.

"Penny, would you mind helping Henry back up to his room?" asked Mrs. Taylor. "Those stairs are challenging."

Henry looked at Penny and shrugged.

"Alex and Sean are getting into town later," added Henry's mom. "They're staying at your hotel. They can bring you back here for dinner."

"That sounds perfect!" said Penny. "It's so wonderful to be here!"

Henry stood and playfully held out an arm to Penny. She hooked it firmly on her own and they ambled to the steps. Once they reached the top, Henry leaned against the wall, out of breath.

"You still remember where my room is?" Henry soon asked, smiling.

"I believe I do. Let's get you there."

"This is what I hate the most, having everyone fussing over

me," Henry apologized.

"We don't mind. In fact, I kind of like this!" Penny tugged Henry's arm and leaned tighter against him.

Henry chuckled. "Yeah, I could get used to this!"

They shuffled over to the bed and Henry sat down cautiously. Looking at Penny, he patted the area next to him.

"I'm really glad you're here," he said as Penny sat beside him. "It's been so long, and now, seeing you, I'm sorry I didn't stay in touch."

"I'm just as guilty. I remember sitting here on this bed when we were little. In some ways, it seems like I never left!" Penny said earnestly.

"I feel exactly the same way!" Henry ardently agreed. "It sounds like there'll be a crowd tonight for dinner. I was hoping we could get some time alone."

"Me, too. We've so much catching up to do. I promise I'll visit again as soon as my work schedule allows." Penny then stood to leave so Henry could get some rest.

"I'll still call you now and then, okay? As you can guess, my calendar is wide open."

"I'd love that." Penny leaned down and kissed Henry on the cheek. "I'll see you this evening."

"Now and then" soon became often. It surprised and delighted them both how quickly and effortlessly they rekindled the friendship of their youth. Penny would listen intently to Henry's account of his years at Fusion Lab. Henry hung on every word as Penny recounted her travels throughout Europe, with stories of the many interesting people she'd met.

A project soon opened in Chicago, and Matt assigned Penny to it. Only a three-hour drive from Henry's house in Indiana, Penny could visit Henry on some weekends. They settled into a contented rapport and familiarity, both relishing the time together.

"When are you going to ask Penny for a date?" demanded Alex. He was in town for the weekend and had taken Henry to the local fitness center. Alex insisted Henry needed a "real gym," not the limited exercise machines at the rehab center.

"You both talk all the time. It's obvious you enjoy each other," added Alex.

"We're good friends again. We haven't seen each other in what, twenty years and we're catching up. I'm not certain she sees us as more than that."

"She doesn't call me or Sean. Or even Kate. We're old friends, too."

"I don't know. It could be dangerous," said Henry. "We're at a good place."

"But you've considered it?"

"Penny's attractive, don't you agree?"

"Yes," said Alex. "Who would've thought that little Penny would become so pretty? I bet she has guys after her all the time."

"We've talked about our past romances. At least the serious ones. She's dated some very successful guys. Puts me at a disadvantage, don't you think?"

"You mean because you're unemployed and live with your parents?"

Henry glared at him.

"Yes, my future's a little murky," he grumbled.

"So, you're saying she'd be better off with someone else?"

"She might be."

"And you're going to make that decision for her?" asked Alex, perturbed.

Henry ignored him. He finished his set of pull ups and headed over to the bench. His shirt was soaked in perspiration, and he used a towel to pat his face. Exercise had always been a part of his routine through the years, that is, until Fusion Lab and Solidane consumed his time. Now, after the accident, the exertion to build back muscle was unlike any he'd ever experienced. What used to be easy, seemed impossible.

Alex grunted as he lifted twin barbels and watched himself perform arm curls in the gym mirror. "See, perfect form. Maybe one day you'll look this good."

"Easy for you to say."

"Did you know I came here with Robby and Sean? It was while you were still comatose. We needed a break from watching you sleep all the time."

"No, I didn't. I was comatose."

"Those two are way too competitive." He pressed a bar saddled with round plates over his head and let out a breath. "Don't you think?"

"And you're not?" asked Henry incredulously. "I guess you somehow matured while I was dozing?"

"Yeah. What's that saying, 'snooze you lose'? The world's passing you by, Henry."

Alex lowered the weights, sat on the padded bench, and rested.

"Anyway, they started out spotting each other and got carried away. They both overdid. Robby was so sore the next day he could hardly lift his arms. Kate was angry because Robby couldn't even lift Ellie into her car seat. Kate had to do everything. Sean and Robby tried to blame me for encouraging them, but it wasn't me that did all those reps. Kate and I agreed they were childish."

"That's scary, you and Kate agreeing on something."

"Like you pointed out, I'm evolving," laughed Alex.

Alex took a towel and wiped his face. He turned toward Henry.

"Kate and I agree on something else. You've run out of time, Henry. Why should Penny wait around for you? She has a new job and should focus on that, not fuss over you."

Alex observed as Henry quickened his pace on the pulley machine. Henry let his momentary annoyance at Alex burn out and gradually returned to his usual rhythm.

"I want the timing to be right. Look at me. Not the best impression."

Alex stopped his movement, lowered the weights to the mat with a thud, and stared at Henry. "Hmm," he mumbled. "You should come here more often."

Henry laughed.

"You don't need more time," said Alex. "You're skinnier and a little more moronic than before, but who cares? You're making excuses."

"I need more time. I want to improve my prospects."

"It's just a date, Henry. You're not asking her to marry you," continued Alex.

"I know that!" said Henry sharply.

Alex sighed, sat down again, and started a new set. "If you don't ask her out soon, I'm going to."

Henry paused as he switched the pins on the machine to increase the resistance. He knew Alex was not serious, but the threat had the desired effect. Yes, he was procrastinating. Yes, he was apprehensive.

He stood up and faced the mirror. He saw a reflection that was not nearly his old self, but certainly miles ahead of the gaunt features that shocked and repelled him many months ago. Henry tilted his head higher and straightened his shoulders. Did he want more than a friendship with Penny?

"Okay, I'll do it," he announced matter-of-factly.

"Really? Alright, buddy. Let's do this," said Alex. "I'll let Kate know. You'll see, this is going to be great!"

"Wait, wait. I said I'll do this. You and Kate stay out of it. Since when did the two of you get so chummy?"

Alex laughed. "As you wish. But first, you have three more sets. I bet I can lift triple the weight you can."

Henry rolled his eyes.

Alex clanged an additional plate onto a curl bar and handed it to Henry. "Try this."

He then hoisted two kettlebells from the rack for his own use. Making a production of his controlled breathing technique, Alex slung the weights behind him and back again. At each change in momentum, he glimpsed over at Henry to make sure he was okay. The grimace on Henry's face told Alex he was doing fine. Pleased with himself, he faced the mirror again and critiqued his form as he counted his reps.

Henry was lost in thought. Anxiety over the commitment he had just made fought against a newfound excitement. The physical exertion helped. With each repetition, the worry melted away, replaced by a growing curiosity. He wondered what he would say to Penny. How would she respond? The apprehension returned. He stepped up the pace.

Weary, but exhilarated from a good workout, they both soon rested on the bench. "I think that's adequate for today, don't you?" asked Alex.

"Yes, I'm done," admitted Henry. He fanned himself lightly with his towel and then downed the rest of his water bottle.

After a few moments, Henry turned toward Alex. "I'll need to get used to this new and improved Alex. I can't believe Sean and Robby would accuse you of goading them into something."

Alex pretended not to hear. "Let's get cleaned up," he grumbled. He began wiping down the mats and machines they had used. He then returned the scattered weight plates to the proper racks.

Henry had gathered up their towels and water bottles and stuffed them in their gym bags. Alex did a quick check of the area and nodded his approval.

As he slung his gym bag over his shoulder, Alex stood aside so Henry could pass in front of him to thread through the rows of fitness machines and treadmills. "Okay, Superman," he said playfully, "Let's get going."

Snapping her laptop shut, Penny gently slid it into its case. She sighed and shook her head. The training module she needed for tomorrow's session was not downloading correctly. As a standard practice of hers, she had always verified the next day's session beforehand. She was glad she did this time. Penny had witnessed others stumbling through a critical lesson in front of a group of questioning people staring at a blank screen. That would not be her.

She had already called IT, and they were looking at the file. Hopefully, they'd text her soon that they had fixed it. Penny would then try the download again and scroll through the lesson. In the meantime, she was hungry and wanted to get back to the hotel. Confident that she had everything packed up in her rolling carry bag, she looked around the large conference room. Yes, she'd be ready.

Penny clicked the handle on the carry bag, and it extended enough for her to grab. She made the long trek through the corridors leading from the conference area of the hotel to the elevator bank. A pleasant "bing" let her know she had reached her floor.

Once in her room, she flicked on a few lights and shook off her shoes. Making a beeline to the small desk, she grabbed the room service menu. Scanning it quickly, she reached for the hotel phone and placed a small order.

Her cell phone rang. It was Henry. Smiling, she shrugged off her hunger and irritation with the file and sat on the bed.

"Hi, Henry," she said affectionately as she propped up her pillows and stretched out.

"Hey, Penny!" Henry answered, equally cheery. "How was your day?"

"Fine, really. The session today was very productive. I have a talented group." She paused for a few seconds. "I'm a little worried about tomorrow, though. Some IT problems." She then waved her hand in the air, dismissing her concerns. "But enough of that. How have you been?"

"I have some good news! My physical therapist discharged me today! He said I can maintain the exercises on my own. He told me if I have any setbacks or problems to call him."

"That's great, Henry!"

"Yeah, I've amazed my doctor at my progress since the accident. I'm determined to get as strong as I once was."

"I know that's been a lot of hard work. You should be proud of yourself!"

"You know, I am!" Penny could hear the confidence in his voice. "I can't wait to see you this weekend."

"Me, too. I should get there early Friday evening."

"Kate invited us all to her house on Saturday. Alex and Sean are in town."

"That'll be fun. I haven't seen those guys in a while."

"Do you have time to talk right now? I want to ask you a question."

"Of course. What's going on?"

"Well," Henry began, "Imagine as your friend, I wanted to set you up on an official date."

Penny's heart sank as she struggled with what she imagined Henry was suggesting. "What? You want to set me up on a date with a friend of yours?"

"Yes, but," Henry tried to interrupt.

"You mean a friend like Alex?" Penny was angry now and didn't try to hide it. "I'm not going on a date with Alex!"

"No, no, no," Henry stammered. "Let me finish. I want to

set you up on a date with me. I'm sorry, I feel like I'm in high school again. I messed this up."

Penny calmed down as she sorted out what Henry was asking. "So, you're asking me on a date?"

"Yes."

"Henry, why didn't you just say so? Don't you know me better than that?" asked Penny.

"It's just very hard. I wanted to ask you in person when you got here this weekend, but then we'd have to wait longer to go on the date. Plus, if you said no, can you imagine how awkward the weekend would be?"

"Henry, why do you analyze things so much? It's not that complicated!"

"For me, it is," answered Henry, frustrated.

They didn't speak for a while.

"I'm sorry," Henry finally offered. "Can I try that again?"

"Go ahead," said Penny, softening.

"Penny Stevens," Henry began, "I've grown exceedingly enamored with you over the last months, so much more than a simple friendship. I think about you all the time, romantically, that is. I'm hoping you feel the same way. Would you go on a date with me?"

Penny giggled. "Yes, Henry, I will."

A gasp of relief came from Penny's phone. They both laughed and then became silent again.

"I guess that was a little convoluted," Henry finally chuckled.

"It's a first for me, I'll give you that," Penny laughed. After a few moments, she added, "I understand, though, Henry. We have a unique relationship. It confuses me too, sometimes."

"I'd like to take you out to dinner Friday night. Does that sound okay?" Henry asked quickly.

"Sure, I'd love that!"

"Great!"

Penny rested her head back onto her pillows. She thought about the weekend, happier and more excited than she had expected.

"So, you don't want to go on a date with Alex?" Henry asked.

Penny laughed out loud as she pictured a devilish smile on Henry's face. "No, I don't!"

"Wait till I tell him that."

"You go right ahead."

A knock at her door startled Penny.

"Room service!"

"Henry, I'm sorry, but I need to go. My food is here."

"Okay, but I'm going to call you again tomorrow to make sure you haven't changed your mind about our date!"

Penny laughed. "Don't worry, I won't. I can't wait."

"Me either! I'll make the reservation for dinner, and we'll figure out the details next time we talk."

Pulling carefully into the small driveway at Henry's house, Penny spotted him waiting out front for her. Dressed smartly for an important night out, he waved. Penny smiled and then hesitated.

Ever since Henry had called and asked her on a date, Penny's emotions were in turmoil. For so long, Henry had been her friend. She loved him. Saying yes to the date had unleashed a cascade of romantic feelings. She had been aware of them for a while, but their potency surprised her. She gasped at how handsome he was.

Henry's smile melted as he watched Penny seem to waver in the car. Maybe dating was more than she really wanted. He walked swiftly toward her. Penny smiled again and hurriedly unbuckled her seatbelt and emerged from the car. Henry offered his hand to help her out. He wanted to apologize for making her feel uncomfortable.

"I'm . . ." he began. But what he blurted out was, "My God, you're beautiful!"

Penny giggled as they hugged.

For Henry, too, their agreement to date brought up unexpectedly powerful feelings. A switch had been flipped, liberating long-buried emotions. They shredded his plan of casually dating while he and Penny grew used to their new relationship.

"Thanks for driving," said Henry, as they headed down the road to the restaurant. "I thought about meeting you there. I'm glad I didn't."

Henry watched Penny as she drove, making her uncomfortable.

"This isn't fair, you know. Why don't you point out some places of interest to me? It's been a long time since I've been here."

They chatted about old, familiar establishments, some that had closed, others still open, until they arrived at their destination. It was a locally owned restaurant, one that Henry's mom had suggested as a quiet place to get reacquainted. She had endorsed its good food, along with its cozy atmosphere that encouraged leisurely eating.

"I wish now we'd done this sooner," said Penny. She tilted her head to the side and glanced at Henry's face as she raised her wine glass to take a sip.

"Yes, long before my accident. I feel like we've wasted years of not knowing each other," answered Henry.

They sat in one of the back booths and had handed their menus to the waiter after deciding on what to order.

"I don't see it like that. We were both doing things that were important to ourselves. Maybe this timing was just right," Penny offered.

"Well, no matter what, we can't change the past. Here we are," said Henry as he spread out his hands and hunched his shoulders.

After the waiter set down a basket of warm bread, Penny held it up to her nose and sighed. "I love the smell of freshly baked bread!"

Henry cut some pieces for them, and Penny hummed her pleasure as she crunched down on the crust.

"I'm happy you're here now. Although I suppose I didn't make the best first impression, did I?"

"You were in a coma, Henry!" protested Penny.

"Exactly! How do I salvage that moment?"

Penny laughed and her smile spread from her cheeks, up through her eyes, and out again to him in the way Henry recollected.

Henry's hand slightly shook as he lifted his water glass. He was mending quickly but still had some gawky moments. He had turned down the waiter's offer of wine. Alcohol was not allowed, and unfortunately, therefore, not a remedy for his nervousness.

Penny noticed. "Doing okay, Henry?" she asked. She grabbed his hand and held it briefly in her own. Henry felt its warmth and relaxed.

"You know, it's funny," they both began.

"I know what you're going to say!" Henry uttered quickly. "We're able to talk with each other as if we're kids again. But then I get rattled because you're so different now. The same but different."

"Exactly!" exclaimed Penny. "It's unsettling. I know absolutely what to say and expect, but then, suddenly, I don't!"

Henry nodded, and they both laughed.

"We still have plenty of catching up to do," added Henry.

"It's unfair, I know," volunteered Penny, "But Kate and I have been talking, too. It's been wonderful. I probably have an advantage on what I know."

"Don't be so sure! You forget she's my twin sister and keeps nothing from me."

They spent the next hour comparing notes on the details furnished by Kate. Each was impatient to fill the immense gap of lost years and relive the experiences of the other, only now through their own voice and own expressions.

"Now that you're here, do you miss Europe terribly?" asked Henry.

"I do. I've always craved adventures. That's why I got so immersed in studying history and culture. I love reading about places and people of so long ago. What were they like? How did they live?"

"I remember you had a lively imagination," Henry smiled

and then sipped from his glass.

"Yes, and it's gotten me into trouble way too often!" Penny laughed. "But the past fascinates me. Did you know there are ruins right near Frankfort, where I worked, that are almost two thousand years old? I touched some stones that someone put in place that long ago."

"That's pretty incredible when you think of it like that," acknowledged Henry in between bites of his dinner. "So why stay over here if that part of the world is so attractive to you? Don't get me wrong, I'm happy you're here!"

Penny shrugged her shoulders. "I suppose I've changed. My priorities have shifted. I'd say the adventures I want now are very different. I also realize no situation is perfect and there're tradeoffs in every circumstance." Penny pensively squinched her face. "I think it's my age and level of maturity. My mom calls it wisdom."

"Ah, wise old Penny," Henry kidded.

"Watch it there," Penny retorted. Her fork clinked as she placed it down abruptly. "You may be walking home."

"Well, I'd call it beauty. You've aged rather nicely." Henry reached over and patted her hand.

"Nice recovery. You're still the smartest person I know."

After a moment, Penny grew serious. "A big factor is family. I'm at the point in my life where I want what my mom and dad have, if that's possible. They've been blessed with each other."

"I understand," said Henry lightly. "At least you know yourself well enough to recognize what you want and do something about it. For me, I had to have the rug pulled out from under me to get me here."

"I'm okay with that," Penny smiled.

"Me, too," agreed Henry, laughing.

Henry could feel his strength dwindling. He reached across the table again and gripped Penny's hand gently. "I hate to say this, but I'd better be getting home. Do you mind?"

"Of course not. I've had an amazing time," Penny reassured him.

"Me, too. So, let's not wait so long before our next date," Henry suggested, grinning at her. Penny chuckled in agreement. Holding hands, they walked unhurriedly out of the restaurant.

CHAPTER 13

Penny rinsed off the dish from her breakfast and quickly dried it. She put it back in the cupboard and refilled her coffee cup. Walking over to her kitchen table, she set the cup off to the side and opened her laptop. Clara had texted her yesterday, requesting a video chat this morning. She was ready.

The computer beeped and Clara's face appeared.

"Hello, Penny! How are you getting along?"

Startled for a second, Penny didn't answer. This was the first time in months that she heard German, instead of English. She made a mental note that she owed Adrianna a call.

"Clara! So great to see you!" said Penny. After staring at the screen for a moment, she added, "You cut your hair!"

"Yes, I finally did. I was ready for a change."

"You look so much younger!"

"Well, that's what my hair stylist promised me to convince me to try it," laughed Clara. "But enough of that. How are you?"

"Very busy. I'm trying to learn all these new faces in the

office, but I'm hardly there."

"Your friend, Henry, is monopolizing your time?"

Penny laughed. "I guess so. We're dating now."

"I knew it!" said Clara. "I'm very happy for you. I want to hear all about it, but that will have to wait for another time. I have some news for you."

"What's going on?" asked Penny. She took a sip of her coffee and then moved her head closer to the screen.

"You remember your project in Vienna?"

"Yes! I love that city."

"I know. And the firm that hired us?"

"Sure. They were one of my better clients."

"Well, they made me an offer. I've accepted."

"What? I'm shocked," said Penny. She leaned back in her chair and dropped her hands to her side.

"I am, too, I guess. The new company has treated me very well, but I'm having a hard time adjusting. Too set in my ways, I guess. The hardest part is how long it takes to get a decision made. I need to go through a committee. That's how they operate."

"I'm sorry, Clara."

"Don't be. My new position is perfect. I know it's the best future for me."

"As long as you're excited about this, I'll be, too. So, you'll move to Vienna?"

"Yes, I've been looking around," said Clara. "Also, I've met someone. He works in Vienna, and is divorced with three older children. We started talking on the train. He's in sales and was headed home from a visit."

"Clara! That's wonderful!" Penny placed her arms on her table.

"I know!" said Clara. Her eyes lit up and she smiled broadly.

"I wish I was there to give you a hug!"

"Me, too. But we both need to get moving. I've got a meeting next, and I know you have to get to the office." Clara hesitated, "But Penny, this new company is expanding. That's why they hired me. I have a position open if you want it."

Penny was silent while she considered what Clara had said. She reached for her cup and took a swallow of coffee. After setting the cup down, she still stared at the screen. "Clara . . ."

Clara laughed. "I thought that's the reaction I'd get. But I'm serious about the offer if it ever comes to that for you. In the meantime, once I'm settled, let's do a longer call where we can trade stories about the new loves in our lives."

"I'd love that," said Penny. "Like old times."

"It's been wonderful to chat with you, Penny. Talk to you soon."

"Bye, Clara."

Traffic inched along the Atlanta freeway. Penny's car was sandwiched among hundreds of others as they converged on the beltway artery of the busy city. Penny had become accustomed to the traffic but today was especially bad. "Must be an accident up ahead," she breathed out loud to herself.

She hit a button on her steering wheel to access her linked cell phone.

"Dial Adrianna."

"Calling Adrianna," her phone answered back.

"Penny?" asked a voice tinged with a German accent.

"Hey, Adri. Yes, it's me."

"Let me guess, you're stuck in traffic again? Seems like I only hear from you from your car. You should be on holiday over here with us."

"I do miss you. Do you have some time to talk?"

"Yes, I'm just finishing up a book. This afternoon sun's getting a little hot for me, so I'm ready for a break," said Adrianna as she placed the book at the foot of her lounge chair.

She had a few hours yet before she needed to meet up with Ida, Mia, and Lena. The women had been fortunate to share the same hotel suite on the Baltic Sea for the past three seasons. This year would be unique without Penny, and they'd be so happy to hear she'd spoken with her.

Adrianna pulled her knees up toward her chest, sitting up straighter. She switched the phone to her other ear to better focus her attention.

"You're calling to tell me you're staying there, aren't you?"

"Well, yes. For now," Penny admitted. "They have an assignment for me in Chicago for just a couple of months. I'd travel back and forth from Atlanta. Also, it's closer to Henry's house."

"Ah, so this is about Henry. You're dating now. How's that going?"

"Perplexing. Henry and I were so close as children. Then my family moved away. Now I'm back here again," recited Penny, catching a breath. "But you know this, I've told you before. I'm rambling here."

"No, no, I'm following fine."

"I've had a fabulous life, and I have a fine future. At this new company, there are many opportunities and possibilities. I'm sure I could come back over there and see all of you."

An artificial voice barked out, "Brake! Brake!" Red letters flashed on the instrument panel on Penny's dashboard as automatic brakes abruptly stopped her car. Penny gasped.

"What was that?" demanded Adrianna as she twisted in her chair and planted her legs on the ground.

Penny hesitated. "I almost ran into the car ahead of me."

"Maybe you should pull over."

"I can't. I'm boxed in." Penny relaxed her grip on the steering wheel and gave a friendly wave to the car in front and behind.

"Be careful," admonished Adrianna. "With your driving, that is. Not with Henry."

"But maybe I should be. I told you how upset I was when I first saw him while he was in that coma. He's mostly recovered now, and it's so wonderful to explore our pasts together. I'm so happy when I get to see him."

"I see. By the way. The girls and I were sitting at the hotel bar the other night telling stories."

"Drinking and gossiping?" suggested Penny.

"A little. I may have mentioned how serious you are about Henry," said Adrianna, stretching out on the lounge chair again. She adjusted her sunglasses and settled back.

"I would've loved to have heard that conversation!" grumbled Penny.

Penny gathered her thoughts while adjusting her rear-view mirror. She tilted it up so she would no longer see the scowling face of the driver behind her. She missed her friends. It bothered her that they were having fun together without her.

Adrianna filled her in further. "Ida searched him on the internet over here. We scrolled through all kinds of information about him. Numerous degrees. CEO of some company. Impressive. Still handsome, too. We approve."

"I guess I should be thankful for that," said Penny reluctantly.

"You don't sound very appreciative," said Adrianna. "What's going on?" She turned her back to better ignore the sounds of children splashing in the large pool near her and concentrate on her call with Penny.

"I have concerns," Penny admitted. "Some stories I've heard make me nervous. Henry's very driven. Very focused. I'm wondering if I should be more cautious."

"You're thinking of Ethan?"

"Shouldn't I?"

"Hmmm. This doesn't sound like you. What happened to my idealistic, starry-eyed friend?" Adrianna chuckled.

"Let's not go there. I remember the last time you called me starry-eyed."

"Yes, you didn't speak to me for a week."

"Well, I wanted you to support me, and instead you said it was my fault," argued Penny.

"No, you were angry with Ethan because he went away for the weekend with that other woman. You assumed you two were exclusive, but he never thought that."

"Well, he should have!" exclaimed Penny. She reached down and massaged her thigh. Her leg was tiring from constantly pressing the brake pedal.

"You'd just begun dating. You know Ethan always pushes the limits. At least you do, now."

"It could be happening again with Henry."

"What do you mean?"

"He told me his old girlfriend from college is visiting this weekend."

"Does he still have feelings for her?" asked Adrianna.

"He said no. But they dated throughout grad school."

"Hmmm. They'll be together all alone in his bedroom. And it has been quite a while since. . ."

"Adri, stop it! You're so mean! Be serious," shouted Penny into the phone.

Laughing, Adrianna sat up in her chair. "I'm sorry. I just had to. You worry way too much."

"But I am worried, like with Ethan. There are some things about Henry that, apparently, aren't on your internet pages. For example, he doesn't even have a job."

"He was successful once. Shouldn't he be again?"

"That's the problem. What if he gets so caught up in his career again and leaves me out?"

"Why don't you talk to him? See what he says?"

"I know I need to, and I will. I just want to be sure, that's all. Ugh, this traffic! I'm going to be so late!" Penny shook her head and then looked out her side window. The other driver smiled at her and shrugged his shoulders.

"Penny, where's all this coming from? Worries, concerns, questions? Again, where did my cheery, optimistic friend go?"

"I don't know," said Penny glumly. After some silence, Penny blurted out, "Adri, I've fallen for him!"

Adrianna let out a quick laugh. "Obviously! But that's a wonderful thing, Penny. You talk as if you're at a crossroads and have some decision to make. I need to tell you; the crossroad was when he woke and smiled at you. You're so far down the way, there's no turning back."

Penny was silent as she considered what her friend suggested. She knew Adrianna was right. She was in love with Henry. Did Henry feel the same way? Yes, she suspected he did, and that thought caused her to wobble in her seat. She chuckled. A quick toot from the car behind startled her.

"Adri, we're moving again. I need to hang up and pay attention here."

"Yes, please do. And as far as Henry goes, just be happy, Penny."

"Thanks for listening to me. I miss you and love you. Say hi to everyone tonight. I hope Henry's name doesn't come up too often."

"We'll see about that," laughed Adrianna. "We love you too, Penny."

Henry anticipated the nightly calls with Penny when they would rehash their days. He'd listen intently and offer encouragement, while Penny would recount the challenges and stresses of her new job. He admired her courage to embrace new adventures and her confidence to produce results.

It did not surprise Henry that Penny was popular at work. Her bosses, clients, and fellow employees sought her out. Knowing Penny was so successful made Henry happy for her, but he vied for her time. He became envious when she recounted lunches or dinners with others. The miles that separated them physically annoyed him.

Penny, too, grew frustrated. She and Henry tried their best to visit one another. However, Henry's priority was to get well. His rehab consumed his daily schedule as he fought to regain his strength and recapture the fitness he remembered. She wondered if their desire to be together put too much pressure on him. Some days, she could hear the exhaustion in his voice.

Henry became cranky and sullen when Penny was away. He struggled with anger over the events that brought him to this predicament. Fusion Lab. Solidane. The accident. His future, at least as how he had once envisioned it, had been snatched from him. He grappled with cloudy, gloomy thoughts and battled to keep negative emotions from steering his actions.

"Grrrrr," Penny sighed as flashes from her TV fleetingly lit her face. Sitting upright on the sofa of her rental apartment, she had been pressing the remote button, trying to find something interesting to watch. Penny hit the off button and tossed the remote solidly onto the cushion next to her. She sighed and glanced at her cell phone, now partially hidden by the remote.

She was angry, and rightly so. It had been almost two weeks since she'd last spoken with Henry. She had called him twice, but he didn't answer or return her call. They had planned for her to visit this weekend. She didn't think that was going to happen.

Penny thought back to the phone call when they had argued. Penny had given Henry the name and contact number of a recruiter she had met. Henry refused to take the information and became very agitated. Startled by the unexpected reaction, Penny pressed, and soon, both were talking with raised voices. The call ended abruptly.

Breathing out a heavy sigh, Penny stretched her legs and arms as she stood. She walked toward the kitchen, but paused and slowly turned back around. No, she wasn't hungry. She peered around the apartment. Nothing familiar. A swift wave of homesickness wafted over her. She missed her flat in Germany. She missed her friends. How nice would it be to stroll out into the busy city where she used to work with its bustle of people? And it had been months since she heard the German language she had grown so accustomed to.

Huffing, she strode back to the sofa and weightily sat down. Retrieving her phone, Penny scrolled through her recent call list and pressed Kate's name.

"Penny! How are you?" asked Kate cheerfully.

"I'm okay. But tell me, how is your brother?"

"Ugh, he's been a bear! I've had to stay away from him. I hope he's not been obnoxious with you, too?"

Penny sat up straighter, relieved that Kate felt the same as her and wanting more information.

"Unfortunately, yes. We had a spat a couple of weeks ago now, and I've not heard from him since."

Kate sighed. "I'm sorry. If it helps, our whole family is at wits' end. And Alex wants to induce Henry's coma again."

Penny laughed. "I'm glad it's not just me. Any idea of what's going on?"

"It's Henry's fault," explained Kate. "He stopped his medications without telling anyone."

"Why would he do that?"

"Henry said he couldn't think as clearly when he was on it," answered Kate. "He thought he could slog through his pain.

Obviously, that didn't work."

"Is he worried about the medication? Like getting addicted?"

"No, the doctor is monitoring doses of anything narcotic. He needs to take muscle relaxers sometimes for spasms in his neck and shoulders. He doesn't like how it makes him feel."

"I see," said Penny.

"But the doctor explained to him that the headaches put stress on his body, causing even more painful headaches that become excruciating. Henry's meds prevent that cycle. The idea is to wind them down slowly, not stop cold turkey."

"I guess that explains a lot." Penny leaned back into the cushions and relaxed her back and neck.

"Well, it's still no excuse. He's back on schedule from what Mom told me. Let's see how he does."

Penny's hand shuddered as another call came in. She tipped her screen to catch the caller id. "Well, I'll let you know shortly. He's calling me now."

"Wow! I'll let you go. Call me back!"

"Henry?" asked Penny.

"Yeah, it's me. I really want to apologize. I've been a jackass."

Penny remained silent.

"I need to explain. Do you have some time to talk?"

Closing her eyes, Penny wrestled a moment with her anger at Henry and her relief that he called.

"Yes, it's good to hear from you," she said more coolly than intended.

"I know, I know. I should have called you back. But I was in a downward spiral and couldn't get out."

"Kate told me about your medications. Are you okay?" asked Penny, now genuinely concerned.

"I think so. It was my own stupid fault. I have too much time to read things on the internet. I thought I knew more than my doctor."

Penny chuckled, "I can see that."

"Hey, be nice. I'm trying to apologize."

"I know, and I appreciate that. I was very worried. Seriously, Henry, are you okay?" Penny swung her legs up from the floor and tucked them under a small mound of throw pillows next to her.

"Yeah, I am. But relief from my headaches was only part of it. When I yelled at you over the phone, I realized I had other issues. You were trying to help, and yet it infuriated me."

Penny stifled a gasp as she recalled the conversation. She steadily calmed back down as Henry continued, "I've been talking to a friend of mine, Sammy, from college. He was a psych major. He's now on staff as a counselor at a large church on the west coast. Sammy heard about my accident and called me months ago. I finally took him up on his offer to talk.

Henry paused to make sure Penny was listening and to think a bit.

"Apparently, Sammy has counseled a lot of others in comparable situations. He asked how I was dealing with anger and frustration, and we walked through my experience. He was surprised at how well I was doing, and how you and I talking about it has been a big help."

"It helps me too, Henry," said Penny. "I hate watching you struggle."

"Sammy gave me some suggestions that I'm trying. I wanted to see what you thought about them."

"Of course," said Penny.

"He's concerned that I don't become bitter. Somehow, I need to release all this anger I'm feeling. Let it go. I want to do that, too, but I'm finding it impossible."

"I understand. That's so hard to do when you're in the middle of it."

"Sammy suggested I turn it on its head, so to speak. He said that from a spiritual standpoint, we're supposed to give thanks in any circumstance we find ourselves in. So that means, in my prayers, I should thank God for my situation. It seems illogical to me, but I'm gritting my teeth and doing it."

Penny shifted her legs back onto the floor and listened intently. "Is it helping?"

"It is," Henry breathed out in relief. "It helps me separate from the rage somehow, add some space between me and it. I find I'm not dwelling on my troubles as much. When I think about Solidane and Fusion Lab, I'm still irritated, but not livid. Sammy hopes I can get to the point of forgiving, but I'm not there yet."

"You will be."

"Besides, I have so many blessings in my life. There are a lot of good things happening."

"Like me?" Penny chuckled as she slouched to the side of the sofa.

"Yes, like you," laughed Henry

"Henry," Penny began, somewhat seriously again. "Thanks for telling me this. I know it's difficult and very personal. I hope you keep up those conversations with Sammy."

"I intend to. For the record, talking with Sammy was challenging. Talking with you is not." Henry paused and then added, "Well, as long as I'm medicated."

They laughed heartily, a soothing sound of contentment for both.

The tough week exhausted Henry. But the promise of a weekend visit from Penny heartened him, and he was determined to get some rest. He showered, shaved, and dressed in comfortable shorts and a t-shirt. With nothing to do until Penny arrived, he stretched out on his bed and fell fast asleep.

He woke to a persistent knock. "Hey, it's me. Are you awake?" Penny asked.

"Sure, come on in," grunted Henry. He rubbed his eyes and sat up in bed. "Hi, sorry, I fell asleep."

He patted the bed and Penny walked over. They hugged tightly, excited to see each other. The sun had set and the room had darkened. The only light was the glow from his clock. He looked at the time and turned on the lamp next to the bed.

"This is a pleasant surprise. I hadn't expected you this early. Was your drive okay?" asked Henry. He rolled back onto his bed.

"Yes, not much traffic," said Penny. She took off her shoes and laid happily onto the pillows. Facing each other, they smiled. "Plus, I was able to leave work a little early."

"How did your meeting go today?" asked Henry. He lifted his arm and arranged it around her waist.

"Really well!" said Penny excitedly. "I shouldn't have worried so much. The clients signed off on the schedule. They're thrilled with us."

"I knew you could do it," confirmed Henry.

"How was your day?" asked Penny.

"Pathetic," mumbled Henry. He raised his arm and rubbed his forehead, breaking the coziness. "I spoke to that recruiter this afternoon. The company that was interested in me declined. I've been floundering in self-pity since then."

"I'm sorry, Henry." Penny reached over, grabbed Henry's arm, and draped it back around her waist. "I'm sure something else will come up."

"I know. I'm dumping my problems on you already. I don't mean to do that."

"Thanks for saying that. We've had some rough conversations lately, but that's to be expected if we're going to stay honest with each other."

"True," sighed Henry. "But I hate taking my frustrations out on you." Henry tightened his arm and pulled Penny closer. "This is much nicer!"

"Mmmm," Penny purred. "Much nicer!"

"Have you realized yet how much I care about you?"

Penny beamed. "You're Enamored? Captivated? Spellbound?" she teased.

"All of those fancy words, yes." Henry searched Penny's eyes for any awkwardness. "But I'd say it more simply. I'm in love with you."

"You're in love with me?"

"Yes."

"I'm in love with you too, Henry," Penny quickly whispered. "I have been for a long time." She rested her cheek on Henry's shoulder.

Henry tenderly brushed his arm up Penny's back and nudged her face toward his. They pressed together. Each caught their breath as their lips met.

Barely tilting their heads back, they searched each other's eyes. Penny giggled. Henry smiled. "Let's do that again," he whispered.

They lay cuddled together until the clock alarm beeped. Henry grudgingly reached over and hit a button.

"I'm supposed to get up now, so I'm ready for your visit," said Henry with a slight laugh. However, he rolled onto his back and closed his eyes.

"And I need to say hi to your parents and go check into my hotel," conceded Penny. She patted Henry's chest.

"You know, you can stay here. We have room," suggested Henry.

"Your mom and dad keep offering, and that's so nice of them. But I don't want to impose. Besides, I'm so used to hotels that I feel right at home in them."

"Okay. But let's do something fun tomorrow. I need to get out of this house," pleaded Henry.

"I'm game!" said Penny happily.

They said goodbye, adding a long, loving kiss to their usual hug.

It was almost four weeks later before Penny could visit again. She "kidnapped" Henry and drove him to an out-of-the-way park. Winding trails cut through thick forest, leading down to a river. There, the fast-moving current sloshed over large boulders, emitting a staticky rumble. Hand in hand, Henry and Penny strolled leisurely through the paths, ending up at a wooden bench facing the river.

"I think this is about as far as we should go," said Henry reluctantly. "We've got to cover the same distance back."

"This is perfect, right here. That rushing sound of the river is so relaxing, don't you think?"

"I do," said Henry. He put his arm around her. "Can we talk about some things bothering me?"

"Sure," answered Penny with a sudden surge of apprehension. "What's on your mind?"

"I'm feeling trapped," began Henry.

"By me?" Penny looked at him in panic. "Did Adrianna call you?"

"No, no, no!" said Henry emphatically. "You are incredible!" Henry squeezed her with his arm, and smiling, kissed her on the cheek. "Why would Adrianna call me?"

Penny laughed. "I'm sorry. I'm jumping to conclusions. We're having such a great time and then you . . ."

"I know, lousy choice of words. My fault. What I meant to say is, I'm frustrated with my circumstances. My bedroom is a jail cell."

"No luck on the job front?"

"None. So, I'm having a difficult time envisioning a future."

"Now that you've brought it up, I wanted to ask you about that."

It was Henry's turn to be unnerved, and Penny felt him shudder. They both ignored it.

"What would you like to know? I'll tell you anything,"

Henry affirmed.

"Well, it's obvious you loved Fusion Lab and your work there. Your career is very important."

"You've been talking to Kate, haven't you?"

"What do you mean?"

"My friends and family, specifically Kate, will tell you how wrapped up I was in the Lab and the quest for the wafer. I admit it. I was relentless." Henry made sure he had Penny's eye. "But," he paused again and gingerly placed a hand on each of her shoulders. "My accident has changed me."

Henry casually dropped his hands to the side. To encourage him to continue, Penny draped his arm around her and leaned next to him.

"I've always tended to get so focused on one thing that I'd block out all else. You could call it an obsession. Kate would say I had blinders on. I remember in high school, I bought this video game. I got pretty good at it but played it way too much. One school night, I was engrossed in the game until three o'clock in the morning. My dad came into my room and flicked on the light. I didn't even pause the game." Henry chuckled lightly and shook his head from side to side.

"My dad walked over, grabbed the control stick, and broke it in half. Then he handed it back to me, turned off the light and walked out." Henry smiled at Penny.

"I can laugh about it now, but I was furious."

Henry checked Penny's face to see if she understood. Her confused expression made his smile fade, and he looked away.

Sensing his hurt feelings, she tried to explain. "Don't worry, I'm following you. I'm just trying to get used to how your mind works. It's very different from mine."

"At least I have one," Henry mumbled.

"Henry Taylor! I can't believe you said that." Penny pushed his arm away.

Henry chuckled. "I'm only kidding!"

"Do you remember the last time you said that to me?" Penny asked indignantly.

"I do. We were kids."

"Mindless jabbering, you said."

"I know, and you were just as offended. I'm sorry. I'm only teasing."

"The reason I remember is I had to ask my mom what it meant." Penny hit him playfully on the chest. "I was quite the chatterbox then," she laughed. "It got me into trouble throughout high school."

Henry put his arm back around her and squeezed gently. "To be honest, I love to listen to you talk. It's comforting."

Penny gave him another quizzical look. When she realized he was serious, she leaned against him. "You said the accident has changed you?"

"Yes, that's right. I'm now spontaneous and rash," said Henry with a wide grin.

Penny tilted her head with a "you-expect-me-to-believe-that" look.

Henry continued, "Well, it's still important to me to have a plan, a path, I admit. But I'm learning how to relax and enjoy more things in my life."

"Does this plan of yours include me?" asked Penny.

"I believe so," answered Henry, tightening his arm.

"I'm okay with that."

"However, you've got a brilliant career with incredible opportunities ahead. I wouldn't want to mess that up."

Penny slowly shrugged her shoulders and made a face that said, "so what?"

"I guess the most important thing would be that we're together," said Henry.

"I'd like that, too," Penny agreed and kissed his cheek. "Besides, you're not that big of a mess," Penny chided him.

Henry laughed. "If you say so."

"Think about all you've been through. You're getting stronger every day."

"True, my headaches are mostly gone, too," Henry added.

They hopped up off the bench and started strolling back to the park entrance, hand in hand.

Penny swung their arms. "You're also looking pretty good," she flirted.

"Oh, you think so, do you?" asked Henry, stretching taller.

"Yes, I do. Maybe there's a bright future for us after all. There's always hope!"

"Now you sound like my grandmother," quipped Henry.

"I'd better not!" Penny put her hands on her hips and scowled at him. Laughing, Henry tried to draw her back to him.

"Please?"

"Don't try to appease me with a hug! Besides, you'll never catch me. I'm still faster than you!"

Penny shrieked with delight and took off running into an open meadow meant for kids games.

Henry chased after her. They only ran a few yards and

plopped to the ground, laughing. Penny toppled onto him. They grabbed each other tightly and kissed. Turning over onto their stomachs, they stretched out, side by side, with their arms propping their chins.

"This seems vaguely familiar," said Henry.

Penny chuckled. "It does. Only you never kissed me back then."

"I wish I had. Guess I'll make up for that now."

Henry rolled onto his side and playfully tugged her close to him, kissing her neck where he knew she was ticklish. Penny howled in fake protest until Henry's lips reached hers, quashing her squeals with delight.

CHAPTER 14

"Should you be driving?" asked Kate as she walked out of her front door and gave Henry a generous hug.

"I still know how to drive," retorted Henry.

"Well, I hope your skills have improved a bunch," Kate teased him.

Henry nudged Kate gently with his shoulder as they walked side-by-side up to her door, knocking her off balance for a second.

"Have trouble walking?"

After a couple of steps, Kate leaned into Henry, retaliating. He didn't budge.

"Hmmm. Perfect reflexes, I'd say," taunted Henry.

Since his accident, Kate had become protective of Henry, to his dismay. Growing up as twins, they had settled into a see-saw relationship, continuously quibbling over roles. Who was older, who was younger? Who led, who followed? Which one was stronger, which one weaker?

Kate stopped and tugged Henry's arm, forcing him to face

her.

“Seriously, Henry. Did the doctor say you could drive?”

“Yes, I’m cleared.”

“No panic attacks?”

“No, Katie. You know I never have those. What happened before has nothing to do with my driving right now.”

“Well, I’d have them.”

“I bet you would.”

“Dad let you use the car?”

“Yes.”

They continued this banter as they entered the house. Kate led Henry to the kitchen table.

“I’m finishing up lunch. Want some?”

“No, I ate already. I’m going to grab a drink though,” said Henry. He walked to the refrigerator and took out a bottle of water.

“I have a couple of hours, then I need to take off to pick up the girls at daycare. What’s on your mind?”

“A couple of things. First, I want to apologize to you for all I’ve put you through.”

Kate stopped in her tracks and faced Henry.

“What are you talking about?” she asked, bewildered.

“You know, ‘Twin brother steals trade secrets and drives off cliff.’”

Kate sat down. “Oh, you mean, ‘What will the neighbors think?’”

“Exactly!” said Henry, as he pulled up a chair to the table. “I see how people look at me when I’m out and whisper.”

“Henry, you know me better than that. In fact, none of us

care," said Kate exasperatedly. "I don't understand why you do."

"It's not about me. I know I've no control over what other people think and speak. But I don't want my mess to bleed over to my family. It makes me angry."

Kate rested her chin on her palm, propped up by her elbow.

"I have to admit, it was tough at first. Only because everyone was asking so many questions. Mainly, they wanted to make sure you were okay. Anyone associated with Mom, Dad, and our family, and that includes you, knows better than to believe rumors. All our friends were so supportive. They were amazing."

"Well, I just had to say that."

"No, you didn't," Kate said strongly. "Besides, all those people have their own drama to deal with in their lives. Let it go."

Kate grabbed a piece of sandwich and waved it nonchalantly at Henry. "Now, what's the other thing you wanted to talk about?"

Biting into her sandwich, Kate's expression told Henry that the subject was closed. Henry remained silent as Kate ate the last few pieces of fruit on her plate. She rose and carried it over to the counter. Together, they moved into the family room.

"I need your help to arrange some things for me," said Henry finally. He sat down on the sofa next to his sister.

"You sound ominous. What things? Are you talking about last will and testament type things? Is there something you're not telling the rest of us?"

"No, nothing like that," Henry chuckled. "Physically, I'm doing really well."

"That's what I thought," agreed Kate. "What's going on?"

"I'm nervous about planning something, that's all. Penny is

between assignments and can take some time off. I want to see if she would go on a trip with me. I'd like to visit Fusion Lab."

"What? I'm sure Penny would love to go anywhere with you, but why there? I can think of a million alternatives," protested Kate.

"I'd like to see the Lab again."

"You mean to say goodbye?"

"Maybe. Sort of. There are some things I left in my office that need to be picked up, too."

"Won't a visit dredge up bad memories? You almost died there."

"But I didn't."

"Thank God," whispered Kate.

"Katie, I can honestly say I experienced some of the best and worst moments of my life there. I want to move on, but I also can't forget."

"I understand. Can't Alex or Sean go with you? I'd go if you can talk mom into helping Robby with the kids."

Henry took a swig of water before answering. "No, that wouldn't work."

"Can you even get in there?"

"According to Matt Granger, the Lab is closed down. They have some security people watching over the grounds. But everyone else transferred to Chemclone's facilities or left. It's vacant. I asked Chester Worthington if I could visit."

"Why don't you skip the Lab?" offered Kate, more an appeal than a question.

"Penny and I talk about the Lab a lot, and it'd be great for her to see the place for herself."

"I've seen it, Henry. It's a nice place, but I don't get the infatuation. Are you sure about this?"

"Yes." Henry tipped the bottle to his mouth and drank. After a few moments, he continued, "Whatever memories or emotions it drags up, I'd like Penny to be with me."

"Okay, I can understand that."

Kate tilted her head and thought for a while. "You know, I think you're right, Henry. I'm sure she feels like she's competing with an old girlfriend sometimes."

Henry laughed. "I can tell you two have been talking."

"Maybe," Kate chuckled.

Henry stood up and faced Kate.

"But that's only a small part of the trip. The Lab is along the way."

"Oh, good. I was hoping you had more exciting things planned than a visit to a lab," said Kate, sighing in relief.

"I do." Henry shifted his weight back and forth.

"Penny misses Europe. She told me how she'd visit the old castles over there whenever she could. She's enamored with them," Henry expressed with budding excitement. "Also, gardens. She loves gardens."

Kate nodded her head nonchalantly, her quizzical expression inviting additional details.

"I've checked out the Biltmore Mansion and the Arboretum south of there. I think they're the best options within driving distance. She'd love it. It could make the perfect setting. What do you think?" asked Henry, his hands upturned in expectation of agreement.

"I'm not sure," answered Kate slowly, certain she had not

gotten the whole story. "Setting for what?"

After some hesitation, she rose and grabbed Henry's shoulder. "What's going on here?"

Henry shrugged and made the face she had seen him do many times as a little boy.

They stared at each other, and then Kate's eyes grew wide.

"Oh, this is big!" she blurted. She threw her arms around him and hugged him tightly.

"You're going to ask her?"

"Yes."

Kate let go and dropped onto the sofa. "That's so romantic!" she said excitedly. Then her expression changed. "Well, maybe it is. Henry, you've thought this through?"

"How can you ask me that? You know me."

"I'm a little perplexed. Your life is unsettled. I mean, you're looking for a job and Penny's career is still evolving. I would've bet you'd wait for some clear answers there."

"That would make more sense," said Henry. He turned away with his hands on his hips, thinking.

He turned back around confidently and stood straighter. "I don't want to wait. I want to marry Penny, and she needs to know that. We can get engaged now and then plan the wedding. That would give us time to figure out our careers. In fact, I think that would make those decisions easier."

Kate stepped back and smiled at him affectionately. "Wow, Henry! Is that impulsiveness I'm hearing?"

"I don't see it that way. It's what I want to do. I need your help to make it work." Henry sat down, reached for his water, and looked up at his sister.

"Sorry," responded Kate. "What can I do?"

Relieved at his sister's response, Henry grew excited. "The first challenge is to surprise Penny. That'll be hard. She knows me pretty well by now."

"Just explain the trip to Fusion Lab and keep it at that. That'll be enough for her to wonder about. Now, can I say anything to anyone else?"

"I'd prefer you didn't. Of course, Robby is okay."

"Alex?"

"Absolutely not. You might as well tell everyone."

"What about a ring?" asked Kate excitedly.

"I already got it."

"Can I see it?" asked Kate expectantly.

"The jeweler is sizing it now. I need to pick it up."

"Did you guess on a size?"

"No, when I hold her hand, her ring finger is this big." Henry held up his hand and showed Kate the space between his two fingers. "Not exact, but I'm hoping it's close."

Kate laughed. "For someone who needs to be so precise in everything else, you're taking a chance there."

Henry laughed back. "I know. But I'm short on time. Let me tell you the trip details and get your opinion."

The two of them huddled together and brainstormed. About an hour later, Kate and Henry rose from the sofa.

"I need to get going," said Kate. She hugged Henry tightly. "This is awesome, Henry!"

"A little scary, too!"

"You and Penny belong together!" declared Kate.

"Yes, we do. But as you pointed out, there are some stumbling blocks ahead of us. I'm not sure what's left of my career and . . ."

"Blah, blah, blah," uttered Kate. She grasped Henry's hand and twirled around. "Love, passion, romance, enchantment! That's what you need!"

Henry rolled his eyes as his sister did a quick spin. After one turn, she hugged him, and they headed out the door.

The timing of Henry and Penny's road trip could not have been more perfect. The fall weather was dry and cool. Henry knew the science behind the changing of the leaves. Chlorophyll breaks down, green recedes, bright colors emanate, and then surrender to brown. But the manifestation of that process, splashed across millions of trees up and down the mountainside, was breathtaking.

It started at the mountain peaks. The heavens had tilted paint cans of various, vibrant colors, and the yellow, red, orange, green, and purple hues drizzled slowly on the mountain tops. There they blended, and each day seeped farther toward the valley floor. The allure to the eye was magnificent.

Henry had rented a full-sized SUV. They had plenty of room, and Henry would agree its size added a sense of safety and protection. For the first few days, they drove lazily, as they had no set timetable. Penny shared the driving as each wanted a turn at savoring the incredible beauty of the foliage. They talked easily, sketching out more highlights of their years apart and telling further anecdotes of the people they had met. Penny's stories captivated Henry. He was even content with the silence that settled between them at lulls in their conversation. Any awkwardness he had sometimes felt with others never emerged.

That morning, they descended from a higher elevation into the valley. As they drew near an intersection in the road, Henry glanced over at Penny. He patted her hand. "Here's where we start our detour," he said as he turned the steering wheel in the new direction.

They drove for the next hour in quiet, each absorbed in thought. Soon, the tall trees separated, and a town appeared in the distance. The road widened into four lanes. Henry's foot on the gas pedal lifted imperceptibly. He scanned the streets as the traffic picked up and pedestrians strolled along the sidewalks. After a few turns, they pulled into an outsized cul-de-sac outlined by townhomes. He stopped in front of one.

"That," he pointed, "used to be my house."

"It's cute!" answered Penny. "It looks perfect for you."

"It was. Before the wafer days. But we got so busy, I was never there. I stayed up at the Lab."

"You're not sorry you sold it?" asked Penny.

"No, I needed the money, and I know I'd never live there again. It's all good."

Henry put the car in gear. They toured through the little town and Henry pointed out various significant spots, those that had special meaning for him. Approaching another intersection, Henry pointed to a sign. It announced in large letters the direction of Fusion Lab.

"Okay, let's go check out the Lab," Henry breathed and aimed the car up the hill.

Neither spoke as they weaved up the incline. About halfway there, Henry looked both in front and back. No one else was in sight. He stopped the car. Turning his head, he peered at an opening between the guardrails that led out onto a ledge. Penny realized where they were and gently grabbed Henry's arm.

"That's where you . . ." she began, but didn't finish her question.

"Yes, I'd like to drive out there, if you wouldn't mind," responded Henry.

"Are you sure?"

"Yes."

"Okay, then."

Henry guided the car through the scarred guardrail. Its tires crawled and crunched across the gravel plateau and toward the edge.

"They've added a barricade," said Henry.

He stopped the car midway from the opening to the edge of the cliff, put it in park, and turned off the ignition. Henry pointed to the newly installed rock and steel railings along the fringe of the plateau.

"Wish they'd done that a little sooner, although I'd have hated to run into that boulder there at the speed I was going."

Penny remained silent. She unbuckled her seatbelt and moved close to Henry. She grasped his hand and leaned her body against his. They stared out into the horizon, where the changing trees outlined the blue water of the lake below them.

"It's actually beautiful, isn't it?" he asked.

Penny didn't reply. She tenderly squeezed his hand.

Henry chuckled for a few seconds. "People keep making jokes about me driving off this cliff."

"Does that bother you?" Penny asked, not sure what to say.

"It did at first. Now, I see the humor. It helps me."

"It helps us, too, Henry, being able to laugh at something so scary. I'm so happy and relieved you're still here."

Penny reached over and gently turned Henry's face toward her. Answering her loving smile, Henry kissed her. Huddled next to each other, they were silent.

"See that sandy patch of shoreline way over there?" Henry asked. He pointed to the left. "That must be where they fished me out. Yes, I can see the Fish and Wildlife access road there."

Penny nodded.

"You know, no one's asked me if I remember anything," mused Henry.

"We're all curious, I admit. But we agreed it's not appropriate. We don't want to trigger any painful memories for you. You've been through enough."

"Even Alex? We know how inappropriate he can be," chuckled Henry. Penny covered her mouth as she pretended to hide her own laughter.

After a few moments, Henry continued, "I clearly remember everything up to this spot, right here. After that, I'm not sure."

They were lost in their thoughts for a while.

"It paralyzed me with fear when I was falling. It's hard to describe. When I hit the water, everything went dark."

Henry paused and closed his eyes. His instinct to blot out every memory battled his desire to remember every detail.

"I had a conversation, it seems. Someone was there to help me. Maybe Jesus. I couldn't say for sure, but I think so."

Penny could sense how difficult this was. She leaned closer against Henry, grasped his arm, and placed it around her waist.

"I was so tired and wanted to give up. I clearly remember

the despair and hopelessness." Henry shuddered. "He gave me courage, though. I had to fight. I chose to fight."

Henry then turned to Penny. "The next I remember, I heard you singing in my room." He squeezed her gently.

Penny smiled. "I was thumbing through a photo album your mom had brought and was reminiscing. I didn't realize I was singing. I hadn't sung that song since we were little."

"I'm happy you did!" Henry exclaimed as he leaned into Penny and kissed her lovingly.

Nestled against each other, lost in thoughts, neither wanted the moment to end. Henry finally announced, "We'd better get going. Lukas is waiting for us." Henry squeezed Penny's hand as she smiled at him and shifted back to her seat. "Let's get to the Lab. Believe it or not, I miss that place."

They buckled their seatbelts. Henry backed the car into a wide turn, maneuvered through the opening in the guardrail, and continued out onto the road.

"Henry! It's great to see you!" shouted Lukas.

Lukas had met them at the gate and was waiting in his truck. He had hopped out and bounded over to Henry's car. He gave Henry an enormous hug. Penny slipped out of the car and smiled at Lukas. Before Henry could introduce them, Lukas hugged Penny.

"This must be Penny! I've heard a lot about you. You're as pretty as I was told."

"Who have you been talking with?" asked Henry, bemused.

"Alex and Sean. They gave me the scoop on you two. Let me say I approve," admitted Lukas.

"Who else!" scowled Henry. Penny and Lukas laughed, and all three hugged again.

"Follow me up to the courtyard. We can sit out there and catch up." Lukas didn't wait for an answer, but walked toward his truck and motioned for Henry and Penny to do the same.

They trailed Lukas up the entrance road toward the outdoor courtyard. Penny breathed out quickly as she studied the various buildings they passed.

"Henry, this is incredible! Look at those huge girders. Did Ted Granger do all this?"

"Yes, he spent a small fortune restoring these buildings. Most are facades leading up to the compound. But the Lab buildings are completely restored and functioning."

Penny gawked at the landscape. They soon approached what looked like a railroad crossing. Penny pointed to it and was about to question Henry when the lights lit up and began blinking on and off. A bell sounded a warning. Lukas didn't bother to brake, and Henry followed him over the tracks. The lights and the bell ceased.

"What was that?" asked a startled Penny.

Henry laughed. "That's also Ted's doing. It was an old crossing back in the day. Ted had it refurbished to working order. It goes off anytime a vehicle approaches. He forewarned guests of the Lab, but Ted liked to tease a few of his friends."

They parked in the spaces in front of the administrative building, and Lukas led them across the path to the courtyard. He had a small picnic spread laid out on the table. They gathered around it and chose some chairs.

"I thought you may be hungry. There's nothing around here

in the way of food. You'd need to go back down into the valley."

"Yes, we are. I didn't think about that," said Henry.

"The commissary is closed and empty. It's mighty quiet around here, Henry." Lukas offered Penny and Henry a beer or soda from a cooler.

"I'm sorry about that, Lukas," muttered Henry.

"Not your fault. They keep me on to watch over the grounds. Everyone else moved on. Even Rhonda. She asks about you."

"I do miss everyone. I miss this place." Henry looked out over the courtyard and sighed.

"You're looking good, Henry. I wasn't sure what to expect. My wife and I've been praying for you."

"Thanks, Lukas. It's helped tremendously."

"I think so! You appear to be healthier now than before you left," said Lukas, smiling broadly.

"Surprisingly so," admitted Henry.

"Now tell me, Penny, what do you think of Henry here?" inquired Lukas.

Penny laughed. "He's okay. A decent traveling companion."

Lukas chuckled. "Keep an eye on him. Don't let him drive you off any cliffs."

Penny hesitated and saw Henry and Lukas look at each other. All three laughed. After more small talk, Lukas stood up and began packing up the remains of their lunch.

"I unlocked the buildings. You know your way around here. Stay as long as you want."

"I'm going to show Penny the campus, and then we need to head back down. We want to get to Asheville tonight."

"If you leave me your key, I'll load those boxes from your

office into your car for you. That's a nice SUV!"

"That'd be a big help, Lukas. I never made it back to get everything. I'm surprised it's still here."

Henry tossed his key to Lukas. Grabbing it out of the air, Lukas held it up and smiled. "I'll leave you two alone now. Call me on my cell when you're ready to clear out."

After Lukas left, Penny and Henry finished their drinks and soaked in the view before them.

"Henry, this is gorgeous. Look at that skyline. I see why you loved it here."

"Yes. Great memories." Henry reached for Penny's hand and held it.

They enjoyed more of the view and then Henry spoke up. "Let's see the facility. I'll show you my office and the lab room where most of the work on the wafer happened. We can swing by the cottage I called home."

They picked up a few remaining belongings and started down the walkway.

"First, let me show you the other side of the campus."

They trekked down a winding road until they approached the old railroad cemetery. Wordlessly, Henry and Penny strolled onto the landscaped paths that led to Ted Granger's grave.

"He was a great man," Henry finally stated as they stood together.

"I wish I could've met him," said Penny softly.

After a few more minutes, Henry tugged on Penny's hand and they meandered back up the hilly path. They reached an outlook area that presented the opposite side view of the mountain from where they had lunch.

"It's so incredible!" exhaled Penny.

"Yes, it is," agreed Henry. "The Lab owns this entire mountainside. Ted wanted to develop part of it. If he were still alive, I'd probably be living in a house right over there." Henry pointed off to a tree-filled nest of hills.

"I could be persuaded," sighed Penny, offhandedly.

"Oh, really?" asked Henry. He grinned at her with an impish look.

They both laughed.

After returning to the main campus, Henry guided Penny through the buildings he remembered as so vibrant, now silent. They drifted from the cottage to the administrative building and then to the Lab research areas, retracing steps that Henry had walked countless times. He talked endlessly, adding layers of details, filling in any gaps in the stories he had told Penny before.

For Penny, the tour gave substance to the vague pictures she had formed during her many conversations with Henry. She could now see him clearly seated at his desk, poring over reports. She could envision Ted bursting into Henry's office, and the research team huddled over the equipment in the Lab.

Evening approached, and they returned to the veranda. Henry pushed two wooden lounge chairs close together, and they rested from all their walking. The sun had begun its slow, certain roll over the hills. The glowing, blended colors of the peaks appeared like a vast bowl of ripening apricots.

Penny reached for Henry's hand and held it. "Thank you," she whispered. "This was amazing. I had no idea."

"I'm glad you think so. I have to admit, it's bittersweet."

"I haven't seen you so animated. You really care about this place, don't you?"

"So much of my adult life happened right here. It's hard to see it go."

Penny squeezed his hand slightly. "You said you had to fight before. Maybe you still do."

"What do you mean?" asked Henry, leaning forward in his seat.

"This place is a gem. There must be something that can be done."

Henry settled back and thought.

"Last time Matt spoke to Chester, he said the bank has everything frozen. The wafer's in production testing, and all that is being done by Chemclone. They've moved everything there. Fusion Lab is no longer needed."

Penny placed her hand on Henry's arm. "I know that still stings," she said gently.

"It does," agreed Henry. "They finished it without me."

"I'm sorry, Henry," said Penny. "I didn't mean to bring all that up and spoil our day."

"No, don't apologize. I now have you in my life. That's well worth it to me."

"I'm happy to hear that!" said Penny, squeezing his arm.

Henry drew in a deep breath and slowly exhaled. "Since my accident, I've avoided any involvement with Fusion Lab as much as possible." He paused, and with a smirk added, "Well, until I had the bright idea to visit here."

They both chuckled.

Penny waved her arm. "I see all this, and I don't understand.

This is so much more than the typical lab I'd envisioned. How could the bank not comprehend the value here?"

Henry forced a bitter laugh. "My frustration for the last two years!"

Penny hesitated, unsure if she should push the matter further. "Wouldn't some investors be interested?"

Henry remembered having the same thoughts. He raised a leg, crossed it onto his other one, and shifted toward Penny.

"The problem is the Lab is so remote. As you can see, access is very difficult, given the distance from major roads and airports." Henry waved an arm outward to the view. "Even all this land has minimal value for most. That's why the railroad had happily sold it to Ted at such a bargain price."

Henry sighed loudly and folded his arms.

"I guess it could be worth exploring again. It's just, I'm not sure it's my fight anymore. I feel I'm ready for a new start. In fact, I was hoping our visit here would help close this episode of my life."

"I understand what you're saying," began Penny. "But I'm not sure I agree. Maybe while things are at a standstill, with the bank and trustees at a truce, an opportunity could pop up." Penny rearranged her legs and tilted her weight onto her side, facing directly at Henry. "Would it be worth it to make some inquiries?"

"I don't want to get sucked up into that again."

"I'm not suggesting that," countered Penny. "The thought of this place crumbling into ruins is so sad. There's got to be a better outcome."

"What've I done?" Henry grinned and sat up. He lightly

squeezed Penny's thigh. "I now have you enchanted with this place."

"I am." Penny placed her hand on his.

Henry beamed. He took Penny's hand, pulled her up, and wrapped his arms around her. "I'll give Chester a call when we get home. I guess there's always hope."

Henry heard his name called.

"I hate to break this up, but I need to lock up. Did everything go okay?" asked Lukas as he approached.

"Yes, thanks, Lukas. Many splendid memories here."

"No thanks, necessary. I'm glad to get the chance to see you. All of us were very worried about you."

"I'm good now," insisted Henry.

"Make sure you stay that way," Lukas scowled, and gave Henry a hug. He turned to Penny and hugged her, too. "I'm going to keep praying for you, Henry. And for this place, too. I can't stop agonizing about what'll become of it."

"I appreciate the prayers. You're a great friend."

"I'm going to call Alex as soon as you leave. I need to tell him he and Sean are right. You and Penny are perfect for each other." He winked at Penny.

Penny blushed, and Henry laughed.

"Bye, Lukas. We'll stay in touch."

Henry and Penny walked to their car and settled in. Lukas did the same and followed them as far as the entrance gate. Waving, they turned onto the main road.

CHAPTER 15

The following three days were occupied by driving and sightseeing. Determined to experience as many new venues as possible, Penny and Henry pushed themselves to near exhaustion. But it was a happy, contented one. They devoted an entire day to touring the Biltmore Estate and its beautiful surroundings. Next, they headed to the gardens at the Arboretum.

"Look at those mums!" exclaimed Penny. She stopped midstep and scanned the incredible display, now on all sides of her. "I love them! There's so many! Let's go over there so we can see them better." Penny tugged on Henry's arm as if to drag him down the narrow path.

Henry laughed. "You go on ahead. My legs are a little sore from all of those steps at the Biltmore."

Penny quickly paused and turned back to Henry. "I'm sorry," she giggled. "I got carried away." She squeezed his hand and smiled. "Thank you again for arranging that private tour yesterday. And for letting me ask so many questions! I know I wore her out."

"No, she was just as excited as you to talk about the history of the house and the people who lived there."

"It was fascinating! I loved it!" Penny exclaimed, turning away from Henry and nearly skipping as she bounded ahead.

Henry laughed.

After some amazed wandering, they found a small alcove on the outskirts of the exhibits. Somewhat private, a trellis covered in sparse, twisted branches guarded a round table and bench. Although the air was crisp, the sun's rays enveloped them in a warm, cozy embrace.

Penny sighed as she scanned the colorful patterns of flowers and trees and watched as the other visitors strolled by. "Henry, this is magnificent. I never dreamed of anything like this. It's perfect. I'm having the best time on this trip!"

"I was hoping you'd say that. I was afraid you might get tired of me," Henry joked.

Penny put her arms around Henry. "That's not possible!"

Henry took the backpack off and opened it. Digging inside, he pulled out a small bottle of wine and some cheese and crackers.

"I know this isn't Paris, Santorini, Vienna, or any of the other places in Europe you love so much," said Henry, "but let's have a snack and pretend."

He opened the bottle and poured the red liquid into two small glasses. They toasted to their fun time and ate while they talked, savoring the brilliant, colorful expanse in front of them.

"Tell me what you're thinking about," asked Henry, as he gathered up the remnants of their snack and stuffed the wrapping into the backpack. He then sat back.

Drawn out of her reverie, Penny leaned back against the bench with Henry. "About you." She placed her hand on his forearm. "You've done all this for me. Thank you for bringing me here. I love you for that."

"You know, I'm surprised at how much I've enjoyed it. This place really is beautiful!" He grabbed Penny's hand and smiled. "So, how about we make a pact that we'll always do things like this?"

"You mean pinky swear, like we did when we were kids?" Penny chuckled.

"I was thinking of something a little more substantial."

Taking a deep breath, Henry shifted his weight away from Penny and, with his free arm, brought the backpack closer. A brief look of worry flashed across Penny's face. Henry leaned further and snatched a small box from the knapsack. He laid it on the table.

Watching Penny's face, Henry grinned broadly. He felt her hand grip his tightly as her wide eyes moved from the table and locked lovingly onto his. He tenderly grabbed her other hand.

"Penny Stevens, I love you. I always have. I never want to be apart from you again."

Henry slowly slipped from the bench onto one knee and opened the box. A ring sparkled out from the soft felt.

"Will you marry me?"

Penny gasped. She nodded vigorously, unable to speak.

"Yes," she breathed at last.

Henry grasped her hand and slid the ring on her finger. As he casually stood up, he pulled Penny to her feet and wrapped his arms around her. Penny nestled her head against his until their delighted eyes met, and they eagerly kissed.

"I love you, Henry," whispered Penny.

"I love you, too."

They leaned their heads together again and looked across the field of color. Both thought about the crazy, convoluted journey that led them to this moment. Both sighed a contented, gratified breath that they had found each other.

"I'm so happy," said Penny.

"Me, too." Henry agreed.

His lips then caught Penny's for a long, loving kiss.

The bliss of the trip blended into the fun and anticipation of telling friends and family. Once headed back home, Penny and Henry tallied the names.

"So, how do we do this, Henry? I don't want to offend anyone." Penny had a pen and pad of paper resting on her lap.

"Well, your mom and dad already know. I called them before we left."

"Thank you for doing that!" she exclaimed, smiling at Henry.

"I was worried that they would want us to wait. For all the reasons we already discussed."

"Well, I appreciate you asking them, but we can make our own decisions."

"I know. I like traditions, though. I wanted to get their blessing. It didn't matter, they were thrilled."

Penny patted Henry's leg and then lifted the pen. "Okay, let's cross them off."

"Kate knows. She helped with some of the planning. Also,

my mom and dad. My dad was with me when I asked my doctor to allow the long drive. Dad knew I was up to something. I walked him through our itinerary, just in case."

"Good!" said Penny. She made another scratching sound on the pad. "We need to call Adrianna, Clara, and my other friends over there. And Alex and Sean."

With their cell phones paired to the car audio system, they progressed down the list. Everyone was delighted. No one seemed surprised.

The calls completed, Penny and Henry returned to the surrounding sights, retracing their trip there. In the stretch of the long week, the vibrant colors had escaped from the mountains. Millions of brownish leaves now drizzled to the ground, filling the air with the crisp smells of fall.

The night before Penny was due to fly back home, the small group of friends gathered at Kate's house to say goodbye. Penny and Henry huddled close together on the sofa with Kate at the other end. Robby sat on the floor, leaning against Kate's legs. Sean slumped into a couch with his feet propped up on an ottoman. Alex sprawled out on the floor with a large throw pillow under his head. They were facing the TV on the wall, but none were watching. Most were sipping from glasses of wine or beer.

"Sean, I'm so glad I got to meet your girlfriend," said Penny. "She fits right in with this motley crew."

Sean laughed. "Yeah, I warned Angie about everyone."

"Well, I hope we get to see her again soon."

"She had to work this weekend but made me promise to bring her back next time you're here," Sean assured Penny.

"Angie wants to talk to you more about Europe. She'd like to visit there sometime."

"I'd love that!" said Penny.

The group was silent for a few minutes. Eventually, Alex raised his head and looked over at Henry. "So, what's next?"

"What do you mean?" asked Henry.

"When's the wedding date?"

Henry and Penny glanced at each other. "We're not sure. It's complicated."

"How?" asked Alex.

"For one thing, I'd like to at least have a job before we get married," said Henry calmly.

"Why?" persisted Alex.

Henry grew irritated and sat forward. "This concerns Penny and me. We're not asking for your advice."

"I'm just saying you don't need to wait for your circumstances to be perfect. I know you, Henry. Do you have a wedding project outline yet?"

A tinge of anger lit Henry's eyes and he stiffened. Penny put her hand over her face as she laughed. She couldn't hide or suppress it, and shortly the rest joined in.

Henry shook his head. Yes, Alex did know him and how to best goad him. It bothered Henry that Alex was right. But gradually, the humor of the remarks sunk in, and Henry smiled. He grabbed the pillow next to him and tossed it at Alex, hitting him on the side of the head, causing even more commotion.

As the laughter dwindled, Henry leaned back into the sofa. "We considered eloping."

"Don't you dare!" blurted out Kate.

"Relax, Katie. Penny nixed that right away. She wants her family, as well as all of you, there. It'll take some time, but we'll manage."

"I might have an option for you," said Alex.

"WE might have an option for you," corrected Sean.

"Yes, Sean and I talked about this."

"It was my idea," interrupted Sean.

"But I verified it," scowled Alex.

"For heaven's sake, what are you talking about?" demanded Kate as she put her hands on Robby's shoulders and leaned forward.

"We've been doing some work for one of our clients," said Alex. "He has a small resort over in the Bahamas. It's being remodeled. Our crew has been shuttling back and forth, and Sean and I were there a month ago."

"It has a group of cottages surrounding a large restaurant," added Sean. "I was describing it to Angie, and she remarked it would be a perfect wedding location."

"So, it was Angie's idea," Kate pointed out.

"That's not important," insisted Alex. "The guy said we can use it. What do you think?"

Henry and Penny looked at each other. Henry shrugged his shoulders.

Penny's face lit up. "That would be wonderful!"

"Talk it over and we'll see if it works," said Sean.

"The challenge will be getting everyone over there," said Alex. "Of course, as your Best Man, I'll take care of that. We're talking May. That's when the renovation will be done, and he then wants to prepare for hurricane season."

"As what?" asked both Kate and Henry together.

"Best Man," Alex repeated.

"God help us!" moaned Kate.

"Seems like I have no say in this," said Henry resignedly.

"I've never been out of the country. Is it safe over there?" asked Kate.

"Yes, very," insisted Alex. "Don't worry, Robby will keep you safe."

"I can take care of myself. Remember the time I saved you guys?"

"What are you talking about?" asked Henry.

"We were playing in that little park and those three boys came up and told us to leave. They said it was their park. Of course, Alex called them a few names, and they grabbed both of you."

"I do vaguely remember that," said Henry.

"I told them to get lost and showed them my Ninja moves. They ran away," said Kate proudly.

"Your Ninja moves?" asked Sean.

"Yes, don't mess with me," chuckled Kate.

"Katie, do you remember Sean walking up behind you?" asked Henry.

"Yes. But it was my moves that scared them," insisted Kate.

"Even back then, Sean was a foot taller than the rest of us," Henry pointed out. They all laughed.

"Where did you get these moves?" asked Penny.

"Henry and I used to watch this show on TV. Then we would fight each other. I'd always win because I was more agile."

Henry turned to Penny, rolled his eyes, and made a face.

"So, Henry has Ninja moves?" Penny asked.

"Sure, come on, let's show her."

Kate stood up and moved toward Henry on the sofa. She made chopping motions with her hands and let out a "hiyaa!"

"How many glasses of wine have you had?" asked Henry.

"Two. Don't worry, Robby is the designated parent tonight."

Robby raised his arm over his head and waved.

"Come on, let's show them," she tried again.

"You're not getting me off this sofa," answered Henry.

Kate made a few more noises and chops, twirled, and kicked out her leg. Her sandal flew off and hit Alex on the nose.

"Ow!" he howled and rubbed the sore spot. The rest of them erupted in laughter. "Would you Taylors stop throwing things at me?"

He reached down for the sandal and lightly tossed it back.

"Sorry, Alex. Do you need some ice for that?" asked Kate.

"No, it's fine," he grumbled.

"You do understand I'm not a Taylor anymore, don't you?"

"I guess you're right. Robby, what were you thinking?" quizzed Alex.

"I know what he was thinking," answered Kate. She began her Ninja moves again in front of Robby, only slowly and slyly.

"Oh my God," squawked Alex. "Robby, as the designated parent, can you please cut her off?"

The group laughed and then settled down.

"Tell us about this resort and what the Bahamas are like," suggested Robby, changing the subject.

"I'll text you the website link and you can check it out," responded Alex. "Henry, you and Penny discuss it. If you're sure, I'll give the client a call."

"Okay," said Penny and Henry together.

"It's beautiful over there. Let me tell you about it."

Their excitement grew as Alex described his experience. Sean, too, recounted his adventure. For the next few hours, the group swapped many more stories before they reluctantly said goodnight.

With dinner over, Penny and her parents hastily cleaned up the dishes and cleared off the kitchen table. While Mr. Stevens refilled their drinks, Penny's mom set an accordion folder marked "wedding" in the middle of the table. The three of them sat down.

Sitting beside Penny, Mrs. Stevens patted the folder. "Now Penny, before we get any further into this, your father and I have some questions for you."

Penny looked from one to the other and took a sip from her glass. "What's up?"

"We want to make sure you're okay with this Bahamas wedding," said her dad.

"Yes," said her mother. "You've always talked about a big, church wedding."

Penny shifted in her chair. "Truthfully, a year ago, I would've told you my wedding would be at a magnificent old church in Europe somewhere. If not, then possibly our church here in Atlanta. And yes, all my extended relatives and friends would be there. I'd always imagined a bigger wedding."

"That has your mother very concerned. What changed? Is it the cost? Your mother and I planned on paying for your wedding, wherever it is."

"Henry and I talked about this. The cost is a factor. That's why we'd planned to wait longer. Henry's accident has been a severe financial burden on his family. Apparently, when Henry resigned from Fusion Lab, the bank canceled his insurance benefits. Henry's attorney is involved, but it's a mess for now."

"My goodness!" said Mrs. Taylor.

"Henry and I don't want to put any more burden on them. But be honest, Mom, are you disappointed? I know you'd like to invite all the family, and your friends from church." Penny choked up. "You both were so supportive of my move to Europe. I know it was hard. I don't want to let you down."

"Penny, no. Don't worry about me. What do YOU want?"

"I promise you, Mom, I'm thrilled with the Bahamas. Henry and I both are. It's an amazing opportunity. We're pinching ourselves!"

Mrs. Stevens suddenly leaned into Penny and hugged her. "I'm so happy you said that! I had to be sure!"

"Really? You were testing me?" asked Penny.

"Yes, I'm sorry."

"You're okay with the Bahamas, then?"

"Of course!" Her mother pulled a handful of paper out of the folder. "Penny, look at these pictures. It's gorgeous!"

Mr. Stevens laughed and pointed to his wife. "She's been talking about this place all week. Your mother has screenshots of most of it there in that folder!"

Penny looked back and forth at them and then shook her head. "You two!"

Mrs. Stevens opened the binder's flap again and drew out

more sheets of paper. "Now Alex gave us the contact information for the resort manager. Your father's already spoken to him. We'll need to cover the food, drinks, and DJ. Everything else is provided."

"According to Alex, getting there is a challenge. He's going to handle that," said Mr. Stevens. "Alex also gave us the name and number of a friend of his, Cubby. Apparently, Cubby and his family have lived in Abaco their entire lives. Alex said that if we need anything, Cubby will know where to get it."

Penny nodded that she understood and turned towards her mother. Penny's mom hunched her shoulders in excitement and grabbed a batch of cards bound by a rubber band. She thumbed through the colorful pages. "I found these wedding invitations. Aren't they tropical looking?"

Penny took a sip of her drink. She could sense her own enthusiasm now racing to catch up with her mom's. "Are you sure we need to send invitations? It's a small group."

"Of course!" said Mrs. Steven. After a pause, she added, "Now, you have the final say, though."

Penny laughed. "Thanks!"

"Okay," said Penny's father. He patted the kitchen table and rose. "I'm going to let the two of you get busy. You've got a lot of decisions to make, and I've got the feeling most don't involve me." He walked around the table. Penny stood and gave her dad a huge hug.

Penny spent the next few hours with her mom, excitedly sorting through ideas and exploring possibilities. Her mom brought her laptop over to the table so they could research each one. With each decision they made, Penny grew more elated with anticipation of a fabulous time.

When Penny next visited Henry, she found him down in the basement of the Taylor house, sorting through the boxes they had brought back from Fusion Lab. Mr. Taylor had protested when Henry asked him to help carry them back down. "I thought I'd finally gotten rid of them!"

The boxes were now empty. Aside from a trash bag of discarded papers, Henry had arranged the remaining items on a folding table. He was browsing through his old notebooks, shaking his head.

"Anything interesting?" Penny asked as she drew up behind him and wrapped her arms around him. Henry turned, and they kissed.

"I guess I'm surprised at some of these experiments. Some are downright impressive."

"I have to admit, I have this troubling visual of you and Alex down here in white lab coats, holding up vials of liquid, your hair sticking out."

Henry laughed. "Maybe Alex's hair. Mine would be neat and combed." He put the notepad down and reached for another.

"What's that big pile there?"

"Oh, you don't want to see that one."

"I don't, huh?" Penny stepped to the table and grabbed a folder. "Bricklebutter Project," she read and opened it.

"Yes, the source of our first big squabble. I'm sure we'll have others, but I don't want to relive that one."

Penny laughed. "It's pretty funny when you think about it."

"Not for me at the time," Henry raised his eyebrows.

"Me either," admitted Penny. She put the folder on the table and looked around. "How about all this other stuff?"

"Over there," pointed Henry, "are old posters from my room and Kate's room. My mom wants to save them."

"Oh, I remember those!" she dashed over and started flipping through them. "Look at these!"

Henry joined her and they laughed as they held up various placards.

"What's this little one?"

"That is my one and only patent," said Henry with a flourish. "Alex's father had our bricklebutter formula patented. He was so proud of Alex."

"You should be proud! You need to get this framed."

"You're right, I should. It's now and forever part of the wafer formula."

"And it's patented?" gasped Penny.

Henry gaped at her, unable to speak. This patent might be a legal and genuine claim on the wafer.

"How could I miss that?" he finally stammered.

"Do you think it's still valid?" asked Penny.

"I believe they're good for twenty years. Based on the date here," Henry paused and held the paper closer so he could better read it. "We have two years to go. I need to call Chester."

"Here, take a photo with my cell. You can text it to him. Maybe you'll get some kind of credit for the wafer after all."

"Could be. Let's see what Chester says." Henry wrapped his arms around Penny. "I'm glad you snooped through my stuff!"

Laughing together, Henry led them in a slow twirl, and they headed up the stairs.

A month later, late in the afternoon, Henry received a panicked call from Matt Granger.

"I just heard from Chester Worthington with some troubling news," began Matt. "The underwriters moved up the date for Solidane's public offering in New York. It might be awkward for you."

It was Ted Granger's fatal heart attack that was the catalyst that set the forces in motion for the power struggle and subsequent public offering of Solidane. With Henry out of the picture, Hyatt Emerson shepherded the wafer project through its final stages. Now that a viable wafer product was ready, the investment bankers pressed to get the company shares available to the public. Interest from pension funds, institutions, and wire houses was intense.

Henry did his best to avoid the topic, but word of the public offering was everywhere. Without fail, every prospective employer would ask Henry about his role at Fusion Lab and the relationship to Solidane. It would leave Henry justifying his time there to skeptical faces or voices. It drained him.

"I've been doing my best to block it out. Why should it be a problem? When is it?" asked Henry.

"The Friday before the wedding."

Henry sighed. After a few moments, he spoke.

"You know, Matt, I'm not going to let it bother me. I'll call Penny and tell her. We'll talk and decide what to do. I doubt it will make any difference to her. She's so excited about the wedding, and I'm not going to disappoint her."

"Good. I'm glad to hear that," said Matt. "I thought you

should know, though."

Henry paused before asking, "What does this mean for you? An initial public stock offering is a big deal. Isn't your family invited?"

"Yes, and I know Mom will definitely go to represent Dad. But I'm not missing your wedding! Don't let that be a factor."

"I appreciate that," answered Henry. "You shouldn't be in this predicament. Seems like Solidane is a black cloud that won't let me alone."

Matt sought a way to cheer his friend. "Chester also said he's still working on a solution for Fusion Lab. He doesn't want to get our hopes up yet, but he's determined to work something out with the bank."

"Chester's the best. I'm sure he'll figure out something."

"Has he said anything about the patent you found?" asked Matt.

"He's still investigating. But Alex and I have signed over permission for him to file any legal claims he thinks might help. It's a long shot, but who knows."

"I'm hoping something comes of it. You deserve it. Let me know if any of the wedding plans change after you talk to Penny," said Matt. "I know she's finishing up the install training in Chicago. Is she still due back tomorrow?"

"Yes, I talked to her last night. The last class was yesterday, and she had some follow-up meetings today. She said it went very well, but she'll be happy to get back home."

"The word around here is that she's been doing a fantastic job since the merger. I'm sorry she's traveling so much, but everyone is asking for her. "

"She's amazing!" beamed Henry. "Thanks for calling me, Matt. Can't wait to see you, Connie, and Marie at the wedding."

Henry opened the favorites on his phone and touched Penny's name. He had hoped to leave a message, and it surprised him when she answered.

"Hi, hon," Penny said hurriedly.

"Hey! I'm surprised I caught you."

"Believe it or not, we're done. I'm headed up to my hotel room. If I get my report filed in time, I should be able to get an earlier flight."

"Great! I'm sure your mom will be happy to have you home sooner. Sounds like you have a lot to do for the wedding."

Henry filled her in on his call with Matt.

"I don't mean to be bitter, Henry, but right now, I couldn't care less what happens with Solidane. I'd like to forget all about them." Penny breathed faster as she walked. "It's you I'm concerned about if it overshadows our wedding. Does this change anything for you?"

"No, not at all. I'm kind of at the same place you are. I can't wait to be married to you, and I don't care about any distractions, interruptions, or complications."

"Me, too, Henry. I love you."

"Yes," said Henry excitedly, "Let's do this! I love you, too."

Part Four

SO, LAUGH AND DANCE AND SING AND SHOUT

CHAPTER 16

Henry woke in a murky contentedness. His alarm had gone off a while ago, and rather than hopping out of bed, he had rolled from his side onto his back, yawned, and leisurely stretched his arms into the air. With a satisfied sigh, he pondered when he had last felt so relaxed and happy. He couldn't remember.

He scanned the contours of the beach cottage, with its half-opened windows facing the blue, teal, and turquoise waters of the Atlantic Ocean. Henry's ears soon registered the sound of waves breaking methodically on the beach.

Henry hastily rubbed his eyes and glanced at the clock. He had to get going. He slid out of the comfort of the bed. Hoping to shake off his sluggishness, he splashed some cold water on his face and then buried it in a towel. Grabbing a swimsuit and a many-pocketed fishing shirt, Henry quickly shaved, showered, and wrestled with his clothes.

He was headed for the door when he heard a knock, followed

by Alex's voice. "Come on, Henry, let's go!"

Alex raised his fist, knocked twice again, and was ready to call out Henry's name when the door opened.

"Finally," said Alex.

"What's your rush?" grumbled Henry as he exited and shut the door behind him.

"We're supposed to leave in fifteen minutes," answered Alex with an emphatic wave of his hand. "You're getting married tomorrow. This is your last day, and we're going to make the most of it."

Alex, Sean, and Robby ended up at Henry's door at the same moment. The plan was to meet Penny's younger brother and her father at the charter boat down at the dock.

All six were going deep sea fishing. Alex believed this was exactly what Henry needed. A well-outfitted charter boat with an experienced and highly regarded captain. Thirty to forty miles off the coast. No cell reception. No news. No reason to even bother about the events that were unfolding, even now, at 11 Wall Street, downtown Brooklyn, home to the New York Stock Exchange. And if Chester Worthington's careful planning succeeded, today might be quite the day, not only here in Abaco, but possibly even in the Big Apple.

"Tell me again where we are?" Henry sleepily joked as the four men walked down a potholed path that led from the cottage to a lot with a dozen golf carts.

"You're in the Bahamas, Henry," answered Alex sarcastically. "This tiny island is called Hopetown. A perfect name because you have none."

Henry slowed his walk to almost a stop. "None of what?"

he asked.

Alex maintained his pace, then turned, and Henry watched the grin spread across his face. "Hope, that's what," said Alex.

All four of them laughed. Alex took advantage of any opening to now rib Henry about his wedding and "the end of Henry's freedom as we knew it."

Henry jogged a few steps and caught up to them. "Really? Are you kidding? Right now, all I have is hope," Henry said, smiling. "I hope Penny shows up tomorrow!"

They laughed again, and Alex glanced at Henry as he drew beside him. Alex saw the laughter briefly drain from Henry's face as the memory of the events of the last two years flashed back. Gratefully, after a few long seconds, Henry's thoughts returned to the present, and the smile was back.

"I guess I'm up for a boat ride," quipped Henry. He turned his head toward Alex and waited for a reaction.

"For crying out loud, Henry. It's not a boat ride. We're going deep sea fishing!"

"Okay, but I've never even caught a fish before," Henry chuckled.

The four squeezed into one cart and Alex drove them down to the harbor inlet.

"Coffee! I smell coffee!" said Henry excitedly and sprung out of the cart. He followed his nose to a fair-sized restaurant built right onto the pier. Boats of all sorts jostled for room to dock and take advantage of the great food. Though mid-May and out of season, the harbor still protected many yachts, sailboats, fishing boats, and dinghies.

"Henry!" someone shouted.

"Hey, Tim, happy to see you up this early!" Henry answered. "Are you guys ready to go? Where's your dad?"

"Over with Penny and Kate," said Tim, as he motioned his arm in their direction.

Henry turned sideways and made his way through groupings of half-empty wooden tables. Kate saw Henry first and waved. She unconsciously tossed back her blond hair.

Penny and her dad saw Kate's wave and turned to greet Henry.

"Good morning, handsome," Penny half whispered as Henry came close and their eyes met.

"Hey, hon," answered Henry, as he hugged Penny and gave her a quick kiss. "Hi, Mr. Stevens. Ready for a boat ride?"

"Matter of fact, Henry, I was just promising Penny and Kate that I'd make sure all of you jokers got back here safely. Kate's sure Robby will somehow fall overboard." They all chuckled. "I was hoping your dad could join us."

"Me, too," answered Henry. "But he volunteered to make the morning run over to Marsh Harbor to pick up the Granger's, Adrianna, and a bunch of supplies. They are all due at the airport within a half hour of each other."

Henry turned to Kate and gave his sister a hug. Sandwiched between Penny and Kate, he stretched an arm around each and squeezed slightly. "This is a pleasant surprise. I didn't expect to see you two here."

"We brought Dad and Tim down. We're going shopping once Adrianna gets here and need the cart," explained Penny as Henry released them.

"Where are the girls?" Henry asked Kate. He couldn't pass

up any opportunity for the tightest hug possible from those little arms.

"Mom has them up at the house," answered Kate. "She has her hands full. They're fascinated by all the water around here, just as I was worried about. Ellie keeps tossing her stuffed animals over the baby barrier and into the pool to see the splash. Dad got tired of fishing them out yesterday, so most of them are still swimming this morning."

Henry and Penny laughed.

"Mom's taking them down to the beach later, and I don't know how she'll keep Ellie from eating the sand."

Henry laughed louder.

Kate swung a hand toward Penny. "Fortunately, Penny's mom offered to help. Between the two of them, that's one-on-one coverage."

"I hope your mom knows what she's in for," chuckled Henry, moving closer to Penny. He unconsciously put his arm around her waist.

Penny loved Henry's laugh, as it always made her smile, too. She had missed it for too long. Penny pressed up against Henry, and he leaned over and gave her a kiss on the side of her neck.

"Henry! Penny! Come on now!" yelled Alex from the boat, trying to get their attention. "You'll have plenty of time for that later. We have fish to catch."

Along with most of the other people in the restaurant, they turned to see where the shout had come from. There was Alex, standing alongside the boat's captain on the stern with his hands on his hips.

"Are you kidding me?" Kate muttered exasperatedly and

turned back to Henry. “Why did you ever agree to make him your best man, Henry? To Alex, that means he’s in charge. He was issuing orders even before we got here. He’ll drive me crazy before this wedding’s over.”

“Come on, Katie,” challenged Henry. “You take him too seriously. You’re in the Bahamas! We’re all in the Bahamas!”

“But he’s such a drill sergeant sometimes,” protested Kate.

“Lieutenant. He was a lieutenant. When you call him sergeant, it makes him angry. And, yes, he got used to telling people what to do and having them listen,” said Henry. “But I’m having a great time. This is amazing. Just what we all needed.”

“I know,” sighed Kate as she quickly glanced around the picturesque harbor. “It is perfect.”

Kate then turned toward Alex, raised her hands, cupped them around her mouth, and shouted loudly, “We hear you, Sergeant Alex. They’re on the way.” She then saluted.

Alex smiled and then saluted back.

Henry and Penny’s dad swiftly said their goodbyes, and, coffee cups in hand, headed for the boat. The engines were started and purring, and the men joined the others on board.

“Where’re we headed, Captain?” asked Sean, as the boat sliced through the crystal waters and out from the mouth of the harbor.

“I’d like to get us up to Green Turtle Cay,” answered a sandy-haired, leather skinned man of about 40 years of age. “We’ll go about 30 miles offshore and drop the lines over the Great Abaco Canyon. We’re seeing a bit of everything running out there right now. I’ve got us set with both 50-pound and 80-pound monofilament, so yeah, I’m expecting some large tuna. Possibly some marlin. Dolphin, too, are hitting our lures most days."

Alex gestured over at Sean and interrupted, "He's talking about dolphin, the fish, not dolphin as in Flipper, Sean."

Sean was just about to set Alex straight with some profanity-laced facts about fishing, when the captain yelled, "Hold on to your hats boys, we're clear of the channel. Ready for some speed?"

The captain didn't wait for, or even expect, an answer. He thrust the throttles forward. The rumble of the four 300 horsepower engines that powered the thirty-eight-foot craft rose to a synchronized roar. The bow of the boat lifted slightly out of the water and soon settled gently onto plane. Scanning all their faces, the captain was quite pleased at the surprise and momentary unease he observed at the power of his boat. He grinned confidently.

He deserved his reputation as one of the best charters in the Northern Bahamas. He was proud of his craft and loved what he did. The captain liked this bunch and resolved to make this an unforgettable day for them. After so many years on the water and meeting hundreds of people, he could instantly get a feel for them. He'd seen it all.

Henry sat in a nicely cushioned pedestal helm chair. He was struck at how comfortable it was and settled back into the padding. After a while, he relaxed in the subtle up and down motion of the boat as it plowed through the various colors of the water.

Henry had never seen such a beautiful expanse. He swallowed the last few slips of the fresh coffee and scanned the horizon. The sun was just beginning to burn a bit yellower as it rose higher off the port side. The rays hit his face and arms, and the warmth felt good as it countered the coolness of the rushing wind from the racing boat.

"How would you ever describe these different shades of blue?" he wondered to himself. Depending on where he looked, sometimes it was difficult to tell the sky from the water as the blues meshed together and the clouds seemed stretched too thin. "Stop thinking, Henry, and enjoy the moment!" he knew Penny would remind him. He decided to do just that.

The outline of the surrounding cays receded as they galloped closer to the undersea cliff and the 5,000 to 10,000-foot drop that was home to some of the best deep-sea fishing you could hope for.

Alex yelled out something, but the wind caught the sound and stole it away. Seeing the futility of talk, Alex gestured to Henry and then held up and offered a can of beer that he had grabbed from the cooler. Henry hesitated. He had jumped out of bed less than three hours ago.

"Enjoy the moment!" Henry prodded himself. He nodded and Alex tossed him the can. They both pulled the tabs and gulped down some of the ice-cold fluid. After a few moments, Henry raised his can to Alex and shouted, "Thanks, and not only for the beer!" as best he could.

Barely audible but received, Alex valued this appreciation from his friend. He glanced at his watch, satisfied with how well his plans were falling into place. The others had all agreed that, today, Henry needed "distraction." Alex was up to the challenge. He ran through the timeline of the day's activities in his head, optimistic that he was shielding everyone here from what would shortly unfold in New York.

Knowing he had done his best, Alex took a deep breath of the fresh air and let go of the burden. He took a big gulp of beer and had just started relaxing when he felt himself thrust forward. The boat, without warning, suddenly slowed to less than half speed.

"Big fish!" shouted the captain and pointed to a splash of churning white water mixed with soft blues and the dark color of fins.

The hum of the gas engine on the weather-worn golf cart gently melted as Kate pulled up to the front of the pale-yellow cottage where Penny and Adrianna were staying. She pressed the horn button slightly and a sudden "toot" sounded. Kate laughed at the sound as she found it playful and pressed the button again. At the second "toot," Penny and Adrianna strolled out of the veranda, smiled, and waved.

"I love driving this!" chuckled Kate, as Adrianna nimbly settled into the passenger side of the cart, as Penny volunteered for the back.

While Henry and the guys were out fishing, Kate, Adrianna, and Penny planned to venture into the town's shops. The golf cart was perfect for getting them wherever they needed to go on Elbow Cay Island's four-mile stretch. And although Hopetown was a tiny village, there were plenty of shops to keep their attention for the afternoon. They drove easily down the blacktopped lane and parked with the other carts across from the Post Office.

The sun had already ascended to where the rays heated the

air and unsuccessfully challenged the ever-present humidity. The three wandered among the boutique stores offering unique clothes, art, jewelry, books, and music. As the mid-morning turned into mid-day, they welcomed the cool blasts of air conditioning in those shops that afforded the relief.

"Let's drop by the restaurant around the corner and out of the sun," offered Kate, as she clung to four or five bags advertising the shops she had just favored with purchases. "I'm melting here." She had never been a fan of perspiration.

They settled into three white, high-backed chairs toward the open-air back of the restaurant. Happily, a continuous breeze from the overhead fan kept them relatively cool. While taking some time to glance through the menu, they each ordered a frozen rum punch.

With their own spectacular view of the water, the three friends briefly looked around to get comfortable with their surroundings and to see what interesting sights or people were nearby.

About fifteen boats of all sizes were moored in the center of the harbor. A few others were plodding through the far channel's no-wake zone and passing in the face of the red and white candy-striped lighthouse, the most famous landmark in Hopetown.

"So, what'd you get?" asked Kate.

Adrianna shifted a bit to rearrange a bag under her seat. "I found this wonderful hat!" She pulled it out of the bag and modeled it for Penny and Kate.

"That's perfect!" said Penny. "I ended up with just a tee shirt for Henry."

"What! With all the amazing clothes there? I could've spent a small fortune, but Robby has us on a budget. I did get some cute outfits for the girls, though."

Penny giggled. "So many enticements, I know. Your girls look so darn cute in the things you get for them, too. How can you resist?"

"Speaking of outfits, Penny, you chose beautiful bridesmaids dresses for us," said Adrianna. "They're perfect for a seaside wedding!"

"Wait till you see the girls in theirs," said Kate. "They're adorable. I had to hide Joy's from her. She wants to wear it all the time."

Adrianna reached over and patted Penny's hand. "I'm sorry Clara couldn't be here."

"I know," said Penny. "We just couldn't make it work. And Raf, as well." She grabbed Adrianna's hand and squeezed it. "But I'm so glad you're here!"

The waiter reached across the table and handed them each a translucent glass stamped with the colorful imprint of the restaurant logo and filled with an orange/pinkish colored liquid. Still slightly perspiring and anticipating the refreshment of the icy cold punch, Kate grabbed the cup. Unfortunately, she overcompensated on raising it and splashed some liquid onto the table.

"Whoa! It's so light. I didn't expect that. I thought it was glass, but it's plastic." Kate interrupted her stammering long enough to blot the small puddle of punch with her napkins, erasing all evidence of the spill.

Penny knew Kate well enough to understand that her sudden

nervousness meant that Kate wished to pose an uncomfortable question but wasn't sure if she should. Finally, summoning some courage, Kate asked, "So, the Solidane IPO is definitely happening today?"

"Yes, Henry gets agitated anytime it comes up. He wants to put the matter behind him and move on," said Penny. "But it's hard to do. I'm glad Alex is keeping him occupied."

Adrianna gave them a blank look. "IPO?"

Penny took the next few minutes to speak in German to best explain to Adrianna. "Sorry, Kate, didn't mean to leave you out, but that was quicker."

"No," said Kate. "Don't apologize. Adrianna, I'm amazed at how well you speak English. How did you learn?"

"It's fairly ordinary over there to hear it. I learned the basics in school, and then I asked Penny to speak English with me. For the last ten years, she's been my instructor."

"I think your English may be better than mine!" laughed Kate.

A waitress sauntered over to take their order. After surveying their menus, they split some conch fritters and fish tacos. Penny then pointed to their drinks and said, "I think we're going to need another one of these as well."

With the help of the second rum punch, they were soon giggling over stories they told to Adrianna about their childhood times.

Penny let out a loud, contented sigh. "This is wonderful! And I can't wait to be married tomorrow. I love Henry, and how can you complain about this setting?" She gestured out over the harbor.

"Thank you for this, Penny. I've never even seen the ocean before. This is fantastic!" said Kate.

"Oh, I know. So unique and different. I'm loving it!"

"You've always liked adventures!" said Adrianna and Kate simultaneously. They all laughed.

"I couldn't have dreamed of a better one!" asserted Penny. She stared out into the harbor. A large sailboat elegantly powered by. Its crew waved to the people in the restaurant as it passed.

Penny took a sweet sip of her drink and turned back to her friends. "I'm so relieved Angie will get here in time. I wouldn't want her to miss it."

"I'm happy for Sean, too. It's frustrating they canceled her flight," said Kate. "This island is so difficult to get to. I hated that tiny little plane we flew in to get here from West Palm. I'd never flown in a propeller plane before and that one was loud, bumpy, and cold, too."

"I know! Alex took great pleasure in that. Anything to annoy you, Kate," laughed Penny.

"I have to admit, Alex's done a fine job so far with travel arrangements," said Kate.

Adrianna finished a bite of food and set her fork down. "What's the schedule for tonight?"

"The minister will walk us through the ceremony this evening," said Penny. "Then we're going to eat dinner right on the beach with a huge bonfire, lots of drinks, and a setting sun. The perfect appetizer for the wedding tomorrow!"

"It is! I'm so excited!" exclaimed Kate.

They finished their meals and lazily stood up. "We're doing great on time. Let's head to the pool," suggested Adrianna. "We can relax for a while."

"Sounds wonderful!" agreed Penny.

"Yes, let's get out of here before Robby, Henry, and the guys come floating into the harbor. They'll be a mess and Alex will probably want us to clean fish," chuckled Kate.

As they headed back from their fishing expedition, the men's excitement over their catch of fish slowly faded, replaced by a drowsiness. They were approximately halfway to Hopetown, and the captain judged it was time for some good food on dry land. He turned the wheel of the boat slowly and the vessel turned ever so slightly to the starboard.

One of the larger cays seemed to grow as they approached it. Eventually, a well outfitted marina appeared in a cut-out among the sand along the shore. The blues of the water grew lighter and brighter as they approached the shoreline. The boat slowed in incremental segments until it completely settled into the water and drifted up to the dock.

"Okay boys," said the captain. "Everybody out. Head on up to that path and follow it to the other side of the jetty. There's a restaurant and bar there, and we'll grab some lunch. Just tell them you're with me and they'll take care of you."

It took a few moments for all to hobble off the boat and adjust to walking on land again. The combination of the early morning start, excitement, and alcohol made the trek a little tiring. The unrelenting sun, now bright from the noontime, did its part in sapping their energy as they slowly made their way along the trail. However, as they approached the bar, they heard lively voices and loud music.

Even though it was the tail end of the season, the restaurant held a sizable number of patrons, even at midday. As the men eagerly entered the cool breeze and shade of the inside, a man in a bright Hawaiian shirt shouted at them from behind an old wooden bar. He made a gesture with one arm to choose any table as he shook a gallon milk jug full of strawberry colored liquid with the other.

As the men pulled out well-worn chairs and sank into them, the bartender made his way around the edge of the bar and across to their table. He carried two jugs of the rose-colored liquid in one hand and a stack of cups in the other.

"I can tell by the looks on your faces that you're with Captain Rick. We've been waiting for you. Drink a glass of this. It'll do wonders for you." He scattered the cups around the table and haphazardly filled them, not caring that some of the liquid ran over or sloshed from one cup to another.

Mr. Stevens, seated near Henry, leaned forward and muttered, "Now we know why the table and chairs are so sticky."

The bartender overheard it and laughed. As with most bars and restaurants on the islands, this one had its signature drink. Many had tried to guess the combination of the liquors and fruit juices and attempted to duplicate the mixture. "Drink up!" he encouraged them.

The potion proved enticing and enjoyable. After only a few swallows, their cups were empty. And in no time, so were the gallon jugs the bartender had placed upon the table. Alex waved one of the drained jugs at the bartender, but he seemed not to see Alex as he tended to his other patrons.

Just then, Captain Rick appeared through the door, followed

by three employees of the restaurant. They were carrying trays heaped with meats, seafood, vegetables, and fruit. An additional tray held breads and condiments. "Okay men," said Captain Rick, "eat all you can. I promise, this is some of the best food around."

As everyone else dove into the food, Alex again shook the empty jug at the bartender. Still ignored, Alex looked at Henry, rose from his chair and said, "I'll take care of this."

As Alex approached the bar, he saw why the bartender was inattentive. Just around a divider, a group of college girls, celebrating their recent graduation, huddled around two high top tables. As Alex approached, the bartender waved and shouted at him, "I'll be right there."

Curious to see who he was talking to, the girls all swiveled in their chairs and turned toward Alex. Almost in unison, they beckoned Alex to join them.

Taking a last bite of his sandwich, Henry wondered what had happened to Alex. He looked up as the bartender slapped two full jugs on the table. Alex was not with him. Henry scanned the room, trying to spot Alex. He saw other tables filled with people also enjoying themselves.

Off to the left, he noticed a man with a gray beard, dressed in the restaurant's Hawaiian shirt uniform, giving a tour to a smartly dressed young woman. He was obviously the owner, engaged in a business meeting.

Henry stood up to see if he could find Alex. He shifted his body so that he could peer around a divider. Alex was there, surrounded by a group of young ladies. He had his sleeves rolled up, arms flexed, showing off his biceps. The ladies took turns squeezing them and giggling. As if he could sense someone watching him, Alex raised his head and saw Henry.

Alex also noticed the owner and the woman walking toward them. As she walked past, the woman looked from Alex to the girls and then caught Alex's eye. She laughed and shook her head. Alex glanced from the woman to Henry and back again. He lowered his arms, turned to the group of young women, and said, "I gotta go."

"What the heck was that?" asked Henry as Alex returned to their table and sat down.

"I was just having some fun," said Alex, his face a little crimson.

Sean joined in, "My God Alex, they're almost half your age. Aren't you embarrassed?"

"I'm not that old," answered Alex.

They continued to mock Alex's flaunting; it hadn't surprised them. He usually was front and center in any group involving fun, laughter, and, of course, women. The mounds of food dwindled, and they drained more jugs of the intoxicating liquid. Captain Rick decided he'd better get them all back to the boat before he'd be unable to.

"Last call, gents," he shouted as he rose from his seat. "We're powering out of here at one o'clock. That's fifteen minutes from now. Be on board by then."

Henry canvassed the group and deduced all were enjoying themselves. Except for Mr. Stevens. He was rubbing his forehead vigorously. Henry shuffled around the chairs to where Mr. Stevens sat. Henry leaned down and touched him on the shoulder. "Want to get some air?" Henry asked.

"Great idea," answered Mr. Stevens, as he gingerly stood up.

They both grabbed a cold bottle of water from the stack scattered on the table and headed to the open-air front of the building. Out near the beach was a grouping of lounge chairs parked underneath a canopy of palm trees. Henry and Mr. Stevens spied them and sat. A pleasant breeze revived them.

"I'm not used to that swaying of the boat," explained Mr. Stevens. "I was fine until we stepped off. But I still seem to be rocking with the waves." He took a deep breath. He then swung his arm across the horizon. "This appears to be working, though. Look how beautiful that is!"

"It's so different from what I'm used to that I can't stop staring at it," agreed Henry. He paused for a moment. "We've had little opportunity to talk, but I wanted to thank you and Mrs. Stevens for supporting Penny and me with this wedding."

Mr. Stevens turned in his chair to face Henry. "Henry, I want you to realize that Ally and I are thrilled for you and Penny. We couldn't be more excited. We're having a fantastic time here."

"Thanks," said Henry.

"It has been quite the year, hasn't it?" asked Mr. Stevens.

Henry suppressed the difficult emotions that still accompanied any examination of the past couple of years and focused on Mr. Stevens' affable smile.

"It has," Henry agreed hurriedly.

Sensing Henry's discomfort, Mr. Stevens changed the subject. "Do I really need to get back onto that boat? Can't I stay here?" he joked.

Henry laughed and took a big swallow of water. "I'm sure they'll be yelling for us soon. Maybe they won't find us?"

"That reminds me of how you and Penny, when you were little, would lose yourselves in that bricklebutter patch in the greenbelt behind our houses. Kate and Alex, too. I can't comprehend what the attraction was, but we adults always knew where to find you."

"It was our own little hideaway," chuckled Henry. "That certainly was ages ago."

Henry soon heard a rising crescendo of voices as the others made their way back to the path. Henry and Mr. Stevens joined them. They all gingerly stepped onto the boat, already quivering from its idling engines.

The trip back to Hopetown was at half the speed of that morning. The captain graciously kept the boat close to any land to not only minimize any rolling or pitching, but to give everyone a steady fix for their eyes.

As they approached a cay in the distance, Sean stood up and moved next to Henry. He pointed to a house up on a hill facing a pale blue lagoon.

"Look, Henry. That's Alex's house!" He started chuckling.

Seeing Henry's puzzled face, Sean waved Alex over. Realizing immediately what Sean was up to, Alex shook his head in disgust.

"It's not my house, Henry," said Alex.

"But you'd like it to be," insisted Sean.

"Yes, I would." Alex then turned his back to Sean. "While we were down here a while ago, Sean and I were hired to do a quick repair on that house. You can't tell from here, but it's in awful shape. It's a foreclosure. The bank's just doing crucial repairs. I'd mentioned to Sean at the time that we should buy it."

Henry glanced at Sean, who was shaking his head with a

"Isn't he nuts?" look on his face. "What would you do with a house in the Bahamas?" asked Henry.

"Fix it up. Live in it. Re-sell it. I don't know," Alex answered. He put his hands on his hips.

"Not going to happen," insisted Sean. He walked over to a cooler, took out a beer, and flopped into a cushioned deck chair.

"You can dream, can't you?" grumbled Alex.

"Yes, there's always hope," sighed Henry. He patted his friend on the back as they both watched the silhouette of the house and then the cay receded into the distance.

After a while, Henry settled back into a chair and stared out at the varying hues of the blue ocean. Mesmerized, he thought about the events that led to this moment and how thankful he was for the people in his life. He soon closed his eyes and breathed out a contented sigh.

He was happy.

He was blessed.

"Thank you, God," he silently said to himself. He then prayed for his future with Penny, his family, and friends. His old co-workers at Fusion Lab. Finally, he asked God to bless Hyatt Emerson, and wondered how the morning had gone for him.

CHAPTER 17

Hyatt Emerson had never seen the inside of the New York Stock exchange. Impeccably dressed, his dark hair, slim build, and air of authority perfectly suited the moment. They directed him out of a small door onto a dais that overlooked the entire floor. A small cheer arose from the assorted traders and anyone else lucky enough to get a pass to one of the most anticipated public offerings of the year. The raised platform was not much larger than a balcony at one of the nicer hotels or of a private box at a concert hall, and probably less ostentatious. The railing, though wide and strong with intricately formed support columns, barely came up to the waist of an average height person.

The dais could only hold so many people. But for this morning's celebration, the demand to join Emerson on the balcony was considerable. Once the attendee list was settled, egos then battled and jostled for their actual position on the podium.

It was now 9:10 a.m. That left another twenty minutes to pack the guests behind and to the sides of Hyatt before he pressed the button to ignite the ten second clanging noise that always marked the opening bell for trading.

Hyatt surveyed the room. It looked a lot smaller than he had expected. With all the screens, brightly colored lights, ornamental casings and, of course, a packed crowd, it reminded him of a casino. Not the modern, flashy, Las Vegas kind, but the genteel, historic ones of Europe that commanded the aura of generational power and money.

"How fitting," he thought.

An initial public offering is always a big deal at the exchange. Many had stood in Hyatt's place at the lectern-like control panel, usually giddy at the staggering realization that they would become instant millionaires that very day. So too, at the fairly young age of forty-two, would Hyatt, as CEO of the newest public corporation.

The company did not yet have a single dollar of revenue, let alone any profit. But that didn't matter. It had developed the technology for possibly one of the greatest breakthroughs in energy in decades. The potential for profits was obvious, and investors wanted a piece.

But unlike most of those that preceded him, Hyatt felt a sudden twinge of inner sadness that rapidly wrestled with his excitement. Solidane would no longer be his domain. He would answer to shareholders, an outside board, and powerful investors. He would no longer have control. And of all, he cherished control the most. Hyatt shifted his weight on his feet as he hastily buried that fleeting emotion to the depths within himself.

As the guests soon filled the dais, a whiff of expensive perfume hit Hyatt's nostrils and caused him to stiffen. He continued to stare straight ahead and refused to acknowledge the presence of Margaret Granger. The event handlers had warned them all to draw tightly together or not everyone would fit. Margaret dutifully complied, and though placed to the right of Hyatt, she nudged her shoulder directly and snugly against Hyatt's arm. Twenty-five years his elder, Margaret possessed a certain grace and poise that made up for a dwindling attractiveness. It was this grace that had drawn Ted to Margaret.

"Was it worth it, Hyatt?" Margaret whispered into Hyatt's right ear. The sound of her voice and the closeness to his neck caused a slight muscle spasm to fire briefly down his side. He had hoped she would re-consider attending, but she insisted on representing her husband.

Margaret regretted accepting Hyatt's offer to buy her vote. Yet, she knew she'd had no choice. To say no meant not only the ravaged reputation of her late husband, but the financial ruin of her family and anyone else connected with Fusion Lab.

And Hyatt knew that without her signature on that agreement, Henry Taylor might, in fact, be standing in this place on the dais instead of him. Hyatt slowly tilted his head toward her, forced a smile, and muttered so only she could hear, "We will know in a few moments, won't we?"

Margaret stiffened and did not respond. She held her head high and smiled broadly at the cameras. She knew that her face in the frame of every reproduction capturing this moment would forever irritate Hyatt. Because neither had any regard for the other, they both hoped that, after today, they would never need to see each other again.

Hyatt's attention was diverted to the rising crescendo of

voices chattering excitedly to each other as they squeezed more and more people onto the dais. At precisely 9:30 EST, Hyatt pressed a knob on the console. A bell clanged, and Solidane Energy Corporation was now a public entity. A tremendous shout arose from the floor of the Exchange and everyone clapped, waved, and cheered for the many cameras. People slapped Hyatt on the back, shook his hand, and sought to get photographed as close to him as possible.

Hyatt struggled to contain himself. This was far better than he ever allowed himself to imagine. A drop of perspiration slowly formed on his brow as he studied the monitor. The ticker whizzed by with an ever-rising price. All buy orders. No one was selling, for who would be fool enough to do so? He saw the exact quote he was looking for dart by in an instant and then chuckled. He was now, indeed, extraordinarily rich.

The adrenaline rush Hyatt Emerson experienced at the start of trading that morning of the Solidane Energy Corporation IPO was fading. He and his entourage had swiftly filed out of the Stock Exchange Building. They needed to stay in a tight group to reach their destination on time, and now bobbed along a New York sidewalk, engulfed in a wave of people. Limos were out of the question, as the traffic would never accommodate even the short distance, down three blocks, and over four.

A crisp breeze buoyed the spirits of the swarm as they pushed and weaved in the general direction of the office building that housed Solidane's new headquarters. Hyatt hurried them.

Hyatt was eager to get back to the expansive boardroom where his legal team and investment bankers waited. Solidane's entire board of directors would be there. Most were part of the cluster of impeccably dressed individuals that now moved more easily as the everyday crowd thinned and they drew within shouting distance of the building.

As the others paraded to the conference room, Hyatt slipped down a hall to his spacious office. A lush, deep blue carpet invited the eye across pale marble tiles on the floor and up to a broad desk. Originally obtained by Hyatt's great grandfather, it was made of English oak and was inlaid with a striped ebony pattern. Windows stretched along the entire wall space with incredible views of the New York City skyline. His CFO, Nora Bromfield, was already there.

"How'd we do, Nora?" Hyatt asked as he made his way around the desk and gently settled into a comfy leather chair.

"The bankers haven't confirmed yet, but I calculate that the net to Solidane, that's with all the offering fees deducted, is about $4.42 billion," answered Nora. "But the stock has already quadrupled from the offering price. I'd say we're all pretty happy right now, and significantly wealthier."

Nora pointed to three leather binders off to the side of Hyatt's desk. "Those are the contracts you asked to have ready," she said.

"Why do you have these? Where is legal on this?" asked Hyatt as his attention turned to his agenda.

"Ben just finished with them. He gave them to me to verify the last amounts. They have been constantly changing," answered Nora.

"The top one is the closing documents to purchase all the assets of Chemclone. Once executed, we will officially own all their production plants and the research facility in Texas. I still can't believe how massive that plant is," Nora continued. "The second one is for the liquid natural gas plant and pipeline network down in Louisiana. Because of the amounts involved in these two, you need board approval."

Hyatt made no movement to open the binders or even show any interest in them as he allowed Nora to summarize their contents. He was aware of each deal and the significance of the Board of Directors assent to the signed and sealed instruments. The first two would mean Solidane was officially in business with a viable product ready for market. The last was tying up a loose end.

"The bottom one is the deal with Fusion Lab," said Nora. "With both Ted Granger and Henry Taylor out of the picture, the Lab is out of operation. Basically, the only value is the property and equipment. We'll offer $3 million to purchase Fusion. Are you sure we want to do that?"

Hyatt swiveled his chair and gazed out at the New York skyline. Without turning to Nora, he said, "I made a promise to Margaret Grainer that we would preserve the campus. It was part of the deal. Everyone is aware of the role of Fusion Lab in our product development, and from a PR standpoint, the purchase makes sense. We'll convert it into our corporate retreat center."

He pivoted his chair and stood. "Let's go get this done," he said. Nora nodded and followed him out.

Still enmeshed in the high from the offering, the Board of Directors meeting proceeded without a hitch. They approved and signed the contracts and initiated money transfers.

The PR department proudly sent out the first official press release: "Solidane Completes Acquisition of Chemclone in addition to Vast New Natural Gas Pipeline Assets and Commences Production of Wafer." When the story hit the financial wires, Solidane's share price doubled again.

Judge George Noble wiped the dressing from his lips as he hurriedly finished his lunch of a generous Caesar salad with pan seared shrimp. His docket had been busy that morning, as was typical for a Friday and the end of the week.

He had promised to be back in his chambers promptly at 12:30 to review a request from one of the largest law firms in the city. The controlling partner had been his friend since law school and would not have asked for the meeting unless it was incredibly important. Yet, his friend intentionally and irritatingly kept him in suspense. "You'll understand when you see it," was all he offered.

Chester Worthington was already pacing impatiently as the judge entered his offices. "Chester! Great to see you!" exclaimed the judge. The two men enthusiastically shook hands. "So, what're you doing here? You haven't been down to the court in ages."

Judge George's eye then caught another person sitting in one of his side chairs. "Who's this?"

He gazed at the female for a brief time before he recognized her. Wendy Wilkens, syndicated financial news reporter. Her blogs and social media posts had been known to move markets.

Not liking surprises, the judge's friendly demeanor changed to mild irritation at his friend. "Chester, what the heck is going on?" demanded the judge as he huffily rounded his desk and settled into his chair.

Chester reached into his coat pocket and brought forth a neatly creased trifold document as he sat down in a chair opposite the judge. “Here, just read this. And I’m asking you to sign it,” answered Chester.

The Judge grabbed the papers of typewritten, double-spaced wording. No one said anything while he read. As he digested its contents, he sat straighter in his seat. Once finished, he shot an angry look at Chester.

“My God, Chester! Do you comprehend what you’re asking? Do you understand the implications of this?” barked the Judge. He looked over at Wendy Wilkens, who stared at him expressionless. He turned back to Chester. “If she’s here, of course you do!”

“George, everything is in order. I stake my firm’s reputation on it. I give you my word this is valid,” stated Chester.

“Did you give notice?” asked the Judge.

“Yes, at precisely 12:30, my firm both faxed and emailed a notice of infringement for the benefit of the client. Also, a personal representative arrived at their corporate offices and handed a copy to one of the executives. We have a signature of receipt.”

“Why did you wait until now? You’ve had this for some time, I’m sure.”

“There was no infringement until they announced production. Here, read their press release. It just came out. See, Solidane is beginning production. That is in violation of my client’s patent,” explained Chester. “This temporary restraining order will prevent that.”

“Why don’t you work it out without this blatant legal maneuver?” asked the judge.

"We considered that George. Of course, we did. But there are many ways for them to squash this unless we have it documented in the public domain. Their legal team, especially now that they have all that cash, could drag this out forever. No, this is the only way."

"Chester, you can't begin to predict the fallout over this," protested the judge.

"George," said Chester calmly. "It really is simple. They announced production. It violates the patent, and my client would like a temporary injunction, giving each party the space to work this out. If the notoriety were not a factor, wouldn't you readily sign this order?" asked Chester.

The judge tapped his fingers on his desk and then slumped into his chair. Yes, without all the acclaim, the legal issue was simple. He read through the papers again and mentally checked all the legal boxes that such a request required.

"How do you know it violates the patent?" asked the judge.

"Read the holder of the patent on the copy there," suggested Chester.

"Henry Taylor. Henry Taylor. Why does that name sound familiar?" murmured the Judge.

"Fusion Lab," sighed Chester.

"I knew Ted Granger," said the Judge softly. "I heard his successor had passed as well. I thought it was such a tragedy."

"I can assure you he is alive and kicking," countered Chester. "We have all the documentation needed to show how the Solidane process violates this patent. We've tried every which way to poke holes in our case. We can't. It's solid. George, I wouldn't be here otherwise."

The Judge twisted his large frame until he faced Wendy Wilkens. "Have you seen this documentation?" he asked.

It startled Wendy for a second to realize that she was no longer just a spectator. She briefly considered the implications of what the Judge had asked and answered, "Yes, I have. Let me just say that I wish my name were on that patent."

The Judge opened a drawer and pulled out a clean handkerchief from among the many stored there. He fluffed it open and wiped the beads of perspiration that had formed on his forehead. He deftly folded it and set it down beside the papers. The Judge trusted his friend and appreciated that, like Ted Granger, Chester ran his firm with integrity.

The Judge grabbed his favorite pen and turned the pages to the third one requiring his signature. With broad strokes, he hastily wrote "Judge George Noble."

"Here, now both of you get out of my chambers."

In the hallway, a long bench provided the workspace that Wendy needed. She separated the pages of the order and spread them out alongside one another. She then took pictures of each with her phone.

Wendy rustled them back together and handed the order back to Chester. "That's all I need," she calmly stated.

She pulled her pre-written article up on her tablet and downloaded the images she had just taken. After a quick check, she gave Chester an excited smile and said, "Here goes!" She hit the send key.

Chester was already back in his office, pacing in front of his desk, when his cell phone chirped. A newsfeed flashed on the small screen.

"Solidane Hit with Injunction. Stock Plunging on First Day of IPO. Exchange Mulls Trading Halt. SEC to Investigate."

"It worked," Chester muttered, almost surprised. He walked behind his desk and calmly sat in a comfy high-backed chair. Gently, he laid his palms on the desk and patted it while staring at the phone.

It wasn't long before the receptionist buzzed.

"Mr. Worthington, I have a call for you from Hyatt Emerson of Solidane Energy."

"Put him through," said Chester.

CHAPTER 18

A slight wisp of smoke from the crackling fire wafted over toward Henry, Penny, and his sister, Kate. Robby had just thrown on two more logs and a burst of sparks exploded out from the fire pit and brightened up the night. The rehearsal for the wedding had gone off without a hitch. Because it was a simple wedding, few instructions were issued or needed to be remembered.

A few at a time, the family and friends had slowly dispersed from the little alcove that overlooked the ocean and headed back up the long sandy path to their cottages. The moon, though only three quarters full, gave off a warm light. The few electric lights that burned added to the sparkling light that bounced off the ocean's surface. A steady parade of waves provided a low-pitched rhythm as they crested and rolled leisurely onto the beach, followed by a higher-pitched static as the foam scurried over the sand and evaporated.

Kate sighed and lifted her head from the beach lounge chair. She dug her toes into the cool sand once more and turned to

Henry.

"This is heavenly! But I guess Robby and I need to get up to the house. Mom said the girls were having trouble quieting down, so I'd better check on them. They're so excited about the big day tomorrow."

"This is fantastic, isn't it?" purred Penny.

Robby walked over to Kate's chair and held out his hand to her. She grasped it and used his help to rise out of the chaise.

"Don't get up. You two just chill for a while," said Kate. "We're having breakfast tomorrow down at the restaurant at the dock, before we go our separate ways. We'll see you then. Good night!"

Robby and Kate gave a quick wave at Henry and Penny and began their ascent to the cottages up the hill.

Penny rolled over from her lounge and onto Henry's. Together, they cuddled for a while and then began talking.

"One more day. Here's your last chance to back out," joked Henry.

Penny smacked Henry playfully on his chest. "Yours, too!" she replied.

"I'm not going anywhere," answered Henry. "But I still think you're getting the bad end of this deal. My career prospects haven't improved in the least and my finances are awful. I was hoping for some good news before we got married."

Henry's financial situation was much worse than his physical condition. Henry had lost all his Fusion Lab benefits. His employee retirement plan, as well as his savings, consisted of Fusion stock options that were now essentially worthless. To help pay medical bills, Henry had sold his townhouse.

"Henry, we've talked about this. We'll be fine. We have my job and my savings, too. That will keep us going until this mess blows over," answered Penny.

"So much for the little pride I have left," grinned Henry.

"Oh, stop it," giggled Penny. "You have lots of friends who believe in you. You're one of the smartest people I know. The bravest, too. It's incredible how hard you worked to get your health back."

"Thanks, I like hearing that. Everyone has helped me so much. I would've never gotten through it otherwise." He gave Penny a gentle squeeze.

"This, right here, right now, is what we both need. I'm ready," said Penny resolutely. She pressed close to Henry's face and kissed him. "Henry, tell me again why you're marrying me," asked Penny. "I like hearing that!"

Henry breathed in deeply and slowly exhaled. He laid back his head and looked up at the night sky. Thousands of stars twinkled down toward him. Even at the Fusion Lab hilltop, the sky did not offer up so many stars.

Henry shifted his weight to his side and caressed Penny's leg.

"I love you. I always have. You give me a happiness I can't explain. When I think about you, my stomach does flips. It happens every time you look at me with those beautiful eyes of yours. No one else does that to me."

They kissed and held each other tightly. The incredible night sky and the rhythmic rush of the waves lulled them into a comforting contentedness. They talked into the night about their crazy journey that led them to this island, to this spot called Hopetown. And for the first time in a long time, Henry really believed there was hope.

The remodeling of the small resort area at the far end of Hopetown included facilities for special events. A scaled-down banquet room sat adjacent to a restaurant and faced the beautiful expanse of ocean. Its floor-to-ceiling glass doors could be pushed to the side and encased in the restaurant's frame, providing open air pleasure when sunny or safety during rainstorms. A chic bar would service patrons not only during events but offer nightly music and dancing for the locals and tourists. Tall palm trees created discreet sandy paths to the beach and sea.

On the day of the wedding, Penny and Henry kept busy throughout the morning. After breakfast, Penny, Kate, Adrianna, and Angie lounged at the resort spa. The guys went snorkeling. While they were preoccupied, the resort event area was being transformed. So many people had wanted to make the day special for Penny and Henry. As the resort's only guests, the staff were dedicated to indulging them.

The numerous containers of colorful potted plants that normally were scattered throughout the grounds were gathered and arranged along the path Penny would walk with her father. The staff strung vibrant bougainvillea and yellow elder across the round grotto area on the beach, creating a canopy underneath of which Penny and Henry would share their vows. They arranged the chairs in a semicircle. The effect was that Henry and Penny's ceremony would take place in a beautiful garden setting bordered by a turquoise sea.

The outside garden led into an inside one. In the event room, the staff arranged three rectangular tables like an upside down

"U." The bridal party would sit at the top, with the friends and family along the sides. They draped them in white linen, and set in place fine china and silver. Rows of multicolored garlands streaked down the middle. Overstuffed baskets of blossoms hung from the rafters. Tall stands of bouquets rimmed the room walls.

The ceremony itself was wonderful. Henry, in his dark suit, fidgeted up in front of everyone, until Penny and her father began walking toward him. Penny's dark hair, pulled up onto her head, contrasted elegantly with her white wedding dress. Henry stifled the urge to run up and embrace her.

Penny smiled gracefully, surprised at her nervousness. She startled for a second when Henry, handsome as she had ever seen him, seemed to step toward her. Her heart raced at his broad smile.

When they were finally face-to-face in front of family and friends, Henry took Penny's hands and held them in his. Henry locked onto Penny's eyes until a soft glint drew his attention to her neck. A delicate necklace gently grasped a tiny, golden bricklebutter branch, its intricate buds sparkling.

"I can't believe you still have that after all these years!" Henry breathed quietly, trying his best to keep his surprise contained with everyone watching. "It looks beautiful on you!"

Delighted at his reaction, Penny, with an expansive smile, shrugged her shoulders and swayed slightly.

The vows were emotional. Both had difficulty putting into words the intensity of their feelings. Their journey away from each other, and then back again, seemed unfathomable. Henry and Penny professed their deep love for one another and their awe of God's incredible blessing. The cheering afterward was loud and joyful.

Everyone moved into the beautiful banquet room for the reception, and the DJ made the official introductions. The staff bustled about filling glasses with champagne, and Alex rose from his seat. He motioned for the DJ to hand him the microphone.

"Do you really need that?" asked Kate as Alex tapped the top of the microphone, making a dull thumping sound. "We're all right here."

Alex ignored her. "If I could have your attention . . ." he began.

Everyone halted their eating, drinking, and conversations to turn toward Alex.

"It was a great honor when Henry asked me to be his best man," he continued.

Kate chortled and looked at Henry, who shrugged. Kate shook her head, as if in disbelief. Penny started laughing. Shortly, all three were laughing out loud, shifting the attention to themselves.

Alex hesitated and gave them a scolding look.

"Oh, sorry," said Kate, flipping her hand at Alex. "Go on."

Everyone laughed, Alex the hardest.

"I've known Penny and Henry since before I could even talk."

"The good old days," interrupted Sean to more laughter.

"I believe I spent more time at the Taylor's house than my own. I remember walking in our back door one summer evening and my mom asking me who I was. Mr. Taylor, do you recall my dad offering to let you claim me as a dependent on taxes?"

Henry's dad grinned and nodded his head.

"I'd like all of you to take a good look at these two," said

Alex as he waved his hand at Henry and Penny. With everyone focused on them, they laughed self-consciously and turned and faced each other. Henry took Penny's hand under the table and gave it a gentle squeeze.

"There it is!" exclaimed Alex. "See that? See that look they give each other? I've watched that gaze since we were kids. They adore each other."

The group let out a mild rumble in agreement.

"In the third grade, I sat in between Penny and Henry. Can you imagine how painful it was for me, at nine years old, to be caught in between that every day?"

Again, the group echoed Alex's amused chuckles. Penny, beaming, rested her head against Henry.

"We all know, sadly, that Penny moved away. When she did, Henry lost that glint in his eyes." Alex paused, and the party grew quiet.

"None of us had seen it since, until Penny's return home blessed us." Everyone clapped.

Alex waited for the sound to die down.

"Now, we can all agree that Henry didn't need to drive a car off a cliff to get Penny's attention. A phone call would have done just fine," said Alex, met with a few seconds of awkwardness, followed by everyone's laughter.

"But who cares how it happened? The important thing is that," Alex pointed to Penny and Henry, "we all now see that look again. I hope someday, someone looks at me like that."

"Let's raise our glasses to Penny, a beautiful bride and wonderful friend, and to Henry, the best guy I know. May that sparkle last forever. We love you guys!"

A fun evening unfurled like splashy, vibrant wrapping paper. Everyone feasted on the delicious food and drink. Penny and Henry cut their wedding cake and told amusing stories. The music and dancing were boisterous.

As the reception wound down, Kate took the microphone from the DJ and quieted everyone. "Penny and Henry, this is a present from your two nieces."

With that, the DJ pressed a button, and music played. Joy and Ellie, Henry's little nieces, shrieked and ran onto the center of the dance floor. They grabbed each other's hands and were soon singing and dancing. "A stitch in time . . ."

Penny and Henry watched, delighted, as the girls sang and twirled.

"Let's all do the Nimmy Nimmy dance!" they practically shouted.

Penny and Henry, along with everyone else, roared with laughter and delight.

"Come on, Henry, dance with me," pleaded Penny, as she shot up out of her chair, pulled Henry's arm, and ran out to join the girls.

"You heard them everybody. Let's get out there," Henry yelled to the group.

Within a few minutes, they filled the entire reception room with laughing, singing, and dancing. "We'll stomp our feet as fast as we can, pump our arms, wave our hands, turn around, we're in a trance, let's all do the Nimmy Nimmy dance!"

A buzz on Henry's cell phone interrupted the contentment

of the lazy morning for Penny and Henry. It was a text from Chester. "Request a conference call with you and Alex ASAP. EXTREMELY IMPORTANT."

An hour later, hand-in-hand, Henry and Penny walked along the path to Alex's cottage. Before Henry could knock, Alex opened the door and gave them both a big bear hug. "Our newlyweds! Don't you look cute!"

"It does feel good!" agreed Penny.

He ushered them into his small living area. The three of them sat down around a circular table.

"Any idea what this is about?" asked Alex.

"Not a clue," answered Henry, shrugging his shoulders. "We'll know in another ten minutes though."

"Want something to drink or eat?" asked Alex.

"No, we had breakfast with our parents. They couldn't stop talking about what a great time they've had. Alex, I can't tell you how much we appreciate this resort," said Penny.

"The owner is happy we're having fun. He says it's been a great test run for his people."

They happily chatted about the wedding and the wonderful time they've had. Henry soon glanced at the clock and set his cell phone on the table.

"Time to call Chester." He hit the green call button, and then the white one for speaker.

"Henry?" Chester's voice bellowed from the phone.

"Hi Chester," said Henry. "Penny and Alex are here with me."

"Hello, Chester," they chimed in.

"Hello everyone. Penny and Henry, congratulations! I'm very excited for you. Now, I hate to interrupt your morning, but I have some big news. I wish I could do this in person, but it just can't wait. It's regarding Solidane."

Penny and Henry shot each other worried glances. No one had mentioned anything to do with Fusion Lab or Solidane this whole time, and they hoped to keep it that way.

As if he could see their faces, Chester quickly added, "Now don't get upset. This is all good. You'll want to hear this!"

"What does Solidane have to do with me?" asked Alex. He rose from the table, grabbed a few bottles of water, and set them in the middle.

"Bricklebutter Boom. The formula that you and Henry patented," answered Chester.

"Oh, that's right." said Alex as he turned to Henry. "Our bricklebutter pod killer."

"Yes," said Chester. "When Henry told me about the patent, he explained the Boom formula helped fix a problem with Solidane's wafer. My people have investigated it thoroughly and without that formula, there would be no wafer."

"Can we really prove that?" asked Henry. "The formula was only a small part. The entire process was hugely complex. It took years."

"That doesn't matter. It didn't work without the Bricklebutter Boom formula," stated Chester firmly.

"I guess that's true," agreed Henry.

"What are you getting at?" challenged Alex.

"Let me explain," began Chester. "Friday, Solidane went public. You knew that was happening, right?"

"Yes," answered Alex. "We all knew. That's why we took Henry deep sea fishing.

"Well, it was an enormous success. They raised billions of dollars."

Henry winced.

"About three hours after the stock opened for trading, we were able to file a patent infringement suit against Solidane. I made sure the financial press was notified. Raised quite a stir."

"You mean you've already filed suit for patent infringement of the Bricklebutter Boom formula?" asked Henry incredulously.

"Exactly!" exclaimed Chester. "I would've loved to have seen the look on Hyatt's face when he got the news. We then presented Solidane with an offer for settlement. They agreed right away. The infringement suit has already been withdrawn."

"Wait. You're saying the injunction was filed and settled within the same day?" asked Henry, rubbing his forehead.

"Yes. Hyatt signed off immediately. I apologize for not telling you my plan earlier, but I didn't want to interfere with your wedding. Also, I didn't expect everything to fall into place so well. It could've taken months."

"We understand," said Henry. "So, there's an agreement?"

On the other end of the call, Chester paused and energetically drummed his fingers on his desk for a few moments, organizing his thoughts.

"There're actually two agreements. The first one involves Fusion Lab. The bank has had everything on hold until the loan is paid. We arranged a deal where, for cash and some Solidane stock, Solidane would acquire any and all rights that Fusion Lab might have related to the wafer. Hyatt agreed. The cash is enough to pay off the loan, plus fund operations for many years. Fusion Lab is now back in the hands of the Trust."

"That's incredible," Henry mumbled. "It's hard to believe."

"The value of the Solidane shares now owned by the Trust is substantial. I'd say the Lab's future is pretty solid."

Henry stood up and paced around the room. He looked at Penny and Alex, and then paced some more. Finally, Penny stood up, grabbed him by the shoulders, and sat him down.

"This is crazy!" proclaimed Henry, shaking his head.

"It's a good deal for everyone." Chester breathed in slowly and picked up a folder. "But there's more."

"Next, to settle the patent infringement, there's another agreement. We wanted to be fair and didn't want protracted negotiations. If Solidane fought, most likely they'd ultimately prevail. So, based on published settlements of similar infringement suits, we offered terms that any outsider would agree were fitting and equitable."

"I'm sure Hyatt didn't see it that way," suggested Henry.

"Believe it or not, he did," said Chester eagerly. "Solidane agreed to pay thirty million dollars to acquire the patent rights."

Chester paused again to listen for their reaction. They were stunned.

"That's a lot of money," stammered Alex, still struggling to absorb Chester's words. He stood and ambled slowly around the table. Then, pulling back a chair, he collapsed into it.

"There's also a royalty paid based on the number of wafers sold," added Chester. "It's only fractions of the dollar, but that could amount to a bundle."

"This is overwhelming," said Henry. He sipped some water and then grabbed Penny's hand.

"My personal feelings, it should've been more," said Chester in a quiet voice. "Henry, they almost killed you. They destroyed your reputation. Look at the toll on your family and friends. Look what they did to Fusion Lab and Ted Granger's legacy."

Henry sighed. "My head is spinning."

"The funds are now in escrow. Once everything is recorded, they'll be released."

"Chester, do you mind explaining this again?" asked Penny. "I'm not sure I digested everything."

"Same with me," agreed Alex.

Chester slowly and calmly recounted the events. He answered as many questions as he could, placating their need for corroboration. Their shock soon ebbed into a hush.

"I'm going to let you discuss this among yourselves," said Chester finally. "It's not that often that I'm able to give such incredible news to my clients. In this case, my friends. I'm thrilled for you. My utmost congratulations!"

"We're speechless, Chester," said Henry. "We can't thank you enough!"

"No thanks necessary. Enjoy your good fortune," said Chester, and he hung up.

In silence, they glanced at each other, searching for what to say.

"Henry, I don't know how to thank you," said Alex.

"This was not me, Alex. A lot of people made this happen. But think about it. This started with our formula."

Alex stared at Henry and Penny. Then he smiled. The smile grew into a chuckle and the chuckle a full-on laugh.

"Henry, you turned out to be quite the catch!" he bellowed.

Penny and Henry looked at each other. They, too, started

laughing.

Penny stood up, followed by Henry and Alex. All three embraced.

“What should we do next?” asked Henry.

“Let’s find the others!” exclaimed Penny.

Part Five

TOMORROW'S ANOTHER DAY

CHAPTER 19

"Hello, Henry!" said Chester into the phone console on his office desk.

"Hi Chester. Good to hear your voice," answered Henry. He rose from the desk in the spare bedroom he and Penny were sharing as an office. He then sat on the couch along the side wall.

"Back from Hopetown?" asked Chester.

"Yes. We had a fantastic time! Penny and I are still in shock, though. Not only that we're married, but the reason I called, the wafer," stated Henry. "I want to thank you again, Chester. You've been a wonderful friend."

"No thanks necessary. I wanted to do that for you. Even more so, I did it for Ted. He and I were best friends. I miss him. There's no way I was going to let them destroy his legacy." Chester thought about his battle with Hyatt Emerson. He shifted in his chair as a wisp of anger burned through him.

"You put a lot of time and energy into this. I appreciate it."

"I've been well compensated with my percentage. Things

turned out much better than anticipated. I would've done it either way, though," said Chester.

"I'm sure we'll get together at some point. We'd all like to thank you in person," added Henry.

"I'd like that. So, you and Penny are in Atlanta now?"

"Yes, we're renting a townhouse in the downtown area until we figure out our longer-term plans. It seems like a good hub for us. Penny's job is here. Her family, too, as well as Sean and Angie. It's working for us so far."

Henry stood and ambled over to the window. He studied the tall buildings and watched as the heavy traffic seemed to ooze through the crisscrossed streets. He'd never lived in a big city. Unwittingly, he frowned.

"You've had a lot of changes to digest. There are things we need to discuss. Do you have some time now?"

"Sure," answered Henry. He moved over to the desk and sat. Hitting the speaker button, he set his cell phone down and grabbed a notepad and pen.

"Well, first, I don't want to bring up unpleasantries, but there is the matter of your accident. We had a forensics team take a look, and they found some tampering."

"The chip," interrupted Henry.

"How did you know about that?" asked Chester.

"Paul from the security company called me."

"What!" exclaimed Chester.

"He apologized. He thought it was a tracking chip that was approved."

"He should go to jail, Henry."

"I'm not sure Chester. I used to eat lunch with him and his

crew when they were doing their security review. He has a wife and four young children. I don't believe he meant any harm."

"You're saying you want me to drop the matter?"

"I believe so."

"You're a better man than me, Henry."

"I'm positive that's not true. Although I am feeling a bit more gracious today than a month ago."

Chester laughed. "Think that over and let me know if you change your mind."

"I'd like to make sure that could never happen again. Is that possible?" asked Henry.

Chester pulled a folder toward him. He flipped through the pages to refresh his memory. They had sent the chip and the data to the manufacturer with legal threats. That had made some gigantic waves.

"We contacted the company involved," said Chester. "They can't conceive how this could've happened. And they can't duplicate the problem. However, they've issued recalls. They're redesigning it. I expect we'll see a compensation offer from them."

"You've been busier than I guessed!" exclaimed Henry.

"Not me so much, the firm. My wife is urging me to retire. I should. I enjoy my work too much, though."

"You sound like Ted," chuckled Henry.

"Two peas in a pod, my wife used to say," murmured Chester. "Margaret, too. That reminds me, I need to call her."

"Say hello for me."

"Will do. By the way, I hear that Hyatt Emerson is feeling some heat. As they say, out of the frying pan and into the fire."

"He called me, too."

"What! Not Hyatt!" bellowed Chester.

"Very awkward call," began Henry. "Said he was glad I was healthy and wished me well."

Henry began doodling on the notepad with heavy pen strokes. Glancing down, he dropped the pen onto the pad. He leaned back in his chair and stared at the phone.

"And you believe him?"

"Does it matter? The call itself had to be excruciating for him."

Chester laughed loudly.

"Also, it helps me to move on. Again, I'm more magnanimous now."

"That brings me to another topic. Henry, your settlement is public knowledge. I'm certain you'll have people coming out of the woodwork to lure your newfound wealth away. I've asked our team to put some financial and legal safeguards together for you, as well as Alex. Would you meet with them? I hope I'm not overstepping."

"Not at all," assured Henry. "Penny and I have discussed how we hope we aren't trading one set of troubles for another. We appreciate any help."

"One reason I bring that up is the real estate transaction Alex just did. Has he mentioned that to you?"

"Yes, the house in the Bahamas. We've had some long conversations about it. I think it'll be good for him. He and Sean have worked projects over there for years now. It's not an impulse buy, if that's your concern."

"Good. As long as he's being smart about these things. My last issue is Fusion Lab."

"Chester," interrupted Henry. "Penny just got home. I'd like her to hear this too. Is that okay?"

Penny had stopped in the doorway. Henry waved her in, and she sat on the couch next to the desk.

"Of course," said Chester. "Hello, Penny! And congratulations again! I'm thrilled at how well things are going for you and Henry."

"Thank you, Chester," said Penny. "We owe a lot to you."

"Nonsense," said Chester. "Henry's been filling me in on some of the highlights of the past month. You've been busy!"

"We have!" exclaimed Penny. "I'd say a frenzy!"

Penny looked at Henry. They nodded at each other and chuckled.

"I'm sure!" said Chester. "But now back to business. I need to let you know what's happening with the Lab. We'll need to schedule some conference calls with the Trustees in a few weeks. Some decisions need to be made and a plan of action outlined. But in the meantime, I'm working on getting all the liens lifted against the Lab's assets. Once that's accomplished, we'll have a clean slate. But I'll need to know what's happening next."

"What do you mean?" asked Henry.

"Well, what's to become of the Lab? Reopen it? Sell it? I'm sorry, but most of these decisions will fall on you and Matt, as Trustees. We also need to examine who owns what at this point. To honor Ted Granger's legacy, the sooner we sort this out, the better."

"I've got plenty of time on my hands, so shoot me a list of things I can do."

"I was hoping you'd offer that," chuckled Chester. "I'm

staring at it right now. I'll email it. Call me if you have questions. I've also got plenty of people here that we can put on task. It's just that they can't do anything unless the Trustees sign off."

"No problem," said Henry. "I'll get started right away."

"Thank you, Henry and Penny. I'll keep in touch. We'll get together soon."

"Thank you again, Chester," said Henry.

"Bye, Chester," added Penny as they hung up.

Penny walked over to Henry and kissed him. He wrapped his arms around her and hugged.

"How was your day?" asked Henry. "Still feel strange being back?"

"More frustrating than anything else. They haven't assigned me to a project. I've been assisting on others," replied Penny. She turned and headed out of the office.

Henry followed right behind, and they moved into the kitchen. Penny opened the refrigerator and pulled out two bottles of water while Henry got two glasses out of a cabinet. They sat at the table.

"I'm slowly getting used to this routine," smiled Henry.

Upon returning from the Bahamas, Henry and Penny had found a furnished townhouse close to Penny's office. She hated driving in traffic and the house was located right near a MARTA subway station. In some ways, the commute reminded her of her old routine. Only everyone spoke English instead of German.

"Me, too," chuckled Penny. "Only when I've had a day like today, I'd bang on that wall. Ten minutes later, Adrianna would be in here with a bottle of wine."

"I can do that!" exclaimed Henry. He jumped up and

exchanged the tall drink glasses for wine ones. He then pulled a bottle of wine from a rack and opened it.

As the cork popped, Penny exclaimed, "My hero!" They both laughed.

"Let's have a glass and then order in dinner. We can talk about Chester's call. Don't you feel like we're being pulled in every direction?"

"More like spinning. Our lives have changed so much, so quickly, that I'm not sure which direction I'm moving."

By the end of the week, Penny was looking forward to a weekend with Henry. They planned to do something fun, just the two of them.

Sitting at her desk in her office, Penny scrolled down to the last page of the report and smiled. She was ready. Matt had scheduled a meeting this afternoon with the Executive Team for a debriefing on the project she had assisted. It all looked good to her. The training for the client was thorough. Now that they were live on the new software, there were only a few hiccups. The meeting should be quick.

Penny heard a knock on the frame of her open door and looked up to see Matt standing there.

"Ready?" asked Matt.

"Yes," answered Penny cheerily. "I'll admit I'm nervous. This is my first meeting with the entire Executive Team."

"No big deal," Matt assured her with a firm voice but avoiding her eyes.

Suddenly concerned, Penny moved in front of Matt, blocking his exit. "Is something going on?" she asked.

"No, no. Everything's fine," said Matt. He looked at Penny's face, her eyes wide in alarm. He reached out and patted her shoulder. "All I'm allowed to say is that your life is about to get more complicated, if you can believe that."

"Now I'm really concerned," Penny mumbled.

Leaving her office, Penny followed Matt down the hall and through the door of the conference room where the men and women of the Executive Team chatted noisily. Helen, the company President rose and greeted Penny with a handshake and smile.

"Penny, so good to see you again," said Helen. She directed Penny to a seat across from her.

The room quieted as everyone chose a seat and turned their attention to Penny. Matt sat beside her. Penny straightened up in her a chair and put on her most confident smile. This was not going as she had imagined.

"So, Penny," began Helen. "I first want to congratulate you on how successful your projects have been. We're pleasantly surprised that someone so new to the company could accomplish what you did."

"Thank you," said Penny. She turned her head a bit to see Matt's expression. She hoped to get a read from him on what was coming.

"Next," continued Helen, "I'd like to fill you in on the discussions we've had here this morning. We've known that, given the growth of the company, we need to expand this team. Our idea is to split the International unit into sections, carving out Europe. Our potential for new business there is exceptional. We'd like you to run it."

Stunned, Penny shivered as if a chilly breeze had just brushed by. "Um, what does that mean?" she asked.

Helen chuckled. "I apologize. I know you expected a very different meeting than this. What this means is that we think you'd be a fantastic addition to this team. You'd be a director. Just like Matt. Only you'd be stationed in Europe. I would guess you'd choose Germany as your base with your many roots there. You'd recruit and hire your own instructors. Bottom line, you'd be responsible for the successful rollout and integration of our software to our clients in Europe."

Penny glanced at the smiling faces around her. They were waiting for her to say something. "I don't know what to say. I'm deeply honored. What an amazing opportunity."

"I'm not expecting a decision from you anytime soon, so relax," smiled Helen. "In fact, I'd like you to take time to discuss with the rest of the team their own experiences. We're all here to help you succeed."

With the meeting over, everyone filed out of the room while congratulating Penny and offering help with her decision. Matt hung back. Once they had the room to themselves, he hugged Penny.

"Congratulations! You deserve this," he said excitedly.

"I'm stunned, to tell you the truth," replied Penny.

"They're very serious about this expansion. And willing to devote a lot of resources to it. You'd be perfect for the position," said Matt.

"Well, you were right. My life just got a lot more complicated. I can't wait to get home to tell Henry."

"Congratulations! This is a monumental accomplishment. I'm

so proud of you!" exclaimed Henry. He hugged Penny tightly, and they swayed back and forth.

"I'm proud of myself, to be honest," Penny giggled. "I worked very hard for this."

They both sat down on the sofa in their family room, Henry's arm around Penny.

"We've been saying how we both feel like we're stuck in some kind of transition. Overwhelmed, and not knowing which direction to go. Maybe this is the answer. The perfect solution. You get to go back to Europe, the place you love, but with me, too!"

"Oh, that sounds so enticing!" said Penny brightly, as she immediately thought of her life overseas.

"Let's go celebrate. I'm taking you out to dinner."

They laughed and talked the rest of the evening, both delighted by this new opportunity.

However, the joy didn't last. Their good fortune soon lost its luster. By Friday, Penny had become sullen with Henry and made excuses to avoid any discussions. She was not sleeping well. Henry, too, was stressed. Not only was Penny distant and withdrawn, but Chester had called, wanting to discuss the strategy for Fusion Lab.

When Penny walked through the door after work, Henry was stretched out on an easy chair in front of the TV, watching a soccer match. Penny plopped her carry bag on the floor with a dull thud, as if it held rocks. Slowly, she peeled off her coat and slumped her shoulders against the wall. She was exhausted, but relieved to be home.

"Oh, hey, hon," said Henry as he sat upward. "I didn't hear you come in. Let me turn this down." He reached for the remote and stood up. "I thought I'd better get up to speed on European sports, so I fit in better," he laughed.

Henry turned to walk over and hug Penny, but saw her face. "What's wrong?" He grabbed her shoulders and sat her down on the sofa beside him.

"I'm frustrated at work. Everyone keeps smiling and congratulating me."

"Oh," said Henry, knowing not to ask why that was a problem.

"They all act like the decision's made. Like I'm a fool not to take the promotion. They've already got me out the door. Well, I haven't decided, and I'm tired of this pressure. It's only been a week, for heaven's sake. They're like crows, constantly pecking at me." Penny shook her head in anguished disbelief.

Henry reached for her hand. "We'll figure all this out."

Penny pulled her hand away and stood up. "No, we won't," she snapped. "There's also your situation. What's happening with Fusion Lab? Isn't that a mess, too?"

"I'm working on it," Henry assured her.

"I bet!" Penny fussed. "Before I got this offer, I'm positive you already had a five-year plan worked out in that computer brain of yours!"

Henry looked away. "Two years," he mumbled.

"See, I knew it!" Penny squeezed her hands into fists and glared at Henry defiantly.

"Let's not worry about Fusion Lab right now. What's going on at work?" asked Henry.

"I just explained that to you!" Penny glared at Henry. "They're smothering me. If I hear 'Congratulations!' one more time, I'll scream."

"I thought you were excited about the promotion?"

This only provoked Penny further. "I don't want to hear any more about that!" She turned her back to him.

Henry stood up with his hands on his hips. "Well, do you want the promotion or not?" he demanded loudly.

Penny turned and shouted at him, "No, I don't!"

They both froze.

"You don't?" asked Henry cautiously.

"Oh my gosh, Henry. I really don't." They stared at each other, both silent. She slumped toward him, and he drew her into his arms. "I really don't," she repeated, and leaned her head against his chest.

They held each other tightly for a few minutes. Then Penny giggled. She lifted her head and smiled at Henry for the first time in days.

"I'm so sorry, Henry!" She grabbed his face and kissed him. "I didn't mean to get so angry. You married a crazy person."

Henry laughed, too. "I'll admit, I hadn't seen this side of you yet."

They both settled down onto the sofa. Henry propped a throw pillow against the padded arm. Wrapping his arms around Penny, he leaned back and pulled her down with him. They lay stretched across the cushions in contented silence.

"I'm sorry I yelled at you, Henry." Penny whispered. "I should've talked to you sooner."

"Apology accepted," Henry whispered back. "Let's promise

to communicate better."

"Agreed."

"You really don't want the promotion?" asked Henry, still surprised.

"I don't. It's so clear to me now," said Penny.

"Really? You seem so happy there and are doing a great job," countered Henry.

"I am. But I'm thinking it's because it's so new and exciting." Penny sighed. She stroked Henry's arm.

"What do you think they'll say when you tell them?" asked Henry.

Penny turned her head to face Henry. "That's the issue, what's been bothering me. I finally realized I don't want to work there," said Penny.

"So, you don't want the promotion. But not only that, you want to quit altogether? I wouldn't have predicted this," said Henry flatly.

"Me either." Penny tugged Henry's arm tighter to her. "Honestly, Information Technology is not my thing. In my old job in Germany, we solved people problems. Each project was different, with diverse challenges. I really don't see my future in software. I guess I tried to convince myself otherwise."

"I can understand that," Henry assured her as he interlocked his fingers in hers.

"Do you want to wait before we tell anyone? Do you need more time to be certain?"

"No, I'm sure. I've been miserable all week. I'm at peace now," voiced Penny. She patted Henry's hand. After a few moments, she turned her face back to Henry's. "I hope Matt isn't too disappointed in me. He's helped me so much."

"He'll understand once you explain your reasons," stated Henry. "He'll be supportive. He's a great friend."

They were both startled by the ringing of Henry's cell on the table next to them. Henry sat up and looked at the caller ID. "Speaking of great friends, it's Alex. Why does he call at the most inopportune times?"

Penny laughed. "Go ahead and answer." She sat up next to Henry.

Hitting a button, Henry placed the phone back onto the table. "Hi, Alex. You've got both of us here on speaker."

"How are you guys?" asked Alex cheerfully. "I hear congratulations are in order, Penny. You're going to be an international bigwig."

Penny and Henry looked at each other and laughed.

"That seems to have changed in the last hour," chuckled Penny. "I've decided not to take the promotion."

"What?" Alex exhaled sharply. "Didn't expect that." He paused for a moment. "I wanted to be excited for you. But, wow, this is great! I'm glad you and Henry are staying put. You're going to make a lot of people very happy with this news."

"I've been so self-absorbed lately that I hadn't thought of that. But you're right."

Penny held a hand to her mouth and whispered to Henry, "I need to call my mom."

"I guarantee you're better off here," Alex asserted. "I mean, what would you have over there that we don't have here?"

"Oh, maybe being surrounded by so many different countries, each with their unique history, architecture, and culture?"

retorted Penny.

"But we've got real football," insisted Alex.

Penny laughed. "Well, that settles it then!"

"What are you up to, Alex?" asked Henry, laughing and shaking his head.

"I'm sitting here on my porch in the Bahamas with an incredible view and a beer in my hand," Alex paused, "wondering why my best friends aren't here to enjoy this with me."

"That sounds amazing!" Penny exclaimed. She turned to Henry. "I wish we were."

"No, seriously," said Alex. "Do you think you could get away? Maybe spend a week here? I need your opinion."

"You've finished?" asked Henry.

"Yep, and I'm really happy with it. Sean thinks I went way overboard and should list it. I'd like you to see it first. It's a complete transformation."

"Where's the house again?" asked Henry, trying to picture the islands he remembered from the wedding.

"It's on one of the small cays west of Abaco, about 200 miles from the mainland. I can get back and forth on my boat, depending on the weather, but it's also got its own private airstrip. That's how I'd get you guys here."

Alex had found the foreclosed house abandoned and considerably damaged from the rain, wind, and salt air. The bank that owned it wanted to get it off their books. With his new financial resources from the Solidane settlement, Alex purchased it and set about refurbishing it.

With the help of Sean and the rest of their crew, he remodeled the house. They installed a new metal roof with solar panels to help save on electricity. They replaced all the windows with impact glass. For peace of mind when he was away, he installed an emergency generator, cameras, and other monitoring equipment around the property.

"A trip back there may be just what Penny and I need. We're feeling overwhelmed right now," said Henry. "Let us talk about it and get back to you. Are there any certain dates you're thinking of?"

"No, whenever. I just want to show it off. Also, I'd like you to meet someone," answered Alex.

"Your boat?" kidded Henry. "Sean told us about it."

Alex had allocated a sizable portion of his remodeling budget to boating capabilities. He tore out the house's old rotting dock and replaced it with a floating one that would rise and lower depending on the tide. He built a steel-reinforced, custom boat house with a hydraulic lift. Next, he bought a boat to fill it.

"No, a real person. And, yes, I love my boat. I've named it 'Bricklebutter Dayz'. That's days with a 'z.' Get it?" asked Alex, proud of his creativity.

"I like that," said Penny. "Do you see Cubby much?"

Cubby and his wife lived in Hopetown and had befriended the group while there for the wedding.

"Yes, in fact, he and Diega are coming over tonight. They're going to spend the weekend with Gracie and me. He's still a character," chuckled Alex.

"So, we'd get to meet Gracie if we visit?" asked Henry. "Sean told us about her, too."

"Yes, and tell Sean to keep his big mouth shut, would you?"

"Yeah," Henry chimed in. "And Penny and I would love to meet Gracie. We knew it wasn't just a house keeping you busy over there. How'd you meet her?"

The first time Alex had seen Gracie was during the fishing trip the day before Henry and Penny's wedding. It was at the bar of the restaurant where the men had eaten after fishing. She had walked past him with the restaurant owner. Alex had been showing off.

They formally met each other at Alex's house. Gracie was a rep for a company that manufactured all types of hurricane protection for buildings. She'd had an appointment to measure the glazed openings of Alex's house and present to him options for covers.

Alex had recognized Gracie the moment she drove up to his unfinished house and waved hello from her golf cart. His face flushed a quick red as he remembered. Her short brown hair still looked the same. Her smile was as warm and inviting as ever, radiating from her eyes and casting a playfulness that seemed to draw Alex toward her.

A flash of recognition also shot through Gracie, and her smile widened further. She almost chuckled, but quickly caught herself. Alex extended his hand in a greeting, and with his other arm raised, held the door open for her. Gracie casually shook his hand and then slowly reached up and squeezed his bicep. Their ensuing laughter grew into a friendship, then a date, and soon a romance.

"Funny story," answered Alex. "I'll let Gracie tell you in person.

I'm going to let you guys go. Get back to me, okay?"

"Sure," replied Henry.

"Great decision, Penny. Bye, guys."

"Bye, Alex. Love you," said Penny.

"You, too," said Alex, and they hung up.

A week later, Henry was picking up glasses filled with ice from the kitchen counter and headed back over to the table to join Penny. His phone chirped, and he hurriedly handed the glasses to Penny.

"It's Kate," he whispered to Penny. He touched the speaker button and set his phone on the table between them.

"Hey, Kate, what's up?"

"I've got great news for you. You're going to be an uncle."

"I already am an uncle."

"You make things difficult. Is Penny there?"

"Right here, Kate. You're on speaker," said Penny.

"Penny, please tell your husband that his awesome twin sister is having a baby."

"What!" shrieked Penny. "Kate, that's wonderful! Congratulations!"

Henry jumped up. "Kate, that's fantastic!" he shouted.

"Yeah, Robby and I are really excited. We'd been trying, but with so much happening, it's been challenging. You know what I mean?"

"Believe me, we do," answered Penny.

"We're pretty sure Hopetown did the trick. I'm due in February. Counting back, it makes sense. That trip was so relaxing and romantic. We had the best time," explained Kate wistfully.

"I wish I could give you a big hug right now," said Henry as he sat back down.

"Me, too," answered Kate. "I'm hoping we'll see each other soon. Robby and I are taking the girls over to Mom and Dad's tonight. We'll tell them then. I had to tell you first."

"Thanks. We wish we could be there," said Henry.

"How are you guys doing?" asked Kate.

"We're good," answered Henry. "Sitting here talking."

"We were just comparing our lives to an amusement park. Roller coaster. Merry-go-round. Bumper cars. Scrambler," laughed Penny. "Depending on the month."

Kate laughed. "I admit, Robby and I are pretty boring compared to you two. So, you resigned, Penny?"

"Yes, next Friday is my last day. Everyone's been so gracious to me."

"Any regrets?" asked Kate.

"Surprisingly no," answered Penny. "I'm feeling good about my choice. Now I need to figure out what to do with myself."

"I'm thrilled for you. That had to be hard. But now you can go visit Alex!" announced Kate excitedly.

"Yes! It's the perfect opportunity and we could use the distraction. I wish you could go, too," pleaded Penny.

"I know, we're disappointed," sighed Kate. "But I'd never be able to tolerate the plane and boat rides. I'm already queasy in the morning."

"There'll be other opportunities," Henry soothed. "I know Alex isn't selling that house. I can tell by the way he talks about it. And he'll insist on visitors."

"I'm counting on it," added Kate. "But let me get going. The kids will be home soon, and I have a mountain of paperwork in front of me. It's the end of the month, and I have to get these invoices out."

"Tell Robby congratulations, and say hi to Mom and Dad," said Henry. "I'm really excited for you, Kate."

"Will do."

"I am too, Kate," added Penny. "Give Robby and the girls big hugs from us."

Henry reached his arm over to end the call, and Penny stood up. She circled around her side of the table, grabbed Henry's arm, and pulled him up.

"Congratulations, Unca Enry," she teased as she put her arms around him.

"You imitate them well!" laughed Henry. He squeezed Penny. "Congrats to you, too! I'm happy for Kate and Robby."

"I want to thank you, Henry. You've been very patient and understanding with me. While Kate was talking, I realized how blessed we are. You know, simply the fact that we're in a position that I can quit my job. We're so fortunate. God's been so good to us!"

"He has," agreed Henry. "It's easy to forget that sometimes."

"I know. We've been barraged with so many changes. At least He's consistent. That's always reassuring to me."

"Let's keep praying about what He has planned for our future. What do you think? Ready for another ride on the roller coaster?"

CHAPTER 20

The intense heat of the summer had broken, and the weather turned tolerable. Sean and Angie had joined Penny and Henry for the visit to Alex's home. Days of boating to various islands, sampling delicious foods, snorkeling, and lounging lazily on sandy beaches sped by. At the end of a wonderful trip, no one wanted to leave.

"I wish Kate and Robby had been able to get here," said Alex as he walked among them with an armful of new beverages. They were scattered in a semicircle on the Alex's stone porch overlooking the shimmering alcove waters. Alex had dimmed most of the lights, and a multitude of stars seemed to sprout out of the sky.

"We all do," agreed Henry. He reached for a beer that was balanced precariously among others against Alex's chest. "But with everything they've got going on, it's understandable. Kate was pretty bummed. This pregnancy's been harder than the first two."

They nodded in agreement, though most couldn't see the faces of the others in the darkness.

"We've had a great time, Alex. Thank you so much," said Penny.

"Why don't you all stay another week?" pleaded Alex.

"Unfortunately, Angie and I need to get back," sighed Sean. "Our flight's tomorrow."

"I know. I'll get you over to Marsh Harbor. Sorry I couldn't get a charter for you from here. How about you, Henry, Penny?"

Penny instantly squeezed Henry's hand. "Can we do that?" she whispered excitedly.

"I'm in heaven here," admitted Henry contentedly. "I'm game if you are." He returned the squeeze.

Three days later, a tropical storm that had developed into a hurricane, dominated the news. Unexpectedly, it had taken a northwesterly track, threatening Great Abaco Island. Cubby called, alarmed.

"Good morning, Cubby," shouted Alex. "I have you on speaker. We're all right here." Alex scraped the waffle iron and poured some batter onto it. It sizzled as he closed the top and yellowish fingers of excess batter tried to escape. Gracie, Henry, and Penny sat around his kitchen table munching on scramble eggs, awaiting the next hot waffle.

"Sorry to mess up your vacation, but that hurricane has become a problem. I think we need to prepare."

"We've been getting the alerts on our phones," said Henry. "It's still a category one, right?"

"Yes, but it's getting stronger really fast. I don't trust it," answered Cubby.

Alex lifted a steaming waffle off the iron and set it on a plate. He joined the group at the table. "Gracie's getting worried, too. She's been through this before. The rest of us haven't. What do we need to do?" he asked.

"I'll text you my list. Follow that."

"No problem," Alex assured him.

"I'd better get going," said Cubby. "I'll keep in touch."

Alex's phone chirped, and a text from Cubby popped up. Alex re-texted it to everyone.

"Well, I'm glad Sean and Angie went home when they did. Are you sure you and Penny don't want to head back?" offered Alex.

"Honestly, Alex, I don't think that's possible now. It's probably a madhouse getting people off the islands. I doubt we'd get a flight. You need your boat, so shuttling us back like we'd planned is out." Henry pushed his plate to the side and examined his phone. "Plus, we've got too much to do here."

"Believe me, I appreciate the help," said Alex as he scrolled through the list. "Gracie, what needs to be done at your place?"

"Not much. I keep it hurricane ready during the summer months. Some doors needed to be secured, though," answered Gracie.

"Okay," said Alex. "How about I'll ferry you over to Hopetown this morning? Henry and Penny, could you take charge of supplies? You'll need to make a run down to Samuel's." Alex drizzled a generous pool of syrup onto his waffle, cut it with his fork, and hastily shoved it into his mouth.

Penny took a last gulp of coffee. "We're on it!"

Gracie watched Alex devour his breakfast and chuckled. "Slow down, Alex. Look, the sun's shining. We've got time."

The next day, with their preparations completed, the group gathered for a light dinner in the kitchen. Afterward, they all helped clear the table.

Henry clinked a plate against the others in the dishwasher.

"Looks like it may come in at a category three or four now," he said, squinting his eyes towards the big screen TV in the family room. He'd been watching the projected track off and on throughout the day.

The kitchen now tidy, Penny walked over and sat on the sofa next to Gracie. "Do you think we'll be okay?" Penny asked her.

"We've done everything we can. All that's left is to keep praying," said Gracie. She reached out and patted Penny's arm.

"Alex's house is sturdy enough?" asked Penny.

"Yes," smiled Gracie. She reached for Penny's hand and held it. "I'm positive about that. I had to design the wind mitigation features for Alex. He likes overkill. I'm very happy he insisted." She watched Alex in an animated conversation with Henry and chuckled. "We'll be fine."

Henry glanced over at Penny and noticed her worried expression. He gestured with his head to Alex, signaling that they should join the others.

"How are things over here?" asked Henry as he approached the sofa.

"A little concerned," admitted Penny. "I don't know what to expect and that bothers me. And I think it would help if we turned that thing off." She gestured to the large screen TV flashing dramatic, up to the minute pictures of the hurricane.

They all turned to see the swirling bands of the immense vortex headed their way, with the announcer warning of impending doom.

"He keeps talking about storm surge. What's that?" asked Penny, drawing in a deep breath.

"The incredible winds of the hurricane push against the water in the ocean," Henry explained. "The water can't move fast enough, so it builds up into a bulge. When that moves onto land, it causes flooding."

"Do we need to worry about that?" asked Penny.

"That's why they built this house on stilts," said Alex. He stood in front of them with his hand on his hips. "I don't think we'll have a problem with surge. All that trudging up the hill from the dock and all those steps up to the porch have a purpose. It's not just for the view." Alex smiled at her, hoping to instill some confidence.

"Although the view is kind of nice," said Penny, feeling a little better.

"Anyway, just in case, there's a box of life vests over there. If you see my boat float past that window there, I'd grab one."

They all laughed.

Alex reached for the remote and the screen on the TV went blank. He walked over to a large built-in cabinet and opened a door. Waving at the rows of multicolored boxes with whimsical names of puzzles and games, he shrugged his shoulders. "Who wants to pick out a game?"

Everyone yelled out their choice and Alex pulled out the most favored. They were soon sitting or squatting around a wide coffee table, laughing, competing, and having fun.

That night, Penny slept tightly in Henry's arms. The wind and rain had both gained strength. Rain bands from the outermost parts of the hurricane passed over the cay, and pelted the windows, doors, and roof of the house. The lights flickered throughout the night as power surges raced through the wires. Fortunately, the emergency generator still had not been needed.

In the morning, the group fixed a big breakfast and ate together at the kitchen table. Eventually, they noticed a slackening in the sounds as the hurricane moved on. The winds grew tolerable, and some rays of sunshine soon shot like searchlight beacons through the fast-moving clouds. They ventured outside.

They were unprepared for the convoluted mess they encountered. Sand, branches, and various sizes and shapes of debris were everywhere. The wind had ripped the corrugated sides of Alex's storage shed off. It scattered the once organized contents of the shelves about. Alex saw that the storm had pulled up the pilings of his dock and deposited it halfway up the path to his house. The hard top of his boat poked out from the roof of the boathouse.

Alex rubbed his forehead. He put his arm around Gracie and squeezed tightly. It could've been much worse, he realized.

"Penny and Henry, I'm really sorry I got you into this. You should've gone back home when they first started talking about the hurricane. I'm pissed at myself for getting outfoxed by this thing. I put you in danger."

"No one expected it to strengthen and turn like that. Penny and I knew what we were doing. Besides, it's over and everyone is fine." Henry kept studying the area, trying to make sense of where things used to be versus where they were now.

"Thanks, buddy. But this," he waved his hand outward, "is overwhelming. Truthfully, I'm glad you're both here. You've been a tremendous help."

"From the look of things, you're going to need a lot more help. I guess the entire island's hurting," said Penny.

She stooped to pick up some branches blocking her path. Henry did the same. He walked up to Penny and hugged her. He then took his thumb and wiped a tear from her cheek.

That evening, Penny and Henry were resting on Alex's porch overlooking the calm, blue bay. They marveled at how beautiful the scene contrasted with the destruction on the land side of the house. They were calling people back home who were worried sick about them. Henry had just reached Kate.

"Thank God you're okay!"

"Yes, we're all fine," said Henry. "For now, we're still processing the shock of the damage."

"What can we do for you? Do you need Robby to come and help?" she asked.

"No, there's no way to get him here right now. Alex said Sean is headed over with the crew on some kind of barge. They're used to dealing with messes. Although this'll be a challenge for them." Pausing for a moment, Henry switched the phone to the other ear. "It'll be a massive cleanup. I'll keep you posted on anything we need."

"Have you spoken with Cubby? Are he and his family okay?" asked Kate.

"Yes, we talked to him a few minutes ago. He lost the roof

to his house. But everyone's safe."

"I'm so sorry. It's agonizing that such a beautiful place endured such destruction."

"Just keep those prayers coming. It's going to take a lot of rebuilding to get this island back to how we remember it."

"There's always hope," said Kate.

"You bet," agreed Henry.

"When will you come home?"

"I'm guessing we'll stay for another few weeks. We're in a pretty good position to help some of the others," answered Henry.

"Stay safe!" appealed Kate. "Give everyone a huge hug from us."

Two weeks later, Alex and Gracie made a run to Marsh Harbor to attend a FEMA meeting. Henry and Penny took the afternoon off. They were tired. Their muscles ached from bending over picking up debris. Although they had worn gloves and long pants and shirts as protection every day, their arms and legs had the inevitable scratches and bruises from the sharp edges of scattered palm branches and other debris.

Hand in hand, Penny and Henry went for a casual stroll down the white, sandy beach that ran behind Alex's house. They came to a small cove where a palm tree had toppled over. It made a perfect bench for them to sit and rest. The colors of the lapping water changed to differing shades of blue as the incoming tide drew small, successive waves toward them. Behind them, a vast patch of tangled vegetation wrestled to catch the sun for revival from the hurricane damage.

Because the storm had stripped the tall palm trees on the edge of the cove of most branches, they provided little shade cover. Henry snapped open a lightweight, pop-up umbrella and wriggled it into the sand behind them. Stepping back over the log, he sat close to Penny.

Penny shook her sandals off and dug her toes into the soft, warm sand. With the magnificent colors and scenery saturating her senses, she let out a contented breath, turned to Henry, and laid her hand on his leg.

"This is so quiet and relaxing, Henry. I needed this. I guess sometimes the right thing to do in life is stop and rest. It helps me think so much more clearly."

"Me, too," agreed Henry. He gazed out over the dune that circled the cove and outward to the immense ocean that reached the horizon. "Beautiful!" he whispered.

"I woke up in the middle of the night and just laid there thinking and praying," began Penny. "Life has thrown so much at us, but I've never been more content."

"I've noticed how calm you've been the last couple of weeks," said Henry.

"It's surprised me," smiled Penny. "But I'm very confident about my future, our future."

"I'm happy to hear that!" Henry grinned. "So, no regrets about Europe?"

"Honestly, no. I admit I miss it. I still have wonderful friends there. Adrianna, Raf, Carla. I'm not going to block them out. I made that mistake once before."

"I think we've both done that," said Henry, smiling as he gave Penny a quick kiss. "How about, next summer, we plan a trip over there? You can be my tour guide."

"I'd love that!" exclaimed Penny. "Let's do it!" Another fast kiss sealed the deal. Penny turned her gaze to the turquoise horizon. "I thought about something else last night. How much longer is the lease on our house?"

"It's month to month. Why do you ask?"

"I think we should move to Fusion Lab." Penny watched Henry's face for his reaction.

"Where'd that come from?" he asked.

"I don't think you can properly plan for the Lab's future from Atlanta. You need to be there. It feels to me like unfinished business."

Staying silent, Henry studied Penny's eyes.

"I've heard your conversations with Chester and Matt and can sense your frustration. I know Chester wants to get this resolved. In a way, it's a drag on us."

Henry took some deep breaths but remained quiet. The sun had shifted westward, and Henry reached behind them and tugged lightly on the umbrella. The shade now covered both again.

"I'd like to go there, too," Penny continued. "I remember being fascinated by that place. I want us to find a real home, Henry. Maybe that could be it." She dug both her feet into the sand and shrugged. "What do you think?"

"Are you sure about this?" Henry asked. He looped his leg over hers so they could face each other.

"Very."

Henry grabbed Penny's hand. "I'd love to go back there. In my mind, I see it falling apart. Crumbling down. Like it's been through its own hurricane. That really bothers me."

"I know. It bothers me, too."

"Chester, Matt, and I have talked about a complete restructure of how the Lab operates. It needs a fresh approach," Henry pointed out.

Henry's toes dug a hole and scattered the sand onto Penny's feet. She smiled at him. "See, you're already getting excited."

"But what about you? Where's that put your career?"

"I don't know what I want to do. I'm okay with that. I need more time. Meanwhile, you can get moving on that two-year plan of yours for Fusion Lab," said Penny teasingly. She nudged him playfully away from her.

"I've got all five years mapped out already. Gotta keep up!" Henry jumped up and grabbed Penny around the waist. He pulled her laughing out into the water. After a few splashes back and forth, they held each other tightly and passionately kissed.

CHAPTER 21

Penny and Henry returned home to Atlanta from the Bahamas surprisingly energized. They'd been encouraged at the progress made in the recovery. The generosity, cheerfulness, and determination of the people they met on the islands amazed them. They hated to leave, but knew they had to get home.

With the decision to move to Fusion Lab already made, events progressed rapidly. After some wonderful visits with Penny's family and a day of packing, Penny and Henry began the journey up to the Lab.

They retraced the route of their last trip when Henry proposed. The long drive, meandering up and down hills and valleys, contrasted sharply with the sights and ordeals of the last month.

"This is so beautiful, Henry," sighed Penny.

"From the ocean, now to the mountains. Quite a difference. We're very fortunate to have experienced both," said Henry.

"We've been through a lot. And here we are, onward to our

next adventure!" smiled Penny.

"It's going to be a lot of work. I talked to Lukas, and he said the place is a mess. I'm grateful that Chester and Matt gave me the go ahead with my plan. Chester has cleared up all the legal restrictions. We can get rolling immediately."

"And Rhonda's on board, too!" Penny reminded him.

"My first decision was to hire her back. She'll be an immense help. She's lived in the valley all her life and had been staying with her sister. I told her she could move into one of the cottages. I'd bet she's already there!" chuckled Henry.

As they turned into the entrance to Fusion Lab, they spotted Lukas and Rhonda standing in front of Lukas' truck, waving their arms frantically. Penny and Henry tumbled out of their SUV and with excited hellos and enthusiastic hugs, the four were re-acquainted.

Penny and Henry followed Lukas and Rhonda for the drive up to the main building. They were stunned at how the landscape had changed since they were last there. Everything was overgrown and untrimmed. The flower gardens were bare and brown, and leafless bushes and dead trees spotted the road borders.

"How sad," sighed Penny.

"What's this?" asked Henry. He saw various trucks and cars parked along the street, and people ambling around the main entrance.

As Henry got out of the car, Lukas walked briskly over to him. Seeing Henry's face, Lukas chuckled nervously and said, "It's all good. Come on in and I'll explain."

He led them to the cafeteria. Lukas had commandeered the

large room as his own. After meandering through a path bordered by boxes and crates, Lukas stopped at a table surrounded by lunchroom chairs. He grabbed a thick binder and waved at them to grab a seat.

"See this, Henry. It's all here. I've been recording every problem with the facilities since the day Mr. Worthington asked me to watch over it. I felt responsible." He handed the binder to Henry.

Flipping through it, Henry saw hundreds of entries, complete with dates and locations. Leaking windows in an office, a mice infestation at one of the lab rooms, potholes in the paths between buildings. The list was extensive.

"Lukas, this is incredible. I'm so impressed you kept this!"

"I tried to keep up with the problems, but they overwhelmed me. But I wrote everything down so we could fix them once Fusion reopened."

"So, you never gave up on the Lab, huh," Henry pointed out.

"There's always hope, Henry," Lukas reassured him.

"I guess the four of us standing here are proof of that!" laughed Henry. The others joined in. "Who are all these people?"

"Our helpers," answered Rhonda. "Once we knew you were on your way, we got them started. Some have been here a week already."

"Between Rhonda and me, we know exactly who to call in the valley. We have plumbers, electricians, and house cleaners. Look at the list there and we'll have a name beside it."

"We have most of the cottages and the offices cleaned. The dust was ridiculous. Penny and you have the cottage you used to stay in. It's ready for you."

"Thanks!" exclaimed Penny and Henry simultaneously.

Lukas paused and shuffled his feet. He tapped his hand on the table. "We have an issue, though. I told these guys you were arriving today. The ones hanging around the front of the building, pretending they're busy, are looking for some assurances about payment. Rhonda and I've made promises, and many of them are our friends. But their confidence seems to evaporate once they get a look at the Lab."

"I understand," said Henry. "Both Penny and I were upset on the drive in. What can I do?"

Rhonda reached down and snatched a group of papers. "Here are some invoices. Some are for completed jobs and some are for work in progress. If you could talk to the workers and give them a date for payment, that would go a long way."

"I can do better than that if we have internet service," said Henry.

"We do," announced Rhonda. "But we need to go up to Ted's office. It's where the router is."

They made their way upstairs. Ted's large desk had been pushed against a wall, obviously for cleaning. A sofa and three easy chairs were gathered in the center of the room. Henry, Rhonda, and Lukas sat down while Penny ambled over to the window.

"It's so beautiful!" she gasped. The day was slightly overcast, and where the sun's rays broke through the clouds, they shone like spotlights on sections of the rolling hills. Penny imagined they were calling to her, "Here, look at me!"

Henry unzipped his backpack and pulled two credit cards out of an express mail envelope. "Chester overnighted these to me before I left. They're in the trust's name. We have plenty of money in the bank account, too. Let's see those invoices."

Most could be paid immediately from the remittance info on them. Some were handwritten receipts. Henry would need to talk to those proprietors in person.

Once done, after a few high fives, they made the office their "control room." Over the next months, more people joined the team. The desk was moved out and another sofa and more chairs were moved in.

The progress they made in the first month was impressive. Lukas remained in charge of the notebook. He scheduled all the workers, keeping the pace of the repairs manageable. Henry's first request was that technicians evaluate the cabling to restore communications throughout the campus.

Rhonda oversaw the lab equipment. An inventory needed to be taken, and each piece tested. Most of her time, though, was spent on hiring. Word of mouth of Fusion's reopening brought in a flurry of calls. Some were from former lab analysts, but mainly new names. When asked why they were interested in Fusion Lab, the typical reply was, "you helped develop the Solidane wafer."

Penny took charge of restoring the cottages. The window coverings, bedding, and most other perishable items needed to be replaced. She found beautiful alternatives in the local craft shops.

Calls and planning meetings consumed Henry's days. Chester recommended they form a foundation to better structure Fusion Lab's operations. They then transferred ownership to it and cashed out the Granger family.

Chester, Matt, Penny, and Henry invested a lot of time on the foundation's structure and bylaws. Henry felt it was important that the board have a diversity of opinion. Henry had detested Hyatt Emerson's arrogance. But, with hindsight, he had to admit some of Hyatt's ideas contributed to the wafer's success.

Penny's experience with effectively integrating people in stressful environments helped them formulate sound operating procedures. Clear rules were needed for how projects were proposed to Fusion Lab, and which were accepted. Methods to assign future roles and responsibilities were considered. Henry was determined to avoid a repeat of his own experience.

One Saturday morning, as the weather was transitioning from the coldness of winter to the warmth of spring, Henry asked Penny to pack a picnic lunch. He drove up to the administrative offices and exchanged his SUV for the Lab's off-road vehicle. When he returned, he loaded some boxes, two folding chairs, and a small folding table into the back. Penny came out with a basket and containers of hot coffee.

"It's a little chilly for a picnic, isn't it?" asked Penny. She surveyed the items Henry had loaded and gave him a quizzical look.

Henry laughed. "I guess it is. Glad you packed the coffee. I think we'll be okay, though."

The large tires with chunky treads whined as they traveled down the paved road toward the back side of the mountain. The noise stopped suddenly when the blacktop ended, and the road transitioned to dirt. Henry continued for a few bumpy miles and then turned down a recently cleared path. He slowed as they burst out from under the tree awning and onto a rolling field. Henry turned the vehicle up a small hill and parked it facing the immense plateau before them.

"We're here," he announced.

"Henry, this is beautiful! I had no idea!"

Narrow at the top, the plateau broadened out as it slowly descended. Henry pointed to the hills. "Looks like a giant plow came through and pushed all the land up along the sides, creating those ridges, doesn't it?"

"I see what you mean," sighed Penny. "It's gorgeous."

"All this land," waved Henry, "up to that small mountain at the far end, belongs to the Lab. This is the parcel that Ted Granger wanted to develop."

"It's enormous! I couldn't have imagined this if you'd tried to explain it," uttered Penny.

Henry tugged the chairs and table out and set them up in front of them. "Here, you grab a seat. I want to show you something, and then we can eat."

Henry sat a large cardboard file box on the table. "When Rhonda and I were going through Ted's files, we found a blueprint. We called the architectural firm whose name was on it. They sent us this box of drawings."

Penny helped Henry spread out a master plan. "Wow," gasped Penny. "It's an entire community!"

"When we reached out to the architect, they called the developer Ted had originally dealt with. They contacted us, too. We're meeting with them about going forward."

Reaching into the box, Penny drew out some renderings. "This is amazing! See how the designs all resemble the railroad features of Fusion Lab!"

Henry shuffled through a stack and picked up a sketch. "This is the master design. The neighborhood roads will meander through the natural rifts in the ground. There are parcels set aside for community centers, shopping, recreation, etc. See these ball fields and soccer fields way down here? The county asked us to donate that land for schools. The neighboring communities have grown so quickly that they're desperate. If we'd do that, they'd help us with the infrastructure, our roads, utilities, sewer. All this here is green belt and conservation areas. And this area, including where we're sitting," Henry waved his hand to the right and left, "will be houses."

"Are you saying we'd be able to live in a house here someday?" asked Penny hesitantly.

"If you'd like. In fact, we're sitting on what would be our back deck." Henry waited for Penny to react.

She jumped up and hugged him. "Oh my gosh, Henry, that would be amazing!"

"Well, say the word, and you'll be the first resident of Granger Village."

Eleven months later, Penny and Henry were sitting on their deck in the exact spot Henry predicted. The noise and bustle of the construction down the plateau were bothersome. But in the evening, all movement stopped. The clouds then descended with the sun, muffling all sound like a blanket.

"Ready to give Kate a call?" asked Henry.

"Sure," answered Penny. She moved closer to Henry on the cushioned lounge.

"Hi, Kate, Penny's with me on speaker. We're calling to see

how our nephew is doing."

"Hi guys!" said Kate excitedly. "He's doing great. He's sitting up now, and I expect him to be crawling any day."

"And the girls?" asked Penny.

"They're still hovering over him constantly. All he needs to do is drop a toy or start crying and they run over. I feel sorry for him when he grows up."

Henry and Penny laughed. "They're so funny!" said Henry. "And Mom and Dad are doing well?"

"Yes, no complaints. We're all over that bout with the flu. It runs through the daycares and schools, and we can't help but catch something."

"That has to be the worst, up and down all night dealing with three sick kids," said Penny sympathetically.

"Four kids if you include Robby," Kate chuckled. "He was the worst."

"I know that's not true," countered Henry, defending Robby.

"Well, you ask Joy and see what she has to say about that," laughed Kate. "How are you two doing?"

"We're good," answered Henry. "We're sitting out back talking."

"How are things at the Lab?"

"Rhonda has taken over operations, and she's doing a fantastic job. We're gaining ground. We now have three projects ongoing. I've been busy with the development of Granger Village. We have over twenty houses under construction, as well as the community areas. Penny and I love our house."

"We need to get up there and check it out. The photos are beautiful. Your view, wow!" exclaimed Kate.

"The developers grossly underestimated the demand. The first townhouse grouping is already spoken for, mainly by Fusion Lab employees. But young families from the valley are interested, too. Ted would be ecstatic with how everything is unfolding."

"Hmmm," replied Kate. "All I can say is, make sure you're following your dreams, not Ted's."

Henry looked over at Penny. "Well, Ted had terrific ideas," said Henry.

"So do you," asserted Kate.

"I know," said Henry. "But I'm enjoying this project and have learned a lot. It's been so different from directing the Lab."

"I'll verify that Henry comes home happy from work, Kate," laughed Penny. "Granger Village has been good for him. For both of us!"

"Like I said, Robby and I need to visit. We miss you!"

"We miss you, too," Penny and Henry said together.

After they hung up, Penny took a sip of her drink and looked questioningly at Henry. "What are your feelings about your future at Fusion Lab, Mr. Executive Director?"

Henry settled back into the lounge, reached for Penny's hand, and interlocked his fingers in hers.

"My first five years at the Lab were my happiest there. Ted was in charge, but I never felt bossed. All of us had a certain amount of independence. I'd say he herded us around more than anything. We had deadlines, challenges, and personality clashes. But there was an overall positiveness and cheerfulness. I know that emanated from Ted. The wafer changed him and the rest of us."

Henry reached for his glass, took a few refreshing sips, and set it back down.

"I feel that way again now. I hope I'm a large part of that. Though I'm not involved in the day-to-day research, there's an overall optimism. Even Rhonda smiles when she comes into my office."

Penny laughed. "We've become great friends. I love her sense of humor."

"With the foundation in place, we've been able to bring more trustees on board," continued Henry. "I'm finding that I can delegate more of my responsibilities. We're growing at a slow, sensible pace. I don't ever again want to be forced down a path that ends up at a cliff's edge."

"I also love your sense of humor," said Penny.

"Financially, you and I are secure. I hope others involved with the Lab don't feel like I'm robbing them of some awesome opportunities by being so careful," continued Henry.

"I hope so, too. I'm glad you feel the way you do. I'm very happy right now. I enjoy having you around here so much," said Penny.

"Still no regrets about your career?" asked Henry.

"Well, some regrets. I used to love the travel. Each new project was an adventure, exciting people to meet. I miss that. But that's okay, I'm content." Penny gazed at Henry. "Like I said, I'm very happy."

Henry nudged his way closer to Penny. "I'm counting on you to let me know if that changes."

Penny leaned against Henry. "So far, so good."

Henry smiled. "You've been pretty busy, too. You and your

mom did a great job on the house. Can't believe we're moved in and settled. I wasn't much help!"

"Well, I've always enjoyed shopping," Penny chuckled. "Neither of us had many furnishings to contribute, so it was fun picking things out."

"Well, I have to say, I love these cozy lounge chairs!" Henry gently grabbed Penny's chin, turned her face to his and kissed her.

A whoosh rushed by Henry as the warmer air of the house sought to escape into the coolness of the garage. He closed the door and listened for Penny.

"Anyone home?" he called. The car was there. He knew she was somewhere in the house.

The clattering of a keyboard led him back to the office area. Penny peered intently at the screen, let out a satisfied, "Hmmm," and then began typing again.

"Penny?" Henry interrupted. He saw her cheerful face reflected on the computer screen and smiled. He walked over to the desk.

Surprised for an instant, Penny jumped. Seeing Henry, she rose from the chair and met him with a hug. "Hey, hon. Glad you're home," she said and then kissed him. "How was your meeting at the Lab?"

"Fine. You're busy at something! What's going on?" asked Henry, shifting his gaze from Penny to her computer screen.

"I think I've figured out what I want to do. I'm pretty excited." Penny shifted her weight onto her other leg and grabbed Henry's arm. "We can do this later, if you're too tired or hungry."

"No, no. I'm good. I haven't seen you this animated in a while. Tell me what you mean." He pulled a chair up to the desk and sat down.

"Well, you know how I've been working with Diega? We've been helping with the hurricane recovery over on Abaco. Let me show you this." Penny clicked some keys, and some photos popped up. "Look at this one first. This guy collected all those ceiling fan motors from rubbish piles. He repairs them. Now, this lady makes cloth paddle fan blades. Aren't they beautiful?" She looked at Henry.

"Sure!" he agreed, and he nodded his head.

"Now these two people buy the fans and blades and then package them together. They then sell them on the island for a reasonable price."

"A nice little network!" exclaimed Henry.

"What I didn't tell you was that Diega and I brought them together. I had to provide some money to get the process started. But Diega's the go between for them. She's amazing! She matches the supply with the need. For example, we buy any fabric, yarn, and electrical parts that aren't available there. She gives me a list and I find it and have it shipped over."

"Sounds like a good team," encouraged Henry.

"That's what I told Diega. This morning we were on a video chat, and she introduced me to three more people who'd like to network. That's when it hit me. We need to expand this!" Penny turned and looked expectantly at Henry. "What do you think?"

"It's a great idea! What a perfect way to help over there," he said excitedly.

"And Diega and I love doing this! I wrote out this business

plan. Could you look at it?"

Henry stood up behind Penny and gently massaged her shoulder as she walked him through the bullet points on the screen. He asked a few questions, but her outline genuinely impressed him.

"I'm not sure you can run this as a business, though, at least not immediately. I don't see a lot of room for profit. How about a charity? You could solicit contributions," said Henry, tilting his head and thinking. "You'd impact more people, faster."

"I thought that, too. When you see how little these people have, it breaks your heart. But Diega doesn't want to simply give out money. That's why she has set them up as mini businesses."

"So, think of yourself as a business incubator," suggested Henry.

"I like that!" exclaimed Penny.

"You could someday expand to other geographical areas that need help to recover from a crisis. You'd need to find someone like Diega in each place."

"I can do that!" said Penny confidently. "Is this idea solid enough to run by Chester?" asked Penny expectantly.

"Let's find out. He'll give you an honest answer on how viable it is. You're sure you want to commit to this?"

"Yes," said Penny beaming. "Could you help me draw up a better proposal?"

"Sure, I'd love to. You should talk to some of our friends, too. Get their opinions." Henry then bent over and kissed Penny's cheek. "But I think it's perfect for you."

Penny sighed. "I hope so." She leaned her head against Henry's arm and stared into the screen, deep in thought.

Henry kissed her cheek again and then moved his lips down to her neck.

"Stop it!" she laughingly protested.

He didn't.

Penny hit the shutdown key on the laptop and turned her face so her lips met Henry's. They kissed until they were startled into laughter when the laptop screeched a final beep and went dark.

Both home for the evening, Henry and Penny were lying on the sofa watching a show on TV. Henry's cell rang, and "Mom" displayed as the caller. He turned it toward Penny so she could read it, too.

"Hey, Mom, what's up?" asked Henry.

"Hi Henry, it's Kate. Mom's right here, and I'm putting you on speaker."

Both Henry and Penny quickly sat up. "Is something wrong?" asked Henry, now alarmed.

"Yes, there is," said Henry's mother emphatically.

"Wait, Mom," interrupted Kate. "Henry, everyone's fine. Is Penny there?"

"I'm sitting next to Henry," answered Penny.

"Good, hopefully Mom will listen to one of you."

"What happened?" asked Henry.

"The house sold," said Mrs. Taylor.

"What?" asked Henry, confused. "That's great! You just listed it last week!"

"Congratulations!" exclaimed Penny.

"Mom's freaking out," said Kate calmly. "She wants to pull

the listing. Dad's fit to be tied."

"I didn't know it would sell this quickly," said Henry's mom.

"I know the real estate agent told you to expect it to sell fast. Your house is in a great school district. Any family with young kids would want to live there," said Henry.

"Yes, she said that. But I thought she was trying to be nice."

"So, why the change of mind?" asked Penny. "Last time we talked to you, you were excited about moving closer to Kate, Robby, and the grandkids."

"I was. I still am. But they want to settle in a month! A month from now! I can't do that," explained Mrs. Taylor.

"So, it's not the fact that the house sold, it's the timing?" asked Henry.

"Exactly! Have you seen our basement lately?"

"Didn't Dad clear most of that out?"

"Some," answered Mrs. Taylor. "There's plenty more."

"Mom," Kate interjected, "We'll all help. The movers will pack the bigger items. We'll get the rest boxed up."

"I spoke with Dad the other day and he told me they're nearly finished with your villa. You can move in there soon. This could work out well," said Henry.

"Your father's over at the villa now. They're installing carpet. I know it's almost ready, but it doesn't have a basement," protested his mom.

"I can see why you'd be overwhelmed," offered Penny.

Henry glanced at Penny and gave her a "you're pandering her" look. She bounced her own "you don't know what you're talking about" glare back at him.

"How about, not this weekend, but the next, Henry and I'll

drive down and help you get organized?" asked Penny.

"That's a great idea!" exclaimed Kate. "We'll have a 'Let's move the Taylors' party! I'll call Alex and Sean to see if they can help, too."

Mrs. Taylor brightened. "That would help so much! Thank you! You're making me feel so much better. I'm sorry I got panicked. It was such a shock!"

"Well, relax, Mom. We'll all be there in two weeks," said Henry. "See you then!"

"What are you doing out here?" asked Kate. The screen door made a whoosh noise as the rusty arm of the closer tried in vain to pull it shut. Instinctively, Kate helped it along with a quick push. She moved gracefully to the edge of the patio where Henry stood. She placed her hand in his, as she had done so many times in their youth.

Henry squeezed her hand ever so slightly and turned his gaze to her. "A lot of memories here," he whispered wistfully. "You look great, by the way. How's the family adjusting to little Luke?"

"Pretty well. The girls are finally getting over the novelty. I don't have an audience every time I change a diaper. They love him, though!"

They both took a few minutes to scan the backyard where they had spent many great times with their friends. "I remember mowing this lawn," chuckled Henry.

"Thank you for not making me do that with you," answered Kate, laughing.

"Well, the one time you did, you left streaks of grass

everywhere. I had to cut it again anyway," chuckled Henry.

"I'm happy for Mom and Dad. At their new place, all the outside maintenance is taken care of. It's perfect for them," said Kate.

"And they'll be close to you, and not far from their friends," said Henry. He turned to Kate and huffed, "Does Mom really want all that stuff?"

"Well, you saw all the boxes, Henry," answered Kate. "She's keeping everything! I've spent hours helping her sort, but I think it's pointless. Dad marked the ones to be donated to the thrift store with a red 'X'. They're all still here."

Henry laughed. "Dad told me he's rented a storage unit."

Kate laughed, too. "I understand how she feels, though. It's difficult to let go. Change is hard."

"Sometimes you don't have a choice. These last years have been wild," said Henry.

Kate squeezed his hand. "Remember when we were little, and we would get into bed at night after Mom left the room? We'd tell each other about our day."

"No, you would tell me about your day. I never got in a word," said Henry.

"Remember what we'd say before we went to sleep?" asked Kate.

Henry thought for a moment and chuckled. "Yes, we'd say, 'Tomorrow's another day.'"

Kate sighed, "So long ago."

Henry spanned the backyard of his youth once more. "I'm going to miss this house."

"Me, too," answered Kate. "How's that saying go, 'sometimes

you need to give up the good to get the better'? I think that'll be the case with Mom and Dad. They'll be super busy for the next few months just getting settled into their new place. Then they have some trips planned. They never traveled much or took many vacations when we were kids. I'm happy for them."

They heard the screen door squeak.

"They're out here," shouted Penny back into the house.

Robby, Alex, and Sean followed Penny out the door.

"Here you are," exclaimed Alex. "We're not finished in there yet."

"We needed a break," protested Kate.

The group gathered near Kate and Henry and peered into the backyard and field beyond. Henry nudged his way behind Penny and unhurriedly wrapped his arms around her. Penny reached up and patted them and rested her head against Henry's chest.

"I remember me and Sean waiting for you to finish mowing this yard. It took you forever. It's not that big," said Alex,

"You could've helped," replied Henry.

They all laughed.

"By the way, Alex," said Kate. "It sounds serious between you and Gracie. At least from what Henry tells me. It's like pulling teeth to get info out of you these days."

Alex laughed. "Yep, I think I'm smitten."

Kate leaned into Alex and nudged him with her shoulder. "I'm happy for you."

"What happened to the bricklebutter hedges?" asked Penny. She held her hand against her forehead to see better into the distance.

Henry froze.

Penny looked at Kate and they began laughing, soon joined by Alex, Sean, and Robby.

"No, it's not what you think," insisted Henry, giving Penny a playful scowl for baiting him. "Some teenagers were smoking out there and set it on fire."

"Would that have been you, Alex, and Sean?" asked Penny.

"No, believe me, you would've already heard about it if so," answered Henry. "This was about five years ago. The city had to bulldoze the hedges."

The group stared in silence as they remembered the past.

Soon, Kate patted Robby on the back and turned toward the screen door. "Let's get back in," she said. "We still have a lot to do. I hope we get everything ready in time."

Robby, Alex, and Sean followed her into the house, leaving Penny and Henry alone. Arms around each other, they continued to peer into the grassy greenbelt.

"Want to walk over to your old backyard?" suggested Henry.

"Sure, one last time might be nice."

They both shuffled through the low blades of grass to the outskirts of a backyard Penny barely recognized. They examined the new features, piecing them into the memories of how it used to be.

"The various owners sure made a lot of changes," remarked Henry.

"Yes," agreed Penny hesitantly. "I love that deck. I wish we'd had that."

"I doubt your mom would agree. I can imagine us jumping off it," laughed Henry. "Or pushing Alex off."

"You know, Henry, I remember being so sad to leave this

house. But if I'm honest, I was excited, too. Our new house was pretty awesome. I wanted your family to move there with us."

"I could tell. Ever the adventurous." Henry grabbed Penny and pulled her close. "You realize, though, that now, wherever your exploits lead, I'm tagging right along with you!"

Penny giggled as Henry squeezed her tighter.

"What's that over there?" asked Penny abruptly. She pointed to a patch of bushes.

"Let's go look," suggested Henry.

They strolled out to a small batch of leafy branches on the edges of the field that they instantly recognized.

"Bricklebutter bushes!" cried Penny.

They both laughed as they checked out the budding stems and forming pods.

"It's amazing how resilient they are," said Henry.

"One day, I bet some little kids will play in a maze of these things!" said Penny. "Maybe our own?"

Penny squeezed Henry's hand.

Henry grabbed Penny by the waist and turned her toward him. "You've heard?"

Penny let out a joyous laugh. "Yes, I got a call with the results while everyone was packing. I wanted to tell you alone. They confirmed it. I'm definitely pregnant!"

Henry couldn't speak. He tried, but the emotions that he could've held back in the past broke through. His eyes grew moist. How did he deserve so many blessings?

"I love you," he finally managed. "This is incredible."

"I love you, too, Henry."

They hugged each other and kissed.

Penny gave Henry a gentle shove backwards. She raised her arms and twirled. Henry laughed.

"Come on, Henry, dance with me," she pleaded and began singing.

She knew he would.

Made in the USA
Columbia, SC
28 August 2023